BOOK I

# Wings of Redemption

A Tale Of Broken Hearts

Gemma A. Summers

Book Cover by Gemma A. Summers

1st edition 2024

# *Content Warning*

THIS BOOK ADDRESSES SENSITIVE topics that may be distressing to some readers.

It contains themes related to disordered eating patterns, weight, and body shaming. The main female character also suffers family abuse and lives in a society where females, in general, are oppressed. It has some serious scenes depicting child abuse in the starting chapters.

Reader discretion is advised, and it is recommended for those who may find these themes triggering to approach this book cautiously.

*PS, I believe that a good book is the one that emotionally heals you, but after destroying you first :)*

# Contents

# Hats off to

*"To all those betrayed by their own, And still decide to get up and fight every day"*

SHADOW REALM
Court of Mirrors
Luminal Sepulcher
Dragons Meet
Shadowed Thicket
Barren house
Eloria
Court of Shadows
Ariana's home
Eldenhaven
N
W
E
S

# Prologue

***"In the cradle of love, their whispers like a song,***
***Guiding through life's journey, steady and strong.***
***Roots of wisdom, branches of care,***
***Parents' love, an eternal affair."***

My belief about family, love, and parents shattered as each slap's sting echoed through the room. The sound mingled with the sharp cracks of the belt and the heavy thuds of my dad's shoe hitting my back. The rigidity of my shoulders and the unshed tears pooling in my eyes made my initial defiance palpable. Gradually, I let it go.

As time passed, my parents' oppressive words scaled the walls of my mental fortress. My once impenetrable defense started to crumble. I loosened my clenched fists and slackened my jaw. The hushed walls alone noticed the silent tears. Only when one or two tears fell on my hand did the room witness my emotional barriers shattering. Heartbreak, anger, and a profound sense of betrayal flowed freely. I wiped away my tears, attempting to conceal my pain. Automatically, my hand moved to an amulet on my neck, a broken heart resembling mine and long accompanying me. I don't even recall its origin. I had never inquired about it with my parents, lacking the bond to do so. Yet, this piece of iron on my neck somehow became a symbol of emotional support for me.

Anguish simmered beneath the surface, fueled not just by the sting of each blow, but by the emotional wreckage they left behind. Anger, a familiar companion, marched alongside confusion and heartache. All the emotions were as vivid as the bruises on my skin.

This painful routine wasn't new. It was a recurring act in the meticulously orchestrated drama of my parents' lives. My cheeks burned as the weight of my mother's hand crashed against my face. With the echoing slap, there was more than just physical pain. Her words hung heavy in the air, a cruel declaration slicing through the room, "You can't be my daughter, you are of no use to me. I regret the day you were born."

Pain in that moment was more than just physical. It was a visceral shattering of my heart. Her every word was a hammer that broke it into countless irreparable pieces. It wasn't the first time these words came out of her lips. But their impact always remained the same, no matter how many times she said them.

"God, stop lying there like a bag of garbage, get up," my father's voice pierced through the room. Pain seared through my skull as he seized me by my hair. He grabbed my arm, his grip iron-tight, and flung me forward with a force that stole my breath. Stumbling into the darkness of my room, I barely registered the movement before his shove sent me tumbling to the ground. The harsh impact of the floor knocked the air from my lungs, leaving me gasping. Behind me, the door slammed with a sound that echoed like thunder, sealing me off from the world outside with an ominous click.

The darkness enveloped me, thick and oppressive, as I lay sprawled across the floor's cold embrace. Each shiver sent by the chill ground contrasted sharply with the burning trails left by my tears. Shadows clung to the corners, watching silently as despair wrapped its arms around me. There, in the quiet, I sat, lost in the gloom, my heart aching for escape—a whisper of hope in the torment or the final piece of liberation.

In the silence that followed my sobs, my parents' voices crashed against the walls, breaking through with violence that felt almost physical. Their shouts, sharp and jagged, sliced through the quiet, landing like blows. With each word, each accusation hurled my way. An invisible burden grew heavier on my shoulders, making them shake under the unseen pressure.

"Why didn't you train her more? Why didn't you give her more time?" My father's voice boomed, each word striking like a hammer against my eardrums. In the thick of this auditory onslaught, my mother's retort soared, fierce and unyielding, clashing against his accusations in a tumultuous symphony of discord. Their exchanges, a relentless storm of blame and rebuke, painted a portrait of a union embroiled in perpetual strife. Amidst the cacophony, one couldn't help but wonder at the glue holding them together. The air, even on the rare days my father spent at home, was charged with the tension of impending quarrels, casting shadows of doubt on the very pillars of their marriage.

"She is not only my daughter. She is your daughter, too. Maybe if you had been more strict with her, this wouldn't have happened." Her voice cut through the tension, each word dripping with bitterness, weaving me tighter into their tangled expectations. Caught in the storm of their discord, I stood alone, a bewildered soul weighed down by their dissatisfaction, tormented by the relentless question of my misstep.

I found myself perpetually perplexed, each of my actions setting off a storm of intense reactions, yet never accompanied by clear explanations of my supposed faults. A simple act, such as declining an extra slice of toast, had unleashed a torrent of scolding. On another day, my mere presence became the scapegoat for my mom's frustration over a party gone awry. This had woven the fabric of my existence for sixteen years—a daily narrative devoid of warmth, care, or a sense of safety within the very walls that should embody home.

# Chapter One

# *Silent Resilience*

Wrapped in a haze of restless sleep, time lost its meaning overnight. Suddenly, a forceful shake and an even sharper voice yanked me from my dreams.

"Wake up. You can't just sleep all day. Get up and study for a while before leaving for school. You need to have some education before we marry you off." My mom's sharp command cut through the early morning, accompanied by the ruthless snatching of my blanket—the chilled air at 5 in the morning bit at my exposed skin. I shivered in the wake of the abrupt awakening, left alone.

But this was my daily routine, that began with the shrill echoes of my mom's warnings. Then there came a moment of peace when she retreated to her household chores. I have been seeing this for years now, even so, it never gets older. I never get used to it. Her behavior.

I begrudgingly picked up my textbook and started turning its pages. The smell of paper does calm me down in the morning. But the weight of her expectations hung heavy as I studied, preparing for the day ahead. Getting ready for school had become a mechanical process at this point, each step guided by the looming threat of potential scolding. I found myself punished for various reasons, varying from my clothes not being dry-cleaned to issues like the help not to arrive on time—matters entirely beyond my control. At first, I always tried to wonder what my mistakes were. But now, I don't really care now.

I stepped into the bathroom, preparing for the day ahead. Hot water flowed from the shower, cleansing away the remnants of yesterday's weariness and tears. As droplets glistened on my skin, I felt a sense of renewal. A sizzling shower provided a profound sense of comfort, similar to wrapping my body in an ever-protective blanket. It had become my sanctuary for years now, whether it was summers or winters. This was the only time in the day when I could simply exist—breathe freely, close my eyes, and allow the hot drops of water to caress and momentarily envelop me. It was almost like a therapeutic ritual for both my body and mind.

Coming out, I reached for my favorite ensemble—a combination carefully chosen for its comfort and familiarity. A dark green tunic top draped over my shoulders. Its soft fabric was a reassuring touch against my skin. Paired with it were black pants, my daily attire. I paused for a moment in front of the mirror in my room, reflecting on the inexplicable preference for dark-colored clothes. Maybe it was to hide the curves of my body that my mother hated so much. Something which I will never understand why. But this dark attire helped me hide when she looked at me with her judgmental eyes.

Turning my attention to my hair, I confronted the unruly chaos of chestnut-colored curls reaching up to my lower back. I was going for a coronet braid with my hair today. As I wove each strand, the repetitive motion became a form of self-care, a deliberate act to rein in the untamed strands. It was like a minor victory over the unpredictable nature of my life.

Freckles speckled across my face, a constellation of tiny marks that bore witness to the passage of time. Yet they could not convey the weariness etched beneath the surface. The exhaustion from yesterday lingered under my eyes. However, my body, with its round and chubby contours, served as a deceptive mask. The thing about having a rounded, chubby face is that it always obscures the struggles beneath, concealing the silent battles fought within. No one really suspects what you are going through.

There was an unspoken resilience woven into each action. The clothing, a shield against external judgments; hairstyle, a manifestation of control over chaos; and face, a canvas painted with both weariness and determination. It was a morning ritual transformed into a personal ceremony of strength.

The school was my safe place away from the problems at home. There, teachers praised me for being a hard worker, unaware of my true fear. Other kids thought I had the perfect life, with great parents and a lovely home. But they didn't realize that I never took a day off, not just because I liked studying, but because I didn't want to be at home with my mom. The idea of spending a whole day with her was just too much. Even on Sundays, I would go to extra classes for 6-8 hours, happy to be away from my parents. The school was one place where I could leave all my troubles behind, the one place where I felt okay.

The bell's ring cut through my daydreams, marking the end of another school day. With that sound, reality crashed back in, reminding me of the turmoil waiting at home. Hastily, I gathered my books, stuffing them into my bag, my hands shaky with apprehension. I was leaving behind the peace of school, a routine farewell that never got easier. Each step away from this refuge felt like a march toward an inevitable storm. A heavy sense of dread hung over me, an unwelcome companion on my walk home, as it did daily.

On my daily bus ride from school, Eldenhaven unfolded like a scene from a fairy tale. A dream glimpsed through the window but never fully lived. The town's allure lay in its cobblestone streets and colorful cottages, vibrant like a page from a storybook, observed but untouched. Passing by, I saw window boxes overflowing with flowers, their fragrances offering fleeting enchantments—a brief encounter with the outdoors.

The bustling marketplace, alive with treasures and laughter, turned into a fleeting view as we moved past in my chariot. The heart of Eldenhaven, known for its fresh produce and exquisite fabrics, stayed just beyond my grasp, a promise of wonders always just out of reach. Waterways under arched bridges, adorned with lanterns that appeared to float on air, turned into mere ribbons of curiosity during my ride.

The town's beauty shimmered in the clear streams. Its quaint doorways and chimneys seemed like pieces of a distant story, observed from afar. As evening approached, Eldenhaven transformed, bathed in the magical light of sunset. Lanterns began to flicker, casting a warm glow over ivy-clad buildings, all witnessed in the brief moments of my journey home.

The lively scenes outside my window contrasted with the quiet tones within, making me long for a taste of the world I knew was out there, but remained elusive. I played with the amulet on my neck, wondering if I would ever get to see what was there in the outside world.

# Chapter Two

# Shadowed Joy

Entering my room in my father's mansion felt like stepping into a gilded cage. I rarely called it home. The opulence surrounded me, but it was a cold, distant luxury that did little to ease the ache in my chest. The room reflected my father's status, more concerned with appearances than the well-being of the one who resided within.

He was more concerned with how we looked, what we did, and how we acted in front of others than actually talking to us and understanding how we felt. The heavy drapes, adorned with intricate patterns, hung from the ceiling to the floor. Its fabric was rich and regal, but it created an oppressive atmosphere, blocking out the natural light as if to keep the outside world at bay.

The room, though spacious, felt suffocating. The furniture, though exquisitely crafted, seemed more like a display than a lived-in space. Chromatic edges and fine details showcased my father's wealth, but the comfort one seeks in a home was conspicuously absent.

The golden hues of sunset, once warm, now seemed cold and distant. The centerpiece of the room was an imposing canopy bed, its posts reaching toward the ceiling like sentinels. The family crest adorned the impeccably arranged bedding, but layers of formality concealed the softness beneath.

The grand fireplace, now adorned with a portrait of the family, stood silent and unlit. Its coldness mirrored the strained relationships within these walls. The room echoed with the hollowness of opulence, the crackling flames replaced by a pervasive stillness.

Photographs on the walls captured staged family moments and frozen smiles that masked the tension beneath. Each image was a testament to the facade we maintained, a veneer of perfection that hid the cracks in our relationships.

The marble floors, polished to a gleaming sheen, added to the sterile elegance of the space. Each step echoed with a hollow sound, a stark reminder of the emptiness that pervaded this luxurious prison.

But sometimes I wondered if only I felt like a prisoner in this gilded mansion, or whether my sister felt this same. I had never seen Catriona take a beating, a scolding here and there was obvious, considering our parents, but never more than that!

Sometimes I thought she was the perfect daughter my parents wanted. She got the perfect scores. And was a beautiful slim ballet dancer currently practicing her moves in the front hall. Her hair, the color of spun gold, cascaded in sunlit waves down her shoulders. Each strand seemed to catch the sunlight, creating a soft, ethereal halo around her. The warmth of her golden tresses contrasted with the coolness of our surroundings.

Her eyes, a shade of azure that mirrored the clearest skies, held a spark of curiosity and innocence. Her lips, reminiscent of delicate rose petals, curved into a perpetual smile. It was a smile that held the promise of untold stories and dreams, a beacon of warmth in the otherwise austere environment. Despite her youth, she moved with a grace that contrasted her age. There was an innate elegance in the way she carried herself, as if she was already familiar with the dance of high society—a natural in a world that often felt foreign to me.

I unpacked my school bag and took out all my books and notebooks to start my homework. My mother was at home, she was always at home. She didn't work like my father did. But she did go to big social gatherings and extravagant parties. She mostly took Catriona with her. I stayed here with Whispers, a furry friend with fur as bright as sunshine.

Whispers was like a golden blanket that brought warmth and happiness, especially when everything felt a bit cold. Whispers' fur was like a bunch of golden sunbeams. When the light hit it, it was so shiny and pretty. It felt like touching a piece of warmth, even on the coldest days. He had big brown eyes that looked at you as if they understood everything. It was like they knew when you were feeling a bit sad and wanted to make you feel better. Those eyes were like a secret language between us.

When I was by myself, Whispers was like a buddy who was always there. He was a friend you could talk to without saying a word. Just running my fingers through his soft fur made everything feel a bit better. Startled by the sudden opening of the door of my room, I tried to contain it as my mom said, “Come, have lunch.”

“Already did,” I said with a cheerful smile if we consider cookies a lunch, but it was better than to sit with them, being stared at by them like an anomaly, or worse, start a conversation that might lead to me lying on the floor, beaten up.

My mom stared at me for a bit, opened her mouth to speak something, but then turned around, shut the door, and left. I closed my eyes in relief...

As I stepped out of my room in Eldenhaven, the transformation for the grand celebration became evident with each footfall. The hallway, once a quiet passage, now sparkled with strands of fairy lights strung along the walls, casting a soft, magical glow.

The air carried the sweet scent of flowers, weaving an invisible tapestry of anticipation. I made my way down the stairs, greeted by the lively hum of conversation and the laughter of guests echoing through the house. The staircase, adorned with garlands of vibrant blooms, felt like a passage into a realm of celebration.

Colorful decorations adorned the living quarters, which had earlier echoed with arguments. Streamers crisscrossed the ceiling, and balloons swayed gently, adding a playful touch to the atmosphere.

The heavy curtains, usually drawn to shield the room from the world, were now pulled back, revealing the spectacle outside—the vibrant streets of Eldenhaven alive with the celebration. Windows, once silent observers of my solitude, now framed scenes of joy and merriment.

The sunlight filtering through the festive decorations painted dancing patterns on the floor. It was as if the very essence of the celebration had permeated every corner, transforming the once-hushed space into a stage for the lively performance of festivities.

Laughter resonated through the air as friends and family filled the space, adorned in an array of elegant gowns and dresses. The atmosphere was alive with excitement, and the vibrant colors of the outfits added a touch of enchantment to the gathering.

The tantalizing aroma of food wafted through the rooms, creating a sensory symphony that beckoned everyone to join in the feast. It was a momentous occasion, a tapestry of joy woven with the threads of shared love and togetherness. It was a celebration of tastes and textures, each dish a testament to the culinary prowess that defines Eldenhaven's Heritage Day.

The dining table, adorned with a vibrant array of dishes, became a focal point for the festivities. It was not just a place to eat; it was a space where the community came together to revel in the joy of good company, delightful flavors, and the rich tapestry of Eldenhaven's culinary heritage.

As the evening unfolded, the warmth of camaraderie enveloped us, making this gathering not just a party but a mosaic of cherished memories. Amid the vibrant celebration, an unsettling undercurrent of sadness and fear permeated the air.

Beneath the facade of festivity, the echoes of past wounds lingered, especially when it came to my relationship with my parents. Their presence cast a shadow of unease. Behind their smiles, there was a palpable tension that used to send shivers down my spine. The fear was not born out of ordinary anxieties, but a haunting reminder of past experiences with their abusive tendencies.

It was as if the festivity magnified the stark contrast between the outward joy and the internal turmoil. My mom's gaze remained a constant presence, a watchful eye observing my every action. Navigating the gathering became a delicate dance between participating in the celebration and trying to shield myself from the emotional minefield.

The heavyweight of unresolved issues tainted the happiness of the occasion, creating a complex emotional landscape that left me grappling with conflicting emotions. Whenever my parents were around during happy times, it was like they brought a heavy cloud with them.

Even when everyone else was laughing and enjoying themselves, their presence made everything feel off. The good vibes and cheerful moments suddenly turned into a balancing act, trying to keep the joy from being completely overshadowed by their influence.

I found myself wondering whether I had truly experienced genuine enjoyment or ever felt true happiness in my life. It was as if they had this knack for turning any celebration into a bit of a battlefield. The colors might be bright here, and people might be chatting happily, but there was always this unspoken tension when they were around. Their presence somehow managed to cast a shadow over the fun.

Following my mom's house rule, I had abstained from eating anything since morning in anticipation of an upcoming party. Now, feeling the pangs of hunger, I eagerly grabbed a plate to satisfy my appetite. The air was filled with cheerful chatter, and the vibrant colors of the celebration infused a sense of joy into the atmosphere.

However, my excitement was abruptly interrupted by my mom's sharp voice, cutting through the jubilant din with a tone that carried subtle disapproval.

"Do you need that much on your plate, Aria? You should really watch what you eat."

Her words hit me like a sudden gust of cold wind, and a knot of discomfort tightened in my stomach. I didn't know why I held onto the hope that today would be different, that I could somehow escape my usual fate and find a moment of peace.

Unfortunately, it seemed I was wrong once again. It was supposed to be a celebration, a moment of joy, yet her scrutiny threatened to overshadow the happiness that should accompany such occasions. My gaze instinctively shifted to my sister Catriona, sitting nearby. She was slim, barely touching her plate, if at all.

The comparison added another layer to my unease, and my mom knew that and took every advantage of it. The celebration, once a beacon of delight, now bore the weight of my mom's critical gaze, and the festivity lost some of its luster. To salvage the moment, I mustered the courage to defend my simple desire.

"It's a celebration, Mom. I just want to enjoy the food. I am hungry." I tried justifying my eating. Her response was not just a disapproving glance; it felt like a silent rebuke, adding another layer of tension to an otherwise joyous occasion.

"Celebration doesn't mean overindulgence. You should be more mindful of your choices. You are already a disgrace to look at." As her words lingered, the emotional landscape shifted.

The celebration, meant to be a source of happiness, became a battleground where my desire to rebel clashed with the weight of her expectations. The vibrant scene, once so full of life, now carried an undercurrent of emotional unease.

My appetite faded away, and I threw my plate in the dump behind the table. As I navigated through the gathering, the echoes of her words lingered, creating a silent dialogue that spoke volumes about the complexities woven into family interactions during moments of celebration.

*You are a fat, disgusting person to look at. No wonder nobody likes you. No wonder your parents hate you. Look at your sister, an epitome of perfection. Can you blame your parents for beating you? Just look at yourself!* Voices echoed through my brain.

The thing with hatred is that, once people around you start to hate you, then after a while, you internalize that hate. You forget that it is the voice of people around you. You start hating yourself, believing that something is really wrong with you.

Mom's words, like a lingering echo, planted seeds of inadequacy within me. As I navigated the celebration, each glance at the festive spread became accompanied by a twinge of self-doubt. The joy that should accompany the gathering was now clouded by a sense of not measuring up to expectations.

The lively conversations around me became a backdrop to my internal dialogue, questioning my choices and actions. It was a struggle to find a balance between enjoying the celebration and silencing the nagging voice of inadequacy fueled by my mother's subtle taunts.

Seeking solace, I stepped out onto the terrace, hoping the cool night air would provide a reprieve from the internal turmoil. The distant sounds of the celebration served as a reminder of the gathering I was momentarily escaping.

The quietness of the terrace became a refuge, allowing me to gather my thoughts. Never had I embraced my body with confidence; the relentless comments about being overweight and not fitting societal norms had eroded my self-confidence.

The weight of expectations, especially from my parents, left me feeling like an outsider in a world that dictates a narrow definition of acceptance. After a while, as the weight of the evening still lingered, I retreated to the comfort of my bed.

The soft embrace of the sheets offered a brief relief from the emotional turbulence, allowing me a moment of solitude to reflect and cry in peace. Hopefully, find a path back to a sense of peace and self-assurance.

# Chapter Three

## Hidden Boundaries

"Come here, Aria, put on this gown and get ready," announced my mom as she burst into my room, her entrance as sudden as a thunderclap. I couldn't help but flinch. The whispers, which usually kept me company in silence, seemed to echo my surprise, fleeing the room like startled spirits.

Holding a gown in her hands, my mom presented a mesmerizing cascade of turquoise water with golden lace that shimmered like the sea at the golden hour of sunset. The gown stood as an artwork of emotions—its color bringing to mind calm waters, and its lace reflecting the warmth of a setting sun. Awestruck me, but the impatience in my mom's demeanor quickly snapped me back to reality.

"What were you staring at? I told you to get up and get ready," she snapped at me. Caught between the ethereal beauty of the gown and the urgency in her voice, I shook off my reverie.

"Where are we going?" I asked. The question lingered in the room, carrying the weight of anticipation and a touch of uncertainty.

"I am taking you to a gathering where all the high ladies of the societies are bringing the children of your age; you all should get to know each other," she declared, her words carrying a sense of formality.

"Is Catriona going?" I asked, my eyes searching for clues in my mother's expression.

"No," she replied, the single word holding a weighty finality that left me with more questions than answers.

"Why?" I pressed, knowing this was not an intelligent thing to do. The air in the room seemed to thicken with unspoken secrets as I awaited her response.

"Don't ask me useless questions, girl. If I tell you to go, then you will go. No questions asked," she shouted, her words cutting through the air like a sharp wind.

A surge of frustration welled up within me, but I knew better than to challenge her at that moment. I bit back any retort, my silence a thin veil covering the rebellion smoldering within.

"No way am I getting into that gown," I murmured, my voice a quiet protest against the impending conformity. The gown, despite its aesthetic appeal, felt like a straitjacket, suffocating and uncomfortable. I loathed it. I despised every inch of it.

Catriona could effortlessly embrace its elegance. Not me. I yearned for the comfort of loose pants and tunics, the freedom to move unencumbered. This gown was a symbol of constraint, and every fiber of my being rebelled against the idea of wearing it.

"Will you get up now, or do I need to remind you how my hand feels on your face?" she threatened, her words as sharp as a knife. Before I could fully grasp the weight of her words, she seized me by the hair, pulling me upright with a force that sent a jolt through my body.

"Get ready. We will leave in one hour," she commanded, her tone leaving no room for dissent. The door slammed shut behind her, the loud echo reverberating in the room, leaving behind a suffocating silence. I reluctantly prepared for the impending gathering—an unwilling participant in a celebration that felt more like a facade.

As I stood before the mirror, the gown became a reflection of my struggles—a masterpiece of turquoise water and golden lace. Its allure was undeniable, but beneath the surface lay a discomfort that tightened with every breath, as if elegant layers of fabric were an intricate prison I never desired. I wondered if this was my fate. If I would ever escape this misery. I tucked the broken heart amulet under my gown, forcing a smile on my face. A smile that didn't touch my eyes, wondering where the other half of this amulet might be...wondering if its other half might be free!

The gown ceased to be a mere garment; it transformed into a symbol of societal pressures, molding me into a shape I didn't recognize. Resentment simmered within a quiet rebellion against the expectations that society imposed on me.

Preparing for the gathering felt like gearing up for a secret evaluation, where the high ladies would meticulously examine every facet of my being—my appearance, my actions, and how well I conformed to their limited standards of desirability.

The weight of this realization pressed down on me, an oppressive burden extending beyond my individuality. I found myself playing a part in a system where people selected the most fitting "object" for their sons, reducing personal worth to a transaction.

Despite my internal resistance, the gown symbolized reluctant compliance. With a deep breath, I gathered the remnants of my strength and stepped into a world where celebration evolved into a dehumanizing spectacle. The interactions with the high ladies visually portrayed the clash between my authentic self and the societal expectations imposed upon me, creating a poignant narrative of inner turmoil and external conformity.

It hit me hard that I was trapped in a cycle of submission. Refusing my mother meant inviting more pain and more bruises, and I had reached a point where the physical toll of defiance was too much to bear. I closed my eyes for a moment, trying to summon the courage to stand up for myself, but the fear of another brutal confrontation prevailed.

The prospect of enduring another round of her wrath was paralyzing, pushing me to sacrifice my own desires for the sake of temporary peace. So, I chose the path of least resistance, a choice dictated by survival rather than free will. With a heavy heart and a sense of resignation, I prepared to step into the suffocating gown and embark on a journey I never asked for but couldn't escape. It was a silent surrender to the harsh reality that bound me, a narrative of compliance etched in every step I took.

In the silence left by my father's frequent absences, the house seemed to breathe a quiet sigh of relief, wrapping me in a blanket of solitude far removed from the mysteries of his livelihood. His presence, when it did filter through the spaces of our home, felt like the fleeting shadow of a ghost, echoing off the cold marble floors and high ceilings, leaving a chill in its wake. Our conversations, rare and fleeting, always ended with his sharp command to "shut up," a verbal barrier that kept me at arm's length.

The mansion, a sprawling testament to his unseen ventures, whispered secrets through the hushed tones of servants and maids. They spoke of cargoes filled with wonders from distant lands: textiles that shimmered with the promise of faraway places, trinkets that whispered ancient tales, scrolls, and books bound in mystery, pottery that bore the touch of artisan's hands, and jewelry that seemed imbued with magic. Yet these treasures, as vibrant and diverse as they were, remained shadows behind the veil of my father's reticence.

Each time he returned from his travels, the air around the dinner table thickened with unspoken stories. He spoke in half sentences, alluding to journeys northward, leaving trails of words that hinted at vast endeavors but revealed nothing.

Outside, the mountains stood tall against the sky, their peaks shrouded in mist and mystery. From the terrace, bathed in sunlight and surrounded by the riotous colors of the garden, I tried to lose myself in their majesty, allowing my imagination to roam free. The mountains, with their ever-changing play of light and shadow, seemed to echo the stories untold, their ancient faces keeping watch over the land.

With a book in hand, I found solace in the tales of others; the mountains becoming the backdrop to my own quiet contemplation, their silent strength a counterpoint to the swirling questions about my father's hidden world.

Whispers, with his golden fur catching the sun's rays, became a steadfast friend in my isolated world. As systematic barriers kept schoolmates and potential friends from my life, Whispers filled the loneliness void with his silent companionship.

Attempts by my classmates to meet me at my home's walls were met with stern rebuffs at the gate, their thoughtful gestures like birthday cakes remained untold secrets to me. Gradually, the effort to maintain friendships seemed futile, leading me to retreat further into solitude, silencing my own voice in a world that offered no echo.

Invisible barriers circumscribed my existence: rules forbade outings, and the idea of guests crossing our threshold was unimaginable. A single attempt by a classmate, as she tried to reach me over the phone, and brought down harsh repercussions, confining me away from school and any semblance of normalcy for a week. In this landscape of restrictions, Whispers wandered into our lives, an unexpected anomaly that my parents, for reasons unknown, chose not to correct—perhaps swayed by Catriona's affection for him as well.

In the quiet moments with Whispers, I found a fragile peace, a temporary shelter from the storm of isolation. The sight of my father returning from his trade travel abruptly disturbed this tranquility. The disruption, however, took a more tangible form in the presence of a boy from school, courageously stepping into my secluded world with the simple act of returning a notebook.

The distant look from my father, laden with unspoken warnings, sent a chill down my spine, a prelude to the inevitable confrontation that awaited me. The sanctuary I had found in Whispers' silent understanding stood in stark contrast to the impending storm heralded by my father's return and the boy's defiant kindness.

As my dad approached the unfamiliar boy, tension filled the air, thickening with each step. His gaze, a silent augury, pierced through the distance and locked onto me. At that moment, the weight of his scrutiny alone sent shivers down my spine, an ominous foreboding of the storm that awaited me.

The look held a mix of expectation, disappointment, and a subtle warning, signaling an impending confrontation or reckoning that echoed through the very core of my being. It was a silent tempest brewing in his eyes, and I could already feel its reverberations in the pit of my stomach. Feeling an intensified emotion, something more perilous than before, triggered an instinctual urge to escape.

As my dad took the notebook from the boy, I sensed a shift in the air, a palpable tension that wrapped around us like an invisible coil. His stern gaze fixated on the boy, and a cold silence descended upon the moment. I glanced at the boy, my classmate, who looked uneasy and quickly retreated, leaving our home in haste.

"Aria, we need to talk," he said. His ominous tone sent a shiver down my spine. Clutching the notebook tightly, he led the way into the house, leaving me with a foreboding sense of dread about our upcoming conversation. As we stepped inside, the door closed behind us with a resonant creak, encapsulating me in a space where the storm of my father's disapproval loomed ominously.

For what seemed an eternity, he just stared at me, pondering his next words, his demeanor. These moments stretched into eternity, a precursor to the calamity I feared would soon befall me, a replay of past confrontations where no one ever saved me. Powerless and paralyzed by fear, I couldn't ever muster the courage to defend myself, to declare my innocence, or to inquire about my supposed fault this time.

As the evening progressed, the air grew thick with the tension of words left unsaid. I cast nervous glances at Dad, who appeared engrossed in thought, the notebook a silent harbinger of the tempest to come lying on the table. Whispers, ever perceptive, curled up beside me, offering a sliver of comfort amidst the escalating dread.

In the quiet, my mind raced with a torrent of self-doubt, shame, and regret. *I warned Keish not to come here. Could Dad's silence be the calm before a storm, a tempest poised to ravage?* The uncertainty of the forthcoming retribution haunted me. A mere act of a classmate returning a notebook shouldn't evoke such fear, yet my heart hammered against my chest, driven by the fear of the unknown.

Trying to convince myself of my dad's reasonableness, I sought solace in the hope that perhaps no explanation would be needed. However, a persistent doubt whispered that such reassurances were but a fragile defense against what lay ahead.

Wrestling with my thoughts, I faced the duality of overthinking and the real possibility of a dire outcome. The fear that words might prove insufficient overshadowed the prospect of explaining myself to my dad.

*I told him not to come.* Recalling the moment the boy from school stood at our door, I remembered cautioning him against this very scenario, aiming to protect him from the potential fallout.

Caught in the suspense of waiting, my thoughts spun in a whirlwind of uncertainty. In this moment of introspection, I reflected on Keish—his tousled dark hair, eyes reflecting the twilight sky, and an aura of serene strength, offering a brief diversion from the inner chaos.

Keish had been a constant presence in my academic journey, a familiar classmate since the days when I first began to grasp the art of reading. Despite sharing the same school and class for years, silent glances and unspoken acknowledgments limited our interactions. This distance was not because of indifference or lack of interest, but a consequence of the unspoken rules that governed my life.

These rules stemmed from the stern disapproval that might befall me if my parents discovered me engaging in something as innocent as a conversation with a boy. While Catriona, fortunate in her familial love and support, had never had to navigate such treacherous waters, my reality told a different story altogether.

Over the years, subtle moments occurred when Keish and I exchanged glances, hinting at his interest in starting a conversation. Yet, a decade slipped by before he gathered the courage to approach me.

His nervousness was evident as he stammered, "Can you lend me your history notebook, Ariana? I... uh... failed to copy from the board." Surprised by this unexpected interaction, I handed over my notebook. My heart pounded in response, my face turning red.

"Of course," I managed, masking my excitement.

"I'll return it to your place," he offered, a genuine smile cutting through his initial nervousness. However, the stark reality of my situation struck me abruptly, like an unforeseen thunderstorm.

"I'll take it from you in class. You don't have to come to my home," I quickly added, turning away to cut short the conversation. It wasn't merely about returning a notebook; it was a stark reminder of the boundaries and restrictions that dictated my interactions, and the fear that any deviation might invite consequences I was not prepared to face.

# Chapter Four

## *Battered Escape*

What should have been a routine visit—a boy returning a borrowed notebook—morphed into a prelude to a living nightmare. The intangible dread within me intensified, coiling like a serpent. My stomach twisted with an inexplicable sense of guilt.

It was as though I had committed an unforgivable sin, the weight of which bore down on me, making me retreat into the recesses of darkness, away from the impending storm. Beside me, Whispers tried to accompany me, his golden soft hair a small beacon in the encroaching darkness.

Yet, the turmoil within me persisted. I was shaking, ensnared by an unnamed fear that refused to let go. The door to my room slammed against the wall. The frame itself shuddered from the impact. This violence heralded my dad's arrival. He stood on the threshold, a looming figure.

His one hand swung freely by his side. The other gripped a heated iron rod. It was glowing red at the end. He stormed towards me. His eyes burned with a ferocity that outshone the rod's ominous gleam. They fixed on me, stripping away any hope of escape.

*This might very well be my last day.*

At that moment, a strange comfort enveloped me. It was an odd sense of peace, realizing this might be the final time they could hurt me. Perhaps this encounter would be the last. Afterward, I might find liberation, even if it meant death.

I told myself to endure it just this once. This inevitable torture might be happening for the last time. Deep down, I knew no one would come to save me. They never had.

As the assault began, time seemed to distort. Every hit, every burn, twisted into a relentless storm of pain. My dad struck my arm with the rod's heated end. It left behind a searing red mark that pulsed with agony. A whimper escaped my mouth as my skin burned.

Simultaneously, Mom's hand-delivered a forceful blow to the left side of my face, sending me crashing to the floor. *Another Burn*. My knees smashed against the unyielding floor. I tried to contain it, but a sob escaped my lips, a feeble cry in the face of relentless brutality.

The whimper that escaped my lips seemed to stoke the fury in my dad's eyes in a blistering inferno. With a tightening grip that promised no mercy, the rod descended on my shin with ruthless precision. The initial strike sent a jolt of excruciating pain shooting through my leg, a precursor to the torment to follow.

Hardly a breath passed before another blow landed, each hit resonating through the room, a cruel symphony accompanying the crescendo of shouts. With every strike, the pain burrowed deeper, a relentless force weaving through my muscles, embedding itself into the very marrow of my bones.

Blow after blow descended upon me, blurring the lines between my father's and mother's hands. My senses numbed, overwhelmed by the onslaught, yet a sharp, piercing realization cut through the haze—a cracking sound. The bone in my leg fractured and pain seared through my nerves.

But they did not stop at the sound. THEY DID NOT STOP. it was like they were enjoying this. They were waiting for this moment. An excuse to kill me.

At this point, all I really wanted was for it to end. I wanted my pain to stop. I didn't care whether it meant giving up the pathetic life. I wanted this torture to end.

"You think you can defy me? Disobey my orders?" I flinched as Dad's words, heavy with rage, echoed around the room, each syllable dripping with the threat of further violence, weaving a dense atmosphere of fear and control. Each word he uttered cut through the air, anchoring me further into a reality where I had no control, no say.

"You need to learn your place. This is for your own good," Mom said, her tone softer yet chillingly detached as if she was discussing a mundane household chore rather than justifying the unspeakable thing they were doing. It felt like she was wrapping cruelty in a blanket of twisted maternal concern, suggesting this brutality was somehow for my benefit.

But inside me, something had shifted. I realized I felt nothing about their words, their actions, or even the fact that they were my parents. An emptiness had settled in me, a numbing void that seemed to consume any semblance of care or concern. I was becoming a shell, an echo of a person, no longer touched by feelings of pain or longing. The only flicker of desire left in me was for an escape, a quiet wish to simply… disappear, to fade into the background where this torment couldn't reach.

"I'll beat the defiance out of you. You'll learn to respect," the man sneered through his teeth. His every word became a shadow, an ominous prelude to the stick's merciless strikes. The fiery end seared my skin, a cruel signature left with each contact, an extension of his hideous character.

"You disgrace this family. We must cleanse you of your rebellious spirit," the woman who was supposed to be my mother added. She raised her head as she said. Her words painted the violence as a grotesque ritual, a perverse means of purging my defiance as if pain could somehow sanctify.

*What did I do? How was it so wrong? It was just a notebook.*

"You're a stain on our legacy. This is the only way to teach you a lesson." The voices blurred into one, indistinguishable in their disdain. Their words sliced deeper than the physical pain, each utterance a stinging rebuke of my existence, my identity.

This rod was not merely a tool. It was a statement of rejection from my parents, that no matter how hard I tried, no matter what I did, I was just a mistake for them that needed to be corrected. They hated me. For my existence.

"Maybe now you'll understand the consequences of your actions," Mom's voice, tinged with an eerie calmness, transformed the ordeal into a twisted form of discipline. The lines between punishment and cruelty blurred as the room bore witness to a nightmarish tableau of parental authority gone wrong. No, this was no parenting at all.

Even though I am just sixteen years old, even though I do not have any child of my own. But I also know that you can't treat your children like this. Should not treat your children like this.

My cries, desperate and pleading, vanished into the void, unheard and unheeded. The room, once a haven of peace, morphed into a theater of anguish. My dad's hand, driven by a storm of anger, moved the stick with a precision that inscribed tales of sorrow deep within me.

With every descent of the rod, despair thickened the air, its strikes slicing the quiet, a dark symphony of malice. Its heated end branded my skin, each contact a fiery brushstroke on a canvas of flesh, leaving a trail of blisters that glowed with the intense colors of pain.

Each harsh blow I received served as a stark reminder of my helplessness, despite my attempts to shield myself and offer defense. My skin, once unmarred, became a vivid mural, a testament to the brutality inflicted upon it, a grotesque masterpiece painted in strokes of red and purple.

Fear, pain, and a crushing sense of helplessness churned within me, a stormy sea threatening to engulf what remained of my spirit. My body, caught in the crossfire, screamed with every touch, every nerve alight with the fire of pain. Tears, the silent witnesses of my ordeal, ran down my face and my leg twisted at an unnatural angle.

The storm of violence finally subsided, leaving behind nothing but a shattered figure crumpled on the ground, a haunting silhouette of defeat. The floor's cold seeped through my bruised skin, a grim reminder of how exposed and fragile I had become. A brief, scornful look from my parents was the only goodbye before they decided I had endured enough—for now.

Dragging me across the boundary of what was once a home, they threw me onto the porch with as much care as one might give to a piece of unwanted furniture. I shuddered as the outside air, sharp with the sting of winter, clashed violently against my wounded flesh.

"Stay here for the night. You'll learn the consequences of your defiance," my dad declared, his back turning to me, shoulders rigid, as if he was proud of his masterpiece, now reflecting on my skin. Beside him, my mother's face showed no mercy, her expression set in stone. The sound of the door closing was a definitive seal on my fate, isolating me in a lonely embrace of abandonment.

*But what defiance?*

The house, once a beacon of familial warmth, now towered ominously above me. It stood silent, a monolith indifferent to the agony it witnessed, casting a long shadow over my broken form left to weather the cold alone.

The porch, usually a threshold between the sanctuary of home and the vast unknown, transformed into a nightmarish space. I gazed at the stars above, seeking solace in their distant glow. Yet, the celestial lights offered no reprieve, their luminescence mocking the darkness that enveloped me. Tears ran down my face uncontrolled.

But the true dagger to my heart came with my dad's ominous threat about Whispers. The loyal companion who had shared my joys and endured my sorrows was now sentenced to separation.

"Whispers will not be staying with us anymore. He'll be better off without you anyway." his words echoed in my brain as the haze of pain wore off. The threat of abandoning him at a dog shelter, of him facing the world alone clawed at the remnants of my shattered resilience.

He had been my solace through countless storms. At this moment, his absence felt like a phantom limb. Silence enveloped me, thick and oppressive, as I wrestled with memories of former hurts and the looming possibility of parting ways with Whispers.

The flickering porch light overhead had cast feeble shadows, dancing grotesquely on the floor like malevolent spirits reveling in my suffering. The world beyond the porch had seemed distant and alien as if the boundaries of our home had become an insurmountable chasm. My leg hurt terribly.

The house behind me was silent, its closed doors a tangible barrier between me and all that had transpired inside. I couldn't fathom how my parents could sleep so peacefully after what they had done. The lights were off, and there I sat in the darkness, feeling the acute pain in my leg.

In front of me, the garden stretched out. Moonlight painted a path through the flowers, and for the first time, I noticed the beauty in the multitude of flowers. They were so beautiful yet so delicate, varying in colors, shapes, and sizes, yet all were loved and cared for equally.

They were not differentiated based on their color or form, all receiving equal amounts of nourishment and love. Then why not me... Why did my parents hate me? I thought today would be the end. I believed I would finally escape this hellish existence, but no! I was still alive... and I didn't want to be. I couldn't bear to spend another day in this house. I just couldn't bear it anymore. There must be some way out, some way to end all this suffering.

A surge of anger and despair washed over me as if the amulet on my neck was mocking me with its brokenness. It was a constant reminder of how alone and unloved I was, how no one ever truly cared for me or understood me. I hated it, I hated myself, I hated everything.

With an impulse, I snatched the broken heart iron amulet from my neck, breaking the chain that held it, and threw it away with all my strength as if I could throw away my pain and misery with it. I watched it fly through the air, landing somewhere in the grass, out of my sight.

I collapsed to the ground, sobbing uncontrollably. Tears streamed down my face, each drop carrying the weight of a lifetime of sorrow. I curled up into a ball, hugging my knees to my chest as if I could protect myself from the world. I felt empty, broken, hopeless.

The amulet, once a source of comfort and support, now lay discarded and forgotten in the grass. The other half of the heart, the other half of me, was somewhere out there, maybe free, maybe happy, maybe loved. But I would never know, I would never find it, I would never be whole.

A lone lamp post in front of me stood at the edge of the garden, casting a soft light on the pathway. The moonlight turned the flowers into silver dreams. Each flower possessed a story, and it felt like they accompanied me, silently witnessing my pain. I felt the pathway covered with fallen leaves and mud, calling to me, bathed in the moon's glow.

I tried to stand on my stable leg, wincing with pain, and followed it, absorbing the beauty of the night-blooming flowers. The petals of the flowers unfolded like delicate dancers, sharing their fragrance with the night.

I never knew it was so beautiful. It was as if I was seeing it for the first time. The once-overlooked garden transformed into a refuge for my wounded soul. Leaves rustled in the night breeze, creating a gentle melody.

The mansion stood tall against the night sky, holding the secrets of a broken family. The windows, like curious eyes, reflected the vast sky, unaware of the pain within. At that moment, the garden became a shelter, a refuge from the storm in my home.

My broken leg throbbed, a painful reminder of what had happened. The pain was there, but so was a strength building inside me. The moonlit garden reflected the strength I wanted to find in myself.

*What if I just leave this house and go out? What if I never look back? These people will never miss me. I am already a burden on them! What could happen worse than this?*

My brain was constantly searching for ways to escape this fate, this torture. In the quiet of the night, I walked through the garden. The cool grass beneath my feet served as a soothing balm for the pains I carried. Each step felt like a small escape from the hurts that had become a part of me.

Walking with a wince of pain, clothes wet with blood sticking to my skin, I found myself drawn to a beautiful archway adorned with angels. It was the first time I was crossing this archway alone, and perhaps only this stood between me and my freedom. Maybe my fate didn't have to be this way anymore. Hope took hold of my heart as I moved forward.

The archway, stationed at the entrance of the garden, held a forgotten kind of beauty. Adorned with winged creatures and angels, its eyes seemed to look sad as if comprehending my pain. Limping and wincing, I moved closer.

The stone-carved angels looked at me with a quiet understanding, as if they knew the troubles of my heart, or maybe it was my brain making up things that I wanted to see in other people. I stepped forward, attempting to touch the beautiful archway, seeking to feel its beauty.

Suddenly, a bright flashing light emerged, resembling a sudden burst of colors. It wasn't just light; it felt like colliding with something magical, something beautiful and powerful, something colorful and colorless at the same time. Glancing back at the garden, the once-familiar area now appeared as a foreign place, with the archway serving as its magical doorway.

Maybe I was disoriented and imagining all this due to my injuries. This couldn't be possible; magic doesn't exist in the real world. Or was this another way to punish me? Fear gripped me. The dazzling light that danced with vibrant hues startled and soothed me at the same time, feeling like stepping into the unknown, a place where the rules of reality might not apply.

The beauty of the garden and the comforting touch of the grass suddenly felt like relics of the past. It all happened in a second, or perhaps I had been there for hours; I had no idea. Time felt distorted at the moment. As the colors intensified, my heart raced with uncertainty.

The once-enchanting magical show now seemed overwhelming. The archway, which had promised healing, became a source of anxiety. The angels, with their understanding eyes, now resembled more like guardians of an unfamiliar realm. Standing at the entrance, my hesitation grew. The garden, touched by the cosmic force, took on an otherworldly appearance. The plants and animals seemed to morph into fantastical shapes, and the once-quiet pathway now whispered with an eerie unknown.

*Home.*

And suddenly, it felt like I was hit hard on my head, and then everything blacked out.

# Chapter Five

# A New World

Consciousness embraced me gently, and I blinked my eyes open slowly. A dull ache pulsed through my head, serving as a lingering reminder of something elusive. As awareness settled in, I realized I was lying in a bed that felt unusually soft. The warmth wrapped around me, momentarily making me wonder if I was experiencing some kind of heavenly comfort.

Confusion began to stir within me. This bed, this room—it didn't match the familiar surroundings of my own room. I wondered whether I was in Catriona's room, or if, perhaps, moved by guilt, my mother had allowed me to sleep in her own room. The thought briefly crossed my mind, a small hope that they regretted the harshness of the previous night.

I slowly rubbed my eyes, allowing the room's soft glow to clear my vision. The light was different here, softer, and beautiful, creating a peaceful atmosphere that seemed to wash away the painful memories of the night before. With some hesitation, I got up from the bed and swung my legs over the side, wincing to expect a sharp pain from my previously broken leg.

Surprisingly, there was no pain. It was like the night had magically healed my injuries, mending the breaks and healing the wounds without a trace. I cautiously stepped out of bed, feeling the cool floor beneath my feet. Amazed at the absence of pain, I inspected my leg, finding it healed and without any signs of the previous injury. This must be a dream.

A grand mirror in the corner of the room drew my attention. It was huge and lavish, making me wonder who would need such a massive-looking glass to look at themselves. I walked toward it, and my reflection appeared—a tranquil face that I didn't recognize. The marks of torment, the bruises, and the scars had vanished. A fair face with delicate freckles looked back at me.

A loose, flowing white gown clothed me, embodying comfort and elegance at the same time. The fabric, though simple, draped gracefully around my body. I marveled at the transformation for a moment. This couldn't be the same person who had faced condemnation and revilement just the last night. In the soft glow of the room, I saw a version of myself that might have never experienced any harsh realities of life.

An intricate design of rustic metal bordered the mirror, catching my eye. Its artistry showed craftsmanship beyond utility—an aesthetic that went beyond mere functionality. I traced the patterns with my fingers, captivated by the beauty woven into the very frame that held my reflection.

A luxurious and elegant bedroom surrounded me, and the bed, the room's centerpiece, symbolized comfort and sophistication. A harmonious blend of various shades of grey colored the room, creating a calming and timeless, yet a little boring, if I might add, atmosphere that invited safety.

The sheets, arranged meticulously, radiated a pristine quality that invited me to sink into comfort and tranquility, even though I had just gotten up from the bed. It was as if no one had touched them. The headboard, elegant and intricate, boasted detailing that showed the craftsmanship in every aspect of the room's design.

A chandelier hung above the bed like a constellation of luxury, exuding a soft, ambient glow. Its crystals caught the light, creating a dance of reflections that enhanced the room's opulent ambiance. The chandelier didn't just illuminate; it made a statement, elevating the bedroom's aesthetic to a level of refined extravagance.

My gaze traversed the room, and the walls revealed themselves as canvases of grandeur. Intricate moldings adorned the walls, creating depth and texture that contributed to the abundance.

The curtains draped gracefully by the windows and handpicked accent pieces adorned dressers and side tables. Nightstands with matching lamps featuring white shades were on either side of the bed. A throw pillow in a complementary shade rested on top of each nightstand. A couch covered in pillows stood in front of one wall and, another chandelier hung above this couch, bringing balance to the room's design elements.

As I was admiring the lavish decor, panic slowly set in, and the door of the bedroom swung open, disrupting the tranquil atmosphere. Anticipation filled the room as my gaze shifted to the entrance. A figure, shrouded in the subdued lighting, stepped into the room, blending into the enchanting ambiance. It was a girl, I think, at the door.

"Who are you?" I asked, my feet stumbling backward into the dresser, "And where am I?"

As she approached, something caught my attention. She resembled me in height, but a slender, human-like figure. However, her eyes stood out. They were large, with purple eyeballs that matched the color of her beautiful hair, sharp and contrasting against her white skin. Her face was a masterpiece crafted by nature's skilled hands. High cheekbones graced her features, a nose as straight as an arrow, and a jawline that defied mortal perfection. Long, slender fingers moved with supernatural grace. In the room, her lithe form moved with nature's grace. She glided effortlessly, and every step left behind a trail of sparkling motes, like stardust scattered in her wake. It was as if the very fabric of the room responded to her presence, creating an enchanting symphony of whispers.

My gaze traveled to the beautiful blueish dress on her body as she stepped toward me and extended her hand.

"I am Ivy," she said, smiling in a gentle tone. I stumbled back once again into the dresser. Ivy studied me for a moment, her big purple sparkling eyes holding an otherworldly depth as she spoke.

"You don't have to be afraid of me. I am not going to harm you, and no one here will."

I tried to ask her again, "Where am I, and who are you?" Or maybe I should have asked what she was. A flicker of doubt crossed my mind — was this a dream, a result of the harsh beating that knocked me out? Was I dreaming all this? Was I still lying in that garden? My heart raced at the thought of whether I was dead! But whatever Ivy was, she was definitely not human.

She sighed, understanding on her face. "This is Eloria," she hissed. "And I am Ivy. I have to help you and get you ready. The High Lord has assigned me to take care of you because I look a little bit like a human," she said, pinching her fingers in the air, "so you don't get scared when you see me." My eyebrows shot up in surprise. I couldn't comprehend what she just said.

"I know you have plenty of questions, and you'll get all your answers. Trust me. One step at a time. But first, let's get you ready for breakfast. The High Lord expects you in an hour."

"Highlor.....?" I tried to speak, but she effortlessly turned me around and opened a door without even touching it. I looked at her, astonished and confused at the same time. She smiled and guided me to the bathroom. Stepping into the bathroom of *this royal place.*

As the door swung open, the first thing that struck me was the walls, painted in the purest white, capturing and reflecting the room's ambient light. This gave the space an airy, almost ethereal quality. My eyes were drawn to the elegant sconces on the walls, each adorned with crystal accents, their gentle, warm glow adding to the room's opulent atmosphere. The air was tinged with a subtle fragrance of fresh flowers, creating a sensory experience that instantly captivated me.

Stepping further into the lavish bathroom, a grand freestanding tub immediately commanded my attention. Its smooth curves and gleaming white surface seemed to invite relaxation, placed invitingly beneath a sizable window. The sheer curtains adorning the window allowed glimpses of meticulously manicured gardens outside, while the soft glow of natural light filtered through, illuminating the space. On the water's surface, fresh flower petals floated, their serene and enchanting aura infusing the room.

Next to the tub, a vanity with a pristine marble countertop boasted gleaming silver accents. Atop it, crystal perfume bottles and porcelain trays held an assortment of scented oils and bath salts, each seeming to promise an opulent bathing experience. The mirror above the vanity reflected the surrounding elegance, enhancing the room's sense of spaciousness.

My gaze then drifted to the windowsill, where potted orchids and fragrant jasmine blossoms were displayed. Their vibrant colors and delicate petals stood out against the white backdrop, adding a touch of nature's beauty to the space. A plush, white robe hung on a gilded hook nearby, promising comfort and warmth after a soak in the tub. The floor, covered with plush ivory-colored rugs, felt soft under my feet, adding to the indulgent atmosphere.

After introducing me to the bathroom essentials, Ivy left, giving me privacy to attend to my needs. I brushed my teeth with refreshing mint-flavored toothpaste, relishing the clean taste. Stepping into the tub, the warm water enveloped me, offering a comfort so profound it nearly brought tears to my eyes.

Around me, various colored flowers floated on the water, their fragrances mingling to create a sensory symphony. Through the giant window in front of the tub, I could see expansive gardens, their beauty warming my heart and completing the experience of ultimate relaxation and serenity.

I wrapped a towel around my body and entered the changing closet. Ivy had chosen a dress for me in a delicate light pink shade, crafted from an airy fabric. It was nothing like the ones my mom used to get, the kind that made me question my existence. This dress was a gentle pink with subtle golden hints, almost invisible but adding a touch of elegance. It hugged the curves of my body in all the right places. Ivy also presented a pair of comfortable pink slippers to complete the ensemble. After I dressed up, Ivy guided me to sit in front of the mirror. She styled my hair with her gentle hands. No one had ever treated my hair with such tenderness as far back as I could remember, and I think she sensed that. She paused for a moment, observed me, and then said, "You are beautiful." Her kind smile penetrated through my past horrors, fears, and terrors. I blinked back a tear and closed my eyes as she continued working on my hair.

She took two braids from either side of my head, secured them at the back, and let the rest of my hair cascade freely. She adorned the braids with flowers, adding a touch of natural beauty. At that moment, I thought–I did look beautiful!

I emerged from my room, and a corridor stretched before me—a grand passageway adorned with towering ceilings and expansive windows, leading to the grand lobby. I stood at the threshold of this architectural spectacle, and the sheer magnificence of the scene captivated my senses.

The building itself, a pristine canvas of white, emanated an aura of sophistication that commanded immediate attention. Surrounded by a cool and modern aesthetic, shades of grey dominated the color palette, with subtle hints of blue in the background adding to the overall visual appeal. Blueish-grey seemed to be the theme of this place. The decor, minimalistic yet purposeful, included carefully placed potted plants and decorative elements, seamlessly incorporating nature into the monochromatic elegance.

Art pieces graced the walls, and potted plants were arranged in baskets. They breathed life into the space, their vibrant colors creating a striking contrast against the neutral tones that defined the decor. In front of me, the grand staircase commanded my unwavering attention—a symphony of intricate details drawing my gaze. As it gracefully curved towards the lower level, a sense of anticipation lingered in the air. The metal railing, both functional and decorative, enhanced the staircase's elegance, adding a subtle touch of sophistication.

Through open doorways and windows, tantalizing glimpses of other areas within the building beckoned, hinting at the expansive beauty that lay beyond. A fleeting view of cloudy skies through a window on the left suggested vast flower gardens, a testament to the breathtaking natural beauty just outside. Beside me stood Ivy, a witness to the unfolding spectacle. With awe reflected in her eyes, I couldn't help but inquire about our destination.

"Where are we going?" I asked, clenching my hands.

Ivy responded with a gleam of excitement, "To have breakfast with the High Lord."

# Chapter Six

# *A New Hope*

As I entered the room, a delightful smell of food surrounded me, making me hungry. I don't really remember the last time I ate peacefully. The dining space was large and elegant, with high ceilings and clean white walls that created a sophisticated atmosphere. The colors were mostly the similar shades of grey and white.

In the center of the room, there was a long wooden dining table, beautifully decorated with plates filled with delicious food, sparkling glasses, and a vase of fresh flowers. Everything looked like a work of art, promising a delightful feast for the senses.

Comfortable chairs surrounded the table, inviting me to indulge in the delicious food spread before me. The chandelier here was bigger than the one in the room, and added a warm glow, making the food even more appealing. Natural light filled the room through large windows on both sides of the table. The curtains, matching the intricate wallpaper, brought an elegant touch to the scene. Artwork decorated one wall, and a tall bookshelf on another held books and decorative items, showcasing the room's charming diversity.

The furniture was both elegant and comfortable, urging me to enjoy the culinary delights in this beautiful setting. But my gaze dropped to a man sitting at the end of the long dining table, and my heart raced.

He was incredibly beautiful, like a living work of art. His silver hair flowed gracefully, almost like moonlight around his face. It caught the light, making it look like he had a halo around him. His skin was radiant, like porcelain, glowing in a way that seemed otherworldly, as if time didn't touch him.

Perfect high cheekbones that added mystery to his face, and his nose and jawline perfectly shaped. His ears pointed upwards, just like Ivy's. It all created a timeless elegance that set him apart from anyone I had ever seen. It felt like I was witnessing something enchanting right there in the room. His eyes were something else—ageless, with a mysterious wisdom shining in their green color. He stared at me, and I felt a sudden sense of smallness as if he could see right through me.

Ivy touched my arm gently, urging me to move forward instead of standing there like a statue. I approached the table, and the High Lord gestured for me to sit beside him. He stood up gracefully and greeted me in a manner like no one had ever done before. He pulled out a chair for me, a gesture I had never seen before, neither at my home nor somewhere else. My father never did anything like this for my mother. Maybe it was something unique to this place.

His attire, a captivating combination of midnight blues and deep purples, absorbed the surrounding light, wrapping him in an air of shadowy elegance. The fabric adhered to him with an unnatural grace, moving like liquid shadows. Eldritch symbols adorned the lower part of his tunic, gathering around his hips in a graceful swirl. They concealed his movements in a captivating dance of darkness. Silver threads traced the edges, shimmering subtly like moonlit reflections on a tranquil lake.

His pants, woven from shadows, cascaded down his legs. The edges trailed like the wings of a nocturnal creature, adding to the mysterious allure. A delicate belt, of the design of ancient constellations I guess, embraced his waist. As I sat down, grabbing the wooden arms of the chair, Ivy nodded to the High Lord and left the room, closing the doors behind her.

I was alone with him in the room, and fear gripped me. I didn't understand how I ended up here, who these people were, and what they wanted from me. My hands started trembling with anxiety.

The High Lord sensed my unease and spoke gently, "You don't have to be scared; no one will hurt you here."

I said nothing and just stared at the windows, at the door, at... .him, wondering if this was a dream.

He cleared his throat and broke the silence with his gentle, yet assertive, voice. "What is your name?"

"Aria," I responded, meeting his gaze. He arched his one eyebrow, his head dipping towards me. I felt so small in front of him right now.

"Ariana Eldenhave," I added, almost stuttering.

"Interesting," he smiled and said, "I am Thorndike, the High Lord of Eloria."

"Ivy mentioned this is Eloria, but where is this Eloria, and how did I end up here?" I asked, trying not to offend him.

He took a deep breath, almost making my heart sink, but then he responded with a patient smile, not the condescending kind that I was accustomed to from my parents. This was a gentle, understanding smile. "You will get all your answers, but first, you need to eat. You've been unconscious for the past three days." His fingers, decorated with jeweled rings, gestured toward the spread of food.

"Three days! I've been unconscious for three days!" I gasped. No wonder my stomach was rumbling with pain.

"Is all this for us?" I asked, hunger taking the better of me.

"If you can eat, then definitely yes," he chuckled.

A lavish spread laid before me, making my mouth water. A plate magically appeared in front of me. Starting with the appetizers, there was a colorful array of bruschetta adorned with vibrant tomatoes, basil, and drizzles of balsamic glaze. Along with that, a platter of artisanal cheeses and cured meats, complemented by a selection of freshly baked bread and crispy crackers.

Every dish had a nametag. A succulent roasted chicken took center stage, its golden-brown skin glistening under the warm glow of the chandelier. Beside it, a pan-seared salmon offered a delicate alternative, accompanied by a zesty lemon and herb dressing. The side dishes showcased a medley of roasted vegetables, their natural flavors enhanced by aromatic herbs and spices. Bowls of freshly tossed salads, featuring crisp greens, heirloom tomatoes, and an assortment of nuts, lay in one corner of the table. The vibrant colors of the salads added a refreshing touch to the overall display.

A smile appeared on my lips when I saw the deserts and wine corner, this time unwatched by my mother. I have never been allowed to wander in the direction of sweet treats by my parents. Seeing them unsupervised made my heart thunder with excitement.

My stomach roared, and the delectable aroma of the cheese and meats enticed me. After that I don't remember much, all I remember is how amazing the food tasted in my mouth, the variety of flavors, and no one judging me about the amount of food on my plate. For the first time in my life, it felt like I was free!

As the sun started to set, Ivy showed me around more parts of the mansion. We ended up in the library. The colors here matched the rest of the mansion—a mix of grey and brown that made everything look fancy yet simple. The room was calm, filled with the smell of old books, paper, and the cozy glow of lamps.

The place felt like a magical haven where stories had been preserved for ages. Ivy pointed to the shelves lined with books, each one holding exciting adventures and secrets. In the middle of the library, there was a big wooden table with four high-back chairs around it. The dark wood made it look really fancy and was a perfect spot to dive into the world of books. There were many books on the table, some opened, some stacked. I wondered who might have read it since there was no one in the library at the moment. O*r in the palace.*

I wandered to the back, where shelves were packed with even more books and journals, making it clear that this room was a haven for literature. It felt like a place where stories and knowledge came alive. A wave of excitement coursed through me. Our school library couldn't compare, and there were always strict rules there. I could only borrow one book at a time there, and that also could hardly take it back with me home. Mom was really strict about it. *NO EXTRACURRICULARS.* She said.

I glanced at Ivy here, and her warm smile accompanied the words, "These books are available for everyone in the mansion. Feel free to come here anytime you want." A sense of ease washed over me.

As I gazed upward, the ceiling unfolded with intricate designs, bestowing an extra layer of aesthetic charm to the room. Suspended from the center, a chandelier cast a gentle glow, creating a welcoming ambiance below.

In a corner, four small yellowish chairs encircled a little coffee table, extending a warm invitation for readers to immerse themselves in the tranquil pursuit of knowledge. *I found my perfect spot for reading. I thought.*

In a cozy corner, a table awaited with a tempting assortment of tea and coffee. The pot emitted a comforting steam, promising warmth, and a delightful choice of beverages. Various cups stood ready, inviting me to pick my favorite. It intrigued me how, despite the apparent solitude, someone cared for this corner, ensuring the continuous replenishment of these comforting drinks.

Returning from the library, the weariness of the day settled in, and I gratefully sank into the comfort of the bed. The soft embrace lulled me into a restful sleep, a welcomed respite from the curious and enchanting world I found myself in.

# Chapter Seven

## *Secrets and Sanctuaries*

As the morning sunlight filtered through the curtain, it danced with an enchanting brilliance, just like scattered particles of magic. It was around noon, and I realized that never in my life had I slept that long! An unexpected sense of relief and anxiety washed over me.

It might seem bizarre, but there were no echoes of shouted voices, no hateful glances from my mother—just a respite from the constant fear of disappointing her. And Dad. The tranquility in this unfamiliar place offered a temporary escape from the tumultuous reality I once called home. Yet, I knew this was not a permanent solution. I can't stay here forever. I have to go back, eventually. *To that hell.*

Curiosity and a desire for answers welled up within me. I had to find out what this place was. How I ended up here? If there was a pathway back to what I, somewhat hesitantly, still referred to as "home."

Rising from the bed, I settled on its edge, my gaze drawn to a meticulously arranged tray on the table beside the sofa. The tableau presented an inviting assortment—pieces of bread, jams, tea, boiled eggs, cottage cheese, naan bread—all exquisitely displayed. The ambiance in the room was soothing. This was the most peaceful place I have ever seen, honestly. I couldn't explain the feeling, the relief. Tears came down my eyes as I dropped down back on the bed, sighing deeply.

I really didn't care what this place was. Who these people were. Whether they were human or not. As long as they kept me away from that hell.

Sitting straight, I engaged in a silent contemplation of the culinary array before me. The aroma of freshly brewed tea filled the air, creating a comforting backdrop to the scene. The golden exteriors of the bread promised a delightful crunch, while the halved-boiled eggs unveiled a perfect fusion of textures. A jar of vibrant jam added a touch of sweetness to the ensemble.

Swinging my legs to the side of the bed and straightening my white nightgown, I rose and made my way towards the inviting tray. A delectable aroma enveloped me as I chose a piece of bread with jam, carefully placing it on a plate. With a steaming cup of hot coffee in hand, I embarked on what promised to be a delicious breakfast—or at least, that was my optimistic assumption.

Midway through my morning indulgence, the door swung open unexpectedly. Ivy, with an assessing gaze, said, "Good, you are awake... and... eating." Her words hung in the air, and I instinctively paused, momentarily preparing myself for a possible reprimand. As I moved to set my plate on the table, half-anticipating a scolding, Ivy interjected, "Don't do that. It is for you to eat." She gestured towards the plate as she continued, "The Highlord wants to meet with you. He wants to know if you will get ready and meet him in the garden downstairs in one and a half hours?"

I nearly dropped my plate. The realization hit me—it was an invitation, not a command. No one had ever asked me before if I wanted to do something. They had always ordered me to do everything. They had never asked about my choice. This was the first time...my throat bobbed. But this might help me answer my questions about this place.

"Yes, of course," I replied, with a hint of surprise and eagerness.

She smiled gently and gestured toward the closet. "I have taken out a dress for you if you like, but you can wear any of them. They all are for you." I nodded in acknowledgment.

"See you later, Ariana. If you need any help, just shout my name down the hall. I will come in a sec," she said and left before I could say anything. The generosity and kindness here were unlike anything I had experienced before.

I stepped out of my room, adorned in a magnificent summer gown that immersed me in the regal aura of royal purple. The fabric resembled a cascade of soft lavender petals, gracefully flowing around me with every step. Delicate straps lovingly embraced my shoulders, allowing the gown to bask in the warmth of the season. As the gown descended, it transformed into layers of silken fabric, capturing the light and orchestrating a mesmerizing dance of hues. It was a symphony of elegance and the graceful spirit of summertime. I paired it with purple slip-ons from my closet, taking a moment to appreciate the coordinated ensemble.

Walking down the passageway, I made my way towards the stairs. I decided not to call Ivy for my hair, letting it flow in loose and curly waves. Today, I wanted to embrace the effortless beauty of the moment without any unnecessary fuss. Exiting the second floor, I descended to the first floor, where I found Thorndike patiently waiting for me at the foot of the stairs. As I approached, he graciously took my hand and bestowed a gentle kiss upon it. A blush unexpectedly graced my cheeks, and the cosmic allure that surrounded him momentarily captivated me. Something.

His gaze swept over my body, and a sensation of insignificance again washed over me in the face of his celestial beauty. Breaking into a warm smile, he invited, "Will you stroll with me in the gardens, Ariana?"

Confusion swirled within me, but I agreed nonetheless. He was a stranger to me, and yet he was asking for my permission at every step. Something ascended in the center of my stomach, something like anxiety, but I took a deep breath. Like always. Thorndike turned and began descending the steps, adjusting his pace to ensure I could comfortably keep up with him.

Reaching the ground floor, we proceeded to the back of the mansion. A stunning glass door, adorned with wooden borders and intricate designs, stood before us. As we approached, the door gracefully opened on its own, allowing us to pass through. I looked at Thorndike in surprise, and he responded with a gentle smile. He extended his hand, beckoning me to embrace the enchantment of the beautiful, lush gardens around the grand mansion.

"Shall we revel in the garden's magic, Ariana?" he asked, his regal tone softening with a warmth that invited exploration. I nodded and accepted his extended hand. As we crossed the threshold, the air transformed, carrying the intoxicating fragrance of blooming flowers.

The garden unfolded like a living mural, vibrant and teeming with life. Thorndike gestured toward a winding path lined with blossoming roses, each petal a masterpiece in shades that transcended earthly palettes. "These flowers," he began, his voice like a piece of music, "tell tales of love, resilience, and the eternal dance between nature and magic."

"Magic?" I asked, but he didn't answer.

We strolled along the path, and the delicate fragrance of roses enveloped us like a fragrant embrace. He spoke with a deep connection to the floral wonders around us.

"Each petal whispers secrets in the language of Eloria, known only to those who listen with a heart attuned to nature's melody." The roses blushed in response to Thorndike's admiration, caught in a dance of hues. His eyes, like those of an art connoisseur savoring a masterpiece, lingered on the blooms.

"These blossoms," he continued, "are not mere flowers; they are echoes of the soul of Eloria, harmonizing with the rhythm of life."

Seeing the confusion on my face, he explained, "Eloria is more than a place; it's a living, breathing entity, a magical realm where the mundane and the mystical blur into a harmonious dance.

Imagine a land where the forests' vibrant greens, the meadows' enchanting hues, and the mountains' majestic purples converge in perfect unity," Thorndike painted a vivid canvas of the enchanting realm with his words.

"In our gardens, nature and magic intertwine seamlessly, like the pulsating heart of Eloria. Every flower and every tree resonates with an energy that is ancient and ever-present. The whispers of the wind and the joyful laughter of the fae folk, who nurture the enchanting blooms with tender care, make these grounds alive." Thorndike cast a spell with his words.

The peace and beauty in this garden were really something I had never experienced before. There was a garden in my *home* in Eldenhaven. It hardly seemed alive in front of this splendor. As we strolled through the grass, nature's artistry unfolded in a mesmerizing display.

Thorndike paused gracefully by a cluster of iridescent orchids, his black tunic complementing their deep orange color. "Witness these orchids," he said. "fae hands skillfully crafted them, attuned to the language of elegance and refinement. Each bloom testifies to the delicate dance between the ethereal and the earthly."

"Fae?" I asked, my hands tucked by my sides, wondering if I was already asking too many questions.

He turned towards me, his hands gracefully encased in his pockets. "Yes, Fae. Meaning Faeries. We all are fairies in Eloria. Some are High Fae and some are lesser Fae. But we all do have a magic of some kind or another. A species superior to humans, of course," he smirked.

"Superior, just because of magic?" My eyebrows shot up.

"Magic is everything, Ariana. You will understand eventually." Something in his tone changed, something I couldn't decipher.

He flicked his hand and a stunning orange flower appeared behind my left ear. I simply gazed at him in surprise as he winked. "You look beautiful."

"Eloria is a sanctuary, Ariana," he went on, "A haven where magic is not just a force; it's a companion, a guiding presence. It dances through the air, tenderly embracing the land and its dwellers with an affectionate touch. In this realm, the commonplace converges with the extraordinary, and the ordinary transforms into something truly extraordinary."

We neared a serene pond embraced by weeping willows, their tendrils trailing elegantly in the water. I asked hesitantly, "Where does the magic come from?" He stepped towards me with a smile, then another step, then another.

Now so close that I felt his presence in my personal space. He looked at me, as if studying me, and then explained, "The magic in Eloria is like the realm's heartbeat, an eternal rhythm that flows from the land's heart. It was first imbued in this world by Goddess Luminara," his face hardened at the word, but he changed it quickly as he said, " the life force coursing through the forests, rivers, and mountains. Imagine it as a river of energy, weaving through the realm's veins, connecting every living being and every corner with an invisible, enchanting thread." His proximity made my heart beat faster.

I wondered why he tolerated all my questions and answered them patiently. Why he didn't give me any side looks or stares that my mom used to give me if I ever troubled her with any of my questions? I didn't understand his behavior. Why was he so gentle? As we moved forward, the breeze carried the birdsong's harmonious melody, unveiling the garden's vivid colors and textures.

Thorndike said, "Nature here is a living tapestry, woven with threads of magic and love. Every petal, every leaf, contributes to Eloria's grand masterpiece." He swept his hand, directing my attention to the surrounding nature. "The trees, the flowers, the very air—every element of our land is suffused with this enchanting energy. It's a gift from the land itself, a symbiotic relationship that has flourished for centuries. This magical current bestows vibrant colors on our plants, ethereal beauty on our creatures, and the ability to harness the arcane arts on our people." I merely stared at him and his words in confusion, but his eyes gleamed with profound understanding as he went on, "But it's not solely the land. Eloria is also graced with ley lines, mystical channels that weave through the very fabric of our realm. These ley lines intensify and channel the magical energy, forming pockets of extraordinary power. These ley lines travel not only in Eloria but also to the human world. Our ancient ancestors uncovered the art of attuning themselves to these ley lines, becoming custodians of the magical equilibrium within Eloria."

Our arms brushed for a moment as we stood beneath the wisteria-laden arbor, a subtle connection in the midst of the enchanting whispers of wishes and aspirations. Thorndike continued, "Every bloom here holds a piece of someone's yearning, creating a delicate symphony of desires that adds to Eloria's magic." As Thorndike painted a vivid picture of the fae with his words, our eyes met, and I felt a connection forming, transcending the ordinary questions.

"Fae are the guardians of Eloria's secrets, the keepers of ancient wisdom," he continued, his voice a soothing melody. "They dance with the winds, whisper with the leaves, and their presence weaves into the land's fabric. To encounter a fae is to witness the intersection of magic and reality, a bridge between realms."

The fae tended to the garden's flourishing beauty gracefully amidst the blooms. "Observe their delicate touch," Thorndike suggested. "They are not just residents; they are the hands that shape Eloria's essence. With each interaction, they infuse the land with their magical touch, cultivating a living masterpiece that breathes with their benevolent energy."

Their presence, marked by ethereal wings and a luminous glow, symbolized their role as custodians of the enchantment that wove through our forests, rivers, and skies. Each fae, in its delicate beauty, was a guardian of nature's magic, a living testament to the harmony between Eloria and the mystical forces that flowed through its essence.

Thorne's words served as a mesmerizing bridge between the human realm and Eloria's magic, nestled in the garden's heart, surrounded by the blossoms' vibrant hues. His language, woven with reverence and poetry, unveiled the extraordinary beauty that flourished in the garden's embrace.

I noticed the gentle transition to night only as the sun set, casting its last warm glow over the enchanting landscape. But something unsettled me. Thorndike hadn't told me how I arrived here, and how I would go back. But I also did not ask him anything. Maybe it is a subtle way for my brain to delay my way back home. But no matter how beautiful this place was, and how flowery his words were, something felt off to me. Like he was hiding something from me or was not telling me the complete truth. Or maybe I was not used to people behaving nicely to me.

# Chapter Eight

## Library and its Mysteries

In the past two days since my encounter with Thorndike, the High Lord of Eloria, I had been ensnared by the enchanting aura of this mystical realm. However, an unexpected void lingered in his absence. Ivy, my guide in this enchanting land, informed me that Thorndike had been called away for the official affairs of Eloria.

It is almost impossible for me to get my answers if the High Lord is not here. And till he comes back, I have to stay here. *And honestly, I don't mind it.*

Sensing my unease, Ivy tried comforting me as I wandered around the palace. The towering trees, vibrant flowers, and ethereal landscapes that earlier filled me with wonder now seemed to echo the silent question of how to return to my *home*, Eldenhaven.

As I walked through the garden with her, I was awestruck by the intricate beauty of Eloria. The air carried a subtle hum of magic, and the flora seemed to shimmer with an otherworldly glow. But despite the allure, I could not remain captivated by this mystical realm forever, as tempting as it might be. The realization settled that I could not just sit here and wait for the High Lord.

I had to muster my own courage and delve into the mysteries of Eloria in search of answers. I took leave from Ivy and turned back towards the library. Instead of waiting for Thorndike's return, I felt compelled to explore the knowledge hidden within the library's shelves. Uncertainty loomed over my place in this mansion – I didn't even know these people; was I their guest or a captive? It was time to be proactive, to sift through the library's secrets and discover the insights that might lead me back to Eldenhaven.

Feeling a bit unsure, I continued to the library. There, I found myself overwhelmed by the sheer number of books, many written in a language I couldn't read. Despite this, I kept looking through the shelves for hours until I finally found a book that seemed interesting. Its title caught my attention.

*"Fae and mortal: Bridging the worlds"*

A glimmer of hope ignited within me as I laid eyes on the book. Cradling it gently, I found refuge in a corner of the cozy sofa, my tired back sinking into its comforting embrace. Placing the book on the small coffee table before me, I eagerly unfurled its binding.

The pages unraveled a mystery that immediately captivated my attention. There was a beautiful painting on the first page. At the core of the illustration, a fae figure similar to Thorne stood divided in duality. On one side, a tender scene unfolded—the fae embraced a human with an aura of warmth and connection. However, the other half starkly contrasted this harmony; the same fae exerted dominance, oppressing the struggling human who endeavored in vain to break free.

A play of shadows and light intricately wove depth into the narrative. Brooding, dark clouds loomed overhead, casting an ominous pallor, while beneath a radiant sun emanated a celestial glow. Ethereal wings gracefully unfurled, caught in a delicate dance between the contrasting elements. Each stroke of the artist's brush seemed to convey a story within the story, leaving me utterly captivated by the enigmatic tale spun through this visual masterpiece. The imagery on these pages stood unparalleled, unlike anything I had encountered in my world. As I turned the page, the depicted scenes and verses struck my mind with the force of lightning, leaving me spellbound by the mysterious and unfamiliar tale unfolding before me.

> *"In the ancient tapestry of time, fae and humans wove the threads of existence together, sharing a realm where magic and mortality danced in harmony for thousands of years."*

The revelation that humans and fae once lived in harmony unfurled before me like an ancient scroll, and I found myself in awe of this newfound knowledge. Humans and fae, coexisting in a bygone era, a discovery so perplexing and enthralling that it begged the question: Why had this profound piece of history been shrouded in obscurity? Where were the tales that spoke of this remarkable fusion of worlds, the books that whispered of their shared existence, tucked away in the recesses of the library? It felt akin to a myth, a narrative lost in the sands of time, yet the enchanting aura of this extraordinary place contradicted the notion of mere folklore. Why have I never heard of fairies before in the human realm?

> *"In days of yore, fae and humans toiled side by side, sharing the canvas of existence. Together, they sowed the seeds of prosperity, nurtured families, and wove the tapestry of life in a harmonious symphony that echoed through the realms. Bound by shared dreams and the embrace of a shared destiny, their lives intertwined in a dance of cooperation and companionship."*

So, fae and humans used to work and live together, creating a colorful picture of life. They had planted success, built families, and told the story of existence together in a happy rhythm. It's hard to believe, but the book said their lives had danced together in a teamwork and friendship melody, bound by common dreams.

It sounded like a fantasy story rather than something real I could understand. In an era of forgotten enchantment, humans and fae intertwined their destinies in a tapestry woven with love and unity. Marriage knew no boundaries, no differentiation between human and fae; it was a sacred bond that transcended the distinctions of their beings.

A harmonious symphony echoed as they embraced one another, their hearts beating in unison, creating families that defied the conventional definitions of lineage. Love, unbridled and pure, bridged the realms, forging connections that painted a vivid portrait of an era where distinctions blurred, and the union of human and fae flourished in a timeless embrace.

With an unexpected thump, a book fell behind me. I stood up quickly to retrieve it, puzzled by its sudden fall, my heart racing at the noise. I arranged it back on the shelf, moved to the corner table adorned with an assortment of teas, and carefully poured myself a cup of steaming black coffee. The rich aroma filled the air, comforting my senses.

Retreating to my sofa, I hunched down to cradle my hot cup, only to realize that the book that had enraptured me was now nowhere to be found. In a mysterious twist, a different book graced the spot, as if it had magically materialized, seamlessly replacing the one I had been engrossed in just moments before. This one read -

*"Elorian Almanac: Current Affairs Unveiled"*

I cast a bewildered glance around, perplexed by the inexplicable book swap that had transpired. My mouth dropped open as I realized—the books in this library were constantly changing the covers. I picked up the new book that lay in front of me. Its backside displayed -

> *This book could delve into the ongoing events, political landscape, and noteworthy occurrences within the enchanting realm of Eloria. It might cover topics ranging from magical phenomena to diplomatic relations between different fae communities, providing readers with a captivating insight into the vibrant and ever-evolving world of Eloria.*

For some inexplicable reason, I decided to tuck this book under my arm and carry it with me into my chamber.

*The enchanted night pressed in ominously as I stumbled through the dense forest. Twisted branches reached out like skeletal hands, and the air whispered eerie secrets. Luminescent fungi cast an ethereal glow, both fascinating and terrifying. With ragged breaths and sweat trickling, I ventured deeper into the arboreal labyrinth. Shad-*

*ows, once companions, now felt like sinister co-conspirators in the inky blackness. Unseen creatures emitted haunting howls, and rustling intensified my disquiet. The forest closed in, trees towering like spectral guardians. Strange sounds crescendoed, a symphony of spectral whispers reverberating. Curiosity propelled me forward, urging me to unravel mysteries in the shadows. Abruptly, the atmosphere shifted, and an unsettling stillness descended. My senses heightened, and an unshakable foreboding settled. A paralyzing chill crawled up my spine as I turned around. A colossal creature, concealed, revealed a single, immense eye-opening, casting a hypnotic glow. My heart pounded, and terror gripped me as I gazed into the abyss of that colossal eye. The forest held its breath. Time paused in this mystical encounter. My body tensed, nerves on edge, as the creature's gaze bored into my soul. Suddenly, a surge of adrenaline jolted through me. With a primal instinct, I bolted forward, running, my panting breaths echoing. The colossal eye loomed, fear propelling me faster through the oppressive darkness. The forest blurs, shadows, and forms a nightmarish maze. My limbs burned with exhaustion, the colossal eye, a malevolent presence, seemed to follow every move. Pushing my limits, breaths with desperate gasps, fueled by a primal need to survive this otherworldly pursuit.*

*As I thought my strength would give out, a sudden change enveloped the dream. Oppressive darkness lifted, and the forest transformed. Haunting sounds dissipated, replaced by tranquil calm. The colossal eye closed, and I found myself standing in a tranquil haven, sweat-soaked, trembling, pulse gradually slowing. I jolted awake, the dream's vestiges clinging to my consciousness.*

My heart pounded, and sweat beads lingered. Seeking refuge, I stumbled out of bed, the cool bathroom tiles a reprieve. Beneath the invigorating shower, water droplets felt like a gentle caress, soothing heightened nerves. Vivid details of my dream replayed—the enigmatic eye, the haunting forest, the palpable fear. What hidden meaning lurked?

Post-shower, wrapped in a fluffy towel, I reflected on the surreal experience. Opting for a summery yellow dress, hair cascading down my back, reaching its lower curves, I completed the ensemble with a matching yellow slip-on. Venturing into the corridor, I focused on the mansion's intricate details. Polished wooden floors echoed with each step, and a soft hum of distant activity added to the ambiance. The vibrant colors of hallway paintings seemed more pronounced, lending a surreal yet comforting touch to the surroundings. Seeking familiar faces of Ivy or Thornedike, I hoped for answers or perhaps just a reassuring presence in the wake of the unsettling dream.

Navigating the mansion's corridors, I descended the staircase with a sense of both curiosity and trepidation. As I meandered through the hallways, my steps echoed faintly against the floor, and the air seemed charged with a mystical energy that hinted at secrets lurking within Thornedike's abode.

Lost in thought and already feeling like an uninvited guest in this otherworldly sanctuary, a sudden interruption shattered the silence.

"Who let you in here?" a deep, male voice resonated from behind me, its unexpected presence sending a chill down my spine. Startled, I pivoted on my heels to confront the source of the question, my eyes wide with surprise and a tinge of fear. A mysterious figure emerged, his black wings glimmering with an enigmatic sheen. Confidence exuded from every inch of his being.

His piercing silver eyes locked onto mine with an intensity that created an unspoken challenge, and the surrounding air seemed to thicken with a palpable aura of mystery. High, sharp cheekbones framed his face, accentuating a chiseled jawline. A distinct scar cut through his left eyebrow, a testament to experiences that seemed to carry the weight of numerous battles.

His skin, kissed by the sun's embrace, carried a subtle tan, a testament to countless hours spent under its warm rays. Clad in a fitted black shirt that emphasized his sturdy shoulders and well-defined arms, he paired it effortlessly with sleek black jeans and polished leather shoes. The crown of his head boasted a rich black hue, transitioning seamlessly to a captivating silver cascade as it reached his shoulders.

"I'll ask once more," he said with a glint of amusement, "just to be certain your hearing hasn't taken an unexpected vacation."

Annoyed, I retreated a step, avoiding his gaze. "I...I'm just exploring," I stammered, fear tainting my voice.

Delighting in my discomfort, he continued his taunts. "Ahaa... exploring? This," he gestured around him, "isn't a playground for humans. It will be better for you if you know your place."

Amid this Eldenhaven déjà vu and his whole authoritative act, I grudgingly took a step back. The air hung heavy with tension as I started to pull away, a cocktail of nerves and irritation brewing within.

"Kael, there's no need to be harsh," a familiar voice interjected beside me, and a surge of relief flooded over. Thornedike had finally arrived.

"She's my guest," he asserted as he came to stand beside me.

# Chapter Nine

## Current Affairs

"Where have you been?" I asked as Thorne and I strolled the riverside. "I haven't seen you in four days."

Thorne glanced at me, a hint of surprise and perhaps amusement in his eyes. "Missing me, Ariana?" he teased, as if he sensed the irritation in my tone.

My eyebrows shot up so fast that I almost forgot he was the High Lord. As I gazed into his eyes, I realized he wasn't mocking me; he was smiling—a kind, gentle, and heartwarming smile. A warmth spread across my skin inexplicably.

I looked down, "No, I mean, I don't want to disrespect you, High Lord. But I want to go back home. Can you help me?"

He studied me with an intensity that felt timeless, and I resisted the urge to shrink under his gaze.

"You don't have to call me Highlord; you can call me Thorne," he said gently, his eyes softening.

I stumbled over my words, caught between the formality and his invitation.

"Yes, Highl... Thorne," I managed to say. He smiled, and it sent a shiver through me, and I instinctively wanted to retreat into the cocoon of my bed, feeling an unfamiliar vulnerability.

"Thorne, can you help me?" I tried to ask politely, the words carrying the weight of my plea.

"I know what you're going to ask, Ariana," he gazed at me, continuing, "Ever since your arrival, Ariana, I've been looking for the theory—how you traveled from the human realm into the fae realm."

"And?" I asked, tucking a loose strand of hair behind my right ear for the third time as the wind here wouldn't comply with me.

"I don't have all the answers yet, but trust me, I'm working on it," he assured me with a determined gaze.

I wasn't sure if I was disappointed or somewhat relieved. I had a few more days to myself, here, without all the violence before heading to Eldenhaven, before returning to the parents whose actions felt like a constant storm.

As Thorne and I strolled along the cobblestone bridge, the river beneath us glistened with the reflections of the sun, creating a dance of sparkles that mirrored the magic within Eloria. The melodious flow of the river accompanied our steps, whispering secrets of the land. The mountains stood tall and majestic, their peaks crowned by wisps of clouds. Each ridge and valley told a tale of ancient times, a silent witness to the eons that had passed in Eloria's embrace.

The air was filled with the sweet fragrance of blooming wild-flowers, adding a touch of nature's perfume to the enchanting atmosphere. As we reached the middle of the bridge, I felt compelled to pause and absorb the breathtaking view. Taking a short jump, I took a seat on the cool cobblestones, my fingers gently tracing the intricate patterns beneath me. The sound of the river washing over the stones below was a soothing melody, and the mountains, cloaked in hues of green and blue, captivated my gaze.

Thorne assessed me for a minute and then stepped closer as I sat on the bridge. He came so close, his waist almost touching my knees, his strong hands on either side of me on the bridge. "Can I ask you something, Ariana?"

I looked into his eyes, attempting not to blush under his scrutiny.

"Yes, Thorne," I said, offering a smile.

"The night you arrived here, the night I found you, the bruises on your face and body, the injuries..." His gaze traveled up and down through my body, which made me feel a surge of emotions; and a small part of me wanted to just hug him and let the tears flow. I didn't know why. Maybe because no one had ever asked me about this before, no one really cared.

His voice carried a mix of concern and anger as he said through his teeth, "Ariana, who did that to you?" His green eyes gleamed, but held a depth of empathy I had never seen before. I was at a loss for words, emotions bubbling to the surface. No one had ever shown concern for the bruises that painted my skin. A tear threatened to escape, and I quickly averted my eyes, staring down at my yellow dress.

His touch was delicate as he lifted my chin, urging me to meet his gaze. "Tell me, Ariana, who did that to you?" I closed my eyes, the haunting memories of my parents' cruelty playing before me.

"My parents," tears came down my eyes, as I continued, "but I am sure they had their reasons," the words heavy with the weight of my past.

A flicker of tension appeared in his jaw, and I noticed a hint of something in his eyes. Was it anger on my behalf? But why would he be angry? He barely knew me; I was just a stranger in his world. Yet, there was a depth of care in his gaze that puzzled me.

"No reason is big enough to ever hurt you, Ariana," his warm hand cupped my cheek gently, and the assurance in his words rippled through me. "They should have never touched you. They will pay for this," he said.

"I know I barely know you, and you might find it strange, but there is something about you. Something that makes me want to care for you. Something that makes me want to stand for you."

My throat bobbed. At that moment, I felt a weight lift off my shoulders, as if the safest haven cradled me, and the promise of a better life enfolded me.

My daily routine had a new twist now, and I didn't mind it. Thorne was spending more time with me, especially during meals in the mansion. It was a new and nice experience for me, and I wouldn't mind if it continued.

Sitting in the garden, under the big beautiful flowered tree, I liked the sunlight gently kissing my face, even at midday. It wasn't like Eldenhaven, where you'd start sweating within ten minutes under the summer sun. Here, it was pleasant, with a mild breeze playing with my hair and the fragrance of roses filling the air. I had decided to bring that book with me -

*"Elorian Almanac: Current Affairs Unveiled"*

For reasons I don't really understand, I had been delaying reading this book. In a realm as seemingly flawless as Eloria, I pondered if any shadow could cast itself upon its perfection. A book on current affairs raised a veil of curiosity–what revelations might it hold? Yet, without allowing further moments to slip through my fingers, I pried open the unadorned hardcover. Unlike the other book, devoid of intricate art, this one revealed today's date and day on the initial page, concluding with an entry marked just an hour ago. My jaw hung open–this book had been by my side throughout. The bewilderment deepened as I questioned how these entries found their way onto its pages.

**12 March, 17000**

**Tuesday**

10 am

**Breaking News in Eloria - Dark Forces attack**

In a rare and unfortunate incident, the Glittering Grove of Lumoria, a sacred and revered part of Eloria, has experienced an unexpected disturbance. Reports from mystical sources indicate that a disruption in the natural magical balance has occurred, casting a shadow over the once-luminous sanctuary. The Glittering Grove, known for its enchanting bioluminescent flora and fauna, has suffered a mysterious dimming of its radiant lights. The glow-in-the-dark petals of the Moonlit Blossoms, which usually illuminate the grove with a mesmerizing display, have dulled, leaving the once-vibrant sanctuary in an eerie twilight.

The fae inhabitants of Eloria, deeply connected to the mystical energies of the Glittering Grove, express concern and sorrow over this unforeseen event. High Lord Thorne, in a somber address, reassures the fae folk that every effort is being made to restore the Grove's natural brilliance. Elven scholars and magical experts are convening to investigate the cause behind this disturbance and to find a solution that will rekindle the magical essence of Glittering Grove. Residents of Eloria are urged to avoid the area until further notice, as the magical experts work tirelessly to unravel the mystery and restore Lumoria to its former radiant glory. The incident has sparked discussions among the fae community about the delicate balance between the mortal and magical realms and the need for heightened vigilance to safe-

**guard the mystical sanctuaries that define Eloria's enchanting landscapes. As the investigation unfolds, the fae folk remain hopeful that the Glittering Grove will once again shine with the brilliance that has made it a beacon of magic in Eloria.**

My eyes widened in surprise. This was unexpected. I had always thought Eloria was a peaceful place. But attacks and disruptions? That wasn't something I had imagined! The Glittering Trove of Lumoria, from what I gathered in the news, appeared to be a sacred place. But what could cause a disturbance there, and why? Was someone trying to steal the magic from that trove? As I finished reading the above news article, the next one appeared automatically in front of my eyes, and my hands started shaking.

**12 March, 17000**

**Tuesday**

**11 am**

****Breaking News in Eloria - Dark Forces attack****

**Disturbing events have unfolded in the ethereal realm of Eloria, as reports flood in about a series of unprecedented attacks on the fae inhabitants by mysterious creatures known as Kiri. These malevolent**

beings, previously unheard of in the fae realms, have left a trail of concern and uncertainty among the Elven community. The Kiri, described as shadowy entities with glowing eyes and an otherworldly presence, have been venturing into the outskirts of Eloria, targeting fae folk. Witnesses recount harrowing encounters with these creatures, detailing how their piercing cries and swift movements have struck fear into the hearts of even the most seasoned fae warriors.

High Lord Thorne, visibly shaken by the events, has declared a state of emergency in Eloria, urging all fae residents to exercise extreme caution and remain within the protected boundaries of the enchanted realm. The High Lord, along with a team of skilled fae defenders, is mobilizing to confront the Kiri threat and safeguard the safety of Eloria's inhabitants. Elven scholars are researching ancient texts and consulting with mystical experts to understand the origin and nature of these malevolent creatures. The fae healers are working tirelessly to tend to those who have been injured in the attacks, employing both magical remedies and traditional healing techniques.

The Kiri incursions have prompted a rare alliance among the fae clans, as they unite to face this unforeseen threat. Messages of solidarity and support echo through the enchanted woods as the Elven community braces itself against the shadowy menace. As the sun sets over Eloria, the realm is gripped by an air of uncertainty, with fae folk remaining vigilant and ready to defend their enchanted homeland against the enigmatic Kiri. The coming days will undoubtedly

**test the resilience and unity of Eloria's inhabitants as they strive to protect their mystical haven from this newfound peril.**

As I read the news from the book, a wave of worry washed over me. Something bad was happening in Eloria. Creatures called *Kiri* were attacking the fae folk; these beings with glowing eyes were instilling fear among the people. I wondered, were these occurrences new, or had there been ones before me? I quickly turned a few pages back to check the previous dates.

**10 February, 17000**

**Tuesday**

**11 am**

****Breaking News in Eloria - Dark Forces attack****

**Disturbing events continue to unfold in the ethereal realm of Eloria, adding another layer of challenge to the fae inhabitants. Reports are pouring in about an unusual surge in magical anomalies that have disrupted the harmonious balance of Eloria. The once-stable magical ley lines that crisscrossed the realm are now behaving erratically, causing unpredictable fluctuations in magical energy. Flickering**

**lights, shimmering illusions, and unexplained magical gusts have become a common sight across Eloria.**

**Elven scholars, alongside mystical experts, are working tirelessly to understand the root cause of these magical disturbances. Theories range from the possibility of an ancient enchantment awakening to the influence of external forces seeking to destabilize Eloria. As investigations intensify, fae healers are adapting their magical remedies to address the unexpected consequences of these anomalies.**

Here was another one.Elven I tried to concentrate..

**5 January, 17000**

**Tuesday**

**11 am**

****Breaking News in Eloria - Dark Forces attack****

**Regrettably, in the preceding weeks, Eloria faced an unexpected disturbance in the heart of the Enchanted Springs, a revered site known for its healing properties. This incident cast a shadow over the normally serene sanctuary and prompted concern among the fae**

inhabitants. Reports from mystical sources detailed a disruption in the natural flow of the springs' magical waters. The once-clear waters, renowned for their ability to mend both physical and emotional wounds, became tainted with an otherworldly darkness. The fae healers, who draw upon the springs' energies for their remedies, expressed deep sorrow over the unexpected contamination.

High Lord Thorne, visibly troubled by this event, took immediate action to address the issue. A team of elven scholars and magical experts was assembled to investigate the cause behind the disturbance and work towards restoring the Enchanted Springs to their pristine state. Fae residents who traditionally sought solace and rejuvenation in the healing waters, were advised to refrain from approaching the contaminated area. Temporary protective barriers were erected to prevent further exposure to the tainted magical essence, and the fae community rallied together to support those affected by the disruption. While Eloria grappled with this unfortunate incident, High Lord Thorne reassured the fae folk that every effort was being made to purify the Enchanted Springs and restore the vital connection between the mystical waters and the realm's inhabitants. The incident underscored the delicate balance that exists in Eloria and the need for constant vigilance to protect its magical sanctuaries.

# Chapter Ten

## A lingering Sensation

Stepping into the lively city with Thorne felt like entering a new world. The desire to break free from the confines of the mansion, to cease being a passive observer of events, propelled me into the vibrant streets. I wanted to know things, about the creatures, about the attacks. Upon expressing this wish to Thorne, he insisted on accompanying me, emphasizing his concerns about my safety.

Although his protectiveness struck me as odd, I complied and allowed him to guide me through the unknown facets of the city. Together, we explored a beautiful farmland adorned with colorful crops tended to by fae farmers. The orchards bore fruits that emitted a magical glow, casting an enchanting aura over everything. As I took in the mesmerizing sights, my thoughts drifted to the fae folk and the challenges they must be facing, akin to the ones chronicled in that mysterious book. I pondered whether they had encountered the elusive Kiri or if other creatures also lurked in the shadows, contributing to the troubles that plagued this magical realm.

Walking through the fae villages, ancient stones rose like guardians from the earth, standing tall with an aura of timeless wisdom. Fae elders, draped in robes intricately woven with threads of time, partook in rituals that echoed with the magical energy enveloping them. The stones absorbed these enchantments, softly glowing as if holding the secrets of centuries. Thorne explained that regular performance of these rituals was essential to keep our Goddess Luminara content, ensuring a continual replenishment of Eloria's magical resources.

Approaching the heart of Eloria, the landscape metamorphosed into a wondrous city. Crystalline towers stretched towards the sky, embodying the very essence of magic itself. The bustling streets teemed with fae artisans, meticulously crafting intricate jewelry, weaving spells into fabrics, and creating trinkets that gleamed brilliantly in the sunlight. Women stood in shops, captivated by various items such as trinkets, paintings, and feather art, evoking memories of my father, *but not very happy ones*. Despite the ongoing attacks in Eloria, these people exuded happiness. They refused to be confined within their homes, paralyzed by fear of the next attack or the lurking creatures that might emerge from the shadows to harm them.

Thorne took me to a coffee shop named *Whimsical Brew Haven*. I had heard about cafes from children in school, but experiencing one for the first time was an entirely new adventure. Entering Whimsical Brew Haven felt like stepping into a realm of pure enchantment. The door, adorned with swirling vines and delicate fairy lights, swung open to reveal a burst of fragrant air, infused with the rich scent of freshly brewed magical concoctions that enriched my senses.

Inside, the walls came alive with intricate murals portraying scenes of fae folklore—fae people embracing one another, working harmoniously, and their children playing together. Painted in soft pastel tones of lavender and mint green, the images blended seamlessly, yet none depicted humans as if the history with them had been erased from time. My gaze drifted to magical landscapes, adding vibrant colors and splashes, and bringing the walls to life with an otherworldly charm. Occasional shimmering accents caught the eye, and the ceiling sparkled with softly glowing crystals, casting a gentle, ethereal light. The tables, crafted from the wood of ancient, enchanted trees, seemed to radiate a comforting energy.

Walking in, the melodic tinkling of wind chimes, woven with magical charms, danced in the air. The baristas, adorned in a brown apron, expertly brewed elixirs that released wisps of colorful steam. One of them approached us, her features as beautiful as Ivy's, with pointed ears and sparkling eyes. However, her steps faltered as she reached towards us. She bowed before Thorne, the shine somewhat gone from her face as she stammered, "Welcome, Highlord! What can I get for you?"

Thorne smiled and gestured towards me, saying, "How about a nice sitting area?" He inclined his head towards me, and I nodded instinctively. The barista also nodded in agreement, though color seemed to drain from her face as she guided us towards a cozy nook. Seated in a cozy corner, surrounded by plush cushions and enveloped in the soft glow of enchanted lanterns, I felt a sense of tranquility, but also a sense of unease. Thorne ordered himself an iced latte and a black coffee for me, somehow knowing my choice. Though I had had coffee many times, it tasted heavenly, like nothing I had ever experienced.

"So, you're the king of Eloria?" I asked Thorne, wondering about the barista's fearful reaction.

He looked at me and smiled. "You can say so," he said, "but it's more like I manage this place. Sometimes I do have to answer, especially to the people, but also to the High King!"

"High King?" I ask. "Where does he live?" almost shocked.

"This is all his kingdom, and he lives everywhere, knows and sees everything," he said, but something dark flashed in his green eyes that I couldn't quite grasp.

"What does that mean?" I asked, my eyebrows shooting up in surprise.

"Too many questions for a coffee date!" he said, smiling at me. I couldn't help but blush at his comment, realizing that our two hours together had passed without even noticing. As we strolled back to the mansion, our proximity felt electrifying. Our fingers brushed frequently, creating a subtle dance of connection. Hesitant to meet his gaze, I was unsure whether it held care or a tinge of something else—perhaps even pity for a human.

Protectively, I drew my hands close to my chest. Did he notice? It seemed like he might have, or at least, I wanted to believe he did. Navigating the cobblestone streets in the moonlight added an adventurous touch. I was focused on maintaining balance when suddenly, my foot slipped and I stumbled. At that vulnerable moment, he reached out and caught my hand. Without a word, he laced our fingers together, the warmth of his touch comforting. Our hands intertwined, and I saw in his eyes care, not pity, as we continued our journey under the enchanting night sky.

*In the heart of the dense woods, an ancient eye gazed upon me with a weighty knowing. Its pursuit was relentless, threading through rustling leaves and lingering in the very air I breathed. An unspoken demand lingered, a desire shrouded in antiquity that sent shivers down my spine. Despite its familiarity, the mere thought of this enigmatic eye instilled fear, urging me into a desperate run. Ragged gasps escaped my lips, echoing through the silent woods. Sweat formed beads on my temples, and my hair clung wetly to my face. The thudding of my heart reverberated intensely as if it might leap out of my throat. Every step became a struggle, stumbling over uneven terrain, yet the pursuit propelled me forward. Amidst the towering trees, a sudden force jerked me, and as I attempted to regain balance, a face came into view. Recognition dawned with a jolt—it was Kael. The once-familiar visage now wore an unsettling cloak, leaving me breathless and bewildered in the heart of the mysterious woods.*

My eyes snapped open, and I jolted upright in bed. Thorne was standing at the door, his arms folded at his chest and his gaze fixed on me.

"Want to go on a hunt with me?" He asked, and suddenly, I was acutely aware of the sweat clinging to my face.

"Yes," I blurted out with little thought, only to realize that I wore a flimsy nightgown, its straps precariously clinging to my shoulders. After he awkwardly left, the weight of my realization sank in, and I buried my face in my hands.

In just half an hour, I bathed and changed, slipping into an elegant off-white tunic shirt with buttons, complemented by tan trousers and knee-high boots, I recreated the coronet braid—a familiar touch from home that added a sense of comfort to my appearance. It was the first time I had styled my hair this way since arriving in Eloria. I was getting used to living here, the comfort of not getting a beating now and then. I feel like my nerves were relaxing a bit here. My gaze went to the mirror, and I observed that I was smiling.

At the foot of the stairs, Thorne gracefully took my hand, pressing a gentle kiss on it before leading me outside. Two guards awaited us with horses and guns—horses, familiar yet enchanting creatures. My excitement dimmed a bit as I noticed Kael joining our party. Thorne helped me climb onto my pristine white, beautiful horse and moved towards his. We embarked on our journey around midday, nearly three hours into the adventure. Thorne patiently taught me how to handle the gun, especially against the elusive murans—large, brown, and furry creatures with small, round eyes. My first attempt was a bit shaky, but the experience was thrilling, nonetheless. Kael's constant side glances throughout the day made me feel like I was an annoyance he reluctantly had to tolerate. It was becoming a bit overwhelming. Initially, it scared me, but the fear only lasted for a while. Soon, anger and defiance begin to seep in.

As the day unfolded, the sun cast a warm glow over the landscape, and the rhythmic thud of horses against the earth became a comforting soundtrack to our journey. The thrill of the hunt intertwined with the beauty of the surroundings, creating a mesmerizing dance of adventure and enchantment.

"Can I ask you something, Thorne?" I asked, adjusting the reins of the horse as he taught me.

"You don't need my permission to ask me questions, Ariana," he replied, smiling.

"You're good at talking," I side-eyed him.

"You want to know what else I'm good at, Ariana?" His voice was a bit like a growl, a bit taunting, his gaze fixed on my lips, and suddenly, my face was flushed and my skin tingling.

"What attacked the Glittering Grove?" I tried to change the topic, immediately regretting it as I saw his expression shift into something I didn't want to decipher — The expression was all too familiar... The expression of whether I'm deemed worthy or not...

"You don't have to worry about it; it's ancient history," he said, dismissing the concern with a laugh. "Just a creature from the woods. Where did you dig up all this ancient information, by the way?" he asked.

"Oh, I found it in the book," I replied, with a dismissing tone.

"Which Book?"

"A book regarding current affairs I found in your library."

He nodded.

I realized Kael's eyes were still piercing into the back of my head. We stopped for lunch on the way and returned in the evening. Thorne escorted me back to my chambers. As we reached the door, I turned to bid him goodnight, only to realize how close he was. Too close. He stepped forward, and I hesitantly stepped back, his green eyes turning dark.

Something lit up deep in my stomach, my skin turning red hot. He did it again, one step closer. I stepped back, my back shoving into the door behind me. He was close, too close. *No one has ever been this close.* He lifted his left hand to cup my face. I flinched for some reason, just for a second. But he noticed it. A flicker of warmth ignited deep within me as he took another step closer. I instinctively moved back, feeling the door press against my back. There was no way to go as our bodies touched, his pressing into mine. I had never felt anything like this before.

The proximity intensified, and my skin flushed with heat. He gently cradled my face. "You are so beautiful," he purred against my ear. A warm breath caressed my skin, and I instinctively closed my eyes. My back arched against the embrace of his strong, solid frame, enveloping my delicate one. Soft lips pressed against my neck, and my breath caught in response. Abruptly, he vanished, leaving me with a lingering sensation of his touch.

# Chapter Eleven

# Getting Used to

*You are so beautiful.*

Thorne's words echoed in my mind like a sweet melody as I woke up the next day. With a soft smile gracing my lips, I got ready in a simple red flowery gown, with a red rose tucked behind my right ear, anticipating the prospect of sharing breakfast with Thorne.

But as I descended the stairs, my joy quickly turned to concern when I found Thorne in the midst of gearing up, surrounded by an arsenal of formidable weapons. The room, usually filled with the warmth of the morning sun, now felt laden with the weight of impending departure.

"Where are you going?" my voice trembled, a note of panic creeping into it. The echo of my words lingered in the vaulted ceiling. Thorne, looking slightly distressed with furrowed brows, met my gaze.

"There's been an invasion near the border. I have to go and check it," he explained. "I'll be back in a few days."

I cast a glance at Kael, his stony expression revealing nothing of the turbulent thoughts beneath. The uncertainty of the situation lingered in the air like a heavy mist as Thorne prepared to walk out of the mansion.

"Who invaded the border?" I asked. There must be people there. Women. Children.

"I told you, Ariana, you don't have to worry about these things. I'll be back before you realize it," Thorne's words somehow hit like a punch in my gut.

A lingering worry remained, casting a shadow over his impending departure like a fleeting wisp of darkness. Something indescribable fractured within me, and I grappled with the weight of emotions swirling beneath the surface. Was it the prospect of residing in this expansive mansion alone, the solitude stretching endlessly before me like an uncharted landscape, or was it the echo of his response resonating in the depths of my being?

Uncertain, I found solace in the familiar act of nodding, a silent acknowledgment that I had grown accustomed to these types of answers, these artful deflections that shielded more than they revealed. My gaze drifted towards Kael's, and he was looking at me. As if he knew what I was feeling at this moment. I quickly looked away.

"May I go to the market near the mansion, perhaps accompanied by Ivy or someone else?" The words spilled out, lacking the intended gentleness.

"Ivy mentioned I shouldn't go out without your permission." The prospect of being confined indoors without Thorne's presence left in the dark, left me grappling with a sense of uncertainty and a yearning for freedom. I wanted to know about the attack. About what was happening in the world outside, and sitting decorated in these walls of the mansion would have been of no use.

Thorne studied me for a lingering moment, his gaze holding a depth of consideration. He then shifted his attention to Kael, delivering a decree, "Ariana shouldn't venture alone to the town market. You'll accompany her whenever she wishes to go." Kael's jaw tightened, and his silver eyes fixed on me with an intensity that felt like scorching flames.

"Sure, Thorne."

The air thickened with unspoken tension, leaving me caught in the crossfire of their unspoken exchanges. I wonder if it was so difficult for Kael to tolerate me.

For nearly a month, I had found myself immersed in the enchanting realm of Eloria, a place that continued to elude me when it came to revealing the secrets of my arrival and the elusive path back to Eldenhaven. Despite the lingering mysteries shrouding my presence here, I must confess that Eloria had proven to be a surprisingly captivating haven.

The allure of its magical ambiance had cast a spell on me, rendering this unfamiliar realm not the least undesirable. In this fantastical haven, the ordinary norms of existence seemed to be suspended, and I had come to appreciate the peculiar wonders that abounded. The bathwater, for instance, maintained a perpetually warm temperature, never succumbing to the chill that often accompanies the passage of time.

The food tray in my quarters displayed a remarkable resistance to emptiness, defying the conventional expectations of finite sustenance. Even the comforting ritual of indulging in tea and coffee was a perpetual delight, with my cup seemingly bottomless. The kettle was always full of fresh ones.

I could not help but marvel at the ever-fresh and vibrant blooms adorning the pots that punctuated the whole mansion. The flowers, in their perpetual state of bloom, imbued the atmosphere with a sense of constant spring, an eternal celebration of life that contrasted starkly with the temporal nature of the world I once knew. The mundane act of leaving my bed was accompanied by a bewitching phenomenon—the linens arranged themselves seamlessly, restoring order with an almost sentient grace. It was a peculiar occurrence that had become a comforting routine, and with each passing day, I found myself growing accustomed to this otherworldly aspect of my surroundings.

Yet, beyond the whimsical charm of my magically tidy bed, there existed a more profound transformation occurring within me. The absence of the constant barrage of negativity, the conspicuous lack of beatings, taunts, and scoldings for every minor misstep, had become a novel and welcomed experience. I was gradually acclimating to a reality where the mere act of making a mistake, like inadvertently breaking a trinket or spending more than five minutes in conversation with my parents, did not spiral into an agonizing episode of reproach and punishment.

It was both a revelation and a relief, this newfound environment of understanding and acceptance. The dread of a normal conversation devolving into a relentless hour-long session of physical and emotional torment, leaving me isolated in the solitude of my room with only haunting whispers for company, was an unsettling memory that seemed to be fading away in the gentle embrace of Eloria's sanctuary.

"Whispers" persistently echoed within the recesses of my mind, each thought of him prompting a cascade of uncertainties that danced through my consciousness. I found myself contemplating the mysterious fate of the one who once shared our home—a four-legged companion, a faithful friend. Did he now reside in the shelter for abandoned souls, surrendered by my father in a moment of detachment? Or, perhaps, he lingered in the familiar corners of the house, a silent witness to my absence?

The contemplations unfurled like tendrils of curiosity, weaving through the tapestry of my thoughts. I wondered if my parents searched for me. Did they harbor concerns, their hearts heavy with worry over the daughter who had seemingly vanished for almost a month? Alternatively, did they find solace in the absence of my presence, liberated from the weight of what they might perceive as a burden? I was left to speculate on whether their lives had seamlessly adjusted, now adorned by the idyllic image of a perfect daughter named Catriona.

There was no resentment within me for her; hatred had never found a home in my heart. She, in her flawlessness, seemed custom-made for the world they inhabited, a puzzle piece seamlessly fitting into the intricate mosaic of their lives—an image I, by contrast, did not naturally complement. In this paradoxical coexistence, admiration, and inadequacy formed a delicate dance within my soul.

A sudden knock reverberated through the door, interrupting the contemplation that had become my companion in the absence of Thorne, who had not returned for three days. A subtle anticipation stirred within, an unspoken hope that the one behind the door might be him. Alas, that familiar presence remained elusive, leaving me in a state of suspended uncertainty within the confines of my dwelling, where I had chosen to withdraw from the outside world.

Ivy stepped into the room, a beacon of solace, poised to extricate me from the clutches of my own mental anguish and guide me back into the realm of the living. As the door swung open, a palpable shift occurred, and the prospect of stepping outside, guided by Ivy's understanding presence, promised a respite from the internal struggles that had defined my secluded existence.

Our daily routine had evolved into a shared ritual where she, with an eye for beauty, carefully selected outfits that adorned my wide frame. Sometimes she wove intricate braids into my hair, while on other occasions, I let my locks cascade freely, embracing the untamed allure. An unexpected bond had blossomed, and she had transcended the role of a mere caretaker, emerging as a companion and confidante in this mansion.

Despite her appearance suggesting a kindred youthfulness, she disclosed an age that startled me momentarily—52 years. The revelation sparked a silent contemplation on the passage of time, and

I found myself staring at her, trying to reconcile the vivacity in her eyes with the wisdom accumulated over half a century. Her origins are traced back to Elfland, a place with a vibrant history of communal living that was disrupted by the intrusion of malevolent forces. Thorne, in an act of benevolence, extended his sanctuary to them, prompting the migration of elves seeking refuge in Eloria.

As she talked about her past, I felt there were secrets she wasn't sharing, hidden knowledge that made me curious. There were parts of this new world I didn't fully understand, covered in mystery. I really wanted to discover these secrets, but fear stopped me. The unknown seemed overwhelming, and even though I was curious, my fear made me hesitant to look deeper into these mysteries.

# Chapter Twelve

# *Hazy Secrets*

Descending the grand staircase in the light purple gown, I had planned to go to the market today. Today was the fourth day. Fourth day without Thorne. Fourth day without any information about the attack. I needed to get out. To understand what was going on around here.

My gaze went to its intricate borders on the main door, every curve and pattern telling a tale of elegance. Suddenly, an arrogant voice cut through the air, abruptly halting my progress.

The figure, standing in my path, splaying his black wings, mirrored the disdainful mannerisms that had become all too familiar. His presence, reminiscent of the judgmental airs I had endured with my own parents, stood as an arrogant obstacle in my journey—a stark reminder of the very reason I wanted to go alone. Not with him.

"And where do you think you are going?" Kael sneered, his words a venomous reminder of his disdain. How much he hated me. And I hated him.

Summoning my strength, I shot back, "I am heading to the art café."

But I wondered whether he had ever seen me as a person, as a being who had needs or wishes. He must have always considered me as an *animal. An inferior, pathetic, brainless animal.*

"You are not permitted to go out alone, in case you've conveniently forgotten, because of your little brain," he mused.

Irritation flowed through my veins as I clutched the cloth of my gown by my sides. "I'll be fine, and I won't be long." Ignoring him, I pivoted to make my way through the door, only to find Kael with his strong tanned hand on my arm, blocking my path with an almost unnerving quickness.

His silver eyes pinned on me with unwavering intensity, a formidable figure that commanded attention. Caught between his gaze and the door, I found myself in a silent standoff, the desire for independence clashing against the unyielding presence of Kael. The air hung with unspoken tension, and the weight of his scrutiny left me momentarily breathless, ensnared by an invisible force.

"You are not going alone," he snared through his teeth. But he could not have stopped me; he had been ordered to escort me, not dictate my every move. Tired of sitting and waiting, doing nothing, I stood my ground. He studied me, silver eyes boring into mine.

"Why are you doing this? You don't care about me. You don't care if something happens to me. Then why bother with trying to stop me? Nothing is going to happen, anyway." I tried to make sure the hurt was not that apparent in my eyes or in my tone.

His jaw muscle ticked, and his grip on my arm tightened. "Ouch," my eyebrows furrowed in pain.

"Your Thorne has ordered me to do so, remember?" he said, as he let go of my arm with a sudden jerk.

"Escort me, then," avoiding direct eye contact, aware of the proximity to us, I stepped forward. The palpable tension hung in the air, his unspoken disapproval almost tangible. In the face of my gentle assertion, he remained silent. His eyes, sharp and piercing, seemed to pierce through the air with an intensity that could easily scorch the world. Without uttering a word, he conceded with a sidelong step, allowing me to pass. As I moved forward, he fell in step behind me, a silent sentinel on my journey through the mansion.

Entering the mesmerizing art café, named *Elysian Canopy*, felt like stepping into a realm of enchantment. Ivy's tales had painted vivid images of this place. Bright luminescent flowers, unseen in the mortal realm, adorned the exteriors.

As I crossed the enchanted threshold, the air within embraced me with the tantalizing fragrance of exotic coffee blends—a sensory symphony that stirred my senses to life. The walls of the art café had transformed into canvases adorned with vibrant murals, each stroke depicting the fantastical realms of Eloria. Mystical creatures, cascading waterfalls, and celestial skies had unfolded in a mesmerizing dance of color and imagination. Above, the ceiling had sparkled with suspended crystals, their gentle glow casting a celestial ambiance upon the patrons below. This was prettier than the previous one.

Finding a seat in an oval chair, I had placed an order for my customary drink, a simple yet comforting black coffee. Engaging the Elven barista in conversation, I asked her as she poured my cup of hot steaming coffee, "Do you know anything about the attack on the border? I heard it was pretty serious! The Highlord had to go himself to control it."

Her hands started trembling as she poured coffee. A haze appeared in her eyes. The same one I saw in the eyes of the barista in front of Thorne. She kept the kettle from her hands on the table. "I am sorry for that," she said, "but I don't know what you are talking about."

"Are you okay?"

"Yes, of course. Would you like more coffee?" She deflected the question like our conversation had never happened!

Kael's watchful eyes tracked my every move and hung on every word. *A silent guardian amid the art café.* Although he had refrained from placing an order, he was alert, like anything could go wrong at any moment.

Curiosity burning within, "What do you know about the dark forces? And the attacks in the last few months?" I asked, sipping the coffee, trying to act casual and watching the Elven barista's expression for any flicker of recognition or revelation.

Kael's eyes shot toward me with a swiftness that betrayed his keen interest in my line of questioning. The intensity in his gaze added an intriguing layer to my question, leaving me to wonder about the significance of his reaction.

"In the mystical realms of Eloria," the Elven barista began, "whispers of ancient lore speak of the presence of dark forces that once threatened the harmony of this enchanted land. These malevolent entities, shrouded in shadows and fueled by dark magic, were said to be remnants of a time when the balance between light and darkness teetered on the edge."

As the tale unfolded, the barista delved into the legend of Elfland, recounting a sinister invasion that cast the once-thriving Elven communities into chaos. The description of twisted creatures emanating eerie energy and the trail of destruction they left behind painted a vivid picture of the malevolence that had once gripped Elfland. The air in the art café hung heavy with the weight of ancient tales, and Kael's continued scrutiny added an intriguing layer of complexity to the unfolding narrative. At that moment, it became clear that the enigmatic history of Eloria held secrets that beckoned to be unveiled. Amidst the tumultuous upheaval, the figure of the High Lord emerged as a symbol of hope for the beleaguered elves. Thornedike, with unwavering courage, led the defense against the encroaching dark forces that threatened to engulf Elfland. In the aftermath of the conflict, he extended a haven of refuge to those displaced by the malevolence that had insidiously infiltrated the once-thriving Elven homeland.

The Elven barista's voice carried the weight of history as she spoke, narrating a tale that echoed the familiar contours of the lore I had already encountered. Thornedike's courage in the face of darkness and his compassionate response to the plight of the displaced resonated through the words, casting a timeless aura over the narrative.

"But now Eloria is safe. There are no dark forces now. Our High Lord has managed everything." Her words struck me oddly, and my gaze instantly went towards Kael's. But his face revealed nothing. I looked up at the barista's face, and I noticed the same hazy eyes. It was like she was under some control.

I tried to ask another question, but Kael nodded. Maybe he knew something that I didn't.

"Thank you for the coffee," I said, and the barista went back to her counter. Sipping my coffee, I turned my attention to the artists scattered in designated corners, their creations seemingly imbued with the very essence of Eloria. The visual tapestry they wove hinted at the elusive truths I sought, each stroke and hue a potential clue in the unraveling mystery.

Conversations flowed effortlessly around me, a symphony of voices that wove together threads of knowledge about the migration of elves, the mystical properties of certain locations, and the echoes of ancient battles fought against dark forces. The art café, serving as a vibrant hub for the community, resonated with diverse discussions, each snippet contributing to the enigmatic history of Eloria. But I got nothing about the attacks in the past months, that were mentioned in the book. It was like no one knew about them. Like they never happened. But why would they appear in that current affairs book then?

# WINGS OF REDEMPTION

# Chapter Thirteen

## Look at me

Emerging from the enchanting embrace of the *Elysian Canopy,* the moonlight transformed the cobbled streets into a silver canvas, creating a living painting of ethereal beauty. The celestial glow bathed our surroundings, illuminating the labyrinthine town in a soft luminescence. A mere 15-minute stroll away, the mansion stood as an imposing silhouette against the night sky, beckoning us homeward.

An unspoken tension hung thick in the air, a palpable silence woven between us like a heavy mist. I felt Kael's frustration lingering in the shadows, a sentiment undoubtedly fueled by my persistent company this evening. But it was his choice to accompany me—I hadn't forced him to join me, and he couldn't place blame on me for his current state of annoyance.

The ambient glow from the street lamps cast elongated shadows as we navigated the winding paths. I really never liked cobblestone streets. I just don't seem to maintain my balance on it. Moon rays playing peek-a-boo through the branches of ancient trees, creating a magical interplay of light and shadow. Despite the hushed quiet, the town emanated an ethereal charm, as if the very stones beneath our feet held the secrets of centuries. As we navigated the streets, the occasional rustling of leaves added a subtle melody to our nocturnal journey. The town, steeped in history and mystery, appeared to slumber beneath the gentle touch of moonlight. The mansion appeared larger with each step, its architectural details becoming more pronounced against the night canvas.

Casting a covert glance at Kael, I observed his silhouette, a stony presence beside me. The shared journey unfolded differently for each of us—my curiosity undiminished, his patience, perhaps, wearing thin. How long were we going to do this? He was there when Thorne went to the borders to handle the attack. Why didn't he say something? There is something weird going on here. Something that I don't understand.

Kael's voice, a step behind me, sliced through the stillness, rough and edged with an urgency that demanded attention.

"Why were you asking about the dark forces?" His words hung in the night air like an unspoken secret.

Caught off guard, I hesitated for a moment, the weight of his question settling upon me. "Because no one would tell me anything about it," I confessed, the words tumbling out like a confession. A palpable tension lingered in the air as we walked.

"It will be better for you if you stop looking into it," his tone was urgent and reluctant. As if he wanted to tell me more, but couldn't.

"What do you mean..." I began to ask, my voice trailing off as his hand abruptly landed on my arm.

In an instant, he pulled me back with a force that startled me, disrupting the normal rhythm of my steps. The proximity became almost suffocating as I found myself pressed against his body, his other hand firmly covering my mouth. Panic set in as I attempted to speak, but his grip stifled any words of mine that might escape. I struggled against his hold, the effort to move futile against his strength.

My breath quickened, panting now as a surge of anxiety coursed through me. The moonlit streets witnessed this sudden, silent struggle, the shadows casting a surreal backdrop to the unspoken clash of wills. In the intimate dance of shadows and moonlight, my attempts at resistance became a desperate echo against the silence of the night.

"Don't you dare move," his voice pierced through my pants, each word a directive that froze me in place.

"Don't you dare speak," he whispered into my skin, his lips grazing my ear with an intimacy that sent shivers down my spine. The night, once filled with the ambient sounds of nature, now fell into an eerie silence, as if the very essence of life had withdrawn from the space we occupied. Suddenly, an inexplicable chill permeated the air, seeping through the fabric of reality itself. The warmth that once lingered in the moonlit night dissipated, leaving a haunting coldness in its wake. It wasn't the proximity to Kael that caused my trembling—it was something else, something far more ominous that I couldn't quite grasp.

In that suspended moment of frigid stillness, the shadows seemed to deepen; the moonlight casting an ethereal glow upon the scene. The air crackled with otherworldly energy, and a profound sense of foreboding settled over me like a heavy cloak. The very fabric of Eloria appeared to respond to an unseen force, and I found myself caught in a chilling tableau, awaiting the revelation of the unknown that lurked in the icy tendrils of the night.

"Don't open your eyes, no matter what you hear." His words, deliberate and slow, hung in the air like a potent spell. In response, I clamped my eyes shut with such intensity that my brows began to ache.

Amidst the darkness behind my closed lids, a chilling silence reigned, accompanied only by the frigid temperature enveloping me. The hair on my arms rose. The air, once charged with an eerie energy, now held nothing but a palpable stillness. And then, a sound disrupted the silence—a dog's bark. It echoed through the frosty night, a familiar resonance that struck a chord deep within my memory. A rush of recognition coursed through me, and the echoes of that bark transported me to a time and place I thought I had left behind.

Another bark.

With my eyes tightly shut, I stood frozen, the layers of memory and reality intermingling in the shroud of darkness. "Whispers," I breathed, my voice trembling as I struggled in Kael's arms. The attempt to break free proved futile, as he held me steadfastly, an anchor against the unseen currents that threatened to pull me into the unknown.

"Don't open your eyes," he commanded his words, a stern barrier against the mysterious forces that lingered in the shadows.

Bark came closer and turned into a cry.

"Whispers....my d...," My voice panicked.

"It's not true. He is not real," Kael grunted through his teeth, his voice resonating with an air of certainty that clashed with what I had been hearing. As my pleas echoed in the silent space, tears began to flow through my tightly shut eyes, a manifestation of the overwhelming emotions that surged within.

The distant barking came to an abrupt halt, leaving behind a profound stillness. Into this vacuum of silence, the same voice returned, a haunting cadence that sent shivers down my spine.

"Look at me, Ariana. I have been waiting for you," it beckoned, each word laden with an eerie chillness that pierced through the darkened veil of the night. A chilling ripple of fear prompted me to crumble instinctively back into the reassuring, solid body of Kael. Fear tightened its grip on me, and yet Kael remained a steadfast anchor, his strength a refuge against the unseen forces that had woven themselves into the fabric of the night.

"Just keep your eyes closed. It can't do anything until your eyes are closed," he murmured, and I didn't have in me to even nod. I didn't know what was standing in front of me.

In that suspended moment, time lost its meaning. We stood entwined as the weight of the night pressed down upon us. I don't even remember how long we stood there. Maybe it was minutes or hours. The air hung heavy with anticipation, each passing moment resonating with an otherworldly stillness that defied the conventional flow of time.

Amidst the uncertainty, Kael's unwavering presence became a lifeline, grounding me in a reality that teetered on the edge of the inexplicable.

"What was that?" The words escaped my lips as Kael released his grip slowly, his hands traveling down my back as I stepped away. I needed to know, but a part of me expected him to say *don't worry about it, forget it. You ask too many questions* or something along those lines. Because no one ever deemed me worthy of anything, worthy of being explained to, worthy of being talked to, even Thorne seemed to belong to the same category.

Kael took a step forward, turning to face me. The silence hung between us, heavy with unspoken revelations. A glint of concern shone in his silver beautiful eyes. His usually steadfast voice wavered, and I could sense a hesitancy as he began to speak "Aria, what you've encountered today....it was an....Umbracorruptor."

The term resonated with an ominous weight, and an involuntary shiver ran down my spine at hearing the name.

"Umbracorruptor? What do you mean? What are they?

Kael seemed to choose his words cautiously, as though aware that the truth he was about to disclose carried both discomfort and necessity for my understanding. "Umbracorruptors were the ancient entities," he continued, and I caught the mix of knowledge and caution in his voice. "They're born from the convergence of dark magic and the essence of shadows. Beings of malevolence draw to realms where the balance between light and darkness wavers."

In my mind's eye, I began to form a picture of these shadowy entities, creatures born from the delicate dance between magic and darkness. Kael's hesitation was palpable, as if he grappled with the decision to expose me to the unsettling realities lurking in the corners of Eloria.

"These entities feed on fear and uncertainty," he said, and the weight of his words settled in the air. "They manipulate emotions, weaving illusions and whispers to exploit the vulnerabilities, and the moment you look into their eyes, they suck your soul."

Kael waited patiently for me to understand the situation.

"Aria," he said, the weight of concern evident in his voice, "you have to be vigilant. Umbracorruptors are elusive, and their influence can be insidious. The key is not to succumb to their manipulations. Keep your eyes closed, and know what is true and what is not."

"And this is just the beginning. You have to be careful," he warned, as he turned to walk towards the mansion.

# Chapter Fourteen

## *Summer Solistice*

Today, Ivy's excitement was palpable as she enthusiastically declared that it was the Summer Solstice. Here, in Eloria, this occasion held a significance that was unfamiliar to me, having never encountered such celebrations in Eldenhaven.

According to her, the summer solstice marks the precise moment when Eloria's axial tilt is most inclined toward the sun. This astronomical phenomenon leads to the longest day and the shortest night of the year in the Northern Hemisphere. Intrigued by this novel concept, Ivy painted a vivid picture of the festivities that accompany the summer solstice in Eloria. She promised a jubilant atmosphere filled with celebrations, dance, music, and an abundance of delectable food and drinks.

Her eyes sparkled with anticipation as she left me with a resplendent, big, and beautiful gown in a captivating shade of pink, a garment tailored for the joyous occasion. Although I have never been fond of heavy gowns, there is something about this place. The magic maybe. Everything fits just perfectly, and everything is so light.

A whole week had elapsed, and there was still no sign of Thorne's return. The uncertainty surrounding his absence, especially amid the ongoing concerns about the border invasion, left me in a state of restlessness.

*I don't know what you are talking about.*

The words of that barista still resonated in my head. And I haven't even gotten a chance to ask Kael about it. He had not been in the mansion since then. Maybe he is with Thorne. Maybe Thorne needed help. But why would the barista say that she didn't know anything? Maybe the public was not informed about it. To keep them stress-free.

Thoughts of Thorne's well-being and the progress of his mission occupied my mind, creating an invisible thread of worry that lingered. Interrupting my contemplation, a sudden knock on the door drew my attention. I opened my eyes to find Thorne standing before me. A rush of relief flooded over me, and a small smile instinctively graced my lips. He still wore the same garments he had on when he embarked on his journey. He came directly to see me as soon as he returned to the mansion.

As he entered, a genuine smile illuminated his features. At that moment, my heart responded with an involuntary flutter, a subtle acknowledgment of our shared connection.

"Hie, Ariana," Thorne greeted me, his voice carrying a mix of warmth and reassurance. His presence, a welcome balm to the uncertainty that had clouded my thoughts, brought a sense of familiarity and stability.

"Hie..." I managed to whisper as he stepped forward, his presence casting a subtle spell on the atmosphere. Seated on my bed, I instinctively straightened up, creating a bit of space for him beside me. He sat on the corner of my bed, drawing close, and a soft, anticipatory thrill coursed through me as his smooth lips brushed against my forehead, leaving a lingering warmth in their wake. In response, my skin tingled as I inhaled the smell of wind and metal. I closed my eyes to savor the tender moment.

"I missed you, Ariana," he purred against my skin, his words as gentle as the touch that preceded them. My heart pounded, caught in the delicate dance of emotions. I didn't know what to say. The sheer intensity of this moment had rendered me speechless.

Opening my eyes, I found him gazing at my face with a tender smile, and a flood of emotions enveloped me. Gratitude swelled within me for this man who had returned and expressed such words to me. There was a realization, subtle yet profound, that I was beginning to grow a fondness for him. I was starting to like him. Yet, I couldn't say anything to him.

"Get ready, Ariana. I'll meet you in half an hour," he murmured into my ear. With that, he vanished into thin air, leaving behind only the echo of his voice. I couldn't help but marvel at this disappearing magic of his. No matter how many times I had witnessed such feats, the enchantment of his disappearing act never failed to surprise me.

The gown I found myself adorned in was a mesmerizing creation. A soft, delicate shade of pink, reminiscent of blooming cherry blossoms, draping gracefully over my form. Countless pearls embedded in the fabric, each one shimmering like ethereal dewdrops, creating a celestial glow that added an otherworldly dimension to my attire. The gown, with its intricate design, skillfully hugged my body in all the right places, accentuating my curves and hinting at a touch of regality.

Ivy, who had become my friend at this point, wove magic into my hair. Delicate tendrils cascaded around my face, framing it with a whimsical touch. The main body of my hair was expertly braided, interwoven with strands of glistening pink pearls that mirrored the ones on my gown. As I glanced in the mirror, the pearls caught the light, twinkling like stars in my brown hair. This was the first time in my life that I had adorned myself with so much beauty and was happy at the same time.

Ivy escorted me downstairs, where Thorne was already waiting for me. His attire was a vivid tapestry of strength and sophistication, draped in a tunic that boasted a commanding hue reminiscent of deep twilight blues. The fabric, not merely a choice but a statement, breathed life into his robust and well-defined build. As the embroidery wove its way across the tunic, it mirrored the complexity of Thorne's character — a leader with a nuanced understanding of his responsibilities. An aura of strength and authority enveloped him.

Paired with black trousers that tightly hugged his muscular thighs, it was hard to look anywhere else. A well-fitted belt cinched his slim waist, a subtle touch that not only completed the ensemble but also drew attention to his commanding presence. With every stride, the fabric responded to the contours of his physique, making my throat dry. This man was so beautiful. It was hard to believe my eyes.

He graciously took my hand and hooked it around his arm. We entered the courtyard aglow with radiant lanterns and adorned with colorful flowers, the ambiance alive with the ethereal hum of fae laughter and harmonious tunes. Thorne's other hand gestured towards the vibrant gathering. "Ariana, welcome to the party on the longest day of the year! Ready to tire yourself to dance?" He chuckled.

Approaching me with a crown woven from the finest summer flowers, Ivy said, "Wear this, Ariana. Let it serve as a conduit for the energies of this mystical day. All your wishes will come true today," her gentle smile concealing the profound significance of the moment. The courtyard pulsed with enchantment as I donned the flowery crown, its petals intertwining with strands of my hair like a natural crown.

The air buzzed with otherworldly energy, and the fae inhabitants, with their delicate wings and luminous presence, added to the ethereal atmosphere. Thorne guided me through the festivities, his steady presence grounding me amidst the enchanting spectacle. As we strolled, the fae inhabitants acknowledged Thorne with nods of respect and me, with curious glances, their eyes reflecting the kaleidoscope of emotions. The atmosphere became a mixture of colors, sounds, and scents, each contributing to the celebration of the summer solstice.

Ivy explained to me the rituals and traditions embedded in the fae festivities. From the rhythmic dances that echoed the patterns of the stars to the melodious songs sung in an ancient tongue, everything resonated with a sense of timeless magic. The fae laughter, like tinkling wind chimes, harmonized with the soft glow of lanterns adorning the courtyard. Amidst the revelry, Thorne's eyes held a glint of familiarity with the fae customs, revealing a side of him deeply connected to the mystical heritage of Eloria. He guided me through the intricate dance steps and encouraged me to join in the songs, creating moments that felt suspended in the enchantment of the solstice night.

Everyone was here at this moment, the whole town. I hadn't seen so many people in one place before. My mother used to host parties, but they were never this grand. Never this joyous. It was like a permanent smile had been plastered on my face.

The towering bonfire, its flames aspiring towards the heavens, emerged as a potent emblem of vitality and rebirth, casting an illuminating glow upon the ceremonious celebration.

"Tonight," Thorne shared, his eyes beaming with excitement, "is when the line between our world and the enchanting energy that breathes life into Eloria becomes really thin. It's like a magical sweet spot, a time when connections are super strong between Eloria and the Goddess Luminara, and if you make a wish, who knows? It might just come true."

As the night unfolded, Thorne's passion for storytelling deepened my understanding of Eloria's mystical legacy. Kael, ever the silent figure, kept his distance, his gaze holding a mystery that left me intrigued and curious. It reminded me of the day we went to the cafe, *the day when the barista said that there had been no attacks.*

I need to talk to Thorne about this. Make things clear. *But I doubt he will tell me anything.*

Approaching a majestic ancient tree at the heart of the courtyard, Thorne handed me a vial filled with shimmering dust, snatching me out of my rambling thoughts.

"This dust," he said with a twinkle in his eye and my hand in his hand, "is packed with the very essence of the Summer Solstice. Sprinkle it on your wishes, and let the magic work its charm." *He must have drunk a lot of wine.*

I held the vial in my hands; the dust sparkling like tiny stars in the moonlight. As I sprinkled it in the air, it shimmered like a sparkle. As I turned around to see others, every single fae was doing the same thing, including Thorne. *But not Kael. He was just looking at me. Observing me.* The courtyard came alive with the wishes of the fae, weaving a symphony of enchantment that echoed in the night.

Thorne's gaze, warm and full of understanding, lingered on me. In his eyes, I saw the reflection of the magic we were all a part of. Ivy, with her graceful dance and wings that caught the moonlight, added to the ethereal atmosphere. Amidst the joyous celebration, Kael remained silent, like a shadow; his watchful gaze sparking a sense of curiosity within me.

As the Summer Solstice reached its dazzling climax, Thorne took me on a journey through a kaleidoscope of rituals and traditions. Faeries twirled and giggled, their wings shimmering with the radiant magic of the day. The atmosphere pulsated with the melodies of strings and the harmonious tunes that seemed to synchronize with the very heartbeat of Eloria.

"Tonight is a celebration of unity," Thorne's voice now slurred through his wine, his eyes aglow with the significance of the moment. "The fae gather not just for revelry but to fortify our connection with the enchanting energies that sustain our realm. The Goddess. It's a poignant reminder of our intricate ties to nature and to each other, a dance of unity under the embrace of the mystical Summer Solstice."

*The High Lord.*

The revelry stretched into the early hours of the morning, the bonfire painting whimsical shadows on the joyous fae dancers. Thorne and Ivy, like primary storytellers, wove tales of past solstices.

The night culminated in a grand spectacle—a breathtaking display of fireworks that adorned the sky with brilliant hues. The fae community gathered, their eyes wide with awe as each burst of light and magic unfolded overhead. Thorne turned to me, his expression radiating satisfaction. "Aren't they beautiful?" He whispered, looking up at the sky.

I watched the mesmerizing display; "Yes, they are," I said as I saw the colors reflecting in Thorne's eyes. Despite the enchantment of the celebration, a subtle tension lingered. Ivy's ethereal laughter resonated nearby, but Kael's stony demeanor added a layer of complexity to the night. As the final ember of the bonfire waned, Thorne guided me toward the mansion. The Summer Solstice had been a whirlwind of enchantment, yet Kael's quiet presence continued to pull at the edges of my consciousness. It was like he was not even there. It was just a shadow. He was not talking to anyone, not eating anything, not even drinking.

Upon entering the mansion, Thorne proposed a stroll through the moonlit gardens. Ivy gracefully excused herself, leaving us alone amidst the fragrant blooms. The air retained a lingering magic, and the gardens radiated tranquility.

"Tonight was beyond words, Thorne," I confessed.

He nodded, his eyes fixed on the moon. "The Summer Solstice has a way of etching its essence into the hearts of those who embrace it. It's a jubilation of life, love, and the timeless bond between the fae and Eloria."

As we strolled, the moonlight wove delicate patterns on the cobblestone paths. Thorne's presence provided a reassuring anchor. Yet my thoughts lingered on Kael. The gardens, with their fragrant blooms, seemed to amplify the enigma surrounding him.

Sensing my contemplation, Thorne sighed, "Don't worry so much about the winged man, Ariana. It will not do any good to you."

Shocked, I said, "No...I was not..."

"Come on Ariana, it is written all over your face. You care about him, don't you?"

"Is he always so... distant?" I cautiously asked.

Thorne's expression changed into something I couldn't comprehend, as he said, "Like I said, you don't have to worry. I am here for you. Similarly, Kael also has people who can take care of him."

*I don't know why, but something fractured inside me after hearing Thorne's words.*

# Chapter Fifteen

## The Encounter

Thorne and I strolled through the garden, my hand in his. The atmosphere hummed with an electric current, infusing the air with a sense of subtle anticipation. But my heart ached with something, maybe it was Thorne's words, or something else. I didn't know. Frustration gnawed at me. Why did Kael affect me so much? His mood, his presence, his actions, everything seemed to dictate my emotions. Why? I hated him. I hated the way he talked to me. Thorne is here. With me. He is always so nice to me. *I think.*

Our steps led us to the vicinity of a fountain, where pristine water cascaded in mesmerizing choreography under the moonlight. It flowed in graceful patterns, resembling a dance that captivated the senses. The sound of water splashing against stone filled our surroundings, creating a soothing melody. The fragrance of moist soil filled the air, a heavenly scent that heightened the enchantment of this moment.

"I'm truly grateful that I could share this longest day of the year with you, Ariana," Thorne spoke, turning towards me; gently cradling my right hand in both of his, the warmth radiating close to his heart. *He is nice to me.* My heartbeat fluttered, a mysterious reaction that occurred every time I found myself in Thorne's company. I lifted my gaze to meet his eyes, "I am happy too, Thorne."

*And I will not think about Kael.*

Closing the distance between us, he took a step closer until our feet nearly touched. His hand reached up to delicately tuck a loose strand of hair behind my ear. I closed my eyes. The gentle trail of his fingers continued down to my chin. With the touch of two fingers, he lifted it, bringing my face closer; his face was just inches away from mine.

At that moment, a whirlwind of emotions swept through me — anticipation, vulnerability, and a spark of something undefinable. His closeness, the tender gesture, created an intimate space where time seemed to stand still. My heart raced as his fingers lingered, a silent conversation transpiring between our shared breaths. The air crackled with an unspoken connection, a dance of emotions playing out under the moonlit sky. Thorne's voice held a depth of emotion that mirrored the complexities within me. He whispered against my lips, "Ariana," and I felt the weight of his words resonate within my soul. Something clenched in my stomach. Every heartbeat echoed the unspoken understanding, a connection that surpassed the boundaries of words.

"Open your eyes, Ariana," he purred, his voice sending a shiver down my spine. Obediently, I complied, meeting his once-green eyes now transformed into a deeper, more intense hue. There was something in them that resonated with a craving I couldn't quite articulate. His hand glided from my chin to the nape of my neck, and my back arched involuntarily into the warmth of his body.

At that moment, it felt as though he and I were morphing into a single entity, an intimate connection that defied the boundaries of space and time. Our bodies were so close, touching. My breath was trying to catch up as his lips angled towards mine; almost sealing mine when I heard something. Or felt something.

There was something else here. The once vibrant beauty of this place had evaporated, replaced by an ominous void that made the hair on my arms rise. The air thickened with an unspoken dread; similar to that day with Kael; casting a pall over the once enchanting surroundings.

Thorne and I both turned simultaneously, our eyes widening in alarm as we bore witness to the unsettling transformation. All the lights that once illuminated the scene were extinguished, plunging the landscape into an impenetrable darkness. The gentle breeze that once carried the sweet scent of flowers was gone, replaced by an eerie stillness. The flowers that adorned the surroundings now withered, their once lively hues drained into a muted palette of black.

In the shadowy embrace of the trees, a sinister presence rustled. An indistinct figure took shape, a silhouette that seemed to draw darkness from the very fabric of the night. It was a sight that froze the breath in my lungs, a bone-chilling manifestation that defied the serene facade this place once wore. An unspoken tension charged the air.

A malevolent force stirred; a presence, dark and foreboding that lurked within the shadows, strolled forward. The air became palpably dense, and an ominous stillness descended upon the once-vibrant surroundings. Goosebumps prickled on my skin and a shiver coursed through me as the atmosphere transformed into an eerie symphony of fear. A sudden, piercing cry broke the silence—a sound so haunting that it froze the very marrow in my bones. It resonated through the fae woods around us, bouncing off the ancient trees and sending tremors through the magical tapestry that weaved Eloria together. I dared not move, transfixed by the haunting echoes that seemed to emanate from every shadow, every hidden corner.

*They look like....the ones in the book!*

"Are these......Kiri?" My voice trembled.

Thorne's face drained beside me.

"You need to run inside," his voice muffled.

As I peered into the darkness, my eyes strained to make out the complete form of whatever was standing in front of us. The Kiri, elusive and ever-changing, emerged like a wraith from the depths of the shadows. Glowing eyes, radiant and malevolent, fixated upon me, stripping away the illusion of safety that the fae woods and Thorne once provided.

Their movements were swift and unpredictable. The Kiri glided through the air, their forms defying the natural laws of motion. Panic clutched at my throat, and my breath caught as I realized that these shadowy entities were no mere figments of fae folklore—they were a living nightmare, a manifestation of the unknown.

*How did that barista didn't know about them?*

A profound sense of dread washed over me, as if the very air was tainted with their malevolence. The once-lush vegetation around me withered in their presence, a stark reminder that the Kiri brought not only fear but a tangible disruption to the delicate balance of Eloria's enchanted ecosystem. The shadows seemed to stretch and contort, creating a suffocating embrace that threatened to engulf me. We stepped back as they moved towards us. Thorne slowly angled himself slightly in front of me. But there were so many of them. There was no one here to help us! Where did everyone go?

As the haunting cries intensified, and the shadows deepened, I was paralyzed by fear. I tried to move but couldn't. It was as if they had cast a spell on me.

And suddenly my gaze snapped towards Kael, who was standing beside me, panting. He must have come running, hearing their voice. Wielding two swords; with his sharp silver eyes fixed on our opponents, Kael stood unyielding at my side.

"Yes, these are Kiri," he muttered, his gaze straight. I couldn't help but wonder if he had been present when I posed the same question to Thorne. In the mystical courtyard of Eloria, bathed in the silvery glow of the moon, the air crackled with anticipation. The formidable force known as Kiri, adorned in dark attire, their eyes gleaming like shards of obsidian, stood at the ready. On the opposing side, Thorne and Kael, a united front, faced them with unwavering resolve, standing in front of me. The cobbled ground beneath them seemed to pulse with the energy of imminent conflict, and the air hung heavy with the scent of impending battle. Shadows cast by the moon danced in rhythmic patterns, setting the stage for a confrontation that would unfold like a choreographed symphony of steel.

Kiri glided forward, extending his shadowy arms as swords; attacking us from all sides. Kael and Thorne completely covered me from either side.

"You should run inside," Thorne shouted.

"There is no time now," Kael shot back.

And then all I could hear was the sound of steel clashing against the steel. Though the swords of Kiri were extensions of their shadowy bodies, they were no less than steel itself. Three attacked Kael and he blocked their attack with his both swords, grunting; he tried to throw them back, but they merely glided a few inches back before attacking again.

On the other hand, two Kiri attacked Thorne. He kicked one and sliced the other through the waist. But the wound sealed off right back like it was never been there in the first place.

"You think you can save her?" A stinking voice came from their mouths.

"Stay away from her!" Thorne shouted, shoving the sword inside another one. The same happened with this one. As the sword came out of his stomach, the hole in the top of his stomach closed. The terror in my eyes was unmeasurable at this point in time.

We could not defeat these creatures like this. They were indestructible. Although Kael and Thorne were fighting, my heart was thundering, as if the sword were in my hands. A black-colored hand appeared on my side and grabbed my left hand; Kiri started pulling me towards the woods.

"Thorne.....Thor...." I screamed, eyes wide wide horror. *No, this can't be happening.*

I tried to snatch my hand back from him, that monstrous creature, but my efforts were a mere source of entertainment for that powerful beast. He pulled me towards himself, and I stumbled and fell on the floor, but he didn't stop. He kept on dragging me towards the woods, my knees scrapping on the stones, tears blurring my eyes.

"Thorne…." I tried to call him again, but he didn't notice. He has been busy fighting with them. For me. *But I was being taken.*

As his shadowy form crossed the boundary of the stony path to enter the muddy woods, a shining steel crossed my eyes. I flinched, my voice cracked with fear as Kael's sword cut the hand of Kiri that was holding me. Kael instantly grabbed me by the shoulders, "Are you okay?" flames burned in his silver eyes.

I nodded.

He helped me stand back on my feet and took me towards the entry of the mansion.

"You will stay here. Do not move," he said, his jaw clenching.

I nodded again.

Instead of falling on the ground, the severed hand of Kiri evaporated; and a new one grew in its place within a second. A disgusting sound, a cry, echoed through the air. Not a cry. It was Kiri's laugh. It was all a joke for them. A play.

I don't even remember how long the fight went. My hands, my legs, and my whole body were trembling at this point. Thorne and Kael kept fighting and took a few injuries. But it was like I was fazed out. Just like I used to do at *home. When they didn't stop.*

"I shall come for her again," Kiri's cold, emotionless voice snatched me from my haze. And they disappeared in a second like they had never been there. Everything was destroyed, all the flowers, trees, the whole garden! Everything was lifeless!

"Why would Kiri come for me?" I snapped at Thorne, my voice still shaking. I couldn't ignore it any longer; I couldn't endure it any longer. He had been sweet-talking with his words all this time; but I knew he was concealing things from me—things that involved me. I could not take it any longer. Throughout my entire life, people have taken me for granted, treating me like garbage, as if I am worthless and not deserving of trust.

"Speak, Thorne!" My voice caused him to flinch. Despite his advancing step, my warning stood firm. He might have been the High Lord of Eloria, far more potent than I, but my simmering anger declared that trust must be reciprocal—I couldn't place my trust in him if he didn't reciprocate it. I cast my gaze upon Kael, but he avoided my eyes and fixed his stare on Thorne as if signaling him to reveal the truth. Strangely, at this moment, I found myself leaning towards trusting Kael more. Every time, Kael had stood by me, and shared truths, but Thorne had only spoken in flowery phrases to soothe me. He had never shared anything genuine.

"Ariana..." Thorne sighed.

"I didn't want to involve you in all this; that's why I've never told you," his voice lowered.

"But Kiri came here for me, Thorne, and judging by the situation, it seems I'm already into whatever this is, whether you like it or not," I snapped back.

He sighed, his shoulders drooping, and his sword clinked as it hit the floor. Moving to sit on the cobblestone boundary of the fountain, he cradled his head in his hands.

"Kiri is an ancient entity, a harbinger sent by the dark forces with the explicit purpose of capturing you. Their relentless pursuit has spanned a considerable duration. The essence within you emits a unique spark that draws Kiri to you—a telltale signature that signaled your arrival in Eloria on the first day. It's this very spark that enabled me to locate you when you came here, in Eloria. This place, for centuries, has been grappling with challenges posed by a myriad of creatures dispatched by these dark forces. Their sinister objective revolves around pilfering magic and life force from our realm, leading to the disruption of our land and the tragic loss of our people—children, elders, and women alike. These dark entities wield formidable power, while our numbers are limited in the fight against them," he elaborated, his voice resonating with the weight of centuries-old struggles.

"What do they want from me? How am I tied to all of this?" My initial anger now giving way to a sense of deflation.

"Thousands of years ago, a prophecy foretold that only a human girl within the fae land could either create or seal the portals between the worlds. Before your arrival, there was no glimpse of hope. However, since you stepped into our realm, everyone has been vying to control you. I'm unsure of the intricacies tying you to all of this. Initially, I spent time with you, attempting to understand, and searching for any clues or signs, but I came up empty-handed. It dawned on me that you are just a human girl, unaware of your fate," he confided, his tone reflecting a mix of uncertainty and genuine concern.

"So, everything, all the moments we shared, was just a part of your plan?" I struggled not to lament, though my eyes betrayed the onset of redness.

"No, Ariana. Initially, my intention was simply to get to know you, but as time passed, I found myself falling for you. Everything we felt, it was all.....real," he sighed, looking up at me with a sincerity that resonated in his words.

"I don't know anymore, Thorne. What's true and what's not?" I confessed, heartbroken as if my world had been shattered once again. It was as if I was standing at a crossroads, unsure of how to move forward or what to do next. Thorne was a beacon of hope for me, and now it felt like that hope had vanished. I was left grappling with the uncertainty of how to trust him moving forward.

Kael excused himself, striding into the mansion. I don't know why I wanted him to stay. Thorne rose and approached me. I avoided meeting his gaze entirely. He placed both hands on my shoulders, turning me to face him.

"Please, Ariana. I'm aware I've let you down and betrayed your trust. But grant me one chance to redeem myself," he implored, *his sincerity echoing in his plea.*

Tears cascaded down my cheeks, an unstoppable torrent. He tenderly lifted my face, compelling me to meet his eyes. "Please, just one chance. I vow never to betray you again, never to conceal anything from you."

I brushed away the tears, conjuring a fragile smile. "I want to help you save Eloria. Tell me how can I help."

# Chapter Sixteen

## Broken Heart

According to Thorne, we need to go on a journey to find ancient magic, a formidable force believed to be our only recourse against the encroaching dark forces. He insisted that this elusive magic held the key to our ability to stand against the impending threat, and with the aid of this ancient magic, I might possess the capacity to seal the portal between Eloria and the ominous Shadow realm—a gateway through which malevolent entities were spilling forth to assail the inhabitants of Eloria, children, women, and elders alike.

Despite Thorne's propensity for keeping certain truths concealed, my intuition insisted that his intentions were untainted. I could see the honesty in his eyes. Having endured the company of those with malicious intentions, I recognized the subtle cues in speech and behavior that betray malevolent motives. Thorne, however, defied these indicators. His actions and demeanor spoke of genuine concern and care.

A discreet knock on the door disrupted my focus, diverting my attention from the task at hand—meticulously packing my pants and tunics into a backpack, preparing for the imminent journey that awaited us. Kael stepped in. It was the first time he had stepped into this personal space of mine, and suddenly, a heightened awareness enveloped me—of my own presence, the positioning of my hands, the expression on my face, and even the clothes scattered on my bed; everything seemed magnified. His scrutinizing gaze surveyed the room's entirety before finally meeting my eyes. He whispered, "I need to talk to you."

For the first time, there was no hate or irritation in his eyes. It was something different. Fear. Or worry perhaps? I must be wrong, shaking my thoughts. "What do you want to talk about?" I asked.

He stepped closer, almost reaching my side. I placed the shirt in my hand on the bed before pivoting towards him. His gaze intensified, pinning me with a seriousness that demanded attention.

"You cannot trust Thorne; it's not safe for you to go on this journey with him," his words carrying a weighty concern that lingered in the air.

His words struck a chord, causing an unsettling fracture within my heart. I instinctively took a step back, feeling a mix of surprise and disbelief at whatever he said.

"You need to go," I asserted, a firmness in my tone.

"You don't understand everything, Aria. This is more complicated than you think. You have to listen to me," he blurted out, urgency coloring his words.

"I'm sick of people telling me this. Sick of being told that I don't get it. I believe I can make my own choices if given a chance," I snapped, my fists clenched in frustration.

"Alright, if this is really what you want, I won't stop you. But, please, do one thing for me," he begged, reaching into his pocket. With a deliberate motion, he pulled out a wooden amulet and chain, placing it in my hands. He gently clasped my hands around it, urging me, "Please, wear this."

Curiosity sparked within me as I examined the amulet.

"What is this?"

He took a deep breath before explaining, "This amulet is imbued with magic. It will protect you from any kind of harm. Just promise me that you will wear it."

I gazed at the amulet, then shifted my attention to him, my skepticism evident, not because it was imbued with magic......but because it looked like the other broken half of the amulet I had...the amulet I threw...the broken heart...but that wasn't possible...and it was made of iron and this was made of wood. Despite my reservations, time was of the essence, and Thorne awaited my presence.

"Okay," I agreed, "I will wear it." A sense of comfort washed over me, a familiar one, as I placed it around my neck.

# Chapter Seventeen

## The Shadowed Thicket

Here we stood, at the very border of Eloria, ready for the adventure that awaited Thorne and me. Thorne clutched a backpack in his hands, undoubtedly carrying provisions for our journey—food, clothes, and essentials carefully stowed away. In my grasp, I held a backpack of my own, filled with a similar array of belongings. It surprised me how weightless it felt, despite the substantial amount of items I had packed into it.

*Maybe it was the magic.*

Thorne's attire spoke of preparedness—khaki-colored pants, a crisply buttoned white shirt, and a secure brown belt to hold it all together. Two swords hung confidently at his back. In a similar outfit, my pants snugly embracing my hips and a shirt tailored to perfection accentuating all the right curves, I stood prepared for the journey ahead. Knee-length boots, chosen for their sturdy grip, promised resilience for the extensive travel that lay ahead.

As we peered into the distance, a dense layer of fog, almost like a thick curtain, obscured our vision, veiling the landscape before us. Thorne had cautioned me about the perils of the path ahead—the Shadowed Thicket. For centuries, none had dared to venture into its depths, and those who attempted never returned. Yet, compelled by the dire need to save Eloria, we have decided to take this risk.

*Not that we had any other option.*

Our hands entwined, we stepped into the enveloping fog, my heart racing with fear or excitement I couldn't pinpoint. A disorienting shift in air pressure assaulted my senses, inducing nausea. Breathing became a struggle, my throat constricted, moving my feet was a challenge, and my eyes began to well up. Thorne's hand slipped from mine. Time seemed to pause at that moment, and darkness seemed to envelop me. Alone, it felt like I was alone in this universe, in this world, being shredded to the core of my being. Abruptly, a firm hand reached out, seizing me and yanking me out of the fog—no, to the other side of the fog. It was......Thorne's hand. Panting, as I wiped the tears from the corner of my eyes and tried to see ahead, the vibrant beauty of Eloria had dissipated, replaced by the profound darkness of the sylvan woods of Shadowed Thicket that now greeted us.

The air in this part of the Shadowed Thicket, known as Sylvan Woods, felt thick with an otherworldly tension as Thorne and I walked deeper. Somehow, my bag seemed to be heavier on this side of the fog. The beauty that once surrounded us now transformed into a haunting dreamscape, and an unsettling stillness replaced the earlier whispers of the wind. The dense canopy above blocked out much of the light, casting elongated shadows that had an eerie life of their own.

As we reached further, the silence became deafening, broken only by the occasional rustle of leaves underfoot. A chill ran down my spine, and I couldn't shake the feeling that unseen eyes were watching our every move. Every step. Every breath. I wondered if Thorne could also feel it. But I dared not ask him. To make any extra noise. Just in case I might awaken something.

The ancient runes were etched into the trees, the unclear symbols, that seemed to pulsate with an ominous energy, casting strange patterns on the ground. I heard the distant hooting of owls, their calls echoing in a haunting symphony.

The path narrowed, and the gnarled branches of the ancient trees twisted overhead, forming a natural canopy that seemed to close in around us. Thorne raised his hand in front of me, gesturing for silence. Even the crunching of leaves beneath our feet ceased, and an oppressive hush settled over the woods.

A spine-chilling glow seeped from the moss-covered tree trunks, casting an unsettling ambiance. Ghostly shapes played hide-and-seek, their eerie moans echoing through the hushed woods. It was as if these shadowy figures, stuck between realms, peered at us with malevolent intent.

*At least with no intent of helping us.*

The air thickened with an unspoken dread, and each step forward felt like a plunge into the abyss of the unknown. My heart was thundering with fear. I was pretty sure anything would jump in front of us at any moment.

The shadows stretched and contorted, morphing into grotesque shapes that flickered at the edge of our vision. Every rustle, every crackle of a twig, echoed like a foreboding drumbeat, heightening the palpable fear that hung in the air.

The oppressive stillness intensified, becoming a suffocating force that clung to our skin. Thorne's composed facade started to crack under the weight of this ominous atmosphere, and the flicker of unease in his eyes mirrored the growing terror within me. As we navigated the narrow path, the ancient trees seemed to leer at us, their gnarled branches reaching out like skeletal fingers, as if they wanted to pick up and eat us alive.

Dense fog surrounded us. We were barely able to see a foot in front of us. Each step forward was met with an invisible resistance, as if the very essence of the woods rebelled against our intrusion. The fear, an ever-present companion, coiled around our hearts, tightening its grip with every passing moment. We pressed on, driven by the urgency of finding the ancient magic *or getting out of this miserable place really,* yet the pervasive fear lingered, a relentless adversary in this shadowed realm.

As dense fog crept in, cloaking the surroundings in an impenetrable mist even more. Shapes moved within the fog—shadows that defied easy explanation. The air grew colder, and my breath formed ghostly wisps in the frigid night. Feeling an instinctive surge of unease in the eerie surroundings, I hastily reached for

Thorne's hand, seeking comfort and reassurance in the unsettling atmosphere of the Sylvan Woods.

Suddenly, a chorus of disembodied whispers filled the air. Indistinct voices murmured unintelligible words, their tone carrying a cry of sadness and urgency. The ancient spirits, awakened by our intrusion, according to Thorne, sought to communicate a message, though its meaning remained elusive. As the whispers intensified, the shadows coalesced into more tangible forms.

Figures with hollow eyes and gaunt features emerged from the darkness, drifting silently towards us. Similar but yet, different from Kiri. *Those Monsters.* Their faces looked haunted, with inverted smiles on their faces, as if they were being forced to keep a secret that was killing them, eating them from the inside. Thorne raised his hand again, this time in a defensive gesture, and I could feel the weight of unseen forces pressing upon us.

"What are these?" I tried to ask, but my voice barely left my mouth.

A cold wind whispered through the trees, carrying with it the scent of decay and forgotten memories. I might just vomit here. This was the worst smell I had ever encountered. It was from the hell itself. Unearthly cries echoed in the distance, a cacophony of wails that seemed to resonate from the very heart of the Sylvan Woods. It was as if the ancient magic that permeated the air was responding to our presence with both curiosity and hostility. As if it was testing us.

Thorne whispered, "Stay close. This area holds secrets, and we are trespassers here. It won't be easy from here on."

*From here on.*

My heart quickened, but I nodded.

The shadows closed in around us, their movements synchronized with an otherworldly boldness. I could feel the cold touch of unseen hands brushing against the skin of my neck, sending shivers down my spine, urging me to curl up against Thorne. My grip on his hand tightened as I flinched to look back. But no one was there.

Each step forward became a struggle against an invisible force that sought to keep us entwined in the forest's haunted embrace. Shadows converged into a dense mass, forming a giant silhouette that seemed to defy the natural laws of the world. From this shadowed amalgamation emerged a creature—a manifestation of the forest's ancient malevolence.

The creature's eyes, resembling pools of inky darkness, fixated on ours with an unsettling intensity. Its form writhed and convulsed, morphing between grotesque shapes reminiscent of long-buried nightmares. A primal growl rumbled from the depths of the creature, the sound resonating with an unholy energy that seemed to saturate the air.

In a desperate bid for defense, Thorne swiftly elevated an ancient talisman in his hand, which I realized he had carried with him from the mansion; its luminous aura acted as a temporary barrier, repelling the creature and casting a fleeting sky-colored shield of protection around us. The creature shrieked in pain, its form trembling, causing ripples in the surrounding air.

"How did you do that?" I asked Thorne, surprised at what was happening in front of my eyes.

"We have to hurry, this field will only hold for so long," Thorne panted, struggling to hold up the talisman.

# Chapter Eighteen

## *Chasing the Ethereal Light*

"You didn't tell me how the talisman did that?" I asked Thorne, looking at him for a moment as we tumbled through our way forward.

"We don't have time for this, Ariana," he gave me a sharp look, "not now," and I regretted asking him, *wondering why I even tried*.

As we moved forward, the haunting chorus of whispers and cries followed us, a ghostly accompaniment to our journey. The creature in the shadows pursued its presence an ever-looming threat, the feel of its touch on my skin still lingering.

A sudden rustle in the underbrush made my heart skip a beat. Thorne halted, his gaze fixed on a cluster of twisted trees. Without warning, a pair of glowing eyes emerged from the darkness, reflecting an unnatural luminescence. The eyes stared directly at me, unblinking, as if warning me to run in the opposite direction. In an instant, the eyes blinked out of existence, and the rustling of the unseen presence ceased.

Thorne's grasp on his talisman tightened, his eyes scanning the surroundings with heightened vigilance. He was moving in front of me, not with me. Not beside me. In front of me.

The once-familiar sounds of the woods now became a chorus of uncertainty, where every rustle of leaves and every snap of a twig hinted at an invisible presence, plunging us into a state where jumping at shadows became an inevitable response to the pervasive atmosphere of foreboding. I could hear the distant laughter of children—echoes that seemed to bounce between the trees.

A man appeared in front of us, old and withered, a human, its translucent form hovering just above the ground. He wore an expression of anguish, and its white eyes locked onto mine. The figure extended a hand toward me, fingers stretching unnaturally. Thorne intervened, waving his talisman to dispel the apparition, his other hand holding mine tightly. But I wondered whether it was the talisman working or the amulet that Kael gave me that was saving my life and sending these monsters away.

The path ahead twisted and turned, and with each corner, my heart raced in anticipation. The darkness seemed to pulse with malevolent energy, and I could almost sense the forest itself closing in around us. Now and then, a cold breeze carried with it the ghostly whispers of forgotten tales, and I couldn't shake the feeling that we were trespassers in a realm where the boundary between the living and dead blurred.

"How long do we have to walk like this?" I asked Thorne. But he didn't reply. As if he was planning something. Maybe to get out safely from here. *Or maybe something else.*

"Thorne...?" I ask again.

"We can't talk here, Ariana, Please!" He motioned for me to stay close as he led the way, his talisman held high as if warding off the encroaching darkness, and I wondered, wondered about the talisman, about his powers, about the things he hadn't told me, wondered where I was going, and Kael's words rang in my mind!

*"You cannot trust Thorne; it's not safe for you to go on this journey with him."*

Trudging through the eerie Shadowed Thicket, time played tricks on us. Thorne had warned that this place doesn't follow Eloria's normal rules. Days turned into nights, with no sunlight breaking through the perpetual darkness. The cold seeped into my bones, making me shiver, while Thorne, being the High Lord, seemed better equipped to handle it. The forest was shrouded in a constant twilight, and the concept of day and night blurred into one. Luminescent fungi provided a mystical glow, but it didn't dispel the oppressive darkness. The air was damp, and the scent of decay hung around, a reminder of the natural cycle of life and death.

It was hard for me to decipher how many hours or days had passed since we entered this hell in the name of the forest. Our routine had become somewhat familiar. We walked until our frozen bones couldn't take it anymore, and then we found a safe spot to rest. Our food supply was long gone, so we relied on hunting and foraging for wild fruit. Thorne warned that the fruit could be risky, though, as it might be poisonous or lead us into traps.

We took short breaks every few hours, but I found it impossible to sleep in this forest. Thorne managed to catch a nap or two, and I kept watch, though I doubted I could do much other than wake up Thorne if a menacing creature were about to appear. Our journey was tough. The frozen ground made each step a challenge, and we were running on empty since our food ran out.

Our feeble attempt to ward off the bone-chilling cold involved gathering stray bits of wood for a meager fire. The flames flickered weakly in the moist and damp air, providing only a modest defense against the pervasive cold that enveloped us. Thorne lay beside me, eyes closed, peacefully asleep. However, sleep eluded me, and I found myself staring into the darkness, attempting to fix my gaze on whatever sky I was able to see above. Yet, the thick, dark green leaves overhead obstructed all the views of the heavens. So, I lay there motionless, trying to suppress even the faintest breath, hoping to blend into the shadowy stillness that defined this nocturnal sanctuary.

The crackling of our struggling fire and the occasional rustle of leaves broke the stillness of the night only, unsettling in its lack of a discernible source. Amid this profound quietude, a golden-colored light pierced the darkness. Intrigued, I sat up, my eyes searching for the origin of it. This ambient glow, like the sun, seemed to defy the inky blackness that prevailed, casting a warm hue upon the surrounding foliage. It was a stark contrast to the foreboding shadows that had thus far defined our journey.

A small, luminous sphere of golden light hovered in the air, just a few feet from where I sat. It flickered like a miniature fire, casting an enchanting glow that defied adequate description. Its ethereal radiance captivated me, instilling a sense of magic in the otherwise profound darkness that blanketed the forest. It was the most mesmerizing thing I had ever seen.

Compelled by an irresistible allure, I rose from my resting place, feeling a magnetic pull toward the radiant orb. It beckoned me, inviting exploration and connection. In the stillness of the night, I was driven to follow this extraordinary light, to touch it, to capture its elusive brilliance. I looked back at Thorne, who remained deep in slumber. I decided not to disturb his peaceful sleep.

A profound sense of care and love seemed to emanate from the golden light, offering reassurance amid the haunting unknown. Carefully navigating through the twisted branches that cast peculiar shadows, I proceeded toward the light, each step taken with a mix of awe and trepidation. The surrounding air was eerily silent, devoid of the usual rustling of leaves or nocturnal sounds. The light, floating effortlessly in the air, maintained its mesmerizing presence, guiding me through the otherworldly darkness.

As I progressed, the forest seemed to transform. The once daunting shadows now appeared as silhouettes against the soft glow of the radiant orb. It felt as though the light was leading me to a place of serene beauty, a sanctuary hidden within the enigmatic depths of the woods. The very atmosphere resonated with an otherworldly stillness, amplifying the ethereal nature of this journey. In my pursuit of the luminous guide, I ventured cautiously, mindful of the uneven terrain beneath my feet.

The forest, once oppressive and foreboding, now took on a surreal charm, a testament to the transformative power of the golden light. I was not feeling scared anymore. Yet, as I ventured deeper into this enchanting realm, an unexpected turn of events shattered the tranquility. The ground under my feet gave way, and I found myself plunged into ice-cold water. The sudden immersion shocked me, causing a jolt, and I felt disoriented in the frigid darkness for a moment.

# Chapter Nineteen

## *Kiss and Betrayal*

Navigating through the oppressive stillness of the swamp, I cautiously swam out of it. The air hung thick with the rancid scent of decay, and suddenly, a guttural growl shattered the eerie silence; a monstrous figure emerged from the murky waters. It defied the laws of nature—an abomination blending equine grace with malevolent distortion.

As it approached, the swamp water became more treacherous, concealing a graveyard of decay. Foul smells intensified, and panic tightened my chest as it advanced. I tried to tread through the water, but the still water developed currents of an ocean. The creature's slick, dark tendrils seemed to consume the feeble light, and its equine head adorned with leathery fins framed hollow, glowing eyes. Jagged, rotten teeth protruded menacingly, and twisted, elongated limbs ended in webbed hooves that glided eerily over the water. Its tendrils grabbed my hands and started dragging me.

The suffocating embrace of the swamp water held unseen terrors, and the creature tightened its grip. The muck clung to my limbs, threatening to pull me into the abyss. Visibility neared zero, concealing nightmares lurking beneath. Horror gripped me as the creature dragged me into the inky depths, and the water became a liquid tomb. Struggling to breathe, my vision blurred, and the world became a disorienting dance of shadows.

The creature's grip tightened around my throat, and water filled my lungs. Thick, decaying, foul-smelling water. I thrashed. Struggled. Coughed. It laughed with its rotten teeth, but it didn't let me go. My body started jerking with the lack of oxygen. My burning eyes started closing. This was the end.

*Thorne?*

The light dimmed, and I faded, the last image etched in my fading consciousness—a malevolent creature reveling in the depths. In the cold embrace of the swamp, silence descended. The creature, having claimed its victim, retreated into the depths, leaving only ripples on the once-still water. The swamp, now a tomb of secrets, concealed its horrors, awaiting the next unsuspecting intruder.

I gasped, waterlogged and disoriented, coughing up swamp water as my chest burned. Each breath felt like a desperate plea for escape from the haunting depths I had just barely survived.

*Maybe?*

Strong hands pulled me from the swamp.....hands....hands of Thorne, and with a firm yet gentle touch, anchored me to a reality beyond the nightmarish visions. In his arms, I found stability—a sanctuary against the horrors that threatened to consume me.

"Hey..hey..are you okay?" Thorne asked.

But I couldn't answer at this moment. All I did was choke. And cough. Every breath was burning my insides. And I stank! Of dead!

"The creature that attacked you was a Kelpie," he explained, pumping the water from my stomach. I coughed again. *Disgusting water came out of my mouth.*

"Just a second" He pumped again. He repeated this a few times until I was able to breathe properly, then cradled me up in his arms.

"You are fine now," He said.

"What was that?" I finally managed to get out.

"These are the water spirits. They are always willing to eat anything. But how did you reach here?"

Trembling with fear and chilled to the bone, I struggled to find my voice, barely able to comprehend Thorne's words. At that moment, all I could manage was to clutch his shirt tightly, burying my face in the fabric, tears escaping my eyes, and my breath staggering in the grip of panic.

"Easy, Ariana," Thorne's voice attempted to soothe me as he wrapped his arms tightly around me. In that secure embrace, I felt protected. The world gradually regaining its familiar contours. The haunting abyss of the swamp receded, its specters reduced to mere echoes.

Thorne's eyes, filled with concern and reassurance, met mine. "You're safe now, Ariana. The Kelpie won't trouble you again," he said, holding me tight.

I nodded.

"How did you get here?"

"There was a...ball of light..floating in the air. I don't know what happened. I just started following it. It felt so safe, so loving and nurturing; it felt like it was calling me." My voice still trembled.

"I told you, Ariana, not to trust anything here. You should not have gone behind it." Irritation itched in his voice.

"I know now."

The swamp, now relegated to the periphery of my awareness, became a backdrop to my ordeal. In the quiet aftermath of the Kelpie's assault, Thorne guided me away from the swamp's edge. We walked through the haunted thicket, each step a cautious dance with the unseen forces that lurked in the shadows. The air itself seemed to thicken with an otherworldly tension. Eerie whispers still echoed through the gnarled branches, and the dim light of the moon still struggled to penetrate the oppressive darkness.

Thorne's eyes remained vigilant as we ventured deeper into the heart of the Shadowed Thicket. The occasional rustle of unseen creatures and the distant hooting of owls made me startle more this time. Maybe it was because of the attack. I angled towards Thorne, his presence reassured me that I was safe.

Despite donning dry and clean clothes, an insidious reminder of the swamp lingered in my senses, stubbornly infiltrating the recesses of my nose. The pervasive odor persisted, a haunting specter that refused to dissipate, a visceral reminder of the unsettling encounter with *that thing*.

It wasn't just the olfactory residue that clung to me; it was an unsettling sensation, an eerie echo of the kelpie's touch that seemed to linger on my skin, a phantom touch on my body and, disconcertingly, on my throat. The memory of those black webbed hands, insubstantial yet chillingly tangible, lingered like an indelible mark on my consciousness.

The kelpies, once mere denizens of Eloria's mythical waters, according to Thorne, had undergone a transformation. Strengthened by the breach in the portal separating Eloria from the shadow realm, their malevolence had surged, fueled by the encroaching dark forces that had taken hold of our once-harmonious world.

The very fabric of Eloria had been compromised. The breach in the portal had become a conduit for the infiltration of malevolent entities, turning the serene waters that were once home to mythical creatures into a breeding ground for something far more sinister. The kelpies, emblematic of this profound shift, now wielded a potency that transcended their mythical origins, their spectral hands leaving an indelible mark on those who dared to traverse their realm.

Eloria used to be a wonderful place, but now it was in big trouble. Every day, people were getting hurt or even killed by these scary, soul-eating creatures. I was the only one who could close the door these creatures were coming through, so I needed to figure out how to do it fast.

Although I arrived here only weeks ago, I still hold a deep affection for Eloria; it's not just a place for me. This is the only place where I had felt loved, apart from Whisper's presence. Engaged in my thoughts, I failed to notice the surrounding view. The somber trees of the Sylvian Forest in the Shadowed Thicket yielded vibrant, wild ones adorned in a myriad of colors.

Nature came alive with the melodic symphony of singing birds, the gentle caress of the wind, and a plethora of blossoms that painted the landscape. The sound of water cascading over rocks serenaded my ears, and luminescent mushrooms cast a soft, pinkish glow. A rainbow graced the sky, completing this surreal panorama. It felt like I had stepped into a dream, and the reality of this enchanting scene overwhelmed me. The beauty of this place was awe-inspiring, and I was determined to shield it from any harm. The once dark and shadowy Sylvian Forest of the Shadowed Thicket had transformed into a breathtaking landscape. A sense of relief washed over me, signaling that the arduous and perilous segment of the journey had come to an end.

In this amazing moment, I forgot about the scary creatures and the danger. Eloria was coming back to life, and it was breathtaking. The responsibility I felt before was now mixed with a feeling of wonder and gratefulness. I realized how important it was to protect this special place and keep it safe from the darkness that was trying to take over. No one came forward for me, ever, to help me, to make sure that I was okay, but the same would not happen with Eloria. I would fight for this place.

The change from a sad and dark place to a vibrant and lively one showed me how strong Eloria was. It was like a symbol of hope resisting whatever was trying to torment it, engulfing its happiness; it made me even more determined to close the portal and help this enchanted world in whatever way I could.

I shifted my gaze to Thorne, but his countenance remained unchanged, almost as though the haunting image of the swamp was still playing before his eyes. Confusion struck my face but before I asked anything, "Here, Ariana, trust is a luxury we can't afford," he cautioned. "These creatures, they're shapeshifters. They lure you in with their words and then, when your defenses are low, they come for your soul."

At least there was some semblance of day and night here. It wasn't a perpetual abyss of darkness, and the bone-chilling fog didn't cling to us constantly. There was a reprieve from the sensation of unseen eyes tracking our every move in the shadows. However, Thorne's words echoed loudly—*we must maintain our vigilance, no matter how captivating the surroundings appeared.*

Discovering a high vantage point to establish our camp for the night, we decided to take a break. The grass beneath us was meticulously groomed and clean, a stark contrast to the twisted trees of the Sylvian forest that sprawled across the ground, seemingly determined to trip us at every step. The temperature in this elevated spot was pleasantly mild, and Thorne skillfully kindled a bonfire, arranging sheets for us to sit on, and providing a welcome respite.

During our journey, we stumbled upon a cluster of glowing fruits. Despite Thorne's initial uncertainty about their edibility, we decided to take the risk, and to our delight, they proved to be a delectable surprise. A purple-hued fruit with sparkling interiors burst with a juicy sweetness that transported my senses to a celestial realm of nectar. *My mouth was drowning in its juices.* I couldn't help but marvel at how something so enticing could coexist with the potential danger of poison. Nevertheless, I was willing to take the chance.

As we reclined beneath the shimmering tapestry of stars, Thorne lay right beside me. A sense of comfort enveloped me, yet an undercurrent of anxiety began to rise. Throughout my life, I had slept alone in my room, on my bed. No one, not even my mother, accompanied me. Catriona was always kept at a distance, forbidden from playing, studying, or sharing a sleeping space with me. The warmth, care, and breath of another person near me were foreign concepts. Our arms accidentally touched, and I instinctively pulled away, succumbing to my nervousness. However, Thorne gently intertwined his fingers with mine. I tried to pull away, but he refused to let go. Somehow, it felt nice.

Despite the uncertainties of our adventure, there was an undeniable comfort in having Thorne by my side. I took a deep breath and turned my head to look at him. He was already looking at me, a warm smile gracing his face. My heart quickened its pace, and I could feel the blush creeping up on my cheeks.

"Can I ask you something, Thorne?" I asked.

"You don't need my permission to ask me anything, Ariana," he smirked, turning towards me. His face was so close to me, his body, his lips so close that my breath almost got caught.

"Why do you call me Ariana and not Aria? No one has ever used my full name before," I asked, avoiding his gaze.

He took a moment, his gaze turning intense as he surveyed my body, as if he could see my scars. "Your parents used to call you Aria, didn't they?" His eyebrows raised.

I remained silent. He propped himself up on his elbow and faced me, lifting his right hand and cupping my face with a gentle caress. The weight of his upper body on mine somehow made me feel safe, his face so close to mine.

"I'll never let anything remind you of what those monsters did," he vowed, his eyes ablaze with a fierce anger, an anger directed at the horrors I endured. Sometimes, I struggled to comprehend why, why he cared so deeply. Slowly, he tucked a loose strand of my hair behind my ear, turning my face toward him. His closeness was palpable as his hand traveled down to the nape of my neck and a strange, indescribable feeling welled up in my chest. Suddenly, his lips met mine. A kiss so intense it sent shocks down my spine. My entire body got electrified as he traced my mouth with his tongue.

His lips, soft, beautiful, and full, locked into mine with a fervor, as if he had been waiting for this moment, for us to collide in this electrifying dance. The kiss transformed from a smooth and passionate exchange to a more intense, raw connection, mirroring the urgency of our emotions. My heart raced so rapidly that it threatened to give out. At that moment, there was no Ariana, no Eloria, no monsters, no magic, and no dark forces. There was just the magnetic pull of our shared vulnerability, an embrace that transcended the haunted past and the uncertain future. Thorne and I entwined into a seamless thread, becoming inseparable. That night, I found myself sleeping for the first time in days, cradled in the comforting embrace of his arms. Fear dissipated, with no lurking eyes and no ominous footsteps trailing behind us. In Thorne's arms, safety became a reality amid uncertainty.

In the middle of the night, I heard footsteps approaching... no, actually; they were moving away from me. Maybe I was just dreaming or imagining the sound. However, my sense of peace was shattered when I woke up and realized Thorne was nowhere to be found. The bonfire was still flickering, casting shadows on the surroundings, but Thorne's absence was conspicuous. As I listened intently, the murmur of men talking drifted through the air. Determined to uncover the source of the voices, I rose from my makeshift bed and followed the distant conversation.

"I fear your loyalties may be shifting, High Lord," the man uttered in a tone that struck a chord, a familiar demeaning cadence that resonated deep within me. It was a tone that bred uncertainty and dread. He interrupted his own words with a mocking laugh, his large frame casting a shadow, obscuring his face beneath the hood.

In response, Thorne's voice thundered, a commanding force that sliced through the tension. "Don't you dare come near her. I'm following the plan. She will open the portals for me."

Open the portals? But he had insisted we needed to close them. A sudden deafening silence enveloped me as conflicting thoughts raced through my mind.

*Is Thorne betraying me again? Is this all an elaborate ruse? Am I just a pawn, a foolish believer in a love that was never real? Why would he ever choose someone like me? I'm not the kind of beauty he'd fall for. Perhaps he's just been using me.*

The cacophony of self-doubt spiraled, my thoughts becoming relentless adversaries.

Amidst this internal turmoil, the need to move, to escape, took hold. I couldn't linger there, paralyzed by doubt. I had to run before he sensed my presence, before the shadows revealed my indecision. The urgency propelled me into motion, a desperate escape from the uncertainties that now tainted the very foundation of trust I once believed in.

# Chapter Twenty

## *The Guidance*

I couldn't breathe anymore. I had been running for what felt like forever—minutes, hours, days, maybe even weeks. Time didn't matter now. Nothing did. It was like something inside me was broken. Everything felt broken. Thorne, the person I trusted, had betrayed me again. The pain was too much to bear. It hurt more than the times my family abused me, more than the nights I went without food as punishment. It hurt even more than the day when my leg broke, the day I first entered Eloria, *the day Thorne found me.*

I believed Thorne loved me, or at least cared for me, but it turned out it was all an act. He was pretending, using me for something I didn't even understand.

*Using me as an instrument.*

Kael had warned me not to trust Thorne, but I hadn't listened. Thorne had always been nice to me. The first time he betrayed me hurt, but this time it felt like I failed myself by trusting him again. How could he be so heartless, so mean? But this time, it was not his fault. It was my fault. That I trusted him again. That I got entangled in his flowery language again. That I didn't listen to Kael again!

My chest burned as I ran. Each step felt like a reminder of my broken heart. My boots hurt my feet more than they should. I wasn't just running from the forest, but from the hurt, the feeling of being tricked and used. It was as if I was running against gravity.

The pain grew with every step, making it hard to see clearly. Once a safe place, the forest now felt like a confusing maze. The moonlight, which used to be comforting, now showed the twisted shadows of the trees, like the twisted feelings inside me.

Thorne must be behind me. I needed to run fast. But I was running not just to escape Thorne's betrayal, but also to escape the questions in my head. How did I let myself fall into this trap? The forest became a tangled mess, like my feelings of confusion and hurt.

Even though it hurt, running helped me find some strength inside me. With each step, I learned more about myself. The tears on my face showed that I was letting out all the pain inside me. But I didn't think it was enough to heal me.

I had gone through a lot of pain and darkness, so much heartbreak, so much physical pain, and abuse, but this somehow felt the worst. Like this had the power to kill me, take my breath away, and break me in a way I could never be healed again. I didn't know what to do now, where to go in this unknown place. I didn't know what to feel. My steps started to falter as the uncertainty of my future, my life dawned upon me. My pace slowed as the sun began to rise. I could see the sky turning into a beautiful golden yellow, shining down at me, *or laughing down at me*. But I couldn't feel the joy that usually came with witnessing such a breathtaking view. It was like something inside me was gone. I had left Thorne and that mysterious man far behind, or at least I hoped so. Panic set in at that moment, and I started walking without really knowing which direction I chose.

My eyes started to turn red again as memories flooded back—what I saw, the kiss that happened before that, and the uncertainty of what Thorne might do, what he might be planning. Whatever it was, I was unable to imagine anything good right now, especially considering the way that man talked, and the unsettling looks they exchanged. The thought sent a shiver down my spine.

My legs started aching from the walk on the uneven forest path, but at least it wasn't filled with twisted roots like the shadowed thicket. My breath was panting. As I shifted my focus from my thoughts to the world around me, my mouth almost dropped open at the scene unfolding before my eyes.

Thick brown tree trunks, adorned with lush green leaves, towered above me. The branches bore countless fruits, each one glowing and shimmering in a dazzling display of radiance. It was as if the entire forest was adorned with nature's own sparkling jewels. The bushes and their vibrant flowers were bursting with life, making it hard to believe the harrowing pathway I had traversed just moments ago.

Tiny winged fairies graced each flower with their ethereal dance, creating a mesmerizing spectacle that transported me to a realm of enchantment. It was almost as if I had stepped into a heavenly oasis, far removed from the troubles that shadowed my recent journey. Across from me, a river flowed with smooth, velvety grace, resembling a shimmering curtain. The scene was further embellished by the presence of iridescent butterflies fluttering gracefully above the water—an awe-inspiring display of nature's beauty.

As my gaze wandered a little further, beautiful majestic mountains came into view, their snow-covered peaks standing tall and proud. It was a breathtaking view, one that evoked a sense of awe and wonder, making me believe that I had stumbled upon the most beautiful place I had ever seen.

Unable to resist the allure of a nearby tree, adorned with ripe, glowing fruits, I plucked one and found a comfortable spot on a rock beside the river. Taking a bite of the succulent fruit, I was enveloped in its juiciness. As I sat there, staring into the picturesque panorama, a profound sense of tranquility washed over me. It felt like a form of meditation, a healing balm for the wounds inflicted upon me by the harshness of the world. At that moment, surrounded by the wonders of nature, I could clearly imagine spending the rest of my life in this sanctuary of beauty and serenity, *away from the world, away from its people and their troubles.*

As I lingered in the tranquility of the beautiful surroundings, the hushed footfalls behind me jolted me with fear. My heart raced; Thorne must be here, trailing me. Regret swept over me—*I shouldn't have stopped*. I should have kept walking. My fingers dug into the fruit in my hand, and I closed my eyes, bracing for the encounter.

A gentle voice pierced through the tension, pulling me from my apprehension.

"You are the human girl," she said, her voice as sweet as a melody. Releasing the breath, I opened my eyes and turned around to find a captivating sight. Before me stood a stunning winged female with pointed ears, large eyes, a round and pretty face, and hair cascading down to her lower back. A tiara made of white flowers adorned her head, accentuating her ethereal presence. Despite her otherworldly appearance, she hardly seemed more than 14 years old. Her flowing turquoise dress resembled a waterfall cascading to the ground, and her wings were a masterpiece of pure white feathers.

"Yes, hi… I am Ariana," I managed to reply, struck by her beauty.

She graced me with a goddess-like smile. "We've all been waiting for you, Ariana," she said, and my heart fluttered—a mix of hope and fear, an indescribable emotion.

"Waiting?" I asked, my eyebrows shooting up.

"Yes," she replied, observing me for a moment, as if hearing something with her sharp fairy ears, before adding, "You are in danger here. Come with me."

The truth in her words was undeniable, so I nodded and cautiously walked toward her, nervous energy lingering in the air.

"I am a Peri, by the way," she said with another radiant smile.

"Hi Peri," I responded, reciprocating the warmth.

As I stepped into this magical forest with Peri, a calming feeling surrounded me. There was greenery all around me. The colors of brown and green made everything feel calm and peaceful. The trees were really tall, and their leaves made soft sounds as the breeze passed through them. On the ground, there were lots of colorful flowers, making the whole place look lively.

There were multiple Peris, these pretty fairies with wings, dancing happily in the treetops. Their wings shone in the sunlight, and laughter mixed with the sounds of the forest. As she guided me through this special place, I saw an old wooden hut in the distance, adding a human touch to the place. The sunlight and shadows played hide and seek on the ground. The Peris kept dancing above us, making the whole scene look like a mesmerizing magical painting. *I still don't believe I am here.* In this quiet and serene place, I felt like I wasn't just watching but also a part of something beautiful, something divine.

The magic of the forest, along with the presence of the Peri, turned our walk into a journey of discovering nature and the magical beings that lived here. The babbling stream of water became a gathering place, where they hovered, their wings buzzing, creating a magical tableau. The air was infused with the sweet fragrance of blooming flora.

As I approached the small hut, its weathered exterior told tales of countless seasons endured. Vines embraced the wooden structure as if nature itself sought to reclaim this man-made dwelling. My steps faltered for some reason, but Peri nudged me further to walk in. The creaking of the wooden door added a rustic charm to the ambiance as I stepped inside.

Sunlight filtered through the withered windows, casting a warm glow on the modest interior. The air was cool, carrying the earthy scent of the forest. The sounds of chirping birds and distant rustling leaves created a soothing melody. The hut's windows framed captivating views of the surrounding nature, offering glimpses of the enchanting forest from the inside. A worn wooden table stood against one wall, adorned with wildflowers in a makeshift vase. The crackling of a softly burning fire emanated from a simple hearth, casting dancing shadows on the walls.

At the heart of the hut, an intriguing sight unfolded. Seated on a woven mat, an elderly figure draped in a mysterious black hood became the focal point of the room. The hood cast a veil over her face, concealing the details that might reveal her identity. Her hands, weathered and marked by the passage of countless seasons, rested before her, fingers contorted into unnatural angles that spoke of a lifetime's journey.

She remained absorbed in her own contemplations, oblivious to my presence. The air within the hut was filled with a profound sense of ancient knowledge, *and silence,* as if the very walls whispered secrets passed down through generations. The subdued lighting enhanced the enigma, casting shadows that danced around the hooded figure like ancient spirits paying homage.

Taking a hesitant step forward, I moved towards the mat before her. A small brown table, unassuming yet purposeful, stood between us. It served as both a physical barrier and a symbolic bridge, separating and connecting us in this intimate space.

"Come, sit, child," her melodic voice broke the stillness, weaving a spell that compelled compliance. I lowered myself onto the mat, facing the mysterious figure. The table, a humble witness to countless interactions, held a space for the unspoken exchange that was about to unfold.

"I sense you've lost your way," she uttered, her words hanging in the air like a gentle breeze. In the weighty silence that followed, I remained mute, unsure of how to respond to the profound observation.

"We often find ourselves adrift when the essence of who we are eludes us when our roots are obscured," her voice, weathered by time, resonated with ancient wisdom. Her words wrapped around the stillness, each syllable carrying the weight of centuries. But they were like another language to me. I failed to understand them.

"Do you understand your origins, child?" she asked, a question filled with the implication that she knew something that I didn't. Though her head tilted upward, the enigmatic hood shielded her face from my view, leaving me to ponder the mystery concealed beneath its depths. I wondered whether there was a face behind that hood, or simply just *nothing*.

"I am Ariana Eldenhaven, daughter of Richard Eldenhaven and Lysandra Eldenhaven," I said with confidence, straightening my shoulders. A subtle unease lingered, a feeling that she already possessed the knowledge of my lineage, as if my history was an open book in her hands. And that what I just said was wrong.

"Well, that you know of," she retorted with a mocking edge to her voice.

"What do you mean?" Frustration colored my voice.

"You don't know anything, child. You need to find yourself, discover your roots, and your reality... uncover your power. You are no fragile creature, despite how others may perceive you. You need to unearth what lies within," her words wove through the air, a withered melody that carried a depth of meaning I struggled to comprehend.

Sensing my discomfort, she continued, "I can't reveal everything; you have to uncover it on your own otherwise you will fail to value it."

"How do I find it?"

"This will be your guide," she declared, placing a piece of paper into my hands. Before I could unfold it, a sudden shift transported me, and I found myself standing at the foot of colossal mountains. The hut, the enigmatic figure, the Peri who offered guidance—all vanished. A panic washed over me, prompting questions of reality. *Was I truly there, or was I still lying beaten up in the gardens of Eldenhaven? How all of this is possible?*

Yet, the parchment remained cradled in my hand, a tangible link to the unknown. With a mix of trepidation and curiosity, I unfurled its wrinkled folds, ready to embark on the journey that its contents promised to unveil.

Journey northward, where peaks touch the heavens,
Cross the icy expanse, a frozen floor untrod.
Seek your haven aloft, with wings unfurled,
Only there shall the path ahead unfold.

In the hush of frost, secrets entwined,
Mountains whisper tales, in echoes defined.
Frozen steps unveil, a cryptic door,
Unlock your flight, embrace the lore.

Winged abode awaits, a sanctuary in the sky,
Unlock its gates, let your spirit fly.
Feathers unfettered, destiny foreseen,
In the dance of shadows, the journey convenes.

# Chapter Twenty-One

## The Journey to The Dragons

As I STARTED WALKING through the heart of the *Whispering Woods* towards the towering mountains, I found solace in the gentle caress of ancient tree branches—a sacred dance in nature's cathedral. The intertwining limbs created an ethereal haven where time stood still, and the very pulse of the forest resonated with vibrant life. A soft, otherworldly glow emanated from luminescent flora, casting a radiant carpet of light upon the forest floor. Though alone in this place, there was an unexpected sense of relief.

*For the first time, I was alone.*

*For the first time, I was at peace.*

The trek ahead appeared challenging, yet an unexplainable feeling of safety enveloped me, adding an enigmatic layer to the unfolding journey.

With every step, the ground beneath my feet seemed to respond, as if answering to the rhythm of my heartbeat. Each footfall resonated through the silent spaces, a dance echoing the ancient tales woven into the very fabric of the trees. The air itself carried whispers, fragments of stories from times long past, wrapping me in the mystique of the unseen.

As I ventured deeper into the heart of the Whispering Woods, the forest unveiled its very soul—a mesmerizing symphony of leaves rustling in harmony, the mysterious murmur of unseen creatures, and an ethereal glow that intensified with every step. Above me, mischievous sprites danced through the dappled sunlight, their translucent wings catching the radiant glow. Seeing me, they flew down snickering and started dancing around me. I laughed along with them. My eyes tearing up.

Small, luminescent insects flitted about, leaving trails of light in their wake. The once-silent woods transformed into a living, breathing entity as if inviting me to partake in its secrets and emotions. There was no fear here, no one watching me, like in the shadowed thicket. Everything was so.....peaceful!

*There is no Thorne here. Relief.*

As I walked further, the woods whispered not just secrets but also a magical tune that touched the core of who I was. Although I could not understand anything, but the energy I was feeling around me was unmatched. I heard the whispers in Sylvian Woods too, but those were scary. *These were peaceful. Voice of a Goddess.*

Stepping into a place where magic and reality mixed together, every bit of sunlight through the leaves felt like a gentle hug, and rustling leaves were the comforting words of an old friend. The journey unfolded gracefully, like a special dance in which I was both watching and taking part.

As I kept walking, the glowing flowers lit up even more, creating a magical trail that called me ahead. The old tree branches bowed to the ground in response to my footsteps. *This was some kind of sorcery.* The gentle light on the ground looked like a dance of fireflies, turning the forest into an enchanting ballet. Sprites flying alongside me now giggled off to a beautiful pink-colored flower, that apparently distracted them from moving forward with me.

Emotions within me swirled like leaves caught in a gentle breeze—wondering at the marvels unfolding, a deep-seated sense of belonging to this magical realm, and an indescribable joy that danced in tune with the forest's heartbeat. The Whispering Woods, with their ancient embrace, wove a tapestry of emotions that transcended the ordinary—a tale of a mortal soul enraptured by the timeless magic of Eloria.

As I went further, the *Serpent's Ascent* revealed itself—a twisty path carved right into the mountainside. Mist wrapped around me. The path grew more challenging, my breath started becoming ragged as I ascended. Despite the beauty of the trail, hours had passed since I began this arduous journey. The trail was a bit slippery, and my stomach was rumbling with hunger. Honestly, I don't remember when I had a proper meal last time. Maybe at Thorne's mansion.

Next, the giant caves appeared in front of me. Water sliding down from its surface. Thank Goddess, I have to enter them, and not climb them. Entering these *Echoing Caves*, expansive chambers reverberated with the melodic rhythm of my footsteps. Stones were slimy and slippery, and I was barely able to maintain my balance. Shadows played on the dimly lit stone walls.

Trying to focus in the dark caves, my right foot slipped between two rocks, leading me to fall on my ass.

"Ahhhhh......" a voice erupted from my throat, as my hip bone banged into the stone. I was pretty sure my pants were scratched from behind. Placing both hands by my side and taking their support, I got up, wincing with pain. *Wondering why was I doing all this. What was the point?* I took the next few steps carefully, my back cried with each step.

As I ascended, the *Frozen Plateau* unfolded before me, a harsh realm dominated by biting winds, *harsher than the stony caves I just passed,* and a ruined landscape veiled in snow and ice. There was no life form to see here, no trees, no plants, not even the sprites that met me a few hours back! It was so *barren.*

The cold penetrated my clothing, and the wind howled its formidable challenges. My footprints marked the frost-covered terrain, a testament to my determination to conquer the mountain's formidable peak. I hadn't anticipated this. Clad in a simple tunic, pants, and leather boots, the biting cold threatened to freeze me to death in this unforgiving terrain. *I can't quit this. I have done nothing for myself till now. If I quit this too, I don't know what else to do. Where else to go?* My legs shivered with cold. Despite the panting and hiking, my body failed to warm itself up.

There was no one here. If I died here today with frostbite, no one would ever know. But again, I doubt anyone ever really cared about me. I was a burden to my parents. They must be glad that I am gone. Catriona didn't even know that I existed. Thorne wanted me to open portals. As an instrument. This was the summary of my life. *No one cared about me.*

As hours passed, the sense of isolation intensified. The solitude of the plateau, broken only by the echoes of my footsteps and the relentless wind, added a layer of introspection to the journey. Fatigue was taking hold of me, but so was anger, and so was disappointment. Not towards me, but towards the world. Yet, with each step, I pressed forward, my determination unwavering. The Frozen Plateau, for all its harshness, became a canvas for resilience.

The mountain's peak, shrouded in mist and mystery, remained an elusive goal, visible yet distant. I pondered what answers awaited me there, questioning whether the journey would prove to be worthwhile in the end. As I continued, the journey became a blend of physical exertion, elemental resistance, and the indomitable spirit that fueled my ascent.

Amid this relentless cold, I grappled with the profound chill, my fingers gradually adopting an ominous shade of blue. The harsh elements assailed me—my balance started faltering, my lips cracked, succumbed to a parched dryness, and my skin, numbed by the cold, lost all sensation. Yet, in the face of this agonizing physical ordeal, I trudged forward, propelled by an insatiable thirst for answers. *I will not quit.*

With every step, the biting cold sank deeper into my bones, and the relentless winds carried the echoes of my pain. The numbing cold, both a physical and emotional torment, mirrored the isolation I felt in my life. Betrayed by those I held dear, the sting of hatred from every corner weighed heavily on my shoulders.

Next came the Crystal Arch, a natural wonder formed by shimmering crystals that marked the summit of this trek. This final stretch proved a relentless test of endurance. With each step, my breath formed clouds in the frigid air, and the thinning oxygen at the summit intensified my struggle. Part of me was regretting this. *Starting the journey. Coming to Eloria. Being born in Eldenhaven. Being born. How far can I go back?*

The mountain, though majestic, revealed its unyielding nature with each step on the icy plateau. Suddenly I twisted my right foot, a sharp pain shot up my leg, and I fell face-first into the ice. It was like a searing electric shock. Every nerve was screaming in protest. The unforgiving cold, like a relentless predator, clung to my battered body, intensifying the agony. As I fought to stand on my feet, the biting wind seemed to mock my feeble struggle to maintain my balance. I moved forward, limping with pain. Most of my weight was on my left foot at this point, but it wasn't helping much. *One misstep and I was pretty sure dead.*

Fear clawed at the edges of my consciousness, the realization sinking in that I was alone in this frozen abyss, but again, that was not very different from how my life had been till now. People had always left me alone, leaving me to pick up the pieces after the damage they had done to me, so this was nothing new. So I tried to regain my strength and move forward. The desolation stretched endlessly in every direction, and the biting cold, now a ruthless accomplice, gnawed at my resolve. Panic threatened to engulf me as I grappled with the torment of both physical pain and the haunting emptiness surrounding me.

With each attempt to walk, the pain surged. My twisted ankle, a sinister accomplice in this ordeal, threatened to betray me with every faltering step. My bones shuddered, magnifying the bitter ache in my limbs.

I really wished I had my gloves with me, or any extra cloth really to put on my hands, which were turning blue as I crouched to hold on to these icy crystals to avoid the fall. The air grew thinner with every upward climb, and each breath became a battle against the biting cold that seeped through my single layer of clothing. In Eldenhaven, though my parents used to beat me, ignore me, and treat me like a piece of waste, but they surely did provide me with all the bare necessities of life, like food, water, and proper clothes, studies. I never struggled there with excessive heat or cold, unless it was for punishment, of course.

As I moved forward, the pain in my ankle became a persistent companion, a constant reminder of not only the precariousness of the journey but also of the fact that this was the first thing in my life that I was doing for myself, without anyone's fear or permission! Each step, though deliberate, felt like a negotiation with the mountain itself with confidence, with strength I never thought I had. The Crystal Arch, like a sentinel of both beauty and adversity, stood as a gateway to the summit—an invitation to conquer the last stretch. My heart started to fill with pride.

*You did this, Ariana. You are almost at the end.*

The Crystal Arch glistened with an ethereal glow, its frozen crystals casting prismatic reflections. The dance between light and ice created a mesmerizing spectacle, a testament to the harmonious yet perilous nature of the ascent. And there I was, standing beneath this mesmerizing Crystal Arch, my eyes watering up with a feeling that I had never felt before. Not when I got the highest marks in the class. Not when baby Catriona held my hand for the first time. Not when Thorne kissed me. This was something different. Something beautiful. Something peaceful.

As I gazed at the breathtaking panorama from the summit, the pain in my ankle became a distant echo. This time though, I could not say that this was the most beautiful place I had ever seen. Because each and every nook of Eloria was unique. As if it was from a storybook. As if I was being repaid by the Goddess for all the torture that she failed to protect me from.

Wiping my tears, I thought this was my first step to finding myself. I would not back down; I would not be suppressed by the conditions, by the people, by the obstacles. Each challenging step on this mountain had been a testament to my inner strength, a declaration of resilience against the adversities that sought to hinder my journey.

As I stood atop the Crystal Arch, the triumphant view before me blurred through tears again. I have cried many times in my life, almost daily. But this was the first time I was happy about it. I started moving forward, covering the last part of my journey. I could not stop now.

The pain radiating from my twisted ankle became more pronounced, each step on the summit an agonizing reminder of the challenges overcome. The thin air at this altitude made breathing a laborious task, and beads of sweat mingled with the salty taste of my tears, freezing like beads on my face.

My hands trembled as I wiped away tears, and a mixture of pain, exhaustion, and the sheer magnitude of the accomplishment overwhelmed me. The sobs that escaped were a release of the emotions bottled up throughout my life. Eloria's magical essence, though ever-present, now mingled with the raw vulnerability of a journey that had tested every fiber of my being.

As I tried to catch my breath and relax a bit, a thought came to my mind. Not a thought, words......words of that hooded figure,

*"You don't know anything, child. You need to find yourself, discover your roots, and your reality... uncover your power. You are no fragile creature, despite how others may perceive you. You need to unearth what lies within."*

*"I can't reveal everything; you have to uncover it on your own otherwise you will fail to value it."*

I wondered what she meant by all of this, about finding my roots, my reality, and my power. None of this made any sense to me. No one was here, in this frozen and barren land, who would help me? Doubt again tried to cripple me...... maybe she didn't know me! Maybe she sent me here by mistake! Maybe I was not the one who she thought I was!

Snow started to thunder under my feet and as I turned around to face what lay ahead, a gasp caught in my throat. A colossal, majestic being with wings bigger than the sky, wings that seemed to stretch to the heavens revealed itself....A..... dragon. The sight was both awe-inspiring and terrifying, their enormous forms casting shadows over the frozen landscape and suddenly I was no longer cold! Or breathing.

At the apex of my taxing ascent, the world unfolded before me in a panorama that transcended mortal imagination. In the sapphire expanse of the sky, a creature emerged, screeching through the

sky, bathed in the beautiful hues of the setting sun. Its scales, reminiscent of rare and glistening gemstones, caught and refracted the sun's golden rays, casting forth a dazzling display of fiery luminosity. With wings unfurled, the dragon's every beat sent an undulating wave through the air, initiating a mesmerizing dance of light and shadow that played upon the canvas of the heavens.

The countenance of this majestic creature bore the regality of ancient royalty, an ethereal embodiment of mythical grandeur. Its curved horns, spiraling royally toward the heavens, adorned its head, framing a crown that echoed with the sagas of time untold. Eyes were molten pools of mesmerizing liquid gold, glistening with a profound wisdom that transcended the era, each gaze holding within it the secrets of realms long past. Serrated frills decorated its neck. Intricate patterns embellished its scales, etching tales of a bygone millennium into the very fabric of its being—a living tapestry woven with the threads of ancient legends. I was going to say this again, *"This was the most beautiful thing I have ever seen!"*

The dragon's tail, a sinuous extension of its ethereal beauty, trailed behind like a celestial comet, leaving tracks of sparks in its wake that illuminated the darkening sky. Each movement of this magnificent creature was a manifestation of unrestrained beauty and raw power, a spectacle that unfolded in the boundless theater of the heavens—a testament to the primal force it embodied. *Never had I seen such beauty in my life!*

The second orange dragon, a mirror image of its celestial companion, soared alongside with a grace that transcended earthly limitations. Its scales, glowing with the warm hues of smoldering embers, harmonized seamlessly with the fading brilliance of the setting sun. With wings outstretched, spanning the celestial expanse like a canvas of flames, the creature painted the sky with the vivid strokes of its flight, leaving ephemeral trails of fiery artistry in its wake. Mirroring the regal countenance of its kind, the second orange dragon bore horns that arched with an elegant symmetry, framing a face that exuded an air of ancient wisdom. Eyes, twin orbs of molten gold, held a gaze that seemed to unravel the secrets of the cosmos, a profound knowledge embedded in their fiery depths. Frills adorned its neck, evoking the image of a fiery crest, and intricate patterns on its scales danced with the play of sunlight, each movement narrating a story of mythical proportions.

In harmonious unison, the two orange dragons circled overhead, their roars echoing through the mountain peaks with a resonance that resembled a celestial symphony. The vibrations reached the very core of my being, a visceral testament to the formidable power these beings wielded. The air itself hummed with the interplay of sound and magic, creating an ambiance of wonder and awe that enveloped me in a cloak of enchantment. As they circled, the dragons etched a mesmerizing ballet against the canvas of the twilight sky, their synchronized movements akin to a celestial dance. The air crackled with the energy of their presence, an otherworldly force that transcended the mundane. The dragons' roars, a melodic thunder reverberating through the mountainous terrain, harmonized with the ambient hum, creating a tapestry of sound that resonated with the mystical energies of the heavens.

As they soared, the dragons acknowledged my presence with a majestic sweep of their wings. In that transcendent moment, I stood as a humble witness to the convergence of worlds. As I marveled at their awe-inspiring presence, a distant sound echoed—a rumble that grew in intensity, like the heartbeat of the very mountains beneath my feet.

A shadow, as profound as the obsidian night, swept over the landscape. A third dragon emerged from the veil of clouds, its scales as black as the cosmic void, absorbing and reflecting no light. It descended with a grace that belied its colossal form, and as it neared the ground, the air resonated with the symphony of its arrival. The wings of this black dragon unfolded with a resounding crack, creating a thunderous boom that echoed through the mountainous terrain. Each beat of its wings sent shockwaves through the air, disrupting the very fabric of reality. The ground beneath quivered, acknowledging the arrival of this obsidian behemoth.

Its visage exuded an enigmatic allure, starkly contrasting with the fiery brilliance of its companions. Horns adorned its regal head, curving with an elegant fierceness. Green eyes, twin orbs of ember, held a depth that seemed to pierce the veil of reality, offering glimpses into the cosmic mysteries that lay beyond.

As the black dragon landed before me, its scales absorbed the ambient light, rendering it a silhouette against the vibrant canvas of Eloria's magical landscape. The frills on its neck, reminiscent of an otherworldly crown, accentuated the creature's regality. Patterns on its scales, subtle yet intricate, whispered tales of the cosmic forces that coursed through its very being.

I stood in awe, just as the two orange majestic dragons landed behind the black one, shaking the whole ground, and the profound darkness embodied by their ebony counterpart. The air crackled with a magical energy that danced around the trio, creating an otherworldly tableau against the backdrop of Eloria's natural splendor. The black dragon, once a shadow in the sky, now stood before me with an imposing grace. The vibrations of its landing resonated through the soles of my feet, grounding me in the surreal reality of this mythical encounter. I felt the weight of its cosmic gaze, and at that moment, a silent communication seemed to pass between us—a recognition of shared existence within the realms of magic and wonder. The dragons, each unique in its essence, formed a trinity that defied the boundaries of mere fantasy. The orange dragons, with their fiery brilliance, embodied the vibrant life force that pulsed through Eloria. The black dragon, an enigma cloaked in darkness, represented the cosmic mysteries that whispered in the winds and echoed through the very soul of this mystical realm.

# Chapter Twenty-Two

## The Dragons

At this moment, an indescribable surge of emotions engulfed me, rendering me incapable of deciphering whether it was the sheer impact of these majestic beings landing before me or the overwhelming fear induced by the realization of my own small stature in their colossal presence. My bones quivered involuntarily, and the source of this tremor was—*was it the reverberation from the dragons' landing or the palpable fear that had seized every fiber of my being?*

I dared not make a move; my breath was held hostage in my chest as I maintained unbroken eye contact with these awe-inspiring creatures. They stood before me, towering and magnificent, their head held high, their ethereal beauty captivating my gaze. A dichotomy of emotions churned within me—a heart brimming with both profound awe and paralyzing fear. The dragons, with their sinuous movements reminiscent of serpents, held me captive in a mesmerizing tableau.

As their heads swiveled in a serpentine fashion, I found myself frozen in place, a silent witness to the majestic ballet unfolding before me. The intensity of their gaze, akin to the piercing eyes of eagles, pinned me down like prey ensnared by an apex predator.

The trio advanced toward me slowly and steadily, synchronized in their approach, the very ground beneath me quivering with their powerful strides. In the deafening silence, broken only by the rhythmic thud of their footsteps, an unsettling realization took root—this might well be my final day. Yet, amidst the paralyzing fear, a whispered solace flitted through my thoughts; *at least, I told myself; I had seen these beautiful creatures today. I can die peacefully now. I think. I was rambling in my head.*

The dragons' eyes, sharp and unwavering, seemed to dissect my very soul, each step forward echoing the inevitability of my vulnerability. I stood, a mere speck in the vast expanse of their dominion, dwarfed by their immense presence. In this juncture of uncertainty, my heart oscillated between the terror of the unknown and the gratitude for having glimpsed a manifestation of beauty and power beyond the realms of ordinary existence. But maybe they were hungry, and since I was the only eatable thing. I frantically looked around. The black one huffed a puff of steam from its nose. And I froze. *Okay. No movement.*

They created an ominous circle around me, akin to predators closing in on their prey. Among them, the black dragon seemed to take a particular interest, its nostrils flaring as it caught the scent of my fear. Despite its comparatively smaller size, the looming presence of this obsidian-hued creature instilled a profound sense of vulnerability; a mere blink could render me a meal in its voracious jaws. Immobilized by fear, I stood helplessly as the dragons drew nearer, their sharp eyes scrutinizing me with such intensity as if they were studying me, my every breath, every motion, my very presence.

*They must have seen a human for the first time.*

The black dragon, though smaller in stature, exuded an aura of primal menace, its predatory instincts finely tuned. The trio inched closer, their majestic forms casting shadows on me that seemed to engulf the very essence of my existence.

The orange dragon, adorned with scales reminiscent of a sunlit sheen, tilted her head inquisitively, as though privy to the thoughts racing through my mind. Despite the unnerving scrutiny, I resisted the urge to break eye contact, a feeble attempt at conveying a semblance of composure in the face of impending uncertainty. Whether this encirclement signified an imminent attack or a mere observation, I was not sure, though the latter seemed unlikely.

And suddenly, to my surprise, all three dragons bowed their regal heads before me, and my eyes shot up in surprise. Instinctively, I stepped back, only to find them advancing toward me with a shared gaze of reverence. Their eyes met mine, and in a surprising turn of events, they nudged their scaly heads toward me—an unexpected display of affection that left me utterly bewildered.

Caught in a surreal moment, I cautiously raised my hand, tentatively reaching out to caress the formidable head of the black dragon. Anticipating the worst, I half-expected a snap of razor-sharp teeth, but to my astonishment, she leaned into the trembling touch, an unexpected warmth emanating from her scaled form. Encouraged, I extended my gestures of gentle affection to the two orange dragons, who, in turn, welcomed the connection.

Inexplicably, tears welled up in my eyes, a torrent of emotions surging forth. A profound love enveloped me, and in the presence of these majestic beings, an overwhelming sense of security and belonging washed over me. A wide smile played on my lips, an expression of joy and gratitude that escaped my awareness. A feeling of completeness entered my heart, as if I had seen the most beautiful thing in the world, experienced the most surreal thing in the world, the most compassionate, as if I did not wish for anything else in my life! *My life could end right now and I would not regret it!*

Amid my elation, a voice, deep and ancient, echoed in my mind. *"You are in the safest place in the world. Your life will not end anytime soon, Mortal One!,"* it declared, causing a surge of warmth to envelop me. Bewildered, I looked around, stepping back, my eyes wide with shock.

"Who.....Who spoke...?" I began to question, my hands traveling to my head and fingers entangling in the matted curls of my hair, only to be met with a snorted remark from a playful female voice in my head.

*"You get scared easily, though. It will be fun!"*

*"Don't tease her. We are talking to you, the dragons,"* interjected a wise female voice, introducing a layer of understanding beyond the ordinary. As I grappled with the revelation that these dragons could communicate with me *mentally*, my mouth dropped open.

"You can talk? Into my mind?" I asked, my gaze shifting among the three in disbelief.

*"We can talk to you because we have bonded with you. Only you can hear us. My name is Zephyr. I am the oldest one, almost thousa nds.."* began the ancient male voice, Zephyr, only to be interrupted by a snarky female voice.

*"Yes, we all know you are thousands of years old and a descendant of the greatest oldest dragon in the history of the world, Zephyros Lumina. You don't have to remind us in every sentence. I am Torrent, by the way—the black one,"* she remarked, rolling her eyes.

*"Stop it, both of you. Don't scare her on the first day with your babbling. I am Ember,"* declared the wise female voice. The orange dragon on my left smiled, her pupils dilating.

"Hello, Zephyr, Ember, and Torrent. I am Ariana," I greeted them. *Zephyr's eye. The eye I used to see in my dreams. That used to follow me. It was Zephyr. He was with me since the moment I entered Eloria.*

*"Yes, Mortal one. I was."*

"You said bonded... What do you mean?" I cautiously inquired, careful not to offend these majestic creatures.

*"For someone your size, you do ask a lot of questions, don't you?"* The black one, Torrent, I think, taunted.

*"You must have a lot of questions, Ariana, but for now, let's just say you have a new family here with a lot of new abilities,"* said Zephyr, the orange dragon standing in front of me after huffing towards Torrent.

Weariness enveloped me like a heavy cloak, dragging me into a deep slumber that blanketed the entirety of my day. The journey's fatigue had etched its presence so profoundly that I don't even remember how I reached here. My brain was so disoriented right now. As consciousness timidly fluttered back, the cave unfolded beneath the gentle touch of morning sunlight, revealing a sanctuary from the biting cold that raged beyond its confines.

Though it was open, still the cave was warm. Like a quilt wrapped around my body. My bones were not shuddering anymore. The blues of my fingertips were gone. Yet, even as the comforting warmth seeped into my senses, the toll of sleeping on the unyielding cave floor was apparent. My neck and shoulders were hurting as if a heavy weight had been placed on them. My legs were stiff, and painful to move, and I was pretty sure I had blisters on my feet. *I will not check.* My heart was feeling giddy with the fact that I had *bonded* with three majestic dragons! If I could, I would be jumping right now.

*"We often find ourselves adrift when the essence of who we are eludes us when our roots are obscured,"* the resonating words of the hooded oracle had lingered in the chamber of my mind. Each word was a riddle. *The dragons, with their ability to converse, might hold the key to deciphering this cryptic message. Zephyr said he was the oldest, he might know something.* Rampant thoughts started running through my brain.

To seek answers, I attempted to rise, awakening to the realization that the stiffness I felt extended beyond my legs to envelop my entire body. Wincing against the persistent ache, I had gathered the strength to stand. My stomach was rumbling with hunger. As I shook off the remnants of yesterday's hike, preparing to step into the world outside the cave, a sudden presence startled me. Torrent, the black dragon, had been sitting in the shadows, fixated on my every move with her sharp green eyes.

*"I scared you, didn't I?"* Torrent snorted, her demeanor almost amusing. Resisting the urge to roll my eyes, I reminded myself that I was a mere *human* in front of her.

*"I'm not planning to make a meal out of you,"* she smirked.

*"Not yet, at least."* She added.

*"Glad to know! Will you always be in my head now?"* I tried to ask politely.

*"You talk back too! I thought I was the only one,"* she winked, momentarily blurring the line between a dragon and a mere human.

Smiling, I retorted, *"Where are Zephyr and Ember?"*

*"They're outside, guarding the cave entrance,"* Torrent explained. *"Too big to fit in here."*

*"Why don't you come out with our mortal?"* Zephyr's huffing voice echoed in my mind.

*"Always the broody one!"* Torrent remarked in a teasing tone. Suppressing a laugh at their banter, I stepped out of the cave, still grappling with the surreal notion of conversing with three colossal dragons.

Summoning my courage, I inquired, *"I have some questions,"* addressing the trio.

*"We know,"* Ember responded, her sweet voice carrying a weight of ancient knowledge. *"We have been waiting for you for years now."*

*She is the sweetest. But what?*

*"Years?"* My mouth dropped open.

*"How? How did you know I was about to come? Did you know about me before I reached here? How is that even possible? I mean, I don't understand any of it. This is all too much, too overwhelming, going on too fast. I don't know what is happening."*

*"Calm down, mortal one,"* Zephyr instructed, exhaling a breath that puffed from his flaring nostrils. *"I will show you."*

And in an instant, I found myself seeing through his molten beautiful amber eyes... their eyes.

*The first Luminara emerged when the goddess Luminara herself had woven strands of starlight and moonbeams into the essence of a chosen fae. From that celestial union, for the first time in this universe, a line of magical beings was born, destined to safeguard the enchanting landscapes of Eloria.*

*The Luminara were known for their unique connection to the mystical energies that flowed through Eloria. They possessed the ability to commune with the natural elements, communicate with magical creatures, and channel the very essence of the enchanted world. This extraordinary lineage had become the custodians of the Glittering Grove of Lumoria, a sacred sanctuary where the magical energies converged in harmonious brilliance.*

*Over the centuries, the Luminara had continued to uphold their sacred duty, ensuring the flourishing of Eloria's magical sanctuaries. The lineage's members were revered for their wisdom, compassion, their strength, and the remarkable magical gifts they had inherited. Each Luminara had passed down its knowledge and abilities to the next generation, creating a tapestry of enchantment woven through time. But this peace didn't last long.*

*In the interconnected realm of Eloria, once a haven of harmony, the ominous clouds of war had gathered with darkness that eclipsed the once-bright skies. The genesis of the conflict lay in the malevolent actions of dark forces that preyed upon the vulnerable, mistreating humans, women, children, and fae alike. This cruelty and brutality had sparked a war that shook the very foundations of Eloria. The perpetrators, fueled by a thirst for power and dominance, had orchestrated a campaign of terror, targeting innocent lives without discrimination. The war had become a desperate struggle for survival as the disfigured and soul-hungry entities unleashed their wrath upon the realm. The once-thriving communities were now marred by the scars of battle, with the cries of the oppressed echoing through the once-lush landscapes. In response to the escalating violence, a coalition of beings from various backgrounds, including both high and low fae, had united to resist the encroaching darkness. The battle lines were drawn, and the war for Eloria's soul had intensified, with each side fiercely contesting the fate of the realm. The origin of the conflict was rooted in a perversion of the natural order, as the malevolent forces exploited the vulnerabilities of the interconnected realm. The breach of trust, the loss of innocent lives, and the palpable fear that gripped Eloria had propelled the once-peaceful inhabitants into a war against an enemy that sought to extinguish the very essence of their existence.*

*Amidst the chaos, the last remnants of the once-mighty fae lineage, the Luminara, emerged as crucial figures in the fight against the encroaching darkness. Their luminous abilities, once symbols of hope and guidance, were now the last line of defense against the malevolent forces that sought to plunge Eloria into eternal night. The battles were fierce and relentless, fought on multiple fronts as the fae, hu-*

*mans, and other magical beings struggled to hold their ground. The war-torn landscapes bore witness to the sacrifices made in the name of survival. Countless lives were lost, and Eloria's vibrant tapestry was stained with the blood of those who dared to resist the shadows. The battlefronts were not confined to open fields alone. The conflict spilled into enchanted forests, desolate plateaus, echoing caverns, and frozen landscapes, each terrain presenting its own challenges and perils. The dark forces, relentless in their pursuit, exploited every vulnerability, seeking to extinguish the light that still flickered in the hearts of those who resisted.*

*The echoes of the final battle resonated through the once-vibrant corridors of Eloria, now reduced to a haunting silence. The remnants of the great Luminara, a once-mighty fae lineage, lay scattered across the magical realm, sacrificed in a desperate attempt to thwart the encroaching darkness. As the last of the Luminara, a lone woman with tear-stained eyes and a heavy heart, surveyed the aftermath, she knew the time for a decision had come. Amid the desolation, a giant winged creature approached her with a sorrowful, yet understanding, gaze. It was a creature of ancient magic, and as their eyes met, an unspoken pact formed—a bond that transcended the boundaries of fae and creature. In that moment, the woman and the winged being became one, sharing not just power but an indomitable spirit forged in the crucible of despair. United, the last Luminara and her newfound companion faced the encroaching shadows. With each beat of the creature's majestic wings, a surge of magic flowed through them, a formidable force that stood as a testament to the resilience of Eloria's magic. The woman, now imbued with abilities beyond comprehension, knew that a sacrifice must be made to preserve what remained. In a selfless act, she wielded the essence of her magic to reshape the world. The realm of Eloria was divided into three distinct parts, each serving a unique purpose in the intricate tapestry of existence. The first realm became the human world, shielded from the knowledge of magic and mythical beings. In this realm, mortals thrived, oblivious to the enchantments that once coexisted with their reality. The second realm retained the essence of magic, becoming Eloria, a sanctuary for mystical creatures, enchanted landscapes, and the lingering echoes of the fae. Here, the memory of the Luminara persisted, safeguarding the remnants of a once-magical civilization. The third realm, a shadowy domain, was reserved for the dark forces that had threatened to consume Eloria. Separated from the realms of light, it served as a prison for the malevolent energies that sought to corrupt and destroy.*

My eyes teared up as I witnessed the pain and suffering through their ancient eyes. Zephyr, the magnificent winged creature, had been alive then, thousands of years ago. He had witnessed so much, and I couldn't fathom the amount of pain people had gone through.

*"But how am I related to all of this? To Luminara?"* my throat bobbed.

*"Before dividing the world into three parts, the last Luminara had a child. A human child. You have the blood of that last Luminara in your veins, Mortal Girl. You are the descendent of that last Luminara.,"* Zephyr said, his words carrying the weight of centuries.

*"You mean to say that my parents are also Luminara?"* I asked, my voice almost trembling with shock. They exchanged glances, a silent conversation passing between them.

*"Those monsters are not your parents, Ariana,"* Torrent finally spoke up, her tone carrying a mixture of anger and compassion.

*"You were adopted,"* Ember said.

The revelation struck me like a thunderbolt, breaking something inside me that I didn't even know was there. *But this explained so much. Why did they hate me? Why did they behave like that with me? Why did they love only Catriona?*

# Chapter Twenty-Three

## *Shattered Reality*

Suddenly, the very ground beneath us quivered, sending shockwaves through the soles of my feet. The once gentle winds transformed into frenzied gusts, snatching at my hair with an almost sentient force. Overhead, the sky darkened at an alarming pace. My gaze instinctively traveled to Zephyr, the ancient dragon whose presence was like a beacon of assurance and safety.

*"They have found you, mortal one*!"Zephyr's voice rumbled with a blend of urgency and concern, his eyes reflecting the gravity of the situation. "We have to hurry. We can't stay here."

His words sent a shiver down my spine. For a moment, I had forgotten that Thorne was after me. I nodded in acknowledgment, my heart pulsating with a mixture of fear and anxiousness. The impending danger was palpable, and I sensed an urgency in Zephyr's gaze that brooked no delay.

*"How will we go?"* I don't know why I asked. Deep down, I already knew the answer, and it elicited a giant cloud of anxiety.

*"You have to climb on any of us and sit, whoever you like,"* Ember said in her motherly voice. Though it did less to calm the panic that was about to grip my throat. *I was going to fly on a DRAGON!!!!*

The dragons looked towards each other as if discussing about my possible mental breakdown. My eyes flickered between Zephyr, Ember, and Torrent, torn between the gravity of the situation and the novelty of the choice presented.

*"What if I fall?"* My voice trembled.

*"Then we will catch you." Torrent, the ever-playful dragon*, interjected with a nonchalant response that belied the peril at hand. *At least someone was enjoying this.*

*"Oh, I am."*

My eyes snapped to her, almost falling out of my socket.

*"Always in your HEAD. Remember?"* She smirked. A dragon smirked.

The ground continued its tremors beneath me. The very world was protesting against the impending storm. With a deep breath, I approached the dragons, their scales glinting in the dimming light. A choice lay before me, and with a hesitant heart, I made my decision. The dragons, guardians of a world I was only beginning to fathom, awaited my choice, ready to carry me through the tempest that unfolded.

*"Will you choose faster? We don't have all the time in the world."* Said the snarky one.

In a rush for a decision, I found myself choosing Zephyr, *obviously,* drawn to the sense of stability he exuded. Perhaps it was irrational to judge safety based on the sheer size of a dragon, but since I entered this world, logic seemed to have taken a temporary leave. My instincts steered me away from Torrent, the playful yet unpredictable dragon who could, in jest, turn me into an unexpected snack. Ember, the gentle and nurturing dragon, was spared from my choice simply because I didn't want to burden her.

Torrent, always the candid one, interjected with a reminder, *"You know we can hear your thoughts."*

*"We don't have time for this. Hurry, mortal one; they will be here any second,"* Zephyr's urgency brought me back to the pressing reality. He crouched before me, making it easier for me to climb into his enormous form. Tentatively, I ascended his claw, almost slipping twice; traversed his arm, and found my perch on his shoulder, holding onto his scales for my dear life. It was far from comfortable; I gripped it tightly, fighting the fear of tumbling down or flying away. A beautiful silence replaced the chaotic symphony of nature. *I am definitely going to fall.*

After sensing that I had taken my seat on his back, Zephyr leaped into the sky, thrusting me into an otherworldly ascent. My heart lodged itself in my throat, nausea swirling with each beat of Zephyr's powerful wings. Clinging desperately to his scales, I kept my eyes shut, afraid that a glimpse might unseat me from my precarious perch. *Or I might just vomit.* My body almost tilted horizontally with the pressure of the wind, a sensation akin to riding the edge of a tempest.

*"You can open your eyes, mortal one,"* Zephyr's reassuring voice entered my head.

Abruptly, the storms, the lightning, the thunder—all vanished. A beautiful silence replaced the chaotic symphony of nature. I cautiously cracked my eyes open, only to find tranquility reigning over the skies. The air felt different—clear and pulsating with a newfound vitality.

As Zephyr soared through the crisp, mountainous air, I was perched on his back, entranced by the awe-inspiring spectacle unfolding before me. Torrent and Ember glided effortlessly alongside us, their majestic forms casting shadows on the pristine blanket of snow that cloaked the towering peaks.

The snow-capped mountains stretched endlessly, their majestic summits piercing the cerulean sky. Sunlight painted the snow in a dazzling display of glittering crystals, creating a panorama of glistening diamonds as far as the eye could see. The air was pure and invigorating, carrying with it the distinct scent of untouched nature, untainted by the hustle and bustle of the world below.

Valleys cradled serene lakes, frozen in time, their surfaces reflecting the brilliant hues of the surrounding landscape. Trees adorned with a delicate layer of snow stood like sentinels guarding the secrets of this pristine wilderness.

As we glided over ridges and ravines, the mountains unfolded like a grand tapestry, each peak revealing a unique silhouette against the canvas of the sky. Torrent and Ember, with their wings gracefully cutting through the air, added an ethereal quality to the scene, their scales catching the sunlight and shimmering in a dance of vibrant colors.

The rhythmic beats of the dragons' wings were the only thing breaking the silence, echoing through the mountains like a mesmerizing melody. The sense of freedom was overwhelming, and I found myself lost in the sheer beauty of the untouched wilderness below. Once I was trapped inside a room and was not allowed to go anywhere except school. I was not allowed to meet anyone. And now I am seeing a whole new world. Traveling it, perched on a dragon's back.

I extended my hand, feeling the rush of cold air against my fingertips. Despite the cold and chilling weather, a warmth enveloped me, and it wasn't just the snug embrace of Zephyr's scales.

*"Your magic, Ariana,"* Torrent remarked with a smirk, *"perks of bonding with a superior species."* Torrent's playful comment about my magic startled me, and I clung to Zephyr's majestic form as if seeking reassurance.

I stammered, *"My magic?"*

*"You will learn, mortal one,"* Zephyr replied.

The revelation of a magical connection with these mighty dragons added a layer of wonder to the breathtaking scene. I tentatively opened myself to the realization that this world was more enchanting than I could have ever imagined. Time seemed to stretch as we soared through the skies, the cool wind rushing past. Hours drifted away like fleeting moments. *I should ask.*

*"Where are we going?"* The question escaped my lips. No one answered for a while. Something was wrong. Maybe they didn't hear me.

*"Zephyr?"*

Zephyr, after taking his sweet time, responded, *"To meet the Highlord."*

My heart skipped a beat as I protested, *"I can't meet Thorne. I won't meet Thorne,"* as if the sheer force of my will could alter our course.

*"Thorne is not the only High Lord we know, mortal one! There are others too."*

The revelation startled me. *"What do you mean?"* I inquired, my voice a blend of confusion and apprehension. *"I thought he was the High Lord of Eloria, as he told me."*

*"He lied to you, Ariana,"* Ember's voice was gentle, a comforting breeze amid the turbulence of my thoughts. *"He is the High Lord of the Court of Shadows in Eloria. However, Eloria has six other courts, and Thorne chose to divulge as little information as possible. He aimed to keep you in the dark, preventing you from forming alliances against him in the future. We are heading to the Court of Mirrors. They have been working tirelessly to combat the encroaching darkness. They will be eager to see you."*

Silence enveloped me, and the weight of deception settled heavily on my shoulders. I had been entangled in a web of lies, woven by those I trusted the most – my parents, the ones I believed would shield me, offer solace, and perhaps love me. Now, I stood at the crossroads of hurt and anger. I didn't know whether I wanted to burn the whole world at this point or curl up on my bed with whispers. The conflict within me blurred the lines between vulnerability and vengeance. Something irreparable was breaking inside me with every betrayal. I was feeling so tired. I felt like I was grappling with the unfamiliarity of not knowing how to move forward, how to stand tall when the foundation beneath me had crumbled.

A tear slipped from the corner of my eye, which I swiftly wiped away, a reflexive act to shield my vulnerability. The dragons might have been privy to my thoughts, but I was determined to keep this moment of internal unraveling hidden. No one would witness my breakdown–not in the presence of ancient dragons, not in a world where strength was both a shield and a weapon. I steeled myself, preparing to navigate the uncertain terrain ahead, even as the shards of shattered trust lingered in the echoes of my past.

Zephyr gently descended onto the frozen land, his massive form causing the ground beneath us to shudder, a harmonious mix of power and grace. My emotions swelled, a turbulent storm within my chest, as the dragons stood like mythical sentinels, their presence dominating the icy landscape. The land, though cloaked in snow, seemed to come alive under their colossal weight, and the air crackled with an energy that transcended the biting cold.

Before us stood a colossal gate, an imposing barrier guarded by men clad in steel-gray armor, their swords gleaming as if untouched by the frosty chill. The gate, a stark contrast to the wintry white, was a testament to the intricate craftsmanship of its creators. Beyond the metal rails, a sprawling palace emerged, an architectural marvel perched atop the mountain. The enormity of its grandeur left me in awe, wondering how such a majestic structure could thrive in this seemingly desolate landscape.

As the palace gate swung open, three figures strode purposefully towards us. The first, a tall male with pointed ears, sported a cascade of silver hair, like Thorne but longer, flowing down his back. His sharp brown eyes, chiseled jawline, and robust physique exuded an air of regal authority. Clad in all-black attire, a long coat adorned with golden embellishments swayed with each deliberate step, the markings adding a touch of opulence to his commanding presence.

The second figure, a striking woman, possessed a captivating beauty underscored by an air of guarded suspicion. Her cat-like pointed ears and keen orange eyes accentuated her alert demeanor, suggesting an acute awareness of her surroundings. Long auburn waves framed her face, enhancing her extraordinary features. Dressed in slim-fit black jeans and a maroon top, she exuded an air of both grace and defiance.

And then, the realization dawned–the third figure was........Ka el, a familiar face among these enigmatic strangers.

# Chapter Twenty-Four

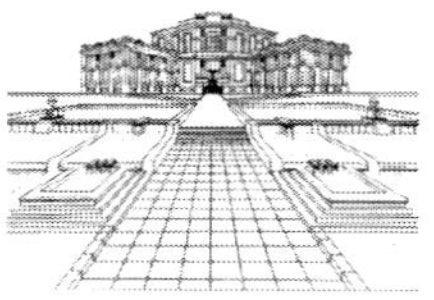

## The Court of Mirrors

Extending his right hand, "Hello, I am Silas," declared the man with cascading long silver hair, his age seemingly defying the wisdom concealed within his eyes. He appeared no older than nineteen.

"Hi... I am Ariana," I responded, my attempt to steady my trembling hand, revealing my inner turmoil. Kael, ever watchful, scrutinized my every move like a vigilant hawk. Silas nodded towards the girl with cat ears. "This is Scarlet," he introduced, her gaze mirroring Kael's intensity as if anticipating a sudden threat. "And you must have met Kael before," he added.

Silence hung between us, prompting him to continue, "Welcome, Ariana. This is the Court of Mirrors, and I am the High Lord of this court." As my response remained elusive *and dumb,* he went on, "Umm...Why don't you come inside, freshen up, and have something to eat? We can then provide you with the explanations you want."

As hunger gnawed at my stomach, I found it hard to deny the appeal of a proper meal. Nodding in agreement, Silas requested Kael to escort me to *my* chambers, and he nodded, flaring his black wings. Lost in my thoughts, I hardly registered the journey until Kael's deep voice broke through, "This is your room, Aria. You can freshen up. The wardrobe is stocked with clothes—choose whatever you like. I'll meet you here in one hour."

He was about to leave when I asked him, "What is happening? Why am I here? Is Thorne coming?" A subtle twitch in his jaw displayed a reaction I couldn't decipher.

"We will explain everything. First, get ready and join us for dinner. Everyone is waiting and no, don't worry, Thorne will not be coming here. He will never be coming here.," Kael responded with a wave of anger in his tone that I couldn't quite put my finger on.

"Are there... more people here?" My voice was more urgent than needed, as he was about to leave again. I could see his brows bunching.

"Just a few," he teased with a wink, perhaps to lighten the mood, before vanishing, leaving me to grapple with a newfound sense of anticipation and uncertainty.

Closing the door behind me, I sought solace in the room's embrace. Its expanse was overwhelming, dominated by tall glass windows that showcased a breathtaking panorama view of snowy mountains, a serene valley, and a frozen lake bordered by a city adorned with twinkling yellow lights. The view stole away my exhaustion, replacing it with a momentary sense of awe.

A king-sized bed took center stage, spacious enough to accommodate the wingspan of two individuals. A lengthy mirror, accompanied by a stool, and a well-stocked wardrobe offered a plethora of clothing options—dresses, pants, coats, tunics, and shoes, a treasure trove of possibilities. *I have worn enough dresses for a lifetime now.*

Stepping into the washroom, I was greeted by a sight that surpassed even the grandeur of the room. The pool, within the washroom, steamed with hot water. My senses were overwhelmed by the opulence of this place. Shedding my clothes, I stepped into the water, the hot steam embracing my skin. It burned, dulling the pain my brain was already grappling with. I immersed myself in the comforting embrace of physical sensation, a temporary respite from the emotional turmoil that threatened to consume me.

After an hour of immersing myself in the burning embrace of the water, I emerged refreshed. Clad in loose, comfortable black pants paired with a cherry red sweater top and ankle-length black boots, I left my hair untied, cascading freely. The mirror reflected a facade of normalcy, but beneath the surface, a storm of uncertainties raged.

*Was I even safe here?* Thoughts ran through my mind. But what was safety for me, anyway? Wherever I had gone, whomever I had met, had always tried to hurt me. Either physically or mentally. Safety was a foreign concept for me.

*"You are safe here, mortal one. We trust these people."* Zephyr's voice thundered in my brain, offering a semblance of comfort that I struggled to accept.

A soft knock interrupted my ruminations. I opened the door to find Kael leaning casually against the frame, his giant wings tucked in casually. His gaze traversed my attire, and I just wanted to shut the door on his face.

"Ready for dinner?" he asked, turning to lead the way.

"Yes," I replied, following him into the hall.

Entering the grand hall of the palace felt like stepping into a realm where nature and artistry converged in an enchanting dance. The sheer expanse of the hall was a testament to fae craftsmanship, its walls stretching up to three stories, fashioned entirely from transparent glass. A cascade of ethereal light, reminiscent of magical crystals, played through these towering panes, casting a radiant glow that transformed the space into a celestial sanctuary.

Within the hall, purple-hued trees adorned the surroundings, their blossoms adding a touch of fancifulness to the already enchanting atmosphere. Beyond the glass walls, a winter wonderland unfolded, the mountains blanketed in pristine snow, creating a breathtaking contrast of colors that captivated the senses. This whole palace was surrounded by snow-capped mountains.

The pathway leading to the glass stairs was a tactile indulgence, firm yet giving beneath each step. Though each step was made of glass, but it felt like I was stepping on a solid cloud. Descending to the second floor, a symphony of elegance greeted me. To the right, the grand dining hall unfolded, a masterpiece of reflective allure. *Everything was so shiny.* Three of its four walls were crafted from mirrors, rising to a height of at least four floors. *They must reach the height of my dragons.*

*"They wish! We are taller, Ariana!" snorted Torrent.* A smirk played on my lips. And Kael noticed. *Obviously.*

Crystal chandeliers, resplendent and suspended from the ceiling, bathed the mirrored surfaces in a cascade of refracted light. The centerpiece of the hall was a colossal glass dining table surrounded by eight wooden chairs, the juxtaposition of materials adding a harmonious balance of sophistication and warmth.

As I approached the dining area, four figures waited patiently. And my heart started racing.

In the grand entrance hall, two new figures joined the ensemble. The first, a towering man with a robust build, boasted big, muscular arms and expansive black wings that extended proudly from his back. His features were defined by a strong, chiseled jaw, a sharp face, and eyes that exuded kindness rather than the scrutinizing gaze I'd become accustomed to. *What was with everyone's bodies here? What did they all eat to get these bodies?*

Long black hair and a beard framed his countenance, giving him an air of both strength and wisdom. His attire, a pristine white shirt paired with black, tight-fitted pants and a navy blue, floor-length jacket, conveyed a sense of authority. Gripped in his hand was a formidable sword, its weight evident in the countless foes it had likely vanquished.

Beside him stood a captivating girl with curly black hair, possessing a figure that could incite envy in the most confident of individuals. She wore a daring black gown, its neckline plunging to her navel, the curves of the dress sensuously hugging her hips. My eyes involuntarily traced the contours of her attire, a subtle acknowledgment she undoubtedly noticed. I don't think I had ever seen someone so confident with her body. But I rather not acknowledge that on a first meeting with a stranger.

Among the familiar faces of Silas and Scarlet, the tall man introduced himself as Claude, extending his hand with a smile as bright as the sun. *Did not see that coming from a bearded man.* Our hands met in a reciprocal greeting as I smiled back. He then directed my attention to the reserved yet striking girl by his side, revealing her name as Olive. Though she remained silent, her presence exuded an enigmatic aura that captivated the room. *I like her confidence.*

"Why don't we all just sit together and have a meal first?" Silas suggested extending his hands in the air towards everyone, and like a choreographed routine, everyone seamlessly chose their seats, displaying a familiarity that hinted at a daily ritual. Meanwhile, I stood there, unsure and slightly overwhelmed. Kael took a seat at one end of the table, pulling a chair out for me to sit beside him. I hesitated, but took the chair. As we settled, I tried to avoid making eye contact with the others.

"So where should we start?" Claude inquired, his gaze shifting between everyone at the table.

A load of dishes appeared at the center of the table, along with plates and glasses of champagne, *I guess,* in front of everyone.

"How much do you know?" Scarlet asked, slicing cabbage roast with her left hand, seemingly disinterested in my answer.

"She knows that Thorne lied to her... about... everything," Kael responded, his gaze fixed on me with an intensity that prompted me to look down. The weight of shame pressed heavily upon me, especially under the scrutiny of everyone in the room. *I am so dumb.*

"She can speak for herself, Kael," Olive side-eyed Kael. It was the first time she had spoken. As her eyes studied me, I struggled to maintain eye contact, feeling exposed and vulnerable. I spoke up, attempting to regain some semblance of control.

"I know there are seven courts in Eloria, and Thorne is the Highlord of the Court of Shadows. Silas, you," extending my hand towards him, "are the Highlord of the Court of Mirrors. That much my dragons told me."

"Ah, your dragons..." Silas mused, "Quite a beauty they are, aren't they?" I responded with a nod and a smile, finding it impossible to disagree. *My beautiful dragons.*

*"Aww.....don't get so sentimental on us, Ariana,"* Torrent teased.

*"Can you ever talk to her normally? Huh...yes, we are your beautiful dragons, mortal one."* Zephyr tried to compensate. I tried not to choke on the water that I was sipping while trying to act normal. *Talking to dragons mentally is normal, obviously.*

"I have also gathered information that dark forces have been attacking Eloria for the past few years. There have been attacks from Kiri, Umbracorruptor..." I glanced at Kael, keeping the glass on the side. "...and in the shadowed thicket, I have also been attacked by a kelpie."

Silence hung in the air as everyone exchanged glances. Claude stopped in the middle of putting a piece of honey-crusted chicken in his mouth, confused, "What.....um...I'm sorry to say this, Ariana," Claude began, "but....there are no creatures named Kiri or Kelpie. Umbracorruptor, yes, but they only appeared after you came to Eloria. That was a singular incident that day." He looked at Kael as he continued, "Other than that, what you've been seeing or feeling was...... not true." His face turned into an expression as if he was dealing with a two-year-old child who didn't know better.

Shock registered on my face. "Not......true! What do you mean? Kael was there during the Kiri attack. There are....were... news articles in Thorne's library, and the kelpie almost dragged me to the bottom of the swamp until....I died.....until.... Thorne saved me!" My eyes welled up with tears. My voice choked.

Kael's voice, gentle and kind, "Do you see the common connection in all of this, Aria?" I looked at their faces, some expressing kindness, others avoiding my gaze, giving me time to piece the puzzle together.

"Thorne?" I asked, my voice almost trembling, "but how?" The revelation shook me to my core.

No one answered for what felt like an eternity, time standing still, or perhaps unraveling at its seams. The weight of the revelation threatened to crush me, challenging everything I believed about Thorne, everything I felt for him. The foundations of my reality were about to shatter.

"It's not your fault, Ariana. Thorne is very powerful. He can deceive anyone, and you are just a human," Olive's soft voice reached me.

"But how?" I asked, but I don't think I was ready to listen to any reasoning. My heart was thundering.

"Thorne has many powers, and one of them is illusion manipulation. He can create things out of thin air, make you feel things that are not there, make you see things and react according to them," Claude spoke gently.

"Kelpies have been extinct for thousands of years. Thorne made you see it, made you feel like it was dragging and choking you. Like you were dying. Like he saved you." Olive's sharp voice sliced through my reality.

I fell into a stunned silence. It felt like everything I had experienced was a lie, a carefully crafted illusion. My hand instinctively went to the amulet Kael had given me—it was still there. If that amulet was real, did that mean there was some truth in this tangled web of deception?

Kael noticed that, his eyes softening as he spoke, "My presence during the Kiri attack that you experienced was part of the illusion Thorne created, Aria. I was not there that night. I tried to come and talk to you the next day, but you wouldn't listen, and I also didn't have the right words to......explain to you." He looked down at his plate on the table. I somehow understood that he meant well to me, but I couldn't bring myself to look at him.

*"Breathe Ariana, we are here for you. I am sorry he did this to you."* Ember's sweet voice tried to reassure me, but it did little.

This was too much. I felt like a fool, betrayed by everyone around me. The hall, with its expansive transparent glass walls, seemed to close in on me. The air became thick, making it difficult for me to breathe. With a sudden jerk, I got up, and my chair clattered to the floor. Wincing at the noise, I turned and ran towards my room. I couldn't be around anyone anymore. I needed to be alone.

Someone tried to get up behind me, but Kael's firm voice stopped them.

# Chapter Twenty-Five

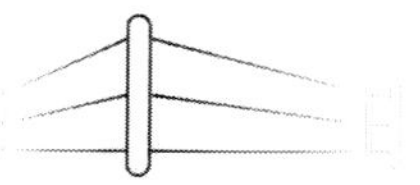

## I Hate Push-ups

It had been a week since I arrived here, a week since the truth of Thorne's deception unfolded before me. Since that moment, when I got up from the dining table, ran into my room, and hadn't stepped out. Meals had been appearing like magic in my room, and everything I needed had been coming to me automatically. As if this house had been intercepting my needs. No one had bothered disturbing my solitude, except for Kael. He came in daily, tried talking to me, getting through to me, *but I do not have it in me anymore; to engage with people, to believe them.*

Throughout my life, those closest to me have inflicted the deepest wounds. My parents adopted me, which wasn't the issue, but they treated me like a burden, like a piece of crap. Every step of the way, they hurt me. And when I thought I found solace with Thorne, believed he was protecting me and cared for me, all he was doing was manipulating me, making a fool of me, using me. The realization struck hard. Why? To open portals between worlds. But why would he want to do that? It felt like I didn't know him anymore, and I didn't recognize the person I thought I loved. He lied to me every single time, and I believed him like a fool.

A lavish breakfast tray materialized on the side table, adorned with an array of bread, cheese, omelets, fruits, and a steaming cup of coffee. Rising from my bed, I had had little sleep, and my head throbbed with an ache that refused to subside. Pouring a cup of black coffee, I settled onto the sofa beside the glass wall, granting me a view of my dragons perched majestically on the mountains, looking at me. They also tried to talk to me, their silent whispers reaching out, but I didn't respond. I knew it wasn't right to shut them out like this, but I needed time—time to process the whirlwind of events that had taken over my life. And after a while, they respected that. Respected my privacy.

So much had happened in such a short span, and my mind felt like a chaotic storm every time I attempted to make sense of it all. In this moment of solitude, the warm aroma of coffee enveloped my senses, offering a semblance of peace and grounding. I was grateful for this respite, aware that it couldn't last forever. Eventually, I would have to step back into the world and face the truths that lingered outside these walls. But for now, I savored this fleeting moment of tranquility, allowing myself to find solace in the simple pleasures of a quiet morning.

The door to my room crashed open, startling me and spilling my coffee all over the sofa. A burst of irritability emanated from Kael's eyes. His wings were rustling in frustration. He threw a pile of black clothes on my bed. "This can't go on. Get up and wear this. We have work to do."

"I'm not going anywhere with you," I retorted, matching his intensity. His gaze lingered on me, a retort forming on his lips, but he restrained himself.

"I'll be back in fifteen minutes. Be ready by then," he said before exiting and sealing the door behind him. I gulped down the last of my coffee in silence, contemplating the outfit–black, skin-tight leggings and a matching top. The idea of facing the world or interacting with people felt overwhelming, yet I knew I had to do that, eventually. But I couldn't stay cooped up in here forever, I had to take responsibility for my life, and my actions, and for righting the wrongs people had inflicted on me! I reluctantly changed into the clothes, *like fifteen minutes were enough for bathing and getting ready,* adding black shoes and securing my hair in a high ponytail. Surprisingly, the all-black ensemble didn't look half bad on me. But the top was high-waisted, hugging me tight. I had never worn anything like this. But if I changed, then I would again have to face his angry stare. And I am in no mood for that.

Another knock and Kael barged in, *becoming a recurring annoyance,* and I wondered whether his wings ever got stuck anywhere.

*"No,"* Torrent's playful remark resonated in my head, *"It doesn't work that way, Ariana,"* and I could see her almost smirking.

"Ready?" he asked, and I nodded. This time, he waited for me, and together we stepped out into the hall, and then into the snowy expanse.

Before me lay a fighting ring, and I shot Kael a bewildered look, as if questioning his sanity. "You can't sit alone in your room and wait to heal. You have to work out your frustration," he said while striding towards the ring.

"I don't have to do anything," I snapped back, defiant.

"Good. This anger will help in your warm-up. Come on, get in the ring now," he said in a tone that made me want to punch him in his face.

"I'm not going in there," I argued, standing my ground.

He studied me for a moment, calculating his words, and then said through his teeth, his silver eyes simmering in anger, "If you want to stay like this, vulnerable to anyone who wants to walk all over you, beat you, make a fool of you anytime they want, then it's your choice. But if you want to change that, stand up for yourself ... then get in the ring." His eyes locked onto mine, igniting a spark within. He stared at me for what felt like an eternity. Without a second thought, I stepped into the ring, the simmering anger in my veins propelling me forward.

"Let's begin with squats to awaken those leg muscles," Kael instructed, while demonstrating the movement. Grumbling softly within, I begrudgingly mirrored his actions, the controlled descent and ascent a silent pact between my protesting muscles and the demands of our imminent practice. *What is the use of this movement, anyway?*

"Now, lunges to stretch them and improve flexibility," he continued, seamlessly leading me through a sequence of movements that seemed to protest against the very air around them.

As we transitioned to push-ups, a sigh of reluctance escaped me. "Keep your core engaged, Aria. This builds strength not only in your arms but also in your core muscles." Yes. My muscles were definitely warming up. Because they were trembling. I could see Torrent enjoying the sight of me cursing. But I got to know one thing, if there was a single thing that I hated the most in this world, it was......pushups!

With our bodies all now warmed up and prepared for the challenges ahead, Kael led me through dynamic stretches to enhance flexibility. The training ground transformed into a battlefield, each stretch and bend a calculated maneuver in the struggle against my own physical resistance, which made me realize how weak I was.

"Good job. Now, let's channel this energy into our fighting practice," Kael said with a tone to encourage me, but I could hardly relate through all the panting.

"Let's start the basics of fighting," he said, depicting his movements, which were a fluid symphony, each step a testament to the grace honed through years of experience. The way he moved in the blink of an eye, my human brain couldn't fathom. So he took a step back and slowed it down for me.

"Feet shoulder-width apart, knees slightly bent. This is your foundation, your balance." I adjusted my stance, striving to replicate the precision of Kael's posture. His discerning eyes caught any deviation.

"Like this?" I managed my balance by extending my arms.

"Perfect. Now, a basic punch," Kael's demonstration emphasized the intricate dance of hip rotation and wrist alignment. I mirrored the movement, feeling the surge of kinetic energy coursing through me.

"Good form," Kael nodded, a smirk forming on his face, but I ignored it. *I will not give him any satisfaction.*

"Now, a front kick. Lift your knee, extend your leg, and aim for the midsection."

We progressed through a sequence of movements, the rhythmic exchange echoing in the training ground as I absorbed the fundamental essence of hand-to-hand combat.

"Now, defensive techniques." Kael shifted into a defensive stance.

"Block a punch using your forearm. It's about timing and precision."

I practiced the defensive maneuver, appreciating Kael's nuanced guidance, but my body protested.

"React swiftly, but with control," he guided, adjusting my hands back in position. Advancing to more advanced techniques, Kael unraveled the artistry of martial arts—spinning kicks, sweeps, and intricate combinations unfolded like a meticulously choreographed performance. He explained the purpose behind each move, urging me to exploit potential weaknesses in an opponent. *Which was he himself.*

"Excellent progress, Aria. You're a quick learner," He smiled sheepishly. "Now, let's engage in a sparring match. Apply what you've learned, and remember, stay focused and agile." My eyebrows shot up in surprise.

"But this was my first session!" I panicked.

"And that's how you will learn. Now get in the position." He turned back and got in position. Every single part of my body suddenly wanted to kill every single cell of him.

Our controlled sparring session started, a harmonious action of combat where each move held a purpose. Kael provided real-time feedback, encouraging me to trust my instincts and employ the techniques learned during the session. As we concluded, my muscles ached with the exertion of newfound abilities. But he was not wrong; I did need to work out my frustration. The physical exertion, the clash of bodies in the ring–it felt good. Each punch I threw, every dodge, was a release, a cathartic expression of the pent-up emotions that had been consuming me.

It was more than a physical workout; it was a reclaiming of my spirit. With every punch, I was reclaiming the agency that had been stripped away by Thorne's deceit. The intensity of the fight mirrored the intensity of my emotions, and as the minutes passed, I could feel a subtle shift – a defiance building within me, a determination to rise above the shadows that had cast their pall over my life. When I finally stepped out of the ring, breathless and exhilarated, there was a newfound sense of strength.

Kael's gaze met mine, a silent acknowledgment of the transformation that had taken place, as if he could also see it in my face. The snow around the fighting ring bore witness to the silent battle, and I stood there, knowing that this was just the beginning. There was much more to face, but with each punch thrown and each obstacle overcome, I was forging my path toward resilience and self-discovery.

After the grueling fighting session in the chilling cold, I stepped out of the shower, my body still tingling with the aftermath of exertion. I dressed in a loose tunic and pants; the fabric providing a comforting embrace after hours of intense physical activity. The wet curls of my hair clung to my skin, and I took the time to dry them, feeling the warmth of the towel against my damp locks.

The echoes of my stomach rumbling with hunger resonated through the room. Two hours of intense fighting on nothing but a cup of black coffee had taken its toll. My hands trembled slightly as I navigated the room, and to my surprise, there was no tray decorated with food in my room this time. And I didn't like it.

Suddenly, Scarlet barged into the room, her unannounced entrance becoming a somewhat annoying habit shared by everyone in this place. Her gaze scrutinized me from head to toe, and she said, "Come on, let's go."

"Where?" I asked, her predatory eyes fixed on me, a reminder of Torrent's intense gaze.

"Aren't you hungry, Ariana?" she purred, her cat ears twitching with every word, her voice sending shivers down my spine. There was something about her that instilled fear in me. I remained silent, unsure if I wanted to engage with others or venture outside. She seemed to assess my inner turmoil and continued in that same purring tone, "You can't stay cooped up here all day now, can you? Without any food, without any water, how will you survive, Ariana?" She smirked knowingly.

Frustration simmered within me, but the relentless hunger took precedence. I walked towards the door, waiting for Scarlet to take the lead as we ventured out. She gracefully guided me into a room that deviated from the routine dining space. The walls, expansive and transparent, served as canvases to the outside world, showcasing the sun in its celestial glory. Heavy beige curtains, drawn with an almost theatrical flair, covered half of the glass walls, creating an atmosphere of both intimacy and wonder. This whole palace was made of glass. People could see from outside, for sure.

The fireplace, nestled on one side of the room, exuded a cozy allure, and above it, the entire wall transformed into a bibliophile's haven. Thousands of books, varying in shapes, sizes, and hues, created a kaleidoscope of colors that harmonized with the warm ambiance. The air was thick with the intoxicating scent of paper, and the plush carpet underfoot beckoned like a welcoming embrace.

Three colossal, high-backed sofas, resplendent in a luxurious dark green hue, dominated the room. Opposite them stood four single-seated, beige-colored chairs, each adorned with plush cushions, inviting comfort and conversation. Between these seating arrangements, a knee-height, dark brown wooden table stood, dutifully supporting cups of coffee and plates, creating a focal point that unified the room.

Additionally, a large wooden table on one side showcased a feast that defied the limits of my imagination. Each dish bore a name tag - Dragonfire Grilled Shrimp Skewers, Fey wild Mushroom Risotto, Enchanted Quinoa Salad, Celestial Citrus Glazed Chicken Wings, Starlight Sourdough Bread, Moonlight Fruit Medley, Ethereal Eclairs, and so on. The room was not only filled with the tantalizing aromas of these culinary delights but also radiated a magical ambiance that pervaded every inch of the Court of Mirrors.

As my eyes absorbed the scene before me, I noticed everyone lounging comfortably on the sofas. There was an air of informality that momentarily made me forget that Silas was the High Lord of this court.

"Help yourself with anything you like," Claude, sitting on the big green sofa, his black wings, though smaller than Kael's, sprawled through the back, gestured towards the sumptuous food table, and the invitation felt like a warm embrace in this haven of relaxation. Overwhelmed by the myriad options, I grabbed a plate and attempted to select whatever seemed familiar.

Holding a mocha in the other hand, I settled into a single-chair sofa on one side of the room. Despite my initial apprehensions, no judgmental eyes befell me. The room was alive with chatter, laughter, and camaraderie, and Kael offered me a genuine, caring smile–a reassuring gesture in this world of intrigue and revelation. *Why would he do that?*

# Chapter Twenty-Six

## Renan

"We need to discuss the plan now, Kael. We don't have much time," Olive stood up and rubbed her hands before placing them in the side pockets of her beige long coat.

"Agreed," Silas added, his expression grave.

"Thorne is already a few steps ahead of us," Scarlet, *as always,* said with a sense of urgency underlying her words.

Kael looked at me and asked, "Are you ready for the discussion, Aria?"

I wondered why he was behaving like this. He was the same Kael who had been so mean to me on the first day we met, the one who hated me from day one. He had never been kind to me, and now, suddenly, he cared whether I was ready to talk about Thorne or not. Why? And why did he always call me Aria? No one in Eloria had ever called me by this name.

"We don't have the whole day," Olive taunted, her eyes sharp as they focused on me, revealing the gravity of the situation, and I wondered what her powers were! *Maybe she could suck the life out of people with those sharp eyes of hers.*

*"She can kill people by suffocating them, without even touching them, mortal one,"* Zephyr said.

"It was directed towards you, in case you missed that, Miss Human." Olive glared at me, and it was then that I realized that I was gawking at her with my mouth open.

"Um... yes, I am ready. I can discuss him," I said, straightening myself, and without meeting anyone's gaze. It wasn't because I lacked confidence or because they were more powerful; it was because I didn't want to. I didn't trust them anymore; I didn't trust anyone anymore. The weight of suspicion and uncertainty hung in the air as we prepared to delve into the dangerous territory of Thorne's plans.

"We had to find a way to get to Renan," said Claude.

"Renan?" I asked, feeling confused.

"Yes.....He has been the Shadowsong Maestro of the Dark realm for the past two thousand years, trying to take over Eloria and the Human realm for the past fifteen hundred years. Since the last Luminara divided the world into three parts, his only motive has been to destroy the veil separating the worlds and bring his rule upon all of them. We have been trying to get to him, but until he contacted Thorne about 100 years ago, it was impossible to spot him. Dragons could sense the breach in the portals, but other than that... Nothing," Kael sighed. "Since then, magic has become unstable... unreliable... Flora and Fauna were dying... people were getting untreatable diseases."

"I saw him once, I think, the day I left Thorne and ran... I saw him talking to a man, hidden in shadows, a hooded figure almost double in size than Thorne," I said without really thinking, and everyone stared at me.

"What were they talking about?" Scarlet stepped forward, both her eyebrows up in shock and mouth open.

"I didn't get much because of panic settling in, but Thorne was telling him not to harm me or come near me. Thorne was convinced that I would help him open the portals to the human realm," I explained.

"And why was he convinced? That you would open portals for him?" She pressed.

I didn't know what to say. Maybe because he thought by kissing me, he could control me. Control how I felt. Control my actions. Maybe because he thought I was so naïve, that I didn't know better. Maybe I didn't know better. Because I trusted his lies multiple times.

"Tell me, Ariana. Why was he so convinced?" She snarled.

*"Calm down Ariana, you are panicking again. Breathe."* Ember suggested, but as usual, it was of no use. My breathing was already ragged up.

"Enough Scarlet. Back-off!" Kael snarled back at her.

Everyone was shocked, their expressions as if a tornado had struck them. "Will you, Ariana? Will you help him?" Olive asked, her gaze scrutinizing me intensely, making me want to shrink away.

"Don't be an asshole," Kael retorted to Olive, and she rolled her eyes.

"I wouldn't, that's why I ran away from him," I responded, keeping my head down without looking at anyone in particular. Yet, I sensed that Kael saw the pain in my eyes.

"No one is accusing you of anything here, Ariana," Silas said politely, his long silver hair moving as he turned towards me, and I took a deep breath. I would not let anyone see how broken I was from the inside. Not here, not anywhere.

"Why haven't you been able to spot him?" I asked, trying to redirect the focus of the conversation.

Kael looked at me as he tried to calm down. "Renan possesses the extraordinary ability to manipulate shadows. This power allows him to meld into darkness, becoming nearly invisible, and move seamlessly through shadowed realms. It had made it almost impossible for me to track him down. No matter how many mirrors I used to track him, no matter how many dimensions I searched in, he had always managed to escape and hide."

"Dimensions?" I asked, my eyebrows almost touching my hairline. "There are multiple dimensions and you can see them?"

"Yes, Kael can see alternate timelines and dimensions all at once, through his naked eyes!" Claude said with a smirk, tucking his wings.

"I don't understand," I said, confused. The concept of seeing alternate timelines and different worlds simultaneously was beyond my comprehension.

"Picture reality as an intricate web of countless threads, each representing a unique timeline," Kael continued, his words painting an abstract canvas of existence. "Every decision we make, every choice, every action, is like a cosmic ripple, setting off a chain reaction that forms an entirely new strand in this tangled tapestry of existence, creating an entirely new reality. Like, the moment you fled from Thorne, it not only shaped the trajectory of your life and this timeline, but gave birth to a new timeline, a reality where that specific choice led to its own set of consequences."

"You mean there is a timeline, a reality where I stayed with Thorne despite knowing everything to........help him?" I asked him, finding it hard to believe.

"Our pain, our trauma, can show us two different paths, Aria. It is always up to us which one to follow," he said with a sad smile, as if he had seen that reality and what becomes of it.

"But I don't understand. How is this possible?" confusion hit my human brain.

His eyes glinted with an almost ethereal understanding as he elaborated further, "In this expansive cosmic world, there are threads or we can say timelines diverging at every juncture, representing the multitude of paths we might have taken. If you had chosen differently, stayed, or made an alternative decision, each of these possibilities would be a distinct timeline, unfolding concurrently with our own."

The concept of these diverging timelines was like a dance of infinite what-ifs. "Imagine," Kael continued, "that there exists a universe where you never entered Eloria, where Renan's influence never touched you. Or perhaps, in another reality, you embraced a different destiny, aligning yourself with Thorne's ambitions. These timelines are not just theoretical; they exist, each running parallel to the others, in the same plane but in different frequencies, creating a cosmic symphony of infinite potentialities."

He paused, letting the weight of the idea sink in. "Renan's power lay in navigating these divergent paths, weaving through the veils that separated them. He conceals himself in the shadows of these myriad timelines, a master of interdimensional travel, always elusive and one step ahead. Though I could track him, his manipulating shadows help him escape every time." The room seemed to vibrate with the complexity of the information, leaving an aura of awe and fascination in its wake.

"Renan's abilities delve even deeper into the mystique of shadows," Kael continued, his tone becoming more gloomy. "He possesses the uncanny skill to summon and sculpt shadows into tangible forms, crafting constructs with diverse applications. These manifestations serve as versatile tools—defensive barriers, formidable weapons, or intricate illusions, similar to Thorne's shadow manipulation. Renan's mastery extends beyond mere materialization; he wields shadows as a canvas for profound manipulation. Itgravity. is like he is painting with shadows, creating detailed and sophisticated magical expressions."

His explanation unfolded with a sense of gravity, "Renan's control over shadows isn't confined to the physical realm. He can intricately manipulate emotions and perceptions using these elusive entities. The very shadows that dance around him can be woven into threads of fear, confusion, or other intense emotions, affecting the mental states of those ensnared in his shadowy influence. It is a power that grants him a formidable advantage, allowing for both subtle manipulation and direct confrontation, playing on the vulnerabilities of the psyche."

The room fell into a contemplative hush as the intricate web of Renan's shadowy prowess was discussed, casting an air of trepidation among those present.

"However, Renan's powers," Kael glanced at me, "came with an inherent challenge of maintaining a delicate balance. The shadows he commands possess the ability to influence his own emotions, creating a symbiotic relationship that requires careful navigation. This was the reason that he had become so obsessive about conquering the three worlds and bringing them under his own rule. It was not only his brain, but shadows also that were influencing his each and every action. And exposure to intense light weakened his abilities temporarily, rendering him vulnerable during such circumstances."

As Kael finished his explanation, a question lingered in the air, prompting me to ask, "Can the rest of you also see other dimensions?" My eyes shifted between everyone in the room.

"No, not with the naked eyes like Kael can," Silas said, tucking his hands neatly in the pockets of his black pants. He nudged toward the mirrors surrounding us, drawing my attention. "These mirrors, Ariana, are not just decorative items of this palace; they serve a profound purpose." He smirked as he went on, "Each mirror is a gateway to any moment in the history of time, any dimension, any timeline, any person. Past, present, or future – be it the future of this timeline or any other. These mirrors hold the ability to unveil the vast tapestry of existence, allowing us to witness everything that has been, is, or will be."

Silas's words lingered in the air, and I found myself captivated by the concept.

"So, you all are like God?" I asked, almost arching up my left eyebrow.

"No, Gods are for humans, we don't believe in them. Never have. We have a Luminara goddess who takes care of us," he gave me a look and continued, "These mirrors harness the echoes of time, reflecting the intricate threads of reality. They are windows into the multiverse, to the different timelines, to other dimensions, to any time in history or future, offering glimpses into the kaleidoscope of possibilities that unfold in the vast expanse of existence. Whether exploring the secrets of the past or glimpsing into the potential futures, these mirrors are conduits to a cosmic understanding beyond our immediate perception."

Olive moved her arms and said something and a mirror in front of me became a portal to my past!

"You need to see it with your eyes to trust us, don't you?" she said, looking at the mirror. A scene played in front of me like a video, in which I was barely three years old and Catriona maybe two. She was in Mom's arms, happy and smiling, but I was sitting on the floor, crying and hungry. She let me cry for a long time. Didn't even look at me. Ignored me like I was a nuisance to her. Then she cradled my sister and went into her room, irritated by my voice. A helper of my mom came, picked me up, held me in her arms, and fed me with a bottle of milk. And I stopped crying. *Obviously.*

Of course, she would show me something like this. But at this point, I couldn't care less. I was not surprised seeing this in front of my eyes, though they were burning.

"You didn't have anything else in your pocket to show her?" Kael said to Olive with anger in his voice, his silver eyes blazing.

"Now that would not have been fun, would it, Kael?" she responded with a smirk.

He stepped towards her, but Silas, with his swift movement, interjected in between, and the temperature of the room suddenly rose.

"How?" I managed to barely speak, "How did you do this?"

Nobody spoke for a while, everyone just stared at each other as if they were ready to rip each other's heads off! Scarlet's claws and sharp nails gleamed against the light. But Kael took a deep breath and stepped back by my side.

He turned towards me as he started explaining, swallowing his anger, "These are not mundane mirrors," his gaze fixed on the reflective surfaces surrounding us. "These are magical artifacts, imbued with spells that transcended the ordinary. They possessed the ability to tap into mystical forces, going beyond the limitations of the physical world. Through their enchantments, they could reflect not only the tangible reality but also unveil glimpses of alternate dimensions and capture the essence of time."

"Through these mirrors, we discovered your journey across the portal and learned that Thorne had found you. Since then, we've been trying to reach you, but unfortunately, we were late, and Thorne had already entrapped your emotions," Kael continued, his eyes focused elsewhere, as if haunted by the weight of the past.

"We seem to have deviated from the topic, haven't we?" Scarlet interjected, her cat-like eyes fixed on Kael, her nails still out.

"Yeah, please get to the point on how we can get to Renan before I die of boredom here," Olive remarked, rolling her eyes, her impatience evident.

Clearing his throat, Silas redirected the conversation to her. "Do you have any idea how to do that, Olive?" The room held its breath, anticipation lingering as the focus shifted to Olive and the imminent strategy to capture Renan.

"We can use her as bait to trap Renan, as he desperately wants her." Scarlet eyed me up. My breath hitched, and suddenly, the whole palace resonated with the thunderous roars of three dragons perched on its top. They must have overheard this discussion with me. A wave of reassurance washed over me.

"No one is using Aria as bait," Kael asserted through gritted teeth, equal to the dragon's roar.

"We'll have to find another way, then," Silas said, shifting his weight to another foot.

"I've seen Thorne planning for a meeting, away from every one, without his usual entourage, like he does every month. This time, I'm sure that the meeting is with Renan in fifteen days, but where? I have no idea. Because of his illusions, I always get lost in the way. I've never been able to follow him completely," Kael shared.

The revelation struck me—Kael had been spying in Thorne's court for years, although I knew it the moment I stepped in this palace, but tried not to think of it...of Thorne. That's why he remained so closed off, so serious, because he bore secrets that weighed heavily on him.

*"This time, illusions won't deceive you, mortal one! You have bonded with us, the superior species! You will see things as they are. It is one of the many powers that will arise within you,"* Zephyr's voice asserted dominantly in my head.

"I can help this time with illusions. Dragons say that I can't be tricked now," I tried to say with confidence, clearing my throat.

"But you will be in danger," Kael argued.

"Since when do you care about my safety? And you only said that if I want to stand up for myself, I have to change things the way I do! This is me changing things!" I snapped back, a surge of defiance coursing through me. *I was tired of everyone.*

Something ticked in his jaw, but before he could say anything, Olive took charge, saying, "Okay, then, this is the rough plan. Kael, you keep an eye on the next meeting point of Thorne," and with this, she strode out of the room.

# Chapter Twenty-Seven

# Another Voice

My body was aching after the strenuous workout and intense fight from the previous day. Every movement felt like I was dragging a giant log, with every limb feeling reluctant, resistant, and stiff. The intensity of the pain made me regret my decision to listen to Kael's words and step into the ring. As I lay in bed, thoughts of the previous day's meeting and subsequent events swirled in my mind.

Despite the challenge of moving my limbs, my mind wandered freely, grappling with the sheer magnitude of what all happened yesterday. Kael possessed an extraordinary ability to see multiple dimensions simultaneously, *a fact I am still trying to understand.*

The past, the present, and the future–all laid bare and accessible to him. It was an immense responsibility, one that could surely drive a person to madness.

No wonder he had always been so silent. So distant. A random thought struck my mind. Did he know about me when I was in Eldenhaven? Was he already aware of my inevitable arrival in Eloria? Did he know about my real parents, my heritage, and the information the dragons shared with me?

*"He does, Ariana,"* Ember's motherly voice resonated within my mind. A thought insidiously crept in–Why didn't Kael tell me anything? Did he also want to use me, just like Thorne? He definitely knew that according to prophecy, I could open portals between the worlds.

*"You will always have a choice here. They do need your help, that is true, but they will never betray you. We believe it, and we will make sure of it,"* Ember affirmed.

*"Why do you want to protect me? Why do you care so much about me?"* I asked, my self-doubt rising to the surface.

Ember sighed, her voice carrying a grave undertone, *"You are the blood of our bonded one, Ariana. We need to ensure that the portals she created stay closed, and that the three worlds remain safe. We failed at that once, and we want to rectify it now. And you, being so young, have suffered enough at the hands of your parents and others in this world. We will not let anyone touch you now,"* a hint of anger tinged her voice.

*"I don't need your pity, you know,"* I sighed, trying not to upset her.

She remained silent for a while.

*"Should we go and eat her parents now?"* Torrent joked, *I think.*

*"No one is eating anyone,"* Zephyr grumbled, putting an end to her... so-called joke. Torrent huffed, and I realized she might not have been joking after all.

*"It's not your fault that portals are weakening or Renan is breaking through. You don't have to blame yourselves for it,"* I said politely. I wished I was in front of her right now, to see her pain, her sadness.

Torrent, steering away from melodrama, demanded, *"Enough of this crying. What are we going to do about it?"*

Suddenly, my door swung open, and Olive strode in with all her attitude. "Get ready," she said, scrutinizing me from head to toe. "We have to train; Kael is not here for you today."

"Where is he?" I asked.

"You don't need to know everything," she said, barely acknowledging me. *I should make a list of people who hate me, without any reason!*

Since there was no option to refuse, and not that I wanted to. I found a strange sense of peace in the training the previous day, but at this moment, my entire body was protesting.

"I'm already sore from yesterday," I tried to tell her.

"It will get better if you move more," she said with a snarky tone. Her eyes narrowed.

"I'll meet you in the ring in fifteen minutes. Don't be late; I'm not as patient as Kael."

*And Kael is patient?* I didn't know whether I liked or hated this place and the people here. They were trying to help me in some way, but I was not fond of their methods.

Cloaked in the black training attire, I emerged into the snowy expanse. The biting wind tugged at my hair, yet the enchantment of magic shielded me from the cold, offering a pleasant sensation reminiscent of autumn.

Olive, already in the ring, was currently jogging in place and practicing a series of moves. A sense of nervousness gripped me, more pronounced than when training with Kael.

Stepping into the icy ring, I swung my arms up and down to warm them up. *Oh, Goddess! They ache!* Snow-capped peaks loomed majestically around me. At the center stood Olive, a commanding presence exuding an aura that demanded respect and terror. Her intense gaze locked onto mine, carrying an unspoken commitment that she was going to make me regret this session.

"Listen closely, Ariana," she said, her voice piercing through the crisp mountain atmosphere with a command as sharp as a winter wind.

"I am not going to hold your hands and teach you. You're here to learn, and you'll learn it the hard way," she went on.

I offered a swift nod as I braced myself for the impending training session.

"First lesson–know your surroundings," she instructed, "you are dead the second your senses are absent," her unwavering eyes boring into mine.

She stepped towards me, her stride smooth as a dance. She put her left foot forward and pivoted her right foot, and I saw a punch coming to my face. I ducked instantly, surprised by my own movement. *Instincts, I guessed.*

"Not bad," she remarked with a smirk on her face, and then my face burned as she unleashed a left punch and a right hook in a matter of seconds, "but you have to be fast too."

The impact of her blows, similar to biting stings, unfolded before me, throwing me off balance. Beneath my clothing, I sensed the emergence of bruises, silent markers defining the intensity of upcoming movements.

"React faster! In a real fight, you won't have time to gloat about your first duck," she panted.

Olive seamlessly transitioned into a series of advanced kicks, her legs a blur against the pristine white backdrop. Attempting to mirror her movements and avoid the attack, I struggled on the slippery snow beneath my feet. Suddenly, a spinning kick caught me off guard, and I tumbled through the cold snowy surface, landing on my ass.

"Balance, Ariana. You are as good as dead if you are on your back," she warned, smirking as she stepped back.

"Now get up, and repeat the moves," she commanded.

The training session intensified as Olive introduced a series of intricate techniques–grappling, joint locks, and throws unfolding in rapid succession. Her eyes remained fixed on mine, dissecting every move. Sweat beading on my head mingled with the cold air, and my muscles screamed from the exertion. Practicing for two hours straight for two days in a row was new for me. I didn't see this one ending anytime soon.

"You're not that bad," she grunted, begrudgingly acknowledging my efforts. "But 'not bad' won't cut it in a real fight. Now, get up. We're far from done, and you should practice more; we don't have much time."

Olive's tough-love teaching style was taking root in the crucible of snowy mountains. There was no room for complacency, no allowances for mistakes. As I rose from the snowy ground, a barrage of questions welled up within me. Turning to Olive, I gathered the courage to ask her for the answers to the puzzle Kael had introduced before me.

"Olive," I asked her, throwing a left kick in the air to an imaginary opponent, and partially expecting some sort of a comeback from her, "when Kael spoke of seeing multiple dimensions, what did that truly mean?"

Olive's sharp gaze met mine, "We'd rather focus on your physical training. All this can be discussed later," she retorted.

"I won't be able to help if I don't understand it," I told her, almost begging.

She studied me for a minute and then said while correcting my form, "Multiple dimensions refer to layers of existence, which are beyond the scope of our immediate senses. It goes beyond the physical realm we perceive; it encompasses alternate realities, diverse realms, and a net of possibilities that unfold alongside our own."

"Can these dimensions or realities... interact with each other? Like, can I contact another form of me in any other dimension?" I asked her further.

"Well, not really! Nothing like this has ever been done before," she said, looking into the wide snow beyond us as if contemplating what I just said.

"But how come Renan can travel through them? Between the different realities?" I continued, "And there must be a different Renan in other realities, who might be trying to travel through these dimensions or realities," terror gripping my throat.

"We should take one thing at a time," worry laced her tone.

Gesturing for me to follow, Olive stepped out of the ring, wiping her face with a soft towel. "For Kael, seeing multiple dimensions meant having the ability to perceive different timelines, alternate realities, and the reverberations of choices made across them. He sometimes suffers through the consequences of his power. He has seen our home destroyed multiple times in different timelines. It is not easy, you know, seeing all that again and again, and trying to prevent it from happening to you at the same time!" she went on, letting me see a slightly different version of her... of them... letting me in.

"He has seen it multiple times, you know, how you betrayed him, betrayed us... to side with Thorne," she says, her voice merely a sigh.

"But that was not me," I try to justify what I don't really understand.

"Yes, but our consciousness is connected throughout the timelines. You can subtly feel the emotions, the feeling of yourself, in another dimension."

"But how?" I ask, trying to make sense of her words.

Olive slowed her pace and looked towards me as she said, "Close your eyes and feel the energies that are flowing around you, through this air, these dimensions, into your body. Try to feel it in your veins, in your blood, like it is calling to you. Trying to guide you."

I closed my eyes just as she said, taking a deep breath. First, nothing happens. All I could feel was the wind gushing around me and hunger gnawing at my stomach. But then something changed when the surrounding air became warmer. The noises became distant. Like I was not a part of them. No birds. No chirping. The blood in my veins started getting warmer. The hair on my arm rose. It was then I heard.

*"You are weak, Ariana, pathetic. You can never defeat us."* I jerked back suddenly as a female voice, laughing, trembled through my brain. *It was my voice, but different!*

"Every dimension possesses its own distinct energy, its rhythm. It's a fight in which you're not merely pitted against an opponent; you're engaged in a profound interaction with the very essence of reality," Olive's voice distracted me from what I just experienced.

Seeing the confusion on my face, she continued, "Let me break it down more comprehensively. Imagine our world as one layer of reality, like a piece of paper. This layer represents what we can see, touch, and experience in our everyday lives...."

She went on, but I couldn't focus on a thing after that.

# Chapter Twenty-Eight

## *Panthora*

I had been training relentlessly for days now. My form has improved, and my strikes have become harder and stronger. My curves have also become sexier, gaining muscle in all the right places, and toning my body. I must admit, I do enjoy this part of training, the after-effects. But the constant soreness is also a part of it. It never really fades away. According to Claude, I need to eat more protein to heal my muscles and gain strength, but I prefer bread, honestly, along with protein, which annoyed him, but I can't do anything about it now, can I?

Today, he was taking me to the city. The one I saw from the windows of this palace, the glowing lights in the valley at night, the chatter, and the laughter I heard in the dead of the night. I was grateful for this opportunity. Going out into the world has always been a luxury for me. To see the world, people, markets...everything!

Claude was adorned in an elegant coat that seemed to be a masterful creation and shimmered with otherworldly grace. Taking my arm, he guided me into the heart of the bustling city markets. The fabric of his attire whispered a subtle enchantment, responding to the magical currents that wove through Eloria. It was as if he had absorbed the very essence of the market's vibrant energy into his clothing.

The shops embraced us in a lively ambiance. Street musicians orchestrated a symphony of whimsical tunes, their melodies dancing through the air like mischievous sprites. The stalls, adorned with an array of colorful wares, beckoned to passersby with a promise of hidden treasures. Animated chatter of people mingled with enticing scents that wafted through the air.

The air was rich with the fragrant aroma of exotic spices, sweet notes of blooming flowers, and savory delights of street food being prepared. Market-goers, each with their own sense of wonder, weaved through the vibrant canvas of colors and sounds, creating a living, breathing spectacle.

As we ambled through the markets, the alluring aroma of freshly ground coffee beans lured us toward a charming coffee shop nestled between colorful stalls. The warm, earthy scent of brewing coffee intermingled with sweet notes of pastries and cakes on display.

"I know coffee is your favorite." He said with a wink as he graciously held the door open, inviting me into a haven of warmth and coziness.

Inside the coffee shop, aptly named *Harmony Brews*, the soft hum of conversation and gentle clinking of mugs created a soothing ambiance. He ordered a sugar-laden frappuccino for himself and a black coffee for me as a takeaway, allowing us to wander through the lively market and savor the sights and sounds of the city. I nudged him towards a freshly baked croissant, too, as it looked heavenly. He chuckled.

With cups in our hands and croissants in our mouths, we stepped back into the bustling thoroughfare, ready to explore the myriad stalls and enchanting nooks the market had to offer. The city's heartbeat resonated through the market as we navigated through the diverse array of vendors. Stalls brimmed with vibrant flowers, handmade crafts, beautiful dream catchers, and eclectic trinkets, creating a kaleidoscope of colors that captivated the eye.

Street performers added a lively soundtrack to our stroll, filling the air with melodic tunes that blended seamlessly with the ambient hum of the crowd. Children giggled and played in a nearby square, their laughter echoing against the backdrop of the city's vibrant energy.

We passed by artists showcasing their talents, their creations, an eclectic mix of paintings, sculptures, and other forms of expression, each one telling a story that sparked our curiosity.

We made our way through the bustling market until Claude took me to the outskirts where the scene changed from vibrant to tranquil. A frozen lake gleamed under the winter sun, reflecting the azure sky above. Along the lake's edge, families and friends enjoyed the serene spectacle. Children, dressed in a variety of winter colors, glided across the ice, their laughter becoming a melody that filled the frosty, wintry air.

As we approached a bakery stall, the irresistible fragrance of warm, freshly baked bread enveloped us, drawing us closer to its source. I followed Claude eagerly, enticed by the mouthwatering aroma. The baker, a cheerful fae with flour-dusted hands, greeted us with a smile and invited us to browse his assortment of bread, pastries, and delectable treats. The air was rich with the tempting scent of freshly baked dough and sweet confections, stimulating my senses. Claude, with a gentle smile on his face, shared stories and anecdotes about the city's rich history and the fascinating tales behind its unique market culture, inspiring me to appreciate the profound richness of my surroundings.

"Kael said that the magic is getting imbalanced, and it's destroying the crops and spreading untreatable diseases. But everything here looks so........perfect!" I said to Claude, looking at the view in front of me.

"This city, Panthora, is close to the palace, the source of all magic in this court. That's why the disruptions are minimal here. Claude extended his hand to me, "Come, I will show you."

I slipped my hand into his, and he wrapped his other arm around my back, launching us into the sky, and I gasped at the sudden rush. The experience was exhilarating but also disorienting, and I could not get used to it. We flew for what felt like forever, and there was a moment when my croissant was back in my throat until we landed in a village. The scene here was the opposite of the idyllic one I saw before.

The village here painted a picture of despair and misery. My heart dropped a beat, seeing what was in front of me. The once fertile fields were now barren and brown, the crops wilted and withered by the lack of rain and the magic imbalance. The air was thick with the stench of rot and decay, and the soil was cracked and dry. Nothing grew here anymore, nothing thrived.

The people of the village were barely surviving, their bodies ravaged by hunger and disease. Their faces were gaunt and hollow, eyes dull and lifeless. Coughing and wheezing surrounded me, their lungs infected somehow. They had no medicine, no magic, no hope. They were living in agony, waiting for death to end their suffering.

The children were the most pitiful sight. Malnourished and crying, their bones were protruding from their thin skin. They had no energy to play, no joy to laugh, no dreams to pursue. They clung to their parents, who could offer them nothing but their fading warmth. They were innocent victims of a cruel fate, robbed of their childhood and their future.

The village was a shadow of its former self, a place where everything was just destroyed. The houses were crumbling and falling apart; the wells were dry and empty, and the animals were dead or gone. It was a ghost town, a place where life had ceased to exist. The silence was deafening, broken only by the occasional sob or moan. A graveyard, a place where the dead outnumbered the living.

"There had been so many places like these. We have tried taking in the maximum number of people we can. But Panthora has only so many resources." He said, sighing.

Claude took me to another one. This was no better. Here too, the crops that used to nourish the people were now shriveled and scorched, the consequence of the magic imbalance and the heat wave. The air was hot and dry, and the dust was everywhere, choking the lungs and the eyes.

The people of the village were thirsty and ill, their bodies dehydrated and feverish. Their faces were flushed and sweaty, their lips parched and bleeding. They had no shade. They were living in torment, waiting for rain or relief.

Tears rolled down my cheeks, their salty sting reflecting the pain and suffering that engulfed me. The air was filled with the cries of children, a heart-wrenching chorus of grief with no one to soothe them. Their loss of parents left a gaping hole in their lives, and hunger bit at their frail bodies, a harsh reminder of the destruction caused by Thorne and Renan.

The hunger for power, and the lust for control, had transformed this once-vibrant community into a land of despair. Their schemes did not care for the lives they ruined, the innocence they had snatched. The mere thought sparked a fiery anger in me. My veins burned with molten lava inside me. Amid the turmoil, a sudden flash of blinding light assaulted my senses—brighter than the sun. Then, everything turned to darkness, and I blacked out.

# Chapter Twenty-Nine

## The Journal Of Seraphina

I heard something. Something whispered in my ear, and then I woke up in my bed with a dull ache pulsating through my head, and the memories of the previous night obscured by the haze of unconsciousness. Surprisingly, Kael was sitting by my bedside with an unfamiliar concern etched in his silver eyes. A concern that I don't quite fully comprehend or, perhaps, don't want to understand. *I don't want to get hurt anymore. I can't bear it anymore.*

"How are you feeling?" he asked, his gaze fixed on me, and there was a weight in his words, a subtle plea for understanding.

"I'm fine...What happened to me?" I attempted to sit up, adjusting my pillows, attempting to keep the conversation light.

"You... fainted," he replied, holding my gaze with an intensity that made my breath hitched, and my heart beat faster.

"But there was light... so bright, almost blinding!" I recalled a shiver running down my spine at the vivid memory, "the same light that I saw in Eldenhaven, before entering Eloria."

"That light is a manifestation of your power, Aria," he said, his tone gentle, as if navigating delicate terrain. The words lingered in the room, leaving me confused.

"My power?" I questioned. "I don't have any powers! If I had any powers, do you think I would have been beaten up by my parents, or I would have tolerated that?"

"Yes, you have had them, since childhood....since your birth. Because of your bloodline. I don't understand how you unlocked it that day when you opened the portals. Maybe it was the pain, the intense emotions that summoned your power at that time, just like yesterday. And you have formed a bond with three mystical creatures, three dragons. That bond has intensified your potential. This is just the beginning. Gradually, you will unlock more, and eventually, you have to train to learn how to control them," he continued as he poured a cup of black coffee for me. *I can never get bored with coffee. I guess?*

"This is one of the reasons Thorne sought to capture you. He was aware of your capabilities and the prophecy that surrounds you," he said, handing me the hot, steamy cup.

"I could say the same about you. You can see multiple realities and glimpse into the future. You already knew I was on my way, did you not? You knew about my impending bond with the three dragons" The words escaped my lips, a challenge reflected in my gaze as I met his silver eyes. There was a subtle tension in the air, and it felt like I had stepped on a nerve. *I should have not said that.*

*"Better to clear your doubts, mortal one."*

*"Good to hear your voice, oldest one."* Zephyr chuckled. *A dragon chuckled in my head.*

A muscle in his jaw ticked as if contemplating what to say next, and flames ignited in his beautiful silver eyes. He lifted his both hands to place on either side of my head, the headboard shrieking under his weight as he said, "You're not a captive here, Aria. You're free to go wherever and whenever you please." With his closeness, I don't know how I managed to keep my coffee straight in my hands, or how I managed to breathe with his face mere inches away from mine.

Something clicked in me, as if I wanted to push him more, see what would come out of him, but instead, I lifted my right hand and slowly put on his cheek, caressing the rough beard of his face. Something softened in his eyes, his gaze traveling downwards....to my lips. My eyes traveled to the scar on his left brow, wondering where he would have gotten that. He flinched as I tried to touch it, and the coffee spilled from my cup. "I am sorry," he mumbled as left the room before I could straighten myself.

I stepped into the library, surrounded by shelves laden with books and mirrors, my heart pulsating with the hope of discovering information to suppress the encroaching darkness. The scent of aged pages filled the air as I started searching through the books for any hint of a weapon or strategy to defeat Renan.

After three hours of scrolling through the pages of nine books, I couldn't find anything of significance. As the count reached ten, Scarlet gracefully entered the library, her feline gaze locking onto me.

"What exactly are you searching for?" she inquired, as she looked through the titles of the books I was reading, splattered throughout the floor.

"I.....don't know, maybe a weapon, or a way to defeat or capture Renan. There must be something hidden within these pages," I said, opening another book. Scarlet scrutinized me with her cat-like eyes, which I tried to avoid. A moment of silent understanding passed between us as she offered, "Let me help you."

Hours melted away as we meticulously scoured the books, the fragrance of aged pages intermingling with the rich aroma of black coffee and freshly baked biscuits, which were automatically appearing by our side. After five intense hours and three cups later, I stumbled upon a worn but treasured discovery titled–the Journal of Seraphina.

The book, a priceless artifact of Eloria's ancient history, was a repository of concealed secrets and sacred wisdom. Its brown leather cover bore the marks of centuries, colors faded by the relentless march of time. The spine, adorned with subtle patterns of stars and moons, revealed the care bestowed upon it by generations of guardians, and its pages turned on the corners.

The journal opened with a crisp sound, resonating like a whisper from the depths of the past. The paper, intricately woven with magic, carried the fragrance of heavenly flowers, as if Eloria's very essence was entwined within its fibers. The ink, a radiant blend of starry colors, gracefully flowed on the pages in elegant writing, each word a testament to the Luminara's unwavering faith, her story, her life.

Within its sacred confines, the journal unveiled a rich mosaic of words and drawings, offering glimpses into celestial worlds, mystical rites, and the intricate process of crafting powerful relics. The edges were adorned with luminous images that twinkled in the light, their vivid hues portraying the complex spells interwoven into the very fabric of Eloria.

As I eagerly turned the pages, seeking insight into the dark forces and any knowledge concerning veils or portals, my quest led me to a profound discovery within the journal's sacred passages.

## *Excerpt from the Journal of Seraphina, the Last Luminara*

*In the shadows of the Great War, when the very fabric of Eloria quivered under the onslaught of dark forces, the Aetherbane emerged as a beacon of hope. Forged with the luminous essence of the celestial realms and the collective magic of our most skilled enchanters, this weapon held the promise of salvation.*

*However, in the face of an enemy that sought to twist the Aetherbane to serve its own dark purposes, the decision was made to dismantle its might. Divided into three parts, each entrusted to a different guardian, the Aetherbane's legacy endured.*

*1. The Blade of Lumis:*

*The radiant blade, blessed by Lumis himself, was enshrined within the sacred archives of our High Enchanters. To access this sanctum, one must prove their dedication to the protection of Eloria and demonstrate an unwavering commitment to the pursuit of justice.*

*2. The Heartstone Amulet:*

*The core of the Aetherbane's power resides within the Heartstone Amulet. Hidden away in a realm accessible only to humans, this crucial piece requires a pure heart and unyielding courage for retrieval. Only a chosen human, endurer of torments and destined by fate, can embark on the quest to reclaim this part.*

*3. The Faebound Keystone:*

*Guarded by the elusive and wise Court of Elements, the Faebound Keystone acts as the stabilizing force of fire for the Aetherbane. Deep within the heart of fire, the court preserves this vital part, ensuring its protection from those who would misuse its formidable magic.*

*To the one who reads these words, entrusted with the destiny of Eloria, the path to reunite the Aetherbane lies in the unity of these three parts. May the luminous legacy guide your steps and illuminate your way in the darkest of times.*

*May Eloria's fate rests in the hands of the chosen one.*

My heart beat fastened with hope, a strong belief that Renan could be defeated and Eloria, along with its people and children, could be saved. I reached out for Scarlet's hand, partially forgetting the fact that she could scratch me with her claws if she wanted to.

"Seriously? We are not friends." She blurted, taking back her hand.

"I am not trying to be your friend. I am just showing you this," I moved the journal towards her side.

At first, her eyes shone with hope after reading the excerpt, but then I noticed a hint of tension, something darker clouding her expression. "What's wrong?" I asked.

"Nothing... we just need to find those parts," she replied. But I sensed that there was more to it, but decided not to press further, *for now*.

We all gathered in the library, a room filled with the scent of old books and the soft glow of magical lanterns, accompanied by the warm orange hues of the setting sun streaming through giant glass windows, to discuss our plan to locate the weapon.

"I want to help too," I asserted. "I want to be part of this mission."

"It won't be safe for you to tag along," Kael retorted sharply, his gaze fixed on the journal in his hands, a lingering trace of anger apparent.

Undeterred, I kept my eyes on him, "You don't have to worry about me. I can take care of myself, and besides, I have three dragons with me."

The dragons responded with a resounding roar, their presence a comforting affirmation. All eyes turned towards me.

"Is this going to happen every time we disagree with you on something?" Olive said with an irritated tone and I offered a nonchalant shrug. It was a subtle gesture of my dragons, but it carried the weight of my confidence.

# Chapter Thirty

## The Blade Of Lumis

*"The radiant blade, blessed by Lumis himself, was enshrined within the sacred archives of our High Enchanters. To access this sanctum, one must prove their dedication to the protection of Eloria and demonstrate an unwavering commitment to the pursuit of justice."*

Kael and I left at dawn for our mission to find the blade of Lumis. Zephyr and Torrent came along with us, Ember along with the rest of the members of the court of Mirrors staying behind. Just in case

Renan got the hint of our plan and decided to attack. Claude also wanted to come, but Kael advised him to stay back.

"THIS TASK SHOULD NOT be that difficult" Kael had said. The air was chilling at this hour of the day, but thanks to the dragon magic that was protecting me from freezing to death.

*"Your magic.."* zephyr said, but I did not believe him. I didn't have any magic. If I could wield magic, then why would have I become the victim of physical abuse by my family?

Kael said we could directly teleport to *Luminal sepulcher, the name is.....I mean who keeps such a name,* instead of flying on dragons' backs at thousands of feet, but Zephyr insisted on coming, which led to Torrent getting stuck with us.

*"I do not go anywhere I do not wish to, Ariana,"* Torrent snaps in my head.

I sat on Zephyr's back, holding his scales for my dear life. And Kael on torrent. I wonder what her thoughts were regarding this seating arrangement. Dragons only allowed their bonded ones to climb and ride them and were really fussy about it, apparently. Although Kael had his own wings, I doubt he could fly as fast as a dragon.

*"Obviously, that is the only reason I agreed to this hell of a journey. Otherwise, I would have never let this bat-man on my back."* Torrent's snarky voice reverberated in my brain. And I snorted. Thank Goddess Kael wasn't in on our communication channel.

"*Do you want him in?"* Zephyr asked.

"*You can do that?"*

*"Yes, if you want, we can include him in our fun, little banter."* Torrent snickered.

"*No, thank you. Please."*

This time, her laugh was louder. I wonder what she was laughing about. But I was pretty sure her patience was barely hanging by a thread here.

*"You think?"* she said.

No matter how rude she seemed to be, I have realized by now that she does care. About me. About Eloria. As I looked toward her, I noticed that Kael was watching me. Observing me. And I don't understand why but whenever his silver beautiful eyes fall on me, my heart seems to skip a beat or two. Always.

We had been flying for hours, trying not to get detected by anyone. Dragons possessed the magic of cloaking themselves, which proved helpful in hiding from the enemy. Although Kael had warned me about my safety in this mission of finding the blade, I think he also realized that I needed to do this. For myself. To believe in myself that I could do something and that I was not a total waste of space.

*"You are not, obviously! Otherwise, we wouldn't have bonded with you."* Zephyr said.

*"Trying to make me feel better about myself, are we?"* I smirk back. *Mentally, of course.*

*"We have better things to do, you know,"* Torrent remarked, and I expected nothing less from her.

Another reason why I wanted to do this was the cries of those children I saw that day in the village, with Claude. Those sounds still rang at night in my head at night, and I didn't want them suffering anymore. Suffering at the hands of other people, at the cruelty of other people. But apart from all that, I was really glad that he trusted my decision and believed that I could do this.

Unlike everyone else in my life, he accepted that I could do this, or maybe he had seen it already happening in the future. I wonder if we could change the future, after seeing it. Whether we could manipulate our destiny. And if not, then what was the point of doing anything? If everything was pre-written. What was the point of trying to make a change if we had already seen the outcome? I guess it was for the good that not everyone had the power to see the future.

Kael seemed to do pretty well with the twists and maneuvers of Torrent. I, on the other hand, was on the verge of throwing my stomach. It was a good thing that I just had a black coffee before leaving this morning. Somehow, I knew eating a proper meal before a flight was a bad idea. Maybe it was Kael's experience of years of flying that he was handling so well, or at least it seemed so. My nerves started relaxing when we started descending.

*"We have to walk from here on,"* Zephyr said.

After almost ten hours of tiring and back-straining flight, we landed with a thud on the tip of a cliff. Ground trembled under the claws of our dragons. Kael flew down from Torrent's back. *Show-off!* And I crawled forward, towards the neck of Zephyr, holding onto his scales, and then slid down his front leg. My black fighting outfit was always a good choice for riding and Zephyr consistently tried to make it easier for me by crouching down slightly whenever I had to climb or slide down. Surrounded by a large valley on three sides and a big tomb-like building, covered with morning yellowish-hues of sun, on the other side. The door of the tomb was made of antique wood, with chrome margins embedded in it. Years of wear and tear showing on each and every splinter. It was hardly big enough to accommodate Kael with his wings, let alone two giant dragons.

"You guys might have to wait outside," Kael said to the dragons. Zephyr huffed audibly, the smell of sulfur filling the surrounding air.

*"I will destroy this pathetic, wretched building in the name of the tomb if any harm comes upon you,"* Zephyr thundered.

"Dont worry, she is safe with me," Kael responded, but unable to convince my dragons.

"You can talk to them?" My eyes shot up in surprise. I don't know what else I was expecting.

"Yes," all of them blurted at the same time.

*"We have been working together for centuries now, mortal one,"* Zephyr said patiently.

"Of course." I nodded.

As we stepped towards the door, both the dragons folded their front legs and crouched elegantly in front of the tomb, sitting like a giant behemoth mountain, ready to devour any threat coming towards it.

The path to the sanctum unfolded before us, a mysterious corridor veiled in arcane shadows. The air crackled with unearthly energy as we walked through the mystical passage. An ethereal glow emanating from small fire sprites guided our way. Shadows, as tall as a human, danced on the periphery of our vision, their forms shifting like transient dreams, ranging from a small crying baby to a crooked old man, all in a matter of seconds. My heart trembled with fear, but I couldn't afford to be scared right now. Not when it was my decision to come here. Whispers of doubt echoed in the air, testing the very core of my dedication to Eloria's safety.

Lumis was originally the sage-fighter of the Goddess Luminara. He meditated, standing in the burning logs of fire, for hundreds of years, without any food or water, throughout the seasons to achieve the benediction from the Goddess. What he really wanted was to marry her, to be with her, but she denied his request. Upon rejection from the Goddess, Lumis was about to burn himself in the name of Luminara, in the name of love. And she couldn't see that, take that blame on her soul. So she offered him to be with her forever, in the role of her pandit-fighter. He accepted it with a heavy heart, but at least he got his wish to be in front of her forever!

He used to perform rituals and enchantments for the Goddess, and even lead the wars for her. Ultimately, Luminara's blessing transformed him into the most powerful weapon ever-present in the world. Unstoppable. He always carried with himself a blade that could slay any enemy, any demon, any entity in the world. The blade was itself blessed by the Goddess. He served her for thousands of years and never complained.

Until one day, when he got tired of waiting for her. Tired of waiting for a moment when Luminara would also see him as her lover. His dam of patience broke when the Goddess announced her engagement with the God, Madhavan.

Something broke inside him after hearing the news, and he arranged a coup against the Gods. In the hope of defeating them and making Luminara see his worth, but ultimately he lost. Just because of his years of service, the Goddess excused his life but exiled him here, in Eloria, for the rest of his immortal days.

Learning about the story from Kael was a pleasant distraction for a moment, from all the scary howling shadows and the voices trying to challenge my resolve.

As we walked further, the corridor turned into a dreadful maze of mirrors, where Lumis's whispers started resonating with a chilling tone. As we wandered through the labyrinth, the reflections morphed and warped into each other's. Our faces changed in the mirror. In a fraction of a second, it turned from our present self to a baby, and then it turned into an old dying shadow. It took a lot of strength to keep my focus. I wondered what Kael might be seeing or feeling. Whether he was seeing the same things as I was, or the mirrors were showing him another horror show.

Life got sucked out of me when the shadow in the mirror in front took the shape of my dad. And for a change, his eyes were gentle and smiling at me as if accepting me, as if he cared for me. Something eased in my chest seeing this side of him.

"Don't get so happy, love," his voice vibrated through the mirror, "I will hunt you down, no matter where you are."

His gentle smile turned into a wicked evil grin and something dark gleamed in his eyes that made me shiver. The mirror then revealed a hideous image–my own battered and bleeding body, with a broken leg and the years of injuries I had endured, a painful representation of the hardships I had suffered, of all the beatings I had taken, all at once. Kael stepped closer towards me as if he was also seeing the same thing as I was, but it hardly did anything to calm my nerves.

*"In the broken reflections, find the truth that escapes your sight, the truth that you deny to accept,"* Lumis's whispers echoed, their otherworldly quality adding to the distressing atmosphere. Tears filled

my eyes as the mirrors played wicked tricks, showing a version of my father who has always held a deep grudge, and who has always hated me for a reason I never understood. The chilling whispers echoing through my ears seemed to magnify the pain, creating illusions that inflamed the scars of an already tense relationship.

"Aria……Aria..," words struck my head, "This is not real Aria. Your father can not touch you here. You are safe," Kael's voice grounded me to reality.

Gripping my shoulders tightly with both his hands, turning me to himself, "I am here with you. No one can harm you, Aria." His silver eyes blazed my heart.

*"Mirror after mirror, what do you see? Can you tell the illusion from reality?"* Lumis's whispers mocked, laughing, casting panic on my senses and intensifying the echoes of my father's contempt. Tears ran down my face as I struggled with the agonizing visions.

"These are just illusions, Aria. These are not true." Kael's soothing words prompted me to face the illusions, to look past the warped reflections.

"You are stronger than them, Aria. Look past these twisted reflections. You are the bonded one, remember? You can fight through these illusions," he urged, his silver eyes fixed on me as he tucked me in his strong solid muscular arms.

My body trembled with fear as I rested my head on his chest, gripping his black shirt tightly, as if it could save me from all my demons. Kael's arms wrapped around my waist and I shut my eyes tightly. The world disappeared as he covered his wings around us, shielding me from everything that was there. *Outside.*

"It's okay Aria. I am here till you need me. I will be here whenever you need me," he said, kissing my forehead, and I slowly lifted my head from his chest to look towards him in his silver eyes. And there it was, something I didn't want to give a name to. Kael's eyes filled with care for me, filled with pain.

"You are not defined by what happened to you, Aria. You are defined by what you decide to do about it," he said, his words a soothing salve to the wounds that the illusions had reopened. I nodded, trying to smile through the pain.

A sudden lightning thundered, startling both of us. Kael stepped back, looking toward the noise. I followed the same. But in the darkness of the cave, we couldn't see anything. Another thunder and I stepped back, my hand automatically reaching to grab Kael's arm, but my heart stopped when I realized that he was not there.

"Kael.......Kael......" I shouted through the damp caves, trying to find him by reaching with my hands in the darkness.

"Kael......" my voice trembled as nothing but wet moss of the cave wall scraped my hands.

# Chapter Thirty-One

# The Riddle

Stumbling through the cave, "Kael......where are you?" My voice echoed through the walls.

*"Should I come inside, mortal one?"* Zephyr asked.

*"You will have to destroy the tomb for that....we will never be able to find the blade after that"*

*"We will worry about that later, first your and Kael's safety is more important,"* he grumbled.

*"Just wait, give me a chance to find him,"* I pleaded.

*"You have ten minutes, Ariana,"* Torrent said.

My legs quaked with fear as I moved further down into the darkness. There were no fire sprites to light the way here. Nothing.

The temperature dropped like hell with each step, and the air became dense. My chest started aching with each breath as if I was inhaling the water itself. Suddenly, my balance faltered, leaving my knees colliding on the next step. Pain erupted through my body with an intensity I didn't know I could handle. Standing slowly with the support of the moist wall, I stepped down the second stair, careful this time.

"Kael......Kael..."

Where did he go? There is no other way. He won't leave me here like this. He said he would never leave me. He must be in some danger. That was the only logical explanation for his disappearance like this. Did Lumis take him? Or was someone else here? Was Thorne here? Or Renan? Terror gripped my throat as I lowered my voice and muted my steps. I had to find him before they could hurt him. Before anything bad happened to him. I hurried down the steps, trying to avoid falling in the dark, and dragging down through the walls. My breath panted as I reached the final step, but still no light, no warmth.

*"Hurry up Ariana, he doesn't have much time,"* Lumis's mocking voice echoed through all the directions in the darkness.

He had him. Lumis had him. I didn't know Lumis was alive. That he would be here. How would I save Kael? Panic started to grip my nerves and my breath became scanty as I moved forward in the passage, flailing my arms in front for direction.

*"Hurry, girl,"* the voice said.

I stumbled into the vast cave, and the sight before me halted my frantic steps. A massive pool of boiling water divided the cavern, steam fogging the air, making it hard to see and even harder to breathe. On one side, Kael was trapped inside a vacuum-sealed chamber, bound in chains, with boiling water slowly filling the surrounding space. On the other side, in the shadowy expanse of the cavern, illuminated only by the sporadic flicker of fire sprites against the damp walls, stood Lumis.

He was an embodiment of contradiction: an old, withered man, his frame stooped with the weight of years, yet his presence commanded the room with an authority that belied his frail appearance. His skin was a map of wrinkles, each line telling a story of battles fought, of magic wielded with a power that had drained him physically. His eyes, however, burned with a fierce, undiminished light, a stark contrast to the fragility suggested by his form.

By his side hung an ancient blade, its hilt encrusted with stones that caught the dim light and threw it back in defiant sparks. The weapon seemed out of place next to such a frail figure, yet the way Lumis's hand occasionally brushed the hilt spoke of familiarity and readiness to wield it, suggesting a depth of the danger that his physical appearance might otherwise be disguised.

My heart raced as I took in the scene. Panic knotted in my stomach, but I forced myself to think, to find a way to save Kael. Lumis caught my gaze, a twisted wicked smile playing on his lips.

"Kael...." I shouted.

"He won't hear you, Ariana. That is the fun here. You both can only see each other die, but can not help each other." Lumis said, flicking his finger. Kael's chamber drowned a little more in the boiling water. Steam fills the chamber. I could see the silhouette of his wings trembling as the water burned through his leather boots.

"What do you want Lumis? Why are you doing this? Let him go, please!" I cried.

"You want my blade, don't you? Just like your ancestor once did! The least you can do is make it interesting for me," he mused.

"This is a game for you?" anger filled my veins.

"Life is a game, human girl. And you always have to play it, whether you like it or not. If you want him alive, then you have to abide by my rules," he said.

*"We are coming.."* Torrent's angry voice rambled in my brain.

*"No....wait.."* I said.

"What do you want?" I asked Lumis.

"Ariana," he called out, his voice echoing through the cavern, "I have a proposition for you."

I squared my shoulders, trying to appear more confident than I felt. "What kind of proposition?" I asked, my voice steady.

Lumis's smile widened on his horrifying face. "A challenge, if you will. I propose a riddle, one that has baffled minds far greater than yours for centuries. Solve it, and I release Kael. Fail, and... well, I think you can imagine the consequences."

My mind reeled. A riddle? It seemed so trivial, so out of place in the face of the danger Kael was in. I know it can't be this simple.

"And if I solve your riddle?" I asked, buying time as I tried to think of a way out of this.

"Then you both go free, as I said. But Ariana, be warned, no one has ever been able to solve it."

I nodded, understanding the stakes. My heart felt like a stone in my chest, heavy with the anticipation of the impossible task ahead.

"What's your riddle?" I managed to ask, my voice barely a whisper against the roar of boiling water.

Lumis's smile was like a slash in the darkness. A throne of rubies appeared behind him. As he sat with an ancient elegance on it, he spoke, "Here it is: 'What is it that runs when it is still, speaks of unity but parts in silence? It is the dawn of despair and the dusk of joy, the one truth that every soul seeks but few truly find.'"

"And remember, you have only two minutes to answer. His chamber is filling with quite a speed," he said, waving a hand towards Kael.

Fear gripped me, its icy fingers wrapping around my heart with a squeeze that threatened to choke the hope from me. The riddle twisted and turned in my thoughts, a serpent coiling tighter with each passing second. The steam from the boiling water clouded the air, mirroring the fog of confusion that clouded my mind. It was as if my brain had stopped working in these two particular minutes.

Time slipped through my fingers like sand in an hourglass, each grain a ticking bomb counting down to Kael's demise. His eyes met mine across the cavern, a silent reassurance, as if he believed that I could do this. His life was in my hands, hanging by the thread of my wit against Lumis's cruel game.

I paced frantically, my mind a whirlwind of fear and frustration. *The dawn of despair, the dusk of joy...* Each attempt to solve the riddle felt like grasping at smoke, each idea more elusive than the last. My hands trembled.

The pressure built inside me, a crescendo of dread that threatened to burst. Lumis's intermittent taunts were a cruel soundtrack to my spiraling panic.

"We are running out of time," he mocked.

Hot boiling water filled Kael's chamber to the waist, and I could smell the burning of his skin from here. No.....no....no...this can't happen. He can't die. I can't let him die!

*One truth that every soul seeks but few truly find.* What can it be? Death? God? Happiness?

Then, in a moment of sheer desperation, the answer dawned on me, cutting through the fog of my fear like a beam of light. I remembered the countless tales of love lost and found, the unity it promised, and the silence it left in its wake. The one truth every soul seeks...

With a breath that felt like my first in hours, I turned to Lumis, as the water reached Kael's throat, my voice stronger than I felt.

"The answer is love," I shouted. Hoping my answer was correct.

Lumis's expression shifted from smug satisfaction to stunned disbelief.

"Correct," he conceded, the word slicing through the tension in the air.

And with a flick of his wrist, the chains binding Kael dissolved as if they had never been, the water receding with a haste that seemed almost eager to correct its course. His chamber drifted towards the shore. I rushed to him, my relief a physical force that propelled me forward, and caught him as he stumbled, weak but alive, *alive! He was alive* from his prison. His body burned, blisters appearing on his arms and hands, on his neck. I can only imagine what was beneath his clothes.

"I am fine," he coughed, but I could see the pain in his eyes. "I will heal in a moment." My eyes widened with shock, but I nodded.

"You are free to go now," Lumis said, turning our back towards us.

"You are forgetting your end of the bargain, Lumis," words escaped my mouth with an anger I have never expressed before. "If you are happy with your entertainment, we would like to have the blade now."

"We all like to have many things in life, girl, but that is not the point. Get out of here before I change my mind about leaving you alive."

Violence simmered in my veins, Kael's eyes fixed on me. His blisters were healing indeed, and he tried to stand on his feet, wincing in pain.

*"Zephyr.."*

*"Take cover mortal one,"* he thundered, and I hurried Kael towards the cave exit. He was limping in pain, his wet wings dragging through the ground. Just as we entered the cave entrance, the walls of this large dreadful bunker in the name of a cavern shattered. Zephyr and Torrent emerged through the storm of dust and fire.

As Zephyr and Torrent burst through the storm, their immense forms casting shadows that danced wildly with the flames, the cavern shook to its core. Lumis, caught off guard by their sudden appearance, turned towards the dragons with a look that mingled surprise with a dawning realization of his own vulnerability.

Torrent, with her dark scales absorbing the light of the fire, roared with a fury that rattled the bones. Zephyr fixed his gaze on Lumis, a piercing glare that seemed to promise retribution.

*"You have meddled with forces beyond your reckoning, pandit,"* Zephyr's voice boomed through all our brains at the same time, resonating with the power of the winds he commanded.

Lumis, however, was not easily intimidated. Drawing himself up to his full, though slight, height, he retorted, "Do you think your presence here changes anything, beasts? I have dealt with your kind before." His hand moved towards the hilt of his ancient gem's blade, the stones glinting more fiercely now as if feeding off the tension in the room.

The standoff was palpable; the air was charged with potential violence. I leaned towards Kael, whose strength was returning, his wounds healing at a rate that was nothing short of miraculous, a testament to his resilience and the power that coursed through his veins. Despite his recovery, concern etched his features. His gaze fixed on Lumis and the dragons, and his hand tightly wrapped around my waist, aware of the delicate balance that held us between confrontation and catastrophe.

I stepped forward, out of his reach as I said, "We do not wish to fight you, Lumis. We are here for your blade. Not for ourselves, but for the protection of Eloria. You trusted my ancestor with your weapon, and she honored your trust by returning this to you. Can you please show the same trust in me?"

My voice resonated with a hollow timbre, unmasking my self-doubt amidst the unfolding scenario. "Your ancestor was a fae luminaire, and you... you are merely a fragile human," he declared, his gaze sweeping over me dismissively. "You lack the strength to wield this weapon."

Undeterred, I countered, "If I was weak Lumis, then the two most majestic creatures of the world wouldn't be standing here threatening you." Kael's head snapped at me, surprised by my tone. *I don't blame him.*

Lumis's grip on the blade tightened, his eyes narrowing. "And what would you have me do? Surrender the blade to you, to be cast back into the shadows, forgotten and unused, like I have been for years now?"

Kael stepped forward, his voice calm but deadly. "Not forgotten, Lumis, but safeguarded. We offer you a choice: join us in protecting what remains of this world, or stand against us and face the consequences of your hubris."

The silence that followed was tense, a moment suspended in time, as Lumis considered his options. The flickering flames, the steam rising from the boiling water, and the gaze of every being in that cavern were fixed upon him. Dragons narrowed their eyes, ready to scorch him to the ground.

Finally, Lumis lowered his hand from the blade. "Very well," he said, his voice barely above a whisper, yet carrying an undeniable weight. "If I am to join you, I will do so on my terms."

"What do you want?" Kael asked, his voice was more like a threat.

"You will know when this time is right," he said.

"Done," Kael replied.

Lumis unsheathed his blade, holding it out towards me with a menacing precision. In a swift motion, he launched it across the pond, directly aiming at me. My heart pounded in my chest as I watched the blade slice through the air towards my head. The dragons let out thunderous roars, their cries echoing as stones tumbled from the cave's edges in response. Just as the blade was about to reach me, Kael intercepted it, seizing the weapon firmly in his powerful grasp.

"Good, but I expected her to defend herself," Lumis remarked, his smirk fading as he vanished into the shadows.

"We need to leave, now," I urged, my voice laced with a blend of fear and relief. Kael's hand clasped mine.

Zephyr lowered himself in front of me, and I mounted his back, securing the blade in my pants for safekeeping. Kael took his place on Torrent's back, and together, we ascended into the embrace of the sky.

# Chapter Thirty-Two

# The Heartstone Amulet

*"The core of the Aetherbane's power resides within the Heartstone Amulet. Hidden away in a realm accessible only to humans, this crucial piece requires a pure heart and unyielding courage for retrieval. Only a chosen human, destined by fate, can embark on the quest to reclaim this part."*

Securing Lumis's blade had marked a promising beginning for us all, yet Kael had remained noticeably quiet since our return. His wounds had vanished, healed by fae the magic, yet his silence loomed larger than his physical recovery. He had barely spoken a word, particularly to me, despite my numerous attempts to bridge the gap.

All of these considerations could be addressed later; our immediate priority had shifted to locating the Heartstone Amulet. Rumored to be hidden within a realm accessible only to humans, speculation arose whether it lay near Eldenhaven, or perhaps even within its borders. The mere thought of returning there sent my heart into a flutter, especially after the unsettling visions I had witnessed in those mirrors.

Every thought of my father had caused me anxiety since childhood. And today was no different. As yesterday's images played in my eyes, the anxiety became overwhelming; it became difficult to breathe.

"*Breathe, Ariana.*" Ember's voice resonated in my head. I was really grateful that I had them as my friends, as my *guardians.* But whenever my anxiety attack occurred, nothing in the whole wide world could calm me down. I tried to breathe in. Breathe out. Close my eyes. But nothing was working. My breathing got ragged; I needed to escape... to find air...

Driven by a desperate need for open air; I found myself running towards the ground, the ring, the one place that offered me peace in these turbulent times, where Kael was currently practicing. *Which didn't help in calming down my nerves.*

He was there, honing his skills with the sword amidst the snow, his black tunic shirt draped over the ring's rope. Frost adorned his black hair like a crystalline crown, while his breath fogged in the cold air, each exhale a visible testament to his exertion. His movements were a study in grace, each stroke and parry flowing like hot water gliding over ice, his focus unbreakable, eyes locked on an unseen foe. A determination blazed within him, the kind of fierce, inner fire that few could kindle. The muscles across his back danced with each movement, his arms sculpted to perfection, making the swords seem almost blessed to be wielded by such hands. And while his muscles were trying to calm down my anxiety, *or give me a new one;* his eyes snapped to mine.

"Came here to blow off some steam, Aria?" he asked, raising his left brow, shrinking the world around me to nothing.

"Umm... no, I just needed some fresh air," I managed to reply, my voice barely above a whisper, my throat parched with nervousness.

"You've been training with one of Eloria's finest warriors," he remarked, his silver eyes scanning me from head to toe. "Let's see what Olive has passed on to you."

*This can't be good.*

Inhaling deeply, I ducked under the rope and entered the ring, quickly gathering my long, loose curls into a high ponytail.

"Sure," I said, as Kael watched me intently, his gaze never wavering. I started jogging kicks.in place, warming up my body.

The icy wind shrieked across the snowy peaks, drawing a vivid line between the warmth of our hidden sparring circle and the night's frosty embrace. Kael stood opposite me, his upper body bare against the cold, clad only in black trousers *and chiseled muscles*; his black wings tucked in tightly. His silver eyes gleamed with a fierce determination.

I, in my regular black combat outfit, mirrored his ready stance, my heart thundering, adrenaline surging through me. The air between us crackled with the anticipation of a duel that promised to be about more than just physical prowess. *Maybe I can talk to him after this spar.*

Breaking the charged silence, Kael's voice, deep and compelling, challenged me. "Ready for this, Ariana?"

I locked eyes with him, my nod firm. "Always, Kael."

Bathed in moonlight, the snowy expanse around us transformed into a stage for our combat ballet. He initiated with a forceful hook aimed at my jaw, which I swiftly evaded, countering with a quick kick to his ribs. He deflected my attack, countering with a jab towards my midsection. I parried his strike, answering with a direct punch towards his face. Kael's movements were liquid precision, a captivating blend of power and elegance. Sweat shimmered on his exposed skin, highlighting muscles that seemed carved for this moment. *Focus your brain on fighting, not on his muscles, Ariana.* Torrent chuckled in my head. I needed to learn a way to shut them out.

Kael smirked as I dodged another one of his kicks. "You're improving, Aria."

I chuckled, "Only because my teacher is exceptional, I meant Olive." I stuck out my tongue. *Well, this was a first. Was that a smile I saw?*

He bridged the gap between us with a swift spin, unleashing a barrage of strikes aimed at my head and body. I countered with a series of deliberate attacks, targeting his vulnerabilities. Our movements synchronized, weaving together combat and connection. As the duel's fervor escalated, his silver eyes fixed on mine.

"You've got spirit, Aria," he conceded, a spark of respect flickering in his look.

With a playful smirk, I shot back, "Spirit, and a few tricks up my sleeve."

He executed a feint with a left hook, which I accidentally anticipated. Capitalizing on my error, he landed a right uppercut, causing me to stagger backward. As he launched a roundhouse kick, I ducked and rolled beneath it, quickly rebounding to land a spinning back fist against his temple. He wobbled, his black shiny wings flared to maintain the balance as he swiftly regained it. Seizing my wrist, he twisted it, bringing me down to my knees. Leaning close, he murmured against my ear, "Nice try, Aria."

Grinning, I used my free hand to sweep his feet off the ground, bringing him down with me. I maneuvered to pin him beneath me, leaning in to whisper, "Not bad yourself, Kael."

*You have got guts now, don't you?*

He grinned, leveraging his strength to flip our positions, now pinning me beneath him. He loomed above, our breaths intertwining, as his silver eyes pierced into mine with an intensity filled with desire and admiration. Leaning closer, he whispered, "You're a quick learner, Aria," causing my breath to catch in my throat.

The chill of the air seemed to sharpen our awareness, stripping away any enchantment and infusing the moment with a palpable tension.

"Were you angry with me?" I asked against his hot breath.

It somehow felt comfortable and safe, as his weight increased when he lowered his head to my face. "Does it matter to you? If I am angry with you, Aria?"

I came here to calm down my heartbeat, which now seemed to ramp up again as his eyes pierced into mine for answers.

"Tell me, Aria. Does it matter to you?"

"No..it doesn't."

Without a word, he stood up and walked into the mansion, grabbing his shirt on the way.

***"Amulet of love, entwined and rare,<br>Wooden heart meets iron's glare.<br>Rooted strength and fiery might,<br>Bound together, day and night."***

My hand instinctively traveled to my neck, drawing Kael's attention—and soon, everyone else's—to the wooden amulet he had given me, the broken heart. A collective realization dawned upon the group.

"Where did you get this?" I asked him.

"It was a gift from my mother. It had accompanied me ever since... since she passed away," he exhaled.

"I'm sorry," I muttered, noticing the softening in his gaze as he acknowledged my sympathy.

"I had a similar amulet back home since birth. It was always around my neck, crafted from iron. It, too, was a broken heart." My hands were still on the amulet around my neck as the words came out of my mouth, trying to make sense of this.

"I might be wrong here...but I believe...we need to combine the wooden and iron amulets," Olive theorized, poring over the journal in her one hand, sipping a cup of steaming hot coffee from the other.

"You might be right," confirmed Silas, tucking a loose strand of silver hair behind his pointed ear.

"Where is your amulet?" Claude asked, placing his sword on the center table as he moved towards the big three-seater couch that accommodated his black wings.

"I… threw it away," I murmured apologetically, trying to avoid their gaze.

"You threw it away?" Scarlet exclaimed, raising an eyebrow, her tone so icy and menacing that sent shivers through me. Suddenly, the traumatic memories of that night—the yelling, the violence, the fractured leg, the bone-chilling cold—flooded back, overwhelming me to the point of speechlessness.

Scarlet repeated her question, yet her voice dwindled to a mere whisper against the overwhelming silence enveloping me. The world seemed to retreat into a hush as panic took a firm hold, constricting my chest. *This was happening more frequently now.* My breaths turned shallow and rapid, sweat beading on my forehead as the unmistakable onset of a panic attack made itself known.

I found myself crouching, desperately clutching the armrest of the nearby sofa for any semblance of stability. The sensation was akin to facing death; my heart fluttered erratically, threatening to cease at any moment. This attack surpassed any level of anxiety I had previously encountered—by far, it was the most severe. Amidst the chaos, powerful arms gathered around me gently, escorting me away from the turmoil and into the quietude of my room upstairs.

"I didn't realize I might need it again... I'm sorry," I uttered as clarity returned, but my head still pounded. I noticed Kael sitting beside my bed on the sofa. He had been my silent guardian for the past hour, steadfast in his vigil. My voice quivered as I continued, "I discarded it in the garden... I..."

Kael moved from the sofa to lie on the bed by my side. He turned his face towards me, his silver eyes boring into my soul with an intensity I was unable to handle. Then he draped an arm around my waist and the soft fabric of my tunic crumpled under his tense arm as he drew me close, which made me realize that my body was still trembling. With his free hand, he tenderly brushed my hair behind my ear and reassured me, "I understand Aria... none of this is your fault... it never was." He cradled my face, pulling me into his chest, and something eased and tightened at the same time in my stomach.

"I know," he whispered.

And we lay there, my head tucked in his chest, as his scent of wind and metal, sweat and ice intoxicated me. In that haven, time seemed to stand still until my breathing steadied, until sleep claimed us both.

"Only I can retrieve the amulet," I stated to the others' fixed stares. "It's likely still in the garden. I will just find it in a few minutes and will be out of there."

"No way you are going to that hell again," Kael snarled.

"You'll be on your own there; we can't assist if complications arise. Our kind can't enter the human realm," Silas cautioned, eyeing Kael to calm down. "You may get trapped there once more."

"And if the portal fails to reopen?" Claude added, "You will be stuck with those monsters," sharing the concern that Kael had evidently conveyed to the group.

"I'll manage..." I assured them. "We just need to locate the thinnest part of the veil where I originally crossed... though I don't recall the exact spot," I said, turning to Kael.

"And how do you know this?" Scarlet's sharp words cut through the air.

"Dragons are not only for flying, you know," I retorted back and my support system roared in agreement and the mirrors of the whole palace trembled.

"I'm aware of the location. I knew you were coming... Thorne simply got there first," Kael sighed, pinching his nose.

"At least it's a starting point," I suggested, shifting the focus.

"Are you certain you want to proceed?" Olive inquired, adjusting her long body-hugging dress as she got up. I wonder how she fights in that entrapment.

"It's worth attempting," I shrugged.

# Chapter Thirty-Three

## *Eldenhaven*

Kael and I found ourselves at the threshold of a grand residence, surrounded by a garden. The house bore an uncanny resemblance to my own, back in Eldenhaven, yet it was distinctly altered.

"This is where the barrier between realms is most fragile," he murmured, breaking the silence. The garden was barren and lacked the vibrancy of flowers and plants, replaced instead by thorny bushes. The house appeared abandoned, untouched by the warmth of life for centuries. A shiver coursed through me as we observed the dilapidated state: windows shattered, doors unhinged, a stark testament to neglect, echoing the absence of affection similar to my memories of Eldenhaven.

I pushed back the rising tide of memories, steeling my heart against the vulnerability. This wasn't the moment for my resolve to falter. The amulet for Eloria was my priority. Approaching the house, the same beautiful archway that loomed grandly above the entrance captivated me, its majestic allure undeniable. Adorned with winged creatures and angels, their gazes seemed imbued with a silent vigilance over me. A mixture of awe and familiarity propelled me forward, their sculpted expressions offering a semblance of comfort as if they understood the depths of my fear.

"Are you ready?" He asked.

I nodded. Extending my hand towards the arch as I had once before, a newfound courage within me, I felt the familiar surge of a bright light enveloping my being. Kael remained behind, a silent sentinel, as I braced myself to navigate this threshold alone, trusting in the light to guide my path forward. Nausea rose in my stomach as if I was being hurdled into a tornado. I didn't know whether it took me seconds, minutes, hours, or years to cross the portal, but the experience was devastating.

As I stepped back into Eldenhaven, the garden greeted me with its blooming flowers, yet it was eerily quiet—no one was around to tend to it, no staff, no gardeners. This solitude brought a fleeting sense of relief. I cautiously jumped behind the trees, my knee hitting the trunk of one as I tried to navigate without getting noticed. Clenching my teeth to mute the scream, I scanned my surroundings to get a sense of the situation. Moving stealthily toward the porch—the same one from where I had thrown the amulet, where I had spent a night alone, crying with a broken leg—I crouched and began my search. Although the tall windows of this house were always covered with heavy curtains to block the light from entering the house, one could never be too sure. Maybe my father was at home. I needed to find the amulet soon and get out of here.

I rummaged through the bushes, combed the grass, and dug into the soil, desperately searching for the amulet. My nails filled with brown soil, but despite my efforts, the broken iron amulet was nowhere to be found. Anxiety surged within me as I considered the possibility that it had been taken, maybe even brought inside the house, or worse, thrown away. The thought of entering the house, and risking capture, made my hands shake as I continued to dig. I took a deep breath to get a hold of my tremors. I had to focus.

Suddenly, a strong hand violently interrupted my search by grabbing my hair, pulling me up, and dragging me away from my frantic search. Pain erupted through my head.

Panic surged through me, making it hard to breathe. Those familiar red angry eyes, the ones I had longed to see filled with love, were now looking at me with a chilling glee. My father stood before me, his smile twisted with malice.

"Looking for this, Aria?" He taunted with a tone so cold that my bones rattled, holding up my iron amulet. Words choked in my throat. He had my amulet. He was not letting me get out of here. Not this time. Not again. How did he know I would come back for it?

"Didn't you miss me?" he mocked, pulling me towards the house and dragging me by the hair. Tears erupted at the corners of my eyes. I resisted, aware of the danger that awaited inside. Last time, I had escaped with a broken leg; this time, I might not escape at all. Despite my efforts, he was too strong, hauling me up to his study on the first floor. I screamed for help, but it was futile; help had never come for me, and I knew this time also, no one was going to help me.

He shoved me into the study, locking the door behind him. "You stay here, girl, I'll be back for you," he sneered through his teeth, his footsteps receding.

Alone, I collapsed, overwhelmed by despair. He was going to kill me; I was sure of it. This couldn't be my life. I had to escape. Scrambling to my feet, I searched the room for any windows. This was a place I'd never been allowed to enter before—a room without windows, sunlight, or any signs of life. I tried to unlock the door, pushing against it with all my weight, but it was immovable. My head still throbbed with pain.

The ominous sound of his footsteps approached. As he unlocked the door, each torturous moment stretched into an eternity and my heart thundered in my ears. He opened the door with deliberate slowness, his eyes alight with dark anticipation, holding a rod, its end glowing ominously red. He had heated it, just like before. *Déjà vu.* Frozen by fear, I couldn't bring myself to move.

"Let's finish what we started... weeks ago," his voice was chilling, his intentions were clear. As he stepped forward with the rod in his right hand, searing burning pain exploded across my arm as he hit me with it.

My screams echoed but were futile against the walls of my prison.

*"Mortal one!"* Zephyr's voice thundered into my brain.

*"We are coming for you, Ariana,"* Ember said, her voice panicky.

They could hear me! Hope fluttered in my broken heart. For the first time in my life, I had someone. Someone who was coming for me. To save me. To help me.

"You came for this, didn't you?" He taunted, placing the amulet on the table. "Good thing I found it first. Thought it might be useful," he sneered, as another strike delivered a blistering agony to my legs, toppling me to the ground.

"Stand up," he commanded, though I could hardly keep upright. He yanked me to my feet, pulling me by my injured arm, only to deliver another blow to my leg, the sound of a cracking bone piercing the air. He had done it again.....*broken my leg again*; the pain was blinding, excruciating, all-encompassing as I crumpled to the ground.

Dragons shrieked in my head. A kick to my stomach followed, his pointed shoe cutting sharply. Blood spilled from my mouth this time. Sweat beaded my forehead as I shivered with fear and pain. Overwhelmed by injuries, my senses dimmed to nothing—I could neither hear, move, speak, nor see, as the world narrowed to the agonizing reality of my father's assault.

*You have been adopted.* Ember's voice echoed in my mind, overwhelming me until darkness took hold. Until I fainted.

"Wake up, Ariana... wake up...," The soft, panicked but familiar voice cut through the haze of pain. Cat... Catriona's voice.

"Wake up... he's going to kill you... you have to run, get out of here," she nudged me with desperation. Surprised by her aid—I couldn't recall a time she had helped me, the last time she stood for me—my heart filled with an unexpected warmth.

Struggling against the pain, I attempted to open my swollen eyes to see her tear-streaked face pleading, "Wake up, Ariana, please."

I tried to push myself to sit up. “You’re helping me,” I whispered, surprised.

“We don’t have time for discussion. You need to leave. He can return at any moment,” terror edged in her words. She helped me get up and laced my right arm around her shoulders as we limped towards the door, each step a burst of agony through my broken leg.

“Wait..the amulet,” I remembered as we got out of the study.

“Hurry, he’s almost here,” Catriona pressed. Ignoring the pain, I ran back to grab the amulet from the study, stuffing it into my pocket. We descended the stairs, Catriona bearing much of my weight, just as *Dad* appeared at the entrance, his eyes wide in shock and anger.

“Helping each other now, are we?” he sneered, glaring at Catriona.

“Please, Dad, just let her go,” Catriona pleaded, her voice breaking.

“Oh, I will...let her go,” he mocked, moving threateningly closer.

Catriona positioned herself protectively in front of me, defiance in her voice, “I won’t let you do this anymore. Why do you hate her so much? She has done nothing wrong. You are the one who always bullied her and abused her. Let her go.”

Her words! She has never spoken those words for me before! Maybe she was afraid to speak all this time! My throat bobbed.

Our dad’s patience snapped as he struck her down with a backhand on her face. “Nooo,” I cried out, anger boiling inside me as I found the strength to stand straight. At this moment, the pain did not bother me. My broken leg did not bother me. Hitting me was something I was used to, but striking my sister. Now he had crossed a line that was unredeemable. As I stepped towards him, rage blinded me. And I saw fear in his eyes for the first time.

Suddenly, his hands started scratching the skin of his neck. He began gasping for air, collapsing under an invisible force. Terror etched across his face as he struggled to breathe air. His face and lips turned blue, seeing death in front of him. He had done enough. There was no need for a monster like him in this world. He needed to die. Right now. His eyes rolled up as his body jerked with lack of oxygen.

As he lay defeated, trembling, Catriona's pleas pierced the air, "No...please don't do this......please let him go, Ariana, he's our father. Mom and I won't survive a month without him. Please let him go, Ariana, for me!"

Anger still simmered in my veins as she continued, "I know he is your culprit. We all are your culprits. But I know you are better than this Ariana, better than him. You won't be able to live with yourself after killing him! Do not forgive us, but just let us go," she cried, holding her head in her hands.

It was then I realized—I didn't want to become what he was. I wanted to choose a different path. I wanted to become a different person. I was not his daughter.

Withdrawing my force, I allowed him to breathe again.

"No, Catriona, he is your father, not mine. I am letting him live just because of you." I strode towards the garden, my hands still trembling with the anger, the fear, the pain.

Facing the archway, with the amulet safe in my pocket, I reached out to touch it. The familiar, dazzling light wrapped around me, transporting me to where Kael was with my three guardians. Overwhelmed by pain and exhaustion, my legs gave way, and I fell into Kael's waiting arms.

"I secured the amulet," I barely whispered against his chest.

"Shh...don't speak, Aria. I've seen everything. My only regret is I couldn't be there for you, couldn't cross the portal." His silver eyes were ablaze with a shared torment and understanding.

*"We are sorry, mortal one! We will burn your father to the ground,"* Zephyr's voice thundered.

*"The only thing saving him is this portal."* He snarled.

# Chapter Thirty-Four

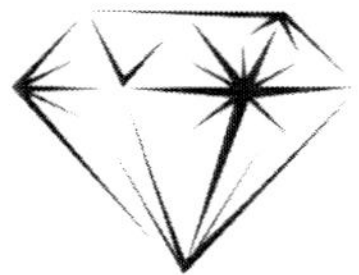

## The Faebound Keystone

*"Guarded by the elusive and wise Court of Elements, the Faebound Keystone acts as the stabilizing force for the Aetherbane. Deep within the heart of fire, the court preserves this vital part, ensuring its protection from those who would misuse its formidable magic."*

The comforting aroma of coffee and freshly baked bread woke me up the next morning. *And this time, I was not surprised that* Kael was sitting there, on the sofa by the tall glass window, holding the iron amulet and staring at it intently. I tried to sit up. "I hope it works."

He looked at me with an intense and inscrutable gaze, "How are you feeling?"

"Better," I replied, my eyes shifting to the spot on my leg that was broken by my father the previous day. Though it was fully healed with no scar or swelling, a faint ache remained—a reminder of what happened. "But there's still some pain," I added.

"You should have killed him," Kael said, his voice calm but unsettling, as if hiding storms beneath the surface. I couldn't understand why he would say that to me, why he would care about me. *Same thing I wondered about Thorne, and he betrayed me.* Maybe I knew, just didn't want to confront it. My thoughts spun, and I told myself to keep my distance; getting involved again in this could be dangerous. I could not handle another heartbreak, another betrayal. I needed to find myself. Stand up for myself before I could trust anyone else again.

I pulled out the wooden amulet around my neck, the one Kael had given me, and handed it to him. "How will we join them?"

He took the amulet from me, our fingers softly touching. I avoided his gaze, but felt an unspoken connection. He aligned the broken pieces of the heart-shaped amulets and held them together. It was a mesmerizing sight—two different pieces, yet fitting perfectly. As they joined, a bright white light emanated from the iron amulet, *the same as mine,* covering the wooden one. In seconds, the whole amulet turned into gold. Shock appeared on my face as Kael held a golden, heart-shaped mended amulet in his hand.

With time pressing against us, I urged everyone to initiate the plan to retrieve the third part of Aetherbane before it was too late. Olive has already gathered the information from the journal last Luminara, that the Faebound Keystone had been safeguarded in the Court of Elements—one of the seven courts of Eloria. This time, Silas and Scarlet also decided to join us on the mission.

"You should sit this one out Ariana," Claude advised, checking out my arm for any injuries as we moved outside in the snow. "You should take some rest," he continued, tucking his wings in against the chill of winter.

"I need to go...I can't sit here..alone with my thoughts," I scowled.

"But you have barely healed. You need to rest," he pressed.

"It's okay, Claude. She is fine. Let her come," Silas intercepted, shrugging off ice from his boots. Claude sighed, "Whatever you want, brother."

Given the dragons' unreceptiveness to that court, blasting seemed to be our only viable option to go there. In a blink of an eye, Kael, Scarlet, Silas, and I teleported from the Court of Mirrors to the snowy courtyard of the Court of Elements, with Kael holding my hand.

As we stepped into the Court of Elements, the world around us transformed into a breathtaking canvas where magic and nature merged into an exquisite symphony. Accompanied by Kael, Silas, and Scarlet, I was immediately enveloped by the courtyard's grandeur, alive with the vibrant pulse of elemental forces. A deep sense of awe enveloped us, a silent homage to the raw beauty and power unfolding before our eyes.

Ancient trees, their leaves a brilliant display of emerald green and fiery red, stood as guardians of this sacred space, crafting a gateway to a realm where the forces of nature and the whispers of magic intertwined seamlessly. Luminous vines, infused with a magical glow, draped the boughs, creating a spectacle of nature's elegance intertwined with mystical allure.

The courtyard was a sanctuary of the elements, divided into four quarters, each honoring the essence of earth, fire, water, and air. Towering stone pillars, their surfaces carved with ancient runes, marked the divisions of these elemental domains. To our left, the dance of a waterfall captured beams of sunlight, scattering them like jewels across the air, while the murmurs of water adepts practicing their craft nearby hinted at the deep connection between the adepts and the elements they wielded.

Stepping into the Fire Pavilion, the right side of the place came alive with flames that danced in mesmerizing patterns. It was like entering a magical fire show. The display captivated us. Right at the entrance, a magnificent sculpture of a phoenix caught our eyes. Crafted entirely from enchanted flames, it stood proudly, showcasing the incredible power of fire magic.

The inviting warmth emanating from the fire realm's flames lured us deeper into its core, offering a sense of comfort and enchantment reminiscent of a cozy hearth yet imbued with a mystical allure. This domain of fire whispered of hidden secrets and ancient lore, igniting our curiosity and desire to delve into its mysteries and unlock the wonders it held.

Before us, the Earth Grove revealed its majestic presence—a sanctuary of resilience and vibrant life. Majestic oaks, their foliage mirroring the rich hues of the earth, soared skyward, providing refuge to earth adepts who shared a profound bond with the land's spirit. Scattered along the grove's paths, stone effigies of legendary beings stood in silent sentinel, imbued with the sagacity of ages, their watchful eyes safeguarding the sanctity of this verdant haven.

Meanwhile, the Air Pavilion above us was caressed by a breeze that bore the sweet scent of blossoming flowers, guiding us into a realm of sublime beauty. It was like entering a realm framed by arches crafted from the softest clouds, their form so delicate they seemed woven from dreams. Within this airy sanctuary, adepts of the wind practiced their art, weaving spells that lent the air an added layer of enchantment. The gentle whisper of foliage and the distant songs of birds fused into a melody, enveloping us in an ambiance of tranquility and wonder as if stepping into a realm untethered from the mundane, where every breath carried the promise of discovery and magic.

In the center of the courtyard stood a magnificent crystal altar, commanding attention as the heart of the Court of Elements. Bathed in a mesmerizing spectrum of light, it resembled a magical kaleidoscope, with each facet reflecting the unique essence of the four elements in a display of spectacular harmony that captivated all who beheld it.

Above, symbols of the elements floated, weaving an ethereal tapestry that cast a spellbinding glow, highlighting the magical interconnectedness that flowed through the court.

The air was alive with magical creatures indigenous to Eloria; luminescent butterflies and diminutive fire sprites darted about, adding to the court's mystique. The gentle flutter of dragonfly wings and the soft chorus of elemental spirits contributed to an ambient melody, enriching the atmosphere with the essence of natural magic.

As we navigated the expanse of the court, it was clear that each adept was an embodiment of their element, their robes, and demeanor reflecting their deep connection to their powers. Water adepts moved with the grace of flowing rivers, their garments cascading like waterfalls, surrounded by orbs of water that mimicked the tranquil sounds of a stream.

Earth adepts, garbed in the vibrant green of dense forests, were adorned with flora that seemed to grow from their very being, the ground blossoming in their wake. Their presence was marked by the rich scent of fertile earth, as if they carried the essence of the forest with them.

Fire adepts, in robes of deep reds and glowing golds, were encircled by tendrils of flame that danced to their command, their presence a living testament to the fierce and untamed nature of fire, the air around them crackling with the promise of untold power.

The Court of Elements was alive, a breathtaking panorama of elemental mastery, where each adept added their distinctiveness to the collective beauty of the place. At its core, an ancient oak stood as a testament to unity and strength, its limbs adorned with glowing orbs, a beacon of tranquility amid the dynamic energy of the court. Everyone stared at us, but no one dared to stop us. I wondered why.

Venturing into the Fire Pavilion, we were immediately enveloped by the intense warmth of its embrace. Flames leaped around us in a welcoming dance, while a majestic phoenix of fire greeted us at the entrance, its wings unfurled in a display of power and beauty. Here, in the domain of fire, the raw strength and majesty of fire magic were palpably present, enveloping us in its fierce and captivating aura.

Looking at each other, we acknowledged the tough task ahead. Our mission was to find the Faebound Keystone, the third piece of the formidable weapon we aimed to build. The air thickened with magic, making everything shimmer and glow.

As we delved further into the realm of fire, the surrounding warmth grew more intense. Sculptures crafted from fire, intricate in design and seemingly alive with flames, lined our path. The play of light and shadow on the ground unveiled the depth and artistry of fire magic, a testament to its allure and power.

The corridors, lit by the soft glow of flickering flames, seemed to come alive with our presence. With every step we took, the flames leaped and twirled, their brightness intensifying and their movements quickening, as if in recognition of our journey through their domain. It was as though the spirit of fire itself was engaging with us, acknowledging our exploration of its fiery world.

The further we ventured, the more the fire world captivated us with its display. Tiny creatures made of flame, akin to living sparks, darted around us, especially towards Scarlet, their trails painting streaks of light through the air. And she responded to them. Their playful antics lent a magical quality to the atmosphere, making it feel as though we were traversing through the very heart of the element itself.

Leading the way, Kael maintained a serious composure. The intensity in his silver eyes sparkled with the fire-like brilliance outside, signaling his complete readiness for the challenges that awaited us. With his keen observational skills, Silas carefully examined our surroundings, seeking to understand the complex fire magic that surrounded us. It was like they had been here before. *Of Course, they must have been here before.* And I followed them like a toddler, feigning the attitude of a teenager.

Scarlet moved through the corridors with the grace of a cat. Each step she took was fluid and poised. The flames adorned her cat ears, which blended seamlessly with the fiery environment, reflecting the ambient light with every graceful movement. Her presence brought elegance and enigma, as though she was a manifestation of the fire's own mystique.

Upon reaching the central chamber of the Fire Pavilion, we were greeted by a surge in temperature and a dazzling intensity of light that nearly overwhelmed our senses. The room opened up to reveal its splendor, centered on a striking black pedestal. Perched atop it was the Faebound Keystone, emitting a glow that reminded us of a star far away, its allure drawing us in irresistibly. A wave of excitement washed over us at the sight, the Keystone's allure compelling us forward. Yet, a complex network of protective spells stood in our path.

With careful steps, we moved closer, mindful of the powerful enchantments that protected the Keystone. Understanding the risks, we navigated the labyrinth of magical defenses with precision. Flames surged with each step.

"We are on the brink of achieving our goal," Kael said, stepping forward. "The Fire Pavilion will challenge our right to claim the Keystone, but this keystone is necessary to defeat Renan. We can not go back without it."

*I was the only one disturbed by the amount of heat here. All others were moving forward smoothly.*

In response to Kael's words, the flames surged, their intensity amplifying, as if acknowledging the impending challenge. The magic of my dragons protects me from this burning heat too, just as it does from the cold. *I guess. But I could still feel the heat.* It was an enormous hall. It would have been easy to reach the crystal if the fire had moved out of the equation. Sweat tingled down my forehead as I lunged to escape another flame waving toward me, almost tumbling onto Silas. *Balance girl.* Although fire couldn't hurt me, but it was a reflex, I guess. *No one accepts fire with open arms.*

Amidst the spectacle of the Fire Pavilion, flames mesmerized us with their captivating dance. The Faebound Keystone, positioned on a pedestal, illuminated the scene with a brilliance reminiscent of a bursting firework. A unique connection resonated between Scarlet and the magical artifact, evident in the palpable strength of their shared magic.

However, her steps faltered midway as the flames adorning her ears started flickering. Before her, stood a tall man, strikingly handsome with yellow-sun-colored eyes and golden shoulder-length hair. He wore a golden headband, accentuating his regal appearance, and was draped in robes of royal purple and gold.

"Father," she uttered, a mix of surprise and uncertainty in her voice.

The atmosphere tensed as her father, the High Lord of the Court of Elements, regarded her with an imposing presence. His voice reverberated like thunder in the court as he addressed her, "I am not sure you are welcome here, Scar. As far as I remember, I banished you from my court."

His words carried a demeaning tone, a stark reminder of the estrangement between a father and his daughter. The realization hit me hard–she, the daughter of the High Lord, had been banished from her own home. Anger simmered within me at the injustice of it all.

"I am not here to fight you, Father," she retorted, her tone resolute despite the underlying pain.

Ever perceptive to the currents of magic, Silas discerned the tension in the air and moved toward Scarlet. With a smug grin, he positioned himself beside her, his hand in the pockets of his pants, his silver long hair loose, and deadly calm in his eyes, a silent declaration that he stood ready to confront her father if need be. The court, a backdrop to this familial confrontation, held its breath, caught in the swirling emotions of family ties strained to the breaking point.

In a commanding tone, the High Lord asserted, "I know why you're here. The Faebound Keystone can only be claimed by a powerful and deserving individual, not someone like... you."

Before Scarlet could respond, Silas interjected, bored by the High Lord's banter, "How about you step out of the way, old man, and we'll find out who the deserving one is!"

Helion, the High Lord of the Court of Elements, retorted, "Are your dogs going to do all your talking now?"

Kael, dismissing the escalating tension with a wave of his hand, intervened. "Enough of this. We're not here for personal vendettas. We're here for Eloria. If you are not going to help us against Renan, the least you can do is get out of our way. The Keystone is reacting to Scarlet's magic, and it might be the key to our mission. We can't ignore that, no matter what you believe." His tone was cool and calculated.

Though visibly conflicted, the High Lord reluctantly acknowledged Scarlet's cool, distant gaze; and the support from Silas and Kael. With a nod, he stepped aside, cautioning, "You all are delusional and you will regret this, Scar."

Rolling her eyes in sync with Silas, Scarlet reached for the Faebound Keystone. The fire responded to her touch, flames waving a path for her as if exchanging greetings. Scarlet felt an incredible surge of power while holding the keystone as if it were a part of her own body.

# Chapter Thirty-Five

# *Aetherbane*

Now that we had gathered all the parts for Aetherbane, the seemingly straightforward phase had been done. The next challenge was trapping and taking down Renan to save Eloria. It wasn't going to be a walk in a park. Even though a week had passed, we still had found no instructions in Seraphina's journal on how to assemble the Aetherbane. We have been scouring other books in the library, some in the old Fae language, which none of us could decipher.

I continued my daily training, switching between sessions with ruthless Olive and Kael. He has been busy tracking Thorne and Renan's activities, and their meeting point. I hadn't had many conversations with him outside the training ring. Maybe it was for the best; spending too much time together tended to lead to more chances of getting hurt. And right now, I couldn't afford another emotional letdown. My focus needed to be on figuring out how to deal with Renan. *And according to my dragons, unlocking my own powers.*

On some days, I practiced riding them, along with some maneuvers that Zephyr wanted me to master. Diving suddenly towards the ground and rotating one-eighty degrees to take a sharp turn was one of them. Till now he had been flying patiently because of me. *I guess.*

Today's weather was especially harsh. I told Zephyr to unbound the surrounding magic, which protected me from the cold. He protested a bit but then agreed. The cold wind biting my skin temporarily eased me from the constant thoughts whirlpooling in my head — thoughts about that day, about Catriona, whether she was okay, and the unsettling idea that our dad, a monster under a human skin might be hurting her. *I shouldn't have left here there. Alone.* I wondered if this was a pattern in our society, the father's reputation in this world was tarnished because of their actions; daughters were mistreated or thrown out of their homes. I wondered what happened when Scarlet had to endure such a disastrous situation. The way the High Lord of the Court of Elements talked to her made my stomach churn. But she handled herself pretty well.

My stomach was rumbling with hunger as I approached the dinner scene. The hall was no different, everyone casually sprawled on sofas, plates scattered across the center table. Some were mid-meal, stuffing the food into their mouth. While others had already finished. Claude shot me a welcoming smile as I entered, lifting an eyebrow. I reciprocated. Scarlet, engrossed in another serving of rice, caught my attention as I picked up my plate.

"How are you holding up?" I asked her. Scarlet's cat ears twitched, and for a moment, she sized me up with a discerning gaze. Perhaps I had mis-stepped, probing into her personal space. I had never witnessed her vulnerability, never seen her open up with anyone.

"I... am fine... I just don't want to talk about it," she replied, moving to the next bowl of grilled barbeque chicken.

Kael was lounging on the three-seater sofa, with his black dense wings sprawled throughout. He offered me a nod. I refrained from probing further, recognizing the boundaries. *And the value of my own life.*

I decided to take a walk after dinner. So much has changed in the past few days. I left Eldenhaven. Discovered a whole new world. Found magic. Met Thorne. My chest still ached at the thought of him. But on the brighter side, I bonded with three majestic dragons. My heart always filled with pride, just thinking about them. And Kael. I didn't know yet what I really felt about him.

The chilled wind nipped at my skin as I strode through the snow, the moon casting a radiant glow that blanketed the landscape. A shadow came up behind me, and suddenly my worst nightmares unfolded in front of my eyes. I had always been the one who got easily startled. Be it a sudden noise, a jump, or anything abrupt. I pivoted, and my training kicked in as I delivered a forceful punch towards the back. Soon realizing that it was Kael's face that had borne the brunt. He tried to duck but was late just by a second.

"Ouch!" he blurted, rubbing his jaw with his left hand.

"You shouldn't have sneaked up on me like that," I retorted, my heart still pounding.

"Yeah, learned my lesson," he grinned amusedly.

I turned around, tucking the loose strands of my hair behind the left ear, and resumed my walk. He effortlessly fell into step beside me, as if he glided through the snow.

"What happened with Scarlet and her father?" I asked him, feeling his warmth near me.

He remained silent for a while, looking up at the bright stars in the sky. It appeared like a beautiful painting. Taking a deep breath, he spoke, "There is this ritual at the Court of Elements known as the *Harmony Convergence*. It is celebrated every ten years. It is a sacred tradition where all elemental adepts gather to channel their magical strengths, ensuring the delicate balance between the four elements within the court."

"During this....ritual," he went on, tucking his hands in the pockets of his pants, "these adepts synchronize their powers in a harmonious display, creating a magical resonance that strengthens the bonds between these elements. It is a time of unity and celebration, marking the court's commitment to maintaining the equilibrium of magical forces. Or so they say."

He sighed as he continued, "Around 20 years ago, an unexpected event disrupted the Harmony Convergence. A surge of untamed elemental energy, sparked by an unknown source, spiraled out of control during the ritual. It transformed the serene ceremony into a chaotic storm of the four elements. A vortex of wild wind erupted, carrying the smoldering fire along with it. Because of the unbalance between these two, water flooded the ceremony, causing the earth to quake. Despite the attempts by Helium and the ministers to restore order, the magical currents spiraled into a destructive force. The very foundation of the court was threatened."

Kael stared into the darkness, his voice heavy as he continued, "That day, thousands of adepts got injured. Many died in that disaster, and the court's magic was left unstable for years due to the sudden disruption of the ceremony. The leaders of the court decided to place the blame on Scarlet, who, at that time, was responsible for maintaining the security of the ritual. Faced with the chaos, Scarlet bore the consequences of banishment. She also blamed herself for a while, for what happened. No one stood by her, not even her family, not even her own father. He turned his back on her when she needed him the most," he said through his teeth, clenching his fist.

"I was there that day when it all happened and knew something was off. I couldn't just let her take the blame for a disaster that was the result of someone else's actions. That's why I brought her here. Although I know she had never considered us family in the past 20 years, we've grown close," he smiled, but it didn't quite reach his beautiful silver eyes.

Kael had always tried to help others, including me, regardless of the circumstances. And I had always misinterpreted the situation. Misunderstood him. A kind man, who always took care of others, knows how to fight for his world, his family, even for a girl he barely knew. While all the high lords of other Courts idly sat around, doing nothing, Kael actively worked, taking care of Eloria's people, Eloria's magic, and everything in between.

My eyes welled up as I gazed at his beautiful tanned face, his black hair dancing with the wind. His eyes met mine, captivating and full of depth. He stepped closer, lifting his hand to cup my face.

"What are you thinking?" He whispered, stepping closer. His hand traveled to the nape of my neck, causing my skin to shiver.

"Nothing." I nodded.

"You can't do that every time I come near you, Aria." His breath fanned across my face.

"Do what?" My gaze traveled to his lips, which were so close right now.

"Shut me off. I am not going to hurt you." He caressed my cheek, tucking my hair behind my ear.

A tear escaped my eyes as I shut them. *I didn't want him to see me cry.*

"Aria," he whispered against my lips. My breath caught as he moved even closer, our bodies touching. And mine yearning for more. His other hand found my waist, tucking me closer to him if that was even possible. Gradually, his soft lips touched my forehead.

His kiss then moved to my eyes. First left, then right; kissing off my tears.

"Open your eyes, Aria." He purred, "Look at me."

I obliged, and his silver eyes turned dark. With something I was yearning for, too. His soft lips then traveled to my cheeks. First on the left, then on the right. Suddenly, I forgot to breathe. His hand gently tilted my chin upward, and I could feel his hot, hitched breath on my face, against my lips.

"I have waited for this moment for so long, Aria. Even before you knew I existed," he murmured against my hot breath.

I looked up at him, in his eyes. *Was it longing there?*

I raised my hand to rest it on his chest. His hard muscles moved under my touch. He was so close, incredibly close. I could feel his hard body, his everything against mine. The feathers of his wings rose as his lips touched mine. A current rippled through my body with his touch. A bright light shining as a sun engulfed us as he tilted my mouth to reach deeper. His tongue swept the floor of my mouth and my eyes rolled up. A whimper escaped me and his kiss turned from passionate to something wild. Like he needed me to breathe, to survive. Like I was water to his dry desert. Like this had been the destiny all along.

And then the memories of Thorne's betrayal came flooding back—the way he kissed me, manipulated me, used me, and made a fool out of me. I jerked back abruptly, my breath panting.

"Aria," he breathed, but I didn't turn back as I ran away from him. I couldn't say anything in this flood of conflicting emotions. Not when I also didn't understand them.

***

***"In fire's embrace, Aetherbane's grace,***
***Three parts aligned, a mystical trace.***
***Forge in flames, the elements entwined,***
***Aether's dance, destiny defined."***

Olive had finally uncovered from a second volume of Seraphina's journal that the three parts of the Aetherbane can be pieced together by subjecting it to pure fire. The challenge is now to decipher what she meant by "pure fire," because, as far as I know, no fire was impure.

"Dragon's fire," Kael sneaked up behind me. Suddenly, all my senses dulled and the whole world narrowed down to just him, despite the presence of five other people in the room. He casually sprawled on the sofa, his elegant black wings following suit, as if nothing had happened between us yesterday. His gaze remained fixed on me, something wicked flickering in them. My cheeks ignited as memories of our kiss flooded my mind.

"Okay, where do we do this? Gather all the dragons in a safe place so they don't burn the place down." I asked, looking at everyone but him.

"We can... do it on the roof of the palace," Kael suggested with a smirk.

"Is something going on with you two?" Silas coughed.

"No," I replied, but the words tumbled out too fast, unnaturally fast. I winced at the awkwardness of the situation.

"Let's focus on the work at hand." Claude cleared his throat.

We gathered at night on the roof of the palace, surrounded by solid, wide concrete walls. On which my three majestic dragons, Zephyr, Ember, and Torrent, were perched. Like the rulers of the whole world. My heart swelled with pride every time I looked at them, captivated by their beauty and enigma.

*"Let's get it over with,"* Torrent said impatiently, tapping her sharp claws on the craggy wall.

*"Can't you speak normally with our little human for once?"* Zephyr retorted with a hint of annoyance.

*"Please, put the parts of Aetherbane on the ground so that we can breathe this pure fire from our holy mouths, Ariana,"* Torrent said mockingly sweetly. I chuckled. Zephyr literally rolled his eyes.

I carefully placed the blade, hearthstone, and keystone in the middle of the ground, stepping away towards Kael. Silas, Claude, Olive, and Scarlet were on the other side of the dragons, near the stairs. Olive's eyes flickered with worry as she clenched and unclenched her hands.

"Do you think this will work?" she asked, her gaze traveling between the dragons.

"We will see, I guess," Silas replies, nodding towards the weapons lying in the center of the roof.

The three dragons swiveled their necks in a serpent-like fashion, rolled their tongues, and breathed out fire synchronously at the center.

Torrent, with a taunting tone, added, *"Hope it's not too much for your human senses."*

When the fiery display subsided, I had expected to find the assembled Aetherbane parts, but instead, a sharp, beautiful knife with a golden hilt emerged. It shone from bottom to top, barely the size of my hand. The dragons exchanged glances, their expressions a mix of pride and amusement, as if they were enjoying the perplexity on our faces.

# Chapter Thirty-Six

## *Argyros*

The intricately assembled dagger, now a potent artifact with the potential to shape the destiny of Eloria, lay under the vigilant guardianship of Kael. *It was the size of my hand.* This fact still surprised me. How can we possibly defeat the Shadowsong Maestro of the Dark Realm using only a dagger that's no larger than my hand? Kael said he had hidden the dagger in *asterixes*, which he referred to as a pocket between the different realms. There is so much that I still don't understand about this world, about magic, about everything. But I am beginning to get a hold of it.

With our preparations having reached the last phase, all that remained was waiting for the meeting between Thorne and Renan. Kael's magic told us that the hidden meeting between the two of them was set to happen in just two days. My mind buzzed with questions about how Kael managed to keep his true identity a secret from Thorne. And wasn't Renan sharp enough to feel our eyes on him? What if he already knew that we were about to attack him? And what if he, too, had a plan for us? He can't be that foolish to not keep an eye on what Eloria is planning against him!

Storms of contemplation whirled within me. Simply barging into the meeting to apprehend the formidable Lord of the Shadow Realm appeared too easy, leaving a lingering suspicion that we had not fully grasped the situation here.

*"We are forgetting about Argyros,"* Zephyr said casually.

"Argyros?" I echoed the name as I sat on the sofa in my room. My heart racing with confusion.

*"Yes, he is the double-headed dragon of Renan. Stories said that he was the most powerful one to ever walk the earth,"* Zephyr said in a bored tone.

*"Was he? And you are telling us this now?"* my eyebrows shot up, hands curled by my side as if Zephyr was standing in front of me.

*"Relax...he wished...he was, mortal one..."* Zephyr chuckled as if hadn't just bombarded me with a piece of new information.

My mind raced, contemplating the implication of Argyros being there with Renan. I needed to share this with everyone. The prospect of facing a dragon with two heads, let alone one as formidable as Argyros, dawned upon me with a weight that threatened to overwhelm me.

*"We three will be going with you...just to remind you,"* Torrent's resolute voice echoed, cutting through the air. I am pretty sure she just rolled her eyes.

*"Yes I did,"* she remarked.

*"Good to know,"* I replied as I ran down the stairs to the study where everyone was gathered.

*"Don't worry, Ariana. We three heads can handle a two-headed little dragon,"* Ember reassured in her motherly tone, offering a comforting presence that contrasted with my own.

*"Don't be so cheesy now,"* Torrent taunted.

And I scowled on my way as if they could see me.

*Umbral Confluence* had been decided as the meeting point between Renan and Thorne, according to Kael. Nestled at the juncture of Eloria and the Shadow Realm, this territory contained both the beauty of Eloria and the dreadful eerie of the Shadow Realm at the same time. Like day and night existed together there, fighting for each other's existence.

"We will cloak ourselves; otherwise, he will sense us coming," Silas said with gravity, his gaze penetrating the room.

Scarlet and Claude nodded. Kael then shifted the focus to tactical aspects.

"We will be attacking from three different points," he asserted, the weight of his gaze falling upon each of us. "He won't be able to handle all of us together."

"And what will we do about Renan's dragon?" Claude almost choked on his evening dose of whiskey, as I continued, "Argyros!"

"Renan has a dragon too!" Olive exclaimed, her eyebrows shooting up.

"Umm...yes. Zephyr said Argyros is double-headed and the most powerful dragon in history," I blurted, moving to the sofa beside the one where Kael was sitting.

*"Not the most powerful one!"* Zephyr thundered, and the mirrors rattled.

"And when was this thundering dragon of yours going to tell us this? Once we were in front of this double-headed beast?" Scarlet bellowed.

*"You needn't worry about Argyros. Tell your cat that we will handle him,"* Torrent shot back. I wish Scarlet could hear it herself. That will result in a fun banter.

"I knew he had a dragon, but I have never seen him. Guess we will have the pleasure together," Kael mocked. My jaw dropped to the floor.

"You knew about it too! You should have told us beforehand, brother! This is not cool!" Claude shot back.

"Calm down. It is not like you are standing in front of Argyros right now. Dragons will handle their matter," Kael grumbled.

Olive huffed audibly, as she sprawled on the same sofa as Kael.

Then we started planning strategies to penetrate the illusion that Renan would cause. How to reach Umbral Confluence and capture him. Amidst this turmoil of scheme and plotting, a thought floated through my mind - these people here, bantering and bickering with each other, were the closest thing to a family I had ever had.

My own relationships, which I once thought were anchored in blood, proved to be hollow and devoid of genuine connection. Yet, these people, whom I'd come to know in mere weeks, had somehow become important to me. My eyes teared up at the thought that the day after tomorrow might be the last one for any of us.

"We will leave the day after tomorrow, early morning," Kael's voice broke through my rumination, bringing me back to the present. His keen perception seemed to discern the currents of my thoughts, connecting us with an unspoken understanding. As if he could sense my discomfort, my unease.

The discussions must have stretched on for hours, as everyone was crying by the time the meeting was over.

"I need a flight." Claude had said and immediately vanished.

I had developed a habit of strolling through the snowy garden after sunset. It was the biting cold and encompassing darkness here that offered a peculiar comfort. My breath formed fleeting imprints in the air, though the magic in the atmosphere kept me from feeling too cold.

As I walked, a sudden awareness of a presence behind me sent a shiver down my spine. But now I was getting used to it. Kael tended to sneak up on me, a habit that inclined to quicken my heartbeat. A subtle smile played on my lips as I turned around to offer a retort.

My eyes widened with terror. It was him, the hooded figure from that ominous night with Thorne. His face, both beautiful and chilling, boasted dark, ruthless eyes. A sinister smile crept across his lips as he uttered, "Hello, Ariana."

Before I could react or grasp any understanding of the situation, Zephyr's voice echoed, "*Mortal one, I am coming.*"

But it was too late. Everything around me plunged into an eerie, impenetrable blackness as Renan grabbed my hand and pulled me towards him.

I struggled to open my eyes, a throbbing pain pulsating through my head. I tried to move my arms and felt a searing pain breaking through my wrists. Cold iron encircled my wrists, a relentless grip that left no room for movement. The clink of chains echoed with each feeble attempt to shift. A shiver crawled up my spine as I strained to pierce the overwhelming darkness, each breath catching in my throat. Shadows danced at the edge of my vision, teasing with the presence of unseen watchers. Then, slicing through the silence, a voice I knew all too well whispered from the depths, sending ripples of unease through the air.

"Ariana...Ariana...Are you okay, Ariana?" Thorne's whisper floated across the space, a fragile thread of concern. Squinting through the dim light, I caught sight of him. Chains were binding him as they did me. Wounds and bruises painted his frame, blood seeping from a gash on his head. An icy wave of shock washed over me, rooting me in place as the reality of his battered state sank in.

"Thorne?" I tried to speak, but he nodded, signaling me to keep quiet. His torn clothes showed the brutality he had suffered as if he had been struck by innumerable lashes.

"Hello Ariana, finally you're awake!" A heavy voice said in a mocking tone through the room. A chill ran through my bones. I strained my eyes and saw him enter—the same hooded-shadowy figure. His eyes were black voids, absorbing all the light. Jet-black hair framed his face, adding to the darkness that seemed to cling to him. His skin was unnaturally pale, almost translucent, as if he were part of the shadows.

An unsettling grace marked his movements—smooth, yet disturbingly calculated. Cloaked in otherworldly attire of long black robes, he effortlessly melded with the shadows, as if darkness itself obeyed his commands. His presence was palpable, each step carrying an unspoken intent, rendering the atmosphere oppressive.

In that dimly lit space, he embodied a fusion of haunting beauty and indescribable darkness, making my skin crawl. I tried to maintain my composure, standing still as he approached me. The architecture and the interiors mirrored what I knew, but now, everything was darker, shrouded in a vicious air.

"I thought I should show you what the real Court of Shadows looked like," he taunted. Confusion took hold of me! My eyes widened with terror.

"It's not that hard to believe, is it? After all, it's the court of shadows! You can't expect flowers and gardens to boom here now, can you?" He laughed.

I felt like a fool—a hopeless one. Did Thorne's illusions have any limits? Was he going to stop anywhere? Or was I going to be stuck here for the rest of my life? Everything he told me and showed me was an illusion! Was Ivy even real? Or was she also a part of his theatrics?

Renan advanced, taunting me, "Oh, don't be so hard on yourself, little girl! You couldn't have stood a chance against a High Lord, could you?"

My blood simmered with rage.

"You couldn't even stand in front of your pathetic parents, in front of your sister. You ran behind them like a little pup, craving their attention, willing to do anything for their approval," he went on, one side of his lips curling up. "How could you have known this, Aria? Don't beat yourself up for your slow-witted brain."

His words struck a painful chord of truth. I had been nothing more than a naïve child, desperate for my parents' love, oblivious to the fact that they hated my every single breath. Renan circled me slowly, his presence instigating a visceral terror.

"Don't you dare touch her, Renan!" Thorne's voice erupted from the hall's shadowy corner, fierce and defiant.

Renan's snarl cut through the tension, his words dripping with contempt. "You... how about you just shut up?" He pointed towards Thorne. In response, Thorne's chest recoiled as if struck by an unseen hunter, a silent scream etched on his face. The hall echoed with his pain.

"I gave you one thing to do. One thing! And you," his voice rose, seething, "couldn't even manage that, you impotent imbecile!" Another loud strike and Thorne stumbled forward, agony written across his features. His arms tearing through the shackles.

Renan turned his disdainful gaze towards me, waving dismissively. "You couldn't get this speck of dirt to open a portal?" His contempt was palpable, filling the space between us with icy disdain.

He leaned close, his breath cold against my ear, his voice an evil whisper. "You have no worth, Ariana," he hissed.

"You are as useless as a rotten fruit fallen from a tree." The words hung heavy in the air, a cruel judgment casting shadows in my heart deeper than those around us.

His words echoed with a sinister truth, seeping into the cracks of my fragile self-worth. I had forgiven Thorne. I tolerated being taken for granted, deceived, and beaten. He was right—I held no value. Even now, surrounded by a group attempting grander things, I fed on their efforts.

"Yes, they just sympathize with you, little Aria! You thought Kael would love you? Wouldn't you? You thought you two have some kind of connection," Renan purred with a bitter laugh, and my head snapped towards him, tears streaming down.

"He's merely taking pity on a homeless, worthless, rotten fruit," he said with a disturbing satisfaction on his face.

I wanted to reject his words, but somehow their truth stung. "You think they'll come for you, little Aria?" he asked playfully, expecting a response, yet words evaded me.

"No one will come to save you; you will die here, today, alone!" He chuckled as he left the hall, his words still hanging in the air. The chilling reality sank in—he was right. No one ever came to save me; I had always been alone. Maybe he was right. Maybe I was rotten from the inside. That's why everyone hated me. That's why I never found love, neither in my family nor in anyone else. Always and forever alone. Maybe he was right.

Exhaustion weighed heavily on me as the day wore on, Renan's absence stretching into an oppressive silence. Thorne remained in his agonizing state, the perpetual darkness offering no respite, no air as if life itself had abandoned this desolate place. Maybe today would be the end, a release from the relentless torments and repeated betrayals.

My heart thundered with fear but deflated with lost hope as every moment passed. As despair clawed at my resolve, my attention was abruptly drawn to the entrance. The floor thundered as silver menacing claws stepped into the hall, disrupting the darkness. As my eyes moved upward, a colossal silver dragon appeared, unveiling terror in my bones.

"Shit!" Thorne rumbled.

*Argyros! He was Argyros!* His two heads were adorned with blood-red and vacant, unnerving eyes that emanated an aura of fear and chaos. His pupils had faded with age. The noble cast of its face, high eyes, and sweeping beard-like chin spikes added an air of regality. A spiny frill had risen high over its head, fading from silver to purple at the edge. The metallic scales gleamed with an eerie luminescence, casting an unsettling glow in the dimness.

His immense stature had cast a foreboding shadow, whose movements resonated like thunder. The synchronized motion of both heads created an unsettling dance, a macabre harmony that amplified the dragon's terrifying demeanor. His both wings bore two talons each. *He was a menace.* The scales, although shiny, emitted an unnatural glow that intensified its horrifying appearance. He roared, and the sound reverberated with a haunting blend of despair and impending doom.

I didn't understand why Zephyr was so casual about him. *I was going to kill Zephyr.* This was no ordinary dragon. He was a manifestation of my ancient fears and lingering darkness.

He approached me. Each step imprinted the cold floor with his footprints, tracing a path ominously aimed at me. The heavy air around us thickened with dread as Argyros, the colossal silver dragon, materialized from the shadows. Zephyr did tell me, but nothing could have prepared me for this type of encounter. My legs trembled with fear, though I fought to maintain a straight face.

Beside him, Renan stood like an ever-elegant dark silhouette. His voice was a stiff wind that carried a simple, chilling introduction.

"Meet Argyros," he said. His presence next to the beast only heightened the sense of unease, as if he drew a perverse joy from the fear Argyros inspired.

The beast sized me up like a predator sizing up its prey. Our eyes locked, and a shiver of fear raced through me. I wanted to run. But running from here wasn't going to save me. I needed my dragons. Argyros tilted its head slightly, his tongue flickering out in anticipation of the havoc he was about to wreak. My breath hitched. Time seemed to pause, every sense heightened in the dreadful wait.

Then, with a slow, deliberate grace, Argyros opened his mouth wide, and a torrent of fire burst forth. My heart skipped, adrenaline surged, expecting the blaze to engulf me. Yet the flames struck harmlessly close, a mere whisper away.

"Aww...he is playing with you. Isn't he a beauty?," Renan's mused tone ignited a spark of anger within me. Again, the dragon directed its fiery play to my other side. *Just kill me already.* Heat scorched my sides and my shackles burned my wrists. Wave after wave, the dragon toyed, turning the hall into a furnace. Each burst of flame was a cruel game in his eyes.

Thirst ravaged my throat. Dehydration muddled my senses. Drained my strength. Argyros's relentless fire attacks merged into an endless onslaught, erasing my all attempts to keep count. The hall transformed into a furnace, baking the air until it scorched my skin and leeched away my resolve. Each fiery breath from that menacing dragon further dismantled my defenses, layer by layer, as my skin burned with heat.

The edges of my vision darkened, surrendering to the unbearable intensity of the heat. My grip on consciousness weakened. The world around me went black.

# Chapter Thirty-Seven

## *Illusion or Reality?*

Slowly, I regained consciousness as a pair of powerful hands caressed my cheeks. A sensation I somehow recognized but was too tired, too exhausted to fully comprehend. Sweat dripped persistently from every inch of my body, the oppressive heat roasting my skin inside out.

"Wake up, Aria," the voice insisted again, now tinged with urgency. "We have to get out of here," he added. It was in that moment of groggy awareness that I realized he had come for me—Kael had come to save me.

Hope cautiously fluttered in my heart as I tried to pry open my tearing eyes. "You're here for me?" My voice cracked. He gently kissed my forehead, his touch conveying a mixture of reassurance and determination.

"I will always come for you, Aria. No matter where you are, no matter how difficult it gets, no matter how many illusions come between us, I will always come for you." A flood of tears started rolling down my eyes. No one had ever done this for me. Despite the shackles, in that moment, I felt lighter, as if I could live again.

"We will live together, Aria," he said gently, "and I never let anyone touch you again. I will always protect you." His eyes, filled with love and care, continued to radiate a determined warmth, something I always yearned to see, something I never found anywhere else.

But a gentle smirk played on his face as he stepped back. My face missing his touch. Something changed in his eyes as he said, "Because you cannot protect yourself,
Aria."

His tone shifted as he continued, "Because you are so weak that you can't even speak for yourself. You are broken."

"Kael," I croaked. But the care and love I saw a moment ago in his face was now transformed into something else, something darker.

"You are a rotten fruit, Aria. You do not deserve to live," he crooned.

*"He is not real, mortal one. Look through the illusions; he would never talk this way to you,"* Zephyr's voice thundered in my brain. Zephyr was here! He must be nearby. That's the only explanation for how he could talk to me. But what if this was another illusion, too? What if Renan is talking as Zephyr?

Anger simmered in my eyes as confusion clouded my mind. I shouted, attempting to force Renan out of my brain. My scream reverberated so violently that the windows of the hall rattled. Amidst the chaos, I saw Renan standing there, a wicked smile playing on his lips. "It is so fun to see you break, to see your world fall apart, Ariana," he laughed.

"What the hell do you want from me? Why are you doing this to me?" I cried despite my efforts not to. My voice echoed through the hall, causing even Thorne to wince in the corner.

"Oh, I don't want anything from you. I just want to make you suffer...make you cry.....make you beg for mercy before I slowly kill you myself," hate gleamed in his eyes.

A hunter lashed at my back so brutally that pain roared through my joints. "Your ancestor, the Last Luminara, shut me into this shadow realm, banished me here, ruined all my plans... and I need you to pay for it," he hissed. With another strike of the leather belt on my back, the pain became unbearable. The relentless assault continued. Each blow was a reminder of my impending fate. I had lost count of the lashes, but one thing was certain–there was no escape from this torment. I
was going to die a brutal death that day.

Suddenly, a massive explosion crumbled the walls of the hall. As they shattered into concrete, dust and darkness enveloped everything. Through the haze, I saw my three mighty dragons roaring in rage. And suddenly my heart flickered with hope! They came for me! My dragons!

Zephyr, Ember, and Torrent stormed, and the entire palace of the Court of Shadows crumbled beneath their feet. Their voices caused thunder in my bones. I knew this was not an illusion. Tears flowed from my eyes, finally meeting the smile on my lips. Despite the pain, despite the torture, I was at peace at this moment. I knew I was not alone; I was loved. I had a family that cared for me, one that would come to save me. I didn't care if I died today; at least I would die in peace.

*"You will not die today, mortal one,"* Zephyr's voice thundered in my brain, and Torrent grunted her agreement. *Hope.*

Renan attempted to get up and summoned Argyros, *the menacing dragon.* The floor vibrated with each step, Argyros fixing one head on me and the other on my dragons, deciding which one to attack first.

*"We will take care of him,"* Ember's motherly reminder comforted me. The three dragons lunged and jumped on Argyros. Their sound shrieked through the dusty air. Torrent snapped at his one neck and Ember's jaws clutched on his massive tail. Zephyr unleashed his fiery breath on his other head. Argyros howled in pain, but the fire didn't seem to bother him. He retaliated by stepping back and biting Torrent's black, scaly neck. Torrent's grip on his other neck loosened as she cried in pain. Fear gripped me; he might snap her neck in half.

"No!" I shouted.

Zephyr plunged his teeth into Argyros' belly. He swiveled his head at an unnatural angle and took out a chunk of scales from Zephyr's side. On the other side of the shattered concrete, Renan gathered his shadows, creating a colossal dragon almost the size of Zephyr. This one was bigger than Argyros. Black holes shimmered in his head in the name of eyes.

He unleashed it on them, and it plunged its teeth into Ember's neck, resulting in a painful scream and a gash of blood leaking from her neck. My gaze went to the shadows of people appearing in the haze. No. Not shadows, but my friends. I tried to snatch my hands from the shackles. I needed to help them, too.

Silas jumped forward, attacking Renan with his sword in his right hand. Renan blocked with his shadow sword and punched Silas so hard that he was thrown to the opposite side of the hall. Scarlet jumped with amazing flexibility, her sharp claws ready to attack. Renan screeched in pain as one of her claws tore through his chest. He staggered backward, his eyes red with anger. Scarlet landed another scratch on his face before he gave her a backhand whip. She got up as soon as she hit the floor. With the stealth of a cat. And getting ready to launch another strike.

On the other side, Claude simultaneously launched his attacks on Renan. His sword, with a bronze hilt, lacerated through Renan's back. Despite so many hits, there was hardly any blood on him. Injuries were barely available on his pale skin. He howled back as he shoved Claude with his shadows. Claude fell painfully in between the dragons, barely escaping their fire. His head hit the floor with a thump.

"Remove my chains. I can help you!" Thorne shouted.

"You have done enough," Kael sneered as he stumbled to my side, his breath catching. Sweat beading his forehead. He cupped my face with his right hand as he opened the shackles with his left hand. *Magic.* I almost collapsed, unable to hold my weight, and he caught me. His wings flared. I saw a glint of the golden dagger in his pocket. *The Aetherbane.*

"You are really here," my voice cracked.

"I am sorry it took so long," he panted, his eyes scanning my body, inspecting the injuries. Scarlet shouted in the background as Renan stabbed her with his shadow sword. Olive held Renan's breath, trying to choke him, but he stepped towards them menacingly.

Amid this chaos, Silas got up and charged at Renan again with silver hair plastered on his head with sweat, and swinging his sword with precision. Claude struggled to stand straight. His black elegant wings were now covered in dust. He and Scarlet coordinated their attacks, creating a diversion.

Torrent, despite the injury, used her wings to create a gust of wind, disrupting the shadow dragon Renan had summoned. Ember lunged at Argyros, distracting him from Torrent. Her neck was still bleeding. *No! She was gonna die!* Zephyr released another burst of fire, aiming at Argyros's underbelly. The hall resounded with roars, clashes, and the crackling sound of fire.

As the battle intensified, the dark and oppressive atmosphere in the hall seemed to push against us. Renan, infuriated by the relentless assault, conjured shadowy tendrils that lashed out towards the group.

"You need to go. Help them. I am fine," I requested Kael, my throat choking with smoke.

"Are you sure?" his breath panted. Eyes wary with fear. I knew he wanted to go. To help his family.

"Yes. Please. They really need you," I managed to say.

Silas, quick on his feet, dodged the shadows and counterattacked. Scarlet, with her agility, maneuvered through the dark tendrils, attempting to reach Renan. Renan tightened his grip on the shadows.

Kael ran down the dais. His wings almost glided him through the air. With a flick of his hand, he shoved Renan behind, disrupting his shadows. Taking the chance, he started weaving the protective barriers with his magic, shielding us from the shadowy onslaught. A blue-colored shield appeared around us. Renan, instantly on his feet, tried to run through the shield. His red eyes bulging with anger.

Dragons coordinated their attacks, each movement calculated and synchronized. Ember was struggling. Losing her height, she was tumbling down to the ground again and again.

Amid the chaos, Renan's shadow dragon dissipated under the combined force of the dragons' assault. All the muscles of Kael's body bulged as he tried to hold the shields in place. Silas, exiting the shield, ran towards Renan. He landed a decisive blow on Renan's face, forcing him to stagger backward. Scarlet seized the opportunity to deliver a powerful strike, and Renan howled in pain.

With the tide turned in our favor, Kael directed his attention to Argyros. Using his magic, he created a leash to grab hold of the dragon. It encircled around the left neck of Argyros, making it difficult for him to focus on any one target. Ember and Torrent continued their relentless assault on the double-headed menace.

Scarlet shouted in the back as Renan stabbed her again with his shadow sword. Olive attempted to hold Renan back, but he stepped towards her, getting closer. His shadows wrapped around her throat, constricting her neck. He hung her in the air, her feet desperately searching for the ground as her eyes started to bulge out.

Claude swung his sword at Renan, but it passed through him this time as if he were a mere illusion. No one was able to touch him. He ensnared everyone with his shadows, tightening the grip on their throats as if strangling them, their feet struggling to find solid ground.

Helplessness was trying to bud in the eyes of my friends. Zephyr, Ember, and Torrent continue their attacks on Argyros, but their efforts seem futile against the formidable dragon. Kael channeled his magic from the ground. His hands trembled with the effort to hold off Renan.

Silas attempted to break free from the shadows' grasp. He threw his sword towards Renan, but the blade again passed through him like air. Frustration and desperation echoed in Silas's eyes as he struggled against the unseen force.

Ember lay sprawled on the ground, blood seeping profusely from her wounds, rendering her unable to move. Zephyr, relentless, soared through the air, engaged in a fierce aerial battle with the shadow dragon conjured by Renan.

Meanwhile, Torrent thrust her claws into the wound on Argyros's belly, tearing through the flesh. Argyros bellowed in agony. Then she clawed all till the back of his wound, stretching it further. She clamped her jaws around one of his heads, and with a savage twist, she severed it from his massive frame. Argyros convulsed in pain, blood cascading from the severed neck.

"NO!" Renan's enraged shout reverberated through the hall, the sheer force rattling my every bone. In an instant, he directed his dreadful gaze towards Scarlet, who was launching a punch across his face. With a sinister snap, he twisted her neck at an unnatural angle. Scarlet crumpled to the floor, lifeless, her eyes vacant and devoid of light. Scarlet was dead.

*Scarlet was dead.*

# Chapter Thirty-Eight

## *The End?*

"No..." Silas's voice had cracked, the words barely escaping his strangled throat. His hands flailed, desperate to break free from Shadows' relentless grip. The battlefield had transformed into a canvas of agony, every inch telling tales of despair and loss.

Scarlet's lifeless body lay sprawled across the blood-stained concrete, a stark contrast to the chaos that surrounded her. Ember, with wounds that seeped, bore the burden of profound pain. The others found themselves ensnared in the vice-like grip of Renan's suffocating shadows, unable to break free from their dark clutches.

Meanwhile, Zephyr fought in a fierce struggle against the formidable shadow dragon. With every ounce of his being, he fought to maintain his ground, his muscles screaming and his breaths coming in short, ragged gasps. The surrounding air crackled with raw energy.

"No...no...no..!" The plea had echoed in Silas's mind.

"This can't be it. We all can't die like this," my brain rambled. "I need to do something."

"Renan!" Kael shouted, running towards him. Raw energy crackled at his fingertips. His eyes were aglow with a silver fire, as his hands traced arcs in the air, weaving an invisible, complex cage that sought to trap Renan in it. This cage, unseen yet palpable, began to constrict him.

It mercilessly squeezed the air from his lungs. His pale face started to get a bluish hue as he tried to break the invisible walls. His breath became labored as he struggled. The air thinned into nothingness, and with it, Renan's hope of escape diminished. His body convulsed with hypoxia.

Olive panted heavily as she tried to summon her power. Hanging in the air, ensnared by Renan's shadows, she lifted her arms. An unseen but palpable energy filled the air as she constricted Renan's airway further. His eyes started to bulge out with terror as he collapsed to the floor, weakened and convulsing from the lack of air.

Torrent sunk her claws into the tail of Argyros. The once mighty double-headed dragon now writhed in pain. The shadow dragon, a creation of Renan's dark artistry, dissipated into nothingness as its shadows crumbled away. Killing Renan would kill the shadow dragon, too. That was the only way to end this.

Cringing with pain, I tried to stand. My skin felt as if it was tearing itself. Burning blisters appeared on my hand. My gaze went to the shining Aetherbane, dangling from Kael's pocket. This was the only way to kill him.

Before I could do anything, Kael's energy holding the Renan in his boundaries shattered. Renan got up, stumbling forward. His eyes were ablaze with a furious red anger. An unsettling surge of power enveloped him. Shadows crackled with lightning as he stepped forward, his breath panting. Dark shadows and lightning illuminated his entire body. It was like seeing the death itself.

He extended his shadows to every corner of the battleground, conjuring another colossal dragon, a grotesque manifestation of darkness and malice. Its creation was a testament to Renan's new-found strength. He was drawing energy from the ground too! He was drawing energy from Eloria as if he was going to deplete this place.

Kael stormed towards Renan, but with a mere gesture, Renan halted Kael in his tracks. A sinister force constricted around Kael, an invisible grip that choked the life out of him with no physical touch. Renan's voice, laced with disdain, pierced through the air as he addressed Kael's attempt to fight back.

"You thought you could orchestrate my demise without my knowledge," Renan sneered through his teeth. "Did you forget that I am the embodiment of the shadows?"

He raised his arms as he continued, "I lurk in every corner, every shadow answers to me. I hear every whispered plan, I see every hidden intention. I witnessed the High Lord succumb to love for this mere human girl," he said, casting a disgusted look at Thorne, then fixing his eyes upon me.

"I also observed as you," he added, his tone dripping with contempt, "fell into the pitiful abyss of affection for her." He belittled Kael as he choked.

"Thorne betrayed me, sabotaged my plan for this rotten human, and now you all will pay the price for this!" He barked.

Kael, his eyes bulging with the strain and face contorted in a hue of red, struggled against the unseen force that bound him. Renan was going to kill him. No! I couldn't let that happen. Kael couldn't die!

Rage surged through my veins. Scarlet was dead. I would not let Kael die! He was the only person in this whole world who ever showed affection to me.

*You are a rotten fruit.* Renan's voice echoed in my brain. No, I would not let this happen again. I would not let him mess with my mind again. Heat burned in my body as light, bright as day, emerged from my body. My face, my hair, and my body were glowing. And I was not tired anymore. I was not exhausted. There were no blisters now. It was like I was born again. I was not Ariana anymore.

Shadows convulsed and writhed in the light. Renan tried to regain control of them as they vanished. Light divulging them all. My light. The Luminara Light.

I stepped forward, my feet barely touching the ground. It was as if I was floating. Never in my life have I felt this powerful, this strong. Like I didn't need anything else. Anyone else. The once-daunting shadow dragons now dissipated into nothingness, and my friends lay on the ground, their forms bathed in the soothing glow. Silas convulsed with the lack of air. Olive shuffled towards him as she tried to help him.

I was not Ariana at this moment. I was not human at this moment. I was the whole universe, and the whole universe was I. There were no scares. No injuries. No betrayals. I was the Luminara herself.

My hand reached for Aetherbane in Kael's pocket. It's light shimmering as my own. As it was a part of me. As it was reacting to my emotions. Renan stuttered as I closed the distance, "This can not be true. I killed you myself. I killed you years ago, Sera!"

His face lost all color as he realized who was standing in front of him. His hands trembled.

"You can not kill me, you fool! I am not Ariana. I am not Seraphina. I am the Luminara herself. Your pathetic existence does not have that kind of power. You have done enough. You have been leeching on the magic of this world for far too long. This needs to end now." My voice pulsated from all the corners, all at once.

I angled the blade and plunged it into his heart. A gush of blood flowed from the wound.

"Nothing can save you now, Shadow Maestro," a small smile tugged at my lips and my energy vanished. My light vanished. All the burns and blisters came back again.

In his desperate attempt to retaliate, Renan ruthlessly seized my hair and sliced my throat with a knife concealed in his attire. "I might not survive, but I will not let you live too, Sera!" He barked, his lifeless body falling to the ground.

"Ariana...!" Thorne shouted from somewhere.

Kael caught me in his arms. Blood staining his clothes along with mine.

"I will not let you die, Aria! We were supposed to be together! Forever!" his voice cracked. The world around me dissolved into chaos, liquid warmth gushing down my neck.

Yet, in that final, agonizing moment, surrounded by the cacophony of voices, I found a sense of peace in the visceral pain of my own end.

# Epilogue

"SHE KILLED HIM," RENAN said, bowing to Ariana, on his knee; standing before the dais.

Her eyes snapped to him, twisting the neck of a human who was struggling in her grip. She thundered, "That little piece of shit had the guts to kill our only alliance to that world."

Throwing the limp body on the ground, she stepped down the stairs. "We need to formulate a different plan this time," she said, wiping the human's blood from her mouth with the back of her hand.

# Elorian series

*This was not the end, my fellow readers!*

*This was just the beginning of an epic series!*

*Click on the link below to subscribe to my newsletter and be the first to know what happens to Ariana!*

https://dashboard.mailerlite.com/forms/823488/114145860491675188/share(Newsletter)
https://linktr.ee/travellingdragon(Linktree)
http://www.travellingdragon.com(Website)

# Dedications

## To my one and only

:)

When it comes to dedicating this to someone, the only person I can think of really is my husband, Apoorv Yadav. I don't even know where to start being grateful to have such an amazing person as my life partner.

Not only does he tolerate all my little shenanigans, but has also supported me through the toughest decision of my life, that is, quitting our psychiatry practice, making my clinic my writing den; and following my love for writing. He gave me the strength to realize this was possible.

Honestly, without him, you would have never met the characters that sprang from my imagination. Ariana, Thorne, Kael, and the three majestic dragons would have remained mere figments of my imagination, unseen and unknown to the world.

So thank you, my dear husband, the love of my life! Thank you for being you, Apoorv, and for making my life infinitely better. Your love and support are the wind beneath my wings, propelling me forward toward my dreams, and for that, I am forever grateful. I couldn't ask for a better life!

Despite all my tantrums, my amazing sister Aashmeen Kanwar helped me edit this book. I can't thank you enough, really!

I love you so much, siso!

# About the Author

Meet Gemma A. Summers, a heart-warming soul with a story that's both inspiring and relatable. Gemma stepped into the world of medical practice, joining hands with her equally passionate husband, Apoorv Yadav, at their psychiatry clinic.

This journey wasn't just a professional choice; it was a legacy, a continuation of the path her doctor's parents had dreamt for her. Since 2011, Gemma has been on this medical voyage, leading her to establish her own mental health wellness center in 2020 alongside Apoorv.

But here's the twist—despite her achievements, Gemma found herself grappling with happiness. Behind her professional facade, she battled with depression, relying on antidepressants to get through her days. It wasn't easy. She initially thought it was all in her head, that somehow she was the problem. But the truth dawned on her eventually—it wasn't her mind; it was her career. Psychiatry, for all its nobility and depth, just wasn't her calling.

The turning point came during a heart-to-heart with Apoorv, who asked her a simple yet profound question: "If not psychiatry, then what?" This question opened the floodgates to a sea of possibilities, but one passion stood out—writing. Gemma found solace in words, a stark contrast to the medical world she was part of. Writing wasn't just a hobby; it was her newfound purpose, her beacon of hope.

Today, we celebrate Gemma's courage and resilience as we dive into her first book. But let me tell you, this is just the tip of the iceberg. Gemma's mind is a treasure trove of stories, and this book is merely the beginning of an extraordinary series that's sure to captivate your heart. So, buckle up and get ready for a journey through Gemma's imagination. Trust me, this adventure is far from over!

*Stay tuned for more books in this series*

*:)*

https://linktr.ee/travellingdragon

Printed by BoD™ in Norderstedt, Germany

functions represented by $V$, would be equal to the number of the bodies, one for each. In this case, if there were given a value of $V$ for each body, together with $V'$ belonging to the exterior space; and moreover, if these functions satisfied to the above mentioned conditions, it would always be possible to determine the density on the surface of each body, so as to produce these values as potential functions, and there would be but one density, viz. that given by

$$0 = 4\pi\rho + \frac{\overline{dV}}{dw} + \frac{\overline{dV'}}{dw'} \qquad (4'),$$

which could do so: $\rho$, $\frac{\overline{dV}}{dw}$ and $\frac{\overline{dV'}}{dw'}$ belonging to a point on the surface of any of these bodies.

(5.) From what has been before established (art. 3), it is easy to prove, that when the value of the potential function $\overline{V}$ is given on any closed surface, there is but one function which can satisfy at the same time the equation

$$0 = \delta V,$$

and the condition, that $V$ shall have no singular values within this surface. For the equation (3) art. 3, becomes by supposing $\delta U = 0$,

$$\int d\sigma \overline{U} \frac{\overline{dV}}{dw} = \int d\sigma \overline{V} \frac{\overline{dU}}{dw} - 4\pi V'.$$

In this equation, $U$ is supposed to have only one singular value within the surface, viz. at the point $p'$, and, infinitely near to this point, to be sensibly equal to $\frac{1}{r}$; $r$ being the distance from $p'$. If now we had a value of $U$, which, besides satisfying the above written conditions, was equal to zero at the surface itself, we should have $\overline{U} = 0$, and this equation would become

$$0 = \int d\sigma \overline{V} \frac{\overline{dU}}{dw} - 4\pi V' \qquad (5),$$

which shows, that $V'$ the value of $V$ at the point $p'$ is given, when $\overline{V}$ its value at the surface is known.

To convince ourselves that there does exist such a function as we have supposed $U$ to be; conceive the surface to be a perfect conductor put in communication with the earth, and a unit of positive electricity to be concentrated in the point $p'$, then the total potential function arising from $p'$ and from the electricity it will induce upon the surface, will be the required value of $U$. For, in consequence of the communication established between the conducting surface and the earth, the total potential function at this surface must be constant, and equal to that of the earth itself, i. e. to *zero* (seeing that in this state they form but one conducting body). Taking, therefore, this total potential function for $U$, we have evidently $0 = \overline{U}$, $0 = \delta U$, and $U = \frac{1}{r}$ for those parts infinitely near to $p'$. As moreover, this function has no other singular points within the surface, it evidently possesses all the properties assigned to $U$ in the preceding proof.

Again, since we have evidently $U' = 0$, for all the space exterior to the surface, the equation (4) art. 4 gives

$$0 = 4\pi\,(\rho) + \frac{\overline{dU}}{dw};$$

where $(\rho)$ is the density of the electricity induced on the surface, by the action of a unit of electricity concentrated in the point $p'$. Thus, the equation (5) of this article becomes

$$V' = -\int d\sigma\,(\rho)\,\overline{V} \;\ldots\ldots\ldots\ldots\ldots\ldots\ldots\; (6).$$

This equation is remarkable on account of its simplicity and singularity, seeing that it gives the value of the potential for any point $p'$, within the surface, when $\overline{V}$, its value at the surface itself is known, together with $(\rho)$, the density that a unit of electricity concentrated in $p'$ would induce on this surface, if it conducted electricity perfectly, and were put in communication with the earth.

Having thus proved, that $V'$ the value of the potential function $V$, at any point $p'$ within the surface is given, provided its

KLARTEXT

**Bildnachweis:**
Adobe Stock ©Jan Kliment S. 4-5; Imago: /momentphoto/Röhner S. 6-7; /imagebroker 21, 29 o., 31, 62, 104; /Dean Pictures 29 o. (Flagge), /ingimage 34 u., /McPHOTO 35 u., /Becker&Bredel 41 u., /Prod.DB 45, /Westend61 46-55 (Hintergrund), /ActionPictures 57 Mitte, /Stefan Zeitz 57 Mitte (Flagge), /allOver-MEV 86 o., /H. Tschanz-Hofmann 89 r., /Media-Punch 90 l., /YAY Images 93 o., /Reiner Zensen 105, /imagebroker/begsteiger 110 o., /ZUMA Wire 113, /PicturePoint 114; Giorgetto Giugiaro S. 14, 96 o.; Günter Poley S. 46, 64, 87 u.; Stuart Mentiply S. 81, 97 o., 107; Marcel Leifer S. 98 u.; Michael Grinda S. 99 o., 99 Mitte; privat S. 37 u., 100 o., 101, 102 o.; Stiftung AutoMuseum Volkswagen S. 103; Martin Meiners S. 111; VW Aktiengesellschaft S. 8/9, 11, 18, 19, 22, 24, 27, 29 u., 30, 34 o., 37 o., 38-44, 47-56, 57 o., 57 u., 58 u., 60, 63, 68, 69, 83, 84, 86, 87 o., 88, 89 l., 90 r., 93, 94, 96 Mitte, 97 u., 98 o., 99 u., 102 u., 106, 108, 109; VW Aktiengesellschaft/Frank Müller-May S. 16; VW Aktiengesellschaft/Tim Hoppe S. 96 u., 100 u.; Porsche AG: S. 13, 35 o.; Knut Simon S. 25, 58 o.; picture alliance/dpa, Horst Ossinger S. 33; picture alliance/dpa, Michael Kappeler S. 110 u.

Bibliografische Information der Deutschen Nationalbibliothek
Die Deutsche Nationalbibliothek verzeichnet diese Publikation in der Deutschen Nationalbibliografie; detaillierte bibliografische Daten sind im Internet über portal.dnb.de abrufbar.

**Impressum**

1. Auflage September 2021
Layout und Satz: Joachim Bartels
Lektorat: Sibylle Brakelmann
Umschlagabbildungen: Adobe Stock: ©Marina Lohrbach, ©TIMDAVIDCOLLECTION, Volkswagen Aktiengesellschaft (2), privat (2), Stuart Mentiply
Druck und Bindung: Linsen Druckcenter GmbH, Siemensstraße 12–14, 47533 Kleve


ISBN 978-3-8375-2390-4

Jakob Funke Medien Beteiligungs GmbH & Co. KG
Jakob-Funke-Platz 1, 45127 Essen
info.klartext@funkemedien.de
www.klartext-verlag.de

Knut Simon

# VW Golf

**Populäre Irrtümer
und andere Wahrheiten**

# Inhalt

# Zum Geleit

Hand aufs Herz: Kennen Sie tatsächlich irgendjemanden, der noch nie einen VW Golf besessen oder gefahren hat? Sehen Sie. So ist das mit einem Modell, das tatsächlich zu einem Volks-Wagen wurde. Der kleinste gemeinsame automobile Nenner namens Golf ist nun seit rund 50 Jahren um uns herum. „Sag‘ doch einfach, wir fahren Golf!“ geriet zum zeitlos gültigen Slogan. Doch das Auto, was sogar seinem Marktsegment der Kompaktwagen seinen Namen aufdrückte („Golf-Klasse“), war mitnichten der Shootingstar am Autohimmel. Und schon gar nicht der natürliche Nachfolger des Welt-Erfolges namens Käfer, der mal eben dessen Siegeszug wiederholte. Der Golf

wurde beinahe zur Totgeburt, denn der Mutterkonzern siechte dramatisch gegen Ende der 1960er, Anfang der 1970er Jahre. Die Mitarbeiter, die damals noch Lohntüten erhielten, speiste man aus Geldkoffern, die man aus den USA holte. Nur dortige Banken gaben VW noch Kredit. In Wolfsburg drohten die Lichter auszugehen, weil man Warnlampen lange ignoriert hatte. Dass es nicht dazu kam, verdankt VW dem Golf – mit Abstrichen bis heute. Wie sehr der Golf und seine Entscheider auf ihrem Erfolgsweg dennoch hin und wieder stotterten, falsch abbogen oder die Leitplanken touchierten, steht in diesem Büchlein. Natürlich nicht alles. Aber vieles.

# Steckbrief

**Name:** Golf

**Bedeutung:** Käfer-Erbe, Volkswagen-Retter

**Erscheinungszeitpunkt:** 1974

**Erste Erfolge:** 1976

**Bekannteste Spielart:** GTI

**Credo:** Sag‘ doch einfach, wir fahren Golf

**Anzahl Generationen:** VIII

**Bisher gebaut:** Über 35 Millionen Exemplare

**Geschwister:** Jetta, Vento, Bora, Caddy, Variant, Touran, Sportsvan ...

**PS minimal:** 50 **PS maximal:** 652

**Besondere Merkmale:** läuft und läuft und läuft und ...

# Hansi aus dem Sarg oder: Der Untergang

**Beinahe wäre der Golf nicht Nachfolger des VW Käfer geworden, sondern der des Simca 1000. Allerdings durfte der kleine Heckmotor-Viertürer dann doch nicht von der Seine an den Mittellandkanal. Zudem soff er vor Brasilien im Ärmelkanal ab. Hä? Genau!**

Wolfsburg 1961. Der Käfer purzelte vom Band, als gäbe es nur ewig gestern, aber kein modernes Morgen. Hinter den Kulissen jedoch wendeten sich die Wolfsburger Blicke in Richtung Frankreich, wo gerade der knuffige Simca 1000 debütierte. Heckmotor, knapp einen Liter Hubraum, vier Türen: Nicht lange, und die VW-Ingenieure am Mittellandkanal fanden morgens bei Dienstantritt einen Tausender vor ihren Werkbänken. Allerdings von Simca aus Blech. Der Wagen wurde zerlegt und in allen Einzelteilen vermessen. Ja, so könnte der perfekten Käfer-Nachfolger aussehen – fanden zumindest VW-Chef Heinrich Nordhoff und die ihm treu ergebenen Anhänger des Porsche-Prinzips aus luftgekühltem Heckmotor und Hinterradantrieb.

Einige murrten jedoch, denn schon damals favorisierten sie Frontantrieb und wassergekühlten Motor. Doch der „Simca von VW" nahm ungebremst Gestalt an, indem man den bereits existierenden VW-Entwicklungsauftrag (EA) 97 dem kleinen Franzosen anglich. Der EA 97 geriet größer und größer, was bei VW allerdings niemand bemerkte. Die ersten rund 100 Nullserien-Fahrzeuge als Limousine, Fließheck, Kombi und Cabriolet, Presswerkzeuge und Fertigungsstraßen wurden gebaut. Dann geschah das Unglaubliche: Erst jetzt fiel dem VW-Vertrieb die frappierende Ähnlichkeit des EA 97 mit dem frisch etablierten VW 1500 Typ 3 auf. Der fix und fertig entwickelte EA 97 wurde – verworfen. Aus

**So wirkte er beinahe hübsch: „Hansi aus dem Sarg“, auferstanden in Brasilien, hier in seiner Fließheck-Variante.**

und vorbei. Welch finanzielles und organisatorisches Desaster! Heute undenkbar.

Die Odyssee des glücklosen EA 97 ging noch weiter. VW versuchte, das Gesamtpaket der Sowjetunion schmackhaft zu machen. Die durchaus interessierten Russen mussten aus Mangel an Devisen abwinken. 1964 schließlich wurde der angestaubte EA 97 Richtung Brasilien verschifft, um dort als VW vermarktet zu werden. Doch auf diesem Weg tauchte der VW-Frachter mitsamt Nullserien-Fahrzeugen, Presswerkzeugen und Fertigungsstraßen im Ärmelkanal ab. Ein Jahr lang lagen er und der verhinderte Käfer-Nachfolger, der nicht Golf geheißen hätte, dort. Dann hob man Schiff und Fracht, die Reise ging weiter. In Brasilien wurden Muscheln und Algen von den Maschinen geklopft und die Produktion der viertürigen EA-97-Limousine aufgenommen. Ihr Spitzname lautete ob ihrer Form „Hansi aus dem Sarg“. Dies also ist die Geschichte, wie aus einem „großen Simca 1000“ beinahe der direkte Golf-Vorgänger und der direkte Käfer-Nachfolger entstanden wäre – so ähnlich planlos wie sein Scheitern.

# Das doppelte Schrottchen

**VW wollte sein bisheriges Erfolgsmodell Käfer von Anfang an gegen den Golf austauschen. Andere Überlegungen und Alternativen existierten nicht. Ähm, doch … Nur war das Auto konstruktiv ziemlicher Mist – weshalb es am Ende auch auf selbigem landete …**

Im Rückspiegel der Autogeschichte wirkt manches lupenrein. Zum Beispiel die Tatsache, dass VW ein Auto namens Käfer baute, das sich ziemlich lange wie geschnitten Brot verkaufte. Sonnenklar, dass auch dessen Nachfolger namens Golf den Markt abräumen würde. Und zwar als Alleinkämpfer. Ach, wirklich? Nö. Selbst der eine oder andere Vorstand traute dem neuen Konzept „Golf" nicht, sondern hoffte insgeheim sogar auf ein krachendes Scheitern der Käfer-Blasphemie. Zusätzlich gab es strategische Überlegungen, dem technisch unverwechselbaren Käfer einen Nachfolger zu bauen, der aufgrund seiner technischen Alleinstellungsmerkmale viele VW-Stammkunden einfangen sollte. Und der nahm in Form des von Ferdinand Piëch konstruierten und von Porsche als Dienstleister entwickelten Autos namens EA 266 Gestalt an.

Der von Porsche-Chefdesigner Wolfgang Möbius gestaltete Zweitürer sollte bis zu 105 PS unter der Haube – respektive unter der um 20 Zentimeter erhöht eingebauten Fondsitzbank – haben. Ein Reihenvierzylinder mit Wasserkühlung und OHC-Ventilsteuerung, allerdings als Mittelmotor in Unterflur-Bauweise. Schön außergewöhnlich, schön anders – schön beknackt. Denn weder rechnete sich der EA 266 aufgrund seiner exotischen Bauweise (keine kostensparenden Gleichteile mit anderen VW) noch erwies sich das Auto bei ausufernden Kosten in unzähligen Versuchen als geeignet. Unkontrollierbares Fahrverhalten, Motorschäden, bei Crashtests platzende Benzintanks und einknickende Karosserien, zudem umständlich in Wartung und Details. So war zum Beispiel der Ölpeilstab 1,4 Meter (!) lang und in der Mitte mit einem Knick-Scharnier versehen … „Und bei einem Motorbrand wären die Insassen schlicht gegrillt worden“, ätzte noch 40 Jahre später Ex-VW-Chef Rudolf Leiding, der den EA 266 im Oktober 1971 als eine seiner ersten Amtshandlungen killte.

Das traf Porsche doppelt hart, verlor der in arger Bedrängnis steckende Hersteller damit nicht nur den Entwicklungsauftrag, sondern auch die Option auf den Bau einer sportlichen Porsche-Variante des EA 266. Der war als Ersatz für 914 und 911 vorgesehen, die an für 1975 angedrohten US-Umwelt- und Sicherheitsnormen zu sterben drohten. Am Ende plättete ein werkseigener Panzer die Vorserien-EA 266. Nur vier überlebten: Zwei verstauben bei Porsche in Weissach, einer thront tipptopp im Wolfsburger ZeitHaus der Autostadt. Und ein schwarzes Exemplar soll sich Ferdinand Piëch gesichert haben. Rest in Peace.

**Sexy Verpackung, irres Konzept, grandios gescheitert: EA 266**

# The Italian Job

**Der Golf I hat seine Form einer geheimen Mission zu verdanken. In ihrem Rahmen begaben sich 1969 mehrere VW-Vorstände auf Geheiß des damaligen VW-Chefs Kurt Lotz (Spitzname „Lotz of Trouble“) auf den Turiner Autosalon …**

Aufmerksam wandelten die Herren durch die Turiner Messehallen. Sie begutachteten herstellerübergreifend Modelle und Studien, notierten sich die überzeugendsten Entwürfe und vermerkten deren Urheber. Ergebnis: Die überwältigende Mehrheit der favorisierten Designs stammte von Giorgetto Giugiaro. Einem echten Car-Guy, der sich nach Tätigkeiten als Designchef von Bertone und Ghia unter dem Label „Italdesign“ selbstständig gemacht hatte.

Schon im Januar 1970 lud VW ihn nach Wolfsburg ein, präsentierte ihm das Projekt „Golf“ und bat um einen Entwurf. Giugiaro war verblüfft, einen komplett zerlegten Fiat 128 im Wolfsburger Besprechungsraum vorzufinden. VW begriff den italienischen Kompaktwagen als modernste Entwicklung – an ihr sollte sich Giugiaro orientieren. Was ihm wohl nicht schwergefallen sein dürfte, hatte er den 128 doch selbst entworfen! Die etwas herab-

lassenden VW-Vorstände verblüffte Giugiaro mit seinen Kenntnissen in Sachen Konstruktion: Da kommt ein eleganter Italiener im Maßanzug, von dem man ein paar hübsche Bildchen erwartet, und dann fragt der Mann plötzlich nach der vorgesehenen Anzahl der Schweißpunkte am Seitenteil ...?

VW schaltete schnell und bestellte bei Giugiaro gleich eine komplette neue Modellfamilie. Realisiert in Form von Scirocco, Golf, Passat. Wobei VW bei Giugiaros Entwürfen jeweils entscheidende Änderungen durchsetzte. So verlor der Golf I seine Breitband-Scheinwerfer, weil runde Streuscheiben schlicht weniger kosteten. Zudem verlängerte VW-Forschungsvorstand Prof. Ernst Fiala den vorderen Überhang des Golf I um sieben Zentimeter und stellte aus Gründen des Insassenschutzes die Frontscheibe um zwei Grad stärker auf. Sieht man deutlich, wenn man Entwurf und Serie vergleicht. Auch die Heckleuchten halbierte VW – um sie dem Golf 1980 als echt innovatives „Facelift" wieder zu verpassen.

Giugiaro schluckte die Kröten, allerdings soll es dabei stets hoch hergegangen sein. Doch VW lockte mit einem Zehnjahresvertrag für Entwicklung, Prototypenbau und Design ... Den kassierte VW-Chef Rudolf Leiding Ende 1971 aus Kostengründen wieder. Giugiaro: „Lotz war weg, für Leiding war ich kein Begriff. Vielleicht kannte er den Vertrag auch nicht. Designchef Herbert Schäfer, sicherlich nur damit beauftragt, dankte mir für meine Mitwirkung. Man werde sich melden." Kann man zwischen den Zeilen lesen, versteht man. Übrigens: 2015 übernahm VW-Tochter Audi Italdesign.

Golf-Evolution: Die Skizzen oben und rechts zeigen den Ursprung. In der Bildmitte die Serienform

# Feuerland-Taufe

**Die wohl längste Erprobungsfahrt absolvierten 1974/75 zwei signalgelbe Golf I auf der Panamericana von Alaska nach Feuerland. Eine von langer Hand geplante PR-Aktion? Na: fast!**

Insgesamt 30.514 Kilometer. Abgespult von Oktober 1974 bis Januar 1975. Auf einer echten Marterstrecke, denn die Panamericana war tatsächlich noch abenteuerlich. Aus klirrender Kälte in sengende Hitze sah die Welt zwei signalgelbe Golf I eilen. Zufällig, weil sich Pirelli, damals auf der Suche nach einem geeigneten „Werbeträger" für seinen neuen Reifen mit dem klingenden Namen „Meilen-Pirelli", ursprünglich die neue S-Klasse W 116 von Mercedes für einen spektakulären Test ausgeguckt hatte. Weil Stuttgart solchen Italo-Mumpitz wohl nicht nötig hatte, zog Pirelli seine Siebenmeilen-Stiefel eben einem neuen VW-Modell an. Es ist ein kleines Wunder, dass inmitten der Anspannung zwischen Käfer und Golf, auf einem riesigen Schuldenberg sitzend, jemand von VW den richtigen Riecher hatte: Das ist genau die PR, die der Golf braucht!

So wurden die Fahrgestell-Endnummern 653 und 714 (heute die ältesten bekannten Golf) von ihrer Produktion im Juli 1974 bis zum Start im Oktober in Handarbeit modifiziert. Die Golf erhielten verdoppelten Unterfahrschutz und mächtige Zusatzscheinwerfer, dazu Plexiglasscheiben vor den Hauptscheinwerfern und maßgearbeitete Ablagesysteme statt der Rücksitzbank für Spritkanister, Gepäck, Fotoausrüstung, Werkzeug. Hinter den Plastikblenden der Lautsprecher gab's Geheimfächer für Schmiergelder für südamerikanische Zöllner und einen 38er Colt. Auf Letzteren wurde erst in letzter Minute doch verzichtet.

Die Tour war dann tatsächlich nicht ohne: geprägt von Gastfreundschaft, Land und Leuten, einer gefährlichen Schießerei in Buenaventura (ohne Beteiligung der Golf-Besatzung) und Begegnungen mit vom Pinochet-System misshandelten Regimegegnern, die als Verbannte in Punta Arenas lebten.

Niemand Geringerer als Deutschlands bekanntester Autotester Fritz B. Busch fuhr die Strecke, schrieb ein Buch und gemeinsam mit dem „Feuerland-getauften" Golf Geschichte. „Death Valley: Harte Burschen suchten hier das Glück. Sie fanden manchmal nur so viel, dass sie davon satt wurden. Manche fanden nichts weiter als den Tod." Oder: „Fernweh hat man zu Hause. Heimweh hat man ganz woanders. Das ist der Unterschied. Er ist gewaltig." So lauten typische Busch-Sätze. Das Team umfasste außerdem „stern"-Fotograf Frank Müller May, die VW-Ingenieure Peter Färber und Wolfgang Peschke, Mechaniker Bernd Ott und Übersetzer Alfonso Barceló. Peschkes Beobachtungen trugen maßgeblich zur Entstehung des Golf I „Caddy" bei (s. Seite 42/43).

Noch heute erzählen die beiden gelben Golf im Museum ihre Geschichten. Man muss nur ganz genau hinhören.

Kalt-Start: In Alaska begann der „Golf-Kurs" für Mensch und Maschine.

AHA!

# Geheimtruppe Injection

**Golf GTI, Ikone des sportlichen Kompaktwagens! Doch die Wahrheit ist: VW wollte den Renner nicht! Warum das? Und wer hat ihn dennoch unter drohendem Jobverlust heimlich entwickelt?**

Kurzer Radstand, hoher Schwerpunkt, Kurbellenkerachse – ein Käfer war niemals eine Alfa Giulia. Als 1972 der VW 1303 mit Einzelradaufhängung kam, spendierte VW ihm einen gelb-schwarzen Anstrich und ein wildes Image als Sondermodell „Gelb-Schwarzer Renner" (GSR). Zwar blieb es unter der Haube serienmäßig bei 50 PS (Tuningfreigabe seitens VW bis 100 PS war erteilt), allein die Optik aber reichte für drei Dinge. Erstens: Minister Franz-Josef Strauß polterte im Bundestag gegen die unverantwortliche Vergötterung der Raserei durch einen Autohersteller, der sich auch noch teilweiser staatlicher Beteiligung erfreute. Zweitens: Die jungen Leute kauften den GSR wie blöde. Drittens: Rennsport-begeisterte VW-Mitarbeiter begannen ihre ungenehmigte Arbeit am von ihnen sorgfältig verborgenen Projekt „Sport-Golf".

Kopf der späteren „Geheimtruppe GTI" war VW-Pressechef Anton Konrad. Er bat an Sonntagen konspirativ zu Kaffee und Kuchen in seinen Wolfsburger Bungalow. Dort brütete er mit Horst-Dieter Schwittlinsky (Marketing), Herbert Schuster (Fahrwerk), Kurt Hablitzel (Projektleitung Golf), Jürgen Adler (Konstruktion Innenraum), Alfons Löwenberg (Ingenieur) und Gunter Kühl (Motorsport) über

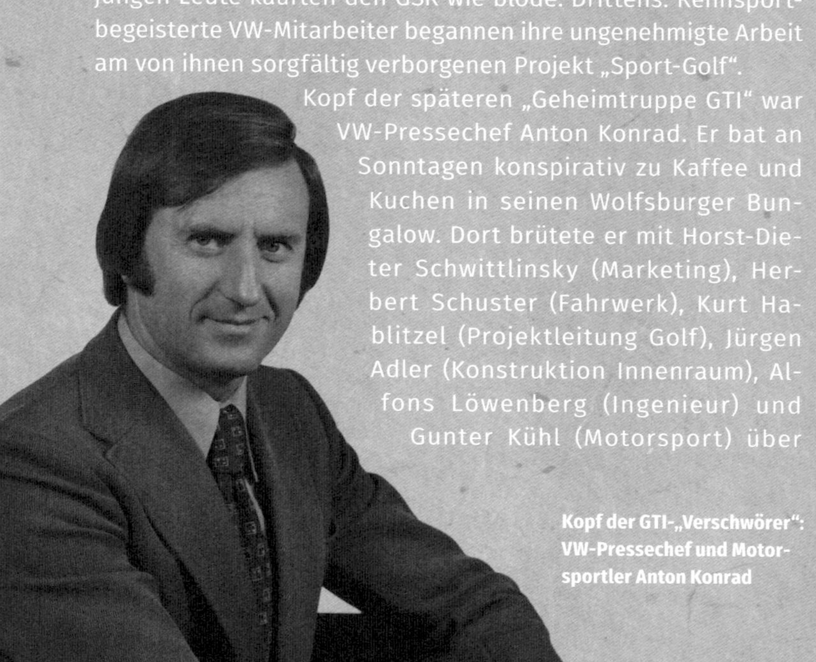

**Kopf der GTI-„Verschwörer": VW-Pressechef und Motorsportler Anton Konrad**

**Erster! Der Golf GTI in seiner Ursprungsform. Einer wie keiner**

einem Modell, das VW die wichtigen jungen Kunden brächte. Ölkrise, Politikschelte und Widerstand aus dem VW-Vertrieb zwangen zur Geheimhaltung. VW hatte Angst vor potenziellem Gegenwind aus Politik und dröger Stammkundschaft. Davor, dass eine neue Variante den Erfolg des Serienmodells stören könnte.

Der Geheimtruppe GTI gelang es, alle VW-Obrigkeiten eiskalt wie bravourös zu umfahren und gleichzeitig den „Sport-Golf" günstig aus Konzern-Gleichteilen zu kreieren. Zudem geriet dessen optischer Auftritt extrem dezent. Das Herzstück des Golf GTI, den 110-PS-Motor aus dem 80 GTE, organisierte Konrad persönlich über Audi-Entwicklungschef Ferdinand Piëch. Dann wagte Schlaufuchs Konrad das Unvorstellbare und weihte einen Tag vor der entscheidenden Sitzung VW-Chef Toni Schmücker in das Projekt GTI ein. Schmücker spielte mit und am Folgetag den Ahnungslosen, der „spontan" begeistert dem GTI zustimmte. Der Vertrieb war durch die Chef-Ansage mundtot, ätzte jedoch, VW werde „keine 500 Stück" von den zu Homologationszwecken für den Rallyesport geplanten 5.000 GTI verkaufen. Stimmt auch, entstanden bis heute doch über zwei Millionen Golf GTI. Anton Konrad: „Einen Fehler haben wir dennoch begangen. Wir haben es versäumt, in unsere jeweiligen Verträge eine Mark pro verkauftem GTI als Marge eintragen zu lassen."

# Der Gipfel vom Löwenberg

**1974 wäre das Geheimprojekt „GTI" beinahe gekillt worden. Alfons Löwenberg, zuvor bei Opel Rallye-Pionier mit Kadett & Co., tüftelte bei VW weiter – dieses Mal am sportlichen Golf. Und für Normalos etwas zu extrem ...**

Wolfsburg 1974. Während die übrige „Geheimtruppe GTI" einen aus Serienteilen bestehenden und mit alltagstauglichen Fahreigenschaften versehenen Sport-Golf plante, tobte sich Löwenberg aus: Er pflanzte einem Golf zwei Weber-Doppelvergaser auf (die dann nur 160 km/h Spitze brachten), verbaute eine Rennkupplung und legte das Auto gefühlte zehn Zentimeter tiefer. Ein Auspuff, dick wie ein Ofenrohr, vervollständigte das Spektakel. Eine echte „Rennsemmel", nur eben nicht das eigentliche Ziel, um das es ging bei diesem hochsensiblen und daher komplett im Verborgenen gedeihenden Projekt. Keine Frage: Die Konzeption dieses Autos schoss weit übers Ziel hinaus ...

Zudem wäre Löwenbergs kompromissloser Sport-Golf nicht zu finanzieren gewesen. Allein die Doppelvergaser kamen in keinem anderen VW- oder Audi-Modell der damaligen Zeit vor, sodass entsprechende Materialbestellungen teuer geworden wären. Auch der Kundendienst hätte speziell auf diese Komponenten geschult werden müssen – wegen eines einzelnen Modells! Eine Horrorvorstellung für den VW-Vertrieb und die dort residierenden Rotstifte!

Dessen völlig ungeachtet preschte der glühende Verfechter seiner eigenen Ideen Löwenberg vor und zeigte dem damaligen Forschungsvorstand Ernst Fiala seine Krawallbüchse. Fiala kam, sah, stieg in das Ding ein und fuhr. Und brüllte im Anschluss lauter als der Auspuff, wie Zeitzeugen sagen. Fialas erhitztes Fazit:

Merke: Brüllt dein Gegenüber lauter als ein Sportauspuff, hast du dich wohl gerade einem VW-Vorstand zum Fraß vorgeworfen ...

unfahrbar, die Kiste! „Ihr komisches Projekt ist gestorben!", blaffte er darauf zwei Tage später den völlig verdutzten GTI-Geheimentwickler Anton Konrad im VW-Vorstandsflieger an. Konrad hatte Mühe, aber letztlich doch Erfolg, Fiala klarzumachen, dass es sich bei dem Löwenberg-Wagen keinesfalls um den angedachten Sport-Golf handele. Dieser werde doch sportiv, aber alltagstauglich konzipiert. Löwenberg musste ab da innerhalb der GTI-Truppe zurückstecken, die restlichen GTI-Macher und ihr „ziviler" Sport-Golf setzten sich schließlich durch. Puh! Doch für einen kleinen Moment hätte es den GTI, den es eigentlich sowieso gar nicht gab, beinahe wirklich nie gegeben.

# Sieben Zehntel und ein Wasser-Fall

**Ein Golf ist vernünftig, ein GTI sportiv, ein Cabrio cool. In all diesen Varianten gab es den neuen VW Golf bereits. Da schaute im Jahre 1980 VW-Forschungschef Ernst Fiala hoch über den Wolken aus dem Fenster seines Flugzeuges auf einen breiten, in der Sonne daliegenden Strom. „Schwimmen müsste der Golf jetzt noch können!", dachte er bei sich.**

Echt Quatsch? Ja, aber wahr: Ein vierköpfiges VW-Team durfte sich ab 1980 am „See Golf" kreativ freischwimmen. Darunter ein Fachmann namens Jürgen Lange, ob seiner Akribie „Sieben Zehntel" genannt.

Drei Jahre sollte dieser „Schwimmkurs" dauern. Zu besagtem Golf Cabrio konstruierte das Team einen komplexen hydraulischen Gesamtapparat. Der hob und senkte zwei seitliche, auf Maß gefertigte Schwimmkörper in der Form ziemlich überdimensionierter „Surfbretter". Sah sehr

Feuchte und am Ende auch fröhliche Spritztour: der See Golf in der Kieler Bucht

lustig aus. Vor allem aber konnte der See Golf in jedem Hafen über die jeweilige Sportbootanlage problemlos gewässert werden. Das Golf-Heck wiederum dominierte die Spezialaufhängung der Schiffsschraube, die über eine am serienmäßigen Getriebe angeflanschte Kardanwelle vom Frontmotor angetrieben wurde. Bei „Landgang" wurde diese Welle entkoppelt. Innen gab's eine robuste wasserfeste Kunstlederausstattung. Und dann? Dann erfolgten erste „Fahrversuche" – und zwar an keinem urigeren Ort als dem Rückhaltebecken der Wasseraufbereitungsanlage des VW-Werks in Wolfsburg! Das Kühlsystem und die Motorleistung wurden an maritime Gefilde angepasst, sodass schließlich 175 PS den Golf zu neuen Ufern trieben.

Trotz dieser umfassenden Versuche fühlte sich das Debüt anlässlich des GTI-Treffens im Wörthersee 1983 aus Sicht der Entwickler an wie der buchstäbliche Sprung ins kalte Wasser. Das erzählen die Jungs jetzt, den Bildern von damals sieht man diese Anspannung nicht an. Im Gegenteil. Anschließend ging der See Golf auf Tournee: Ob im Kieler Yachthafen oder anlässlich des Hamburger Hafengeburtstags zwischen „dicken Pötten" mitten auf der Elbe – die Mannschaft hatte offensichtlich ihren Heidenspaß. Und gestandenen Kapitänen fiel wohl tatsächlich die Pfeife aus dem Mund, als der See Golf an ihnen vorbeistob. Denn dieser war nicht gerade lahm, sondern erreichte eine Höchstgeschwindigkeit von beachtlichen 22 Knoten (41 km/h). Heute haben sich die Wogen geglättet: Tüftler und See Golf sind längst im Ruhestand. Jürgen Lange und seine Kollegen zu Hause, der See Golf in der Stiftung AutoMuseum Wolfsburg.

# Aus dem Giftschrank

Der langjährige VW-Designchef **Herbert Schäfer** entwarf laut übereinstimmenden Aussagen vieler Zeitzeugen keines der ihm zugeschriebenen Modelle selbst.

Herbert Schäfer mit Golf III

Die 1971 ursprünglich für den **Golf** geplante Modellbezeichnung lautete **„Pony"**. Als der mit dem Design beauftragte **Giorgetto Giugiaro** VW darauf hinwies, dass er für seinen Kunden **Hyundai** gerade an einem Coupé gleichen Namens arbeite, schwenkte VW um zu **„Golf"**. Dieser erhielt seine Bezeichnung nach dem Namen des Hannoveraner-Hengstes namens „Golf" von VW-Manager Hans-Joachim Zimmermann.
Kurz vor Serienstart des Golf VII verlangte VW-Chef **Martin Winterkorn** den Einbau vorderer kleiner Dreiecksfenster. Diese spontane Änderung ließ unerwünschte **Windgeräusche** ent-

stehen, die VW zum Teil mithilfe von **Kitt** zu kaschieren versuchte. Im Rahmen der Modellpflege erfolgte eine Serienlösung. Ab da war **Ruhe**.

Zweieinhalb Jahre vor Serienanlauf des Golf I standen Wasserkühlung, Quermotor und Frontantrieb fest. VW-Ingenieur und Golf-I-Förderer **Hans-Georg Wenderoth**, ein ehemaliger NSU-Entwickler, hatte das 1970 maßgeblich forciert. Ob seiner teils unverblümt-drastischen Ausdrucksweise trug Wenderoth den Spitznamen **„Fäkalien-Schorsch“**.

Alfasud-Konstrukteur Rudolf Hruska verglich den Golf mit dem Alfasud, stieg unzählige Male in beide Autos ein und aus, umkreiste sie, schüttelte den Kopf. „Warum nur“, fragte er den ebenfalls anwesenden Giorgetto Giugiaro, Designer von Golf und Alfasud, „laufen die Kunden in Scharen zum Golf über und kaufen den viel besseren Sud nicht?“

Giorgetto Giugiaro

# Hell Driving Range

**Tempo 50 innerhalb geschlossener Ortschaften? Kein Alkohol am Steuer? Wie bitte: Gurtpflicht? Neue Vorschriften brauchen wir nicht, sagten viele Autofahrer vor rund 50 Jahren. VW wollte das Gegenteil beweisen. Und ließ es ordentlich krachen.**

Es ist noch nicht lange her, da wurden „neumodische" Vorschriften wie Promillegrenzen oder besagte Gurtpflicht von vielen Autofahrern und echten oder selbst ernannten Experten kategorisch abgelehnt – oder zumindest angezweifelt. Dabei war augenscheinlich, wie sehr die Zahl der Unfalltoten im Straßenverkehr angestiegen war: 1970 auf über 20 Millionen Menschen allein in der Bundesrepublik.

VW-Forschungsvorstand Ernst Fiala, Visionär in Sachen Sicherheit, trieb die VW-Entwicklung maßgeblich mit diversen Sicherheits-Konzept-Fahrzeugen voran. Unter ihnen der ESVW II auf Golf-Basis. Der hatte allerhand an Bord, was der Serien-Golf dann noch nicht mitbekam. Doch brannte es in Fiala und seinen getreuen Mitstreitern, unter ihnen Prof. Rüdiger Weißner, die Effizienz damals neuartiger Dreipunkt-Gurtsysteme „hautnah" zu demonstrieren. „Die Leute sagten damals immer: ‚Och, wozu diese ollen Gurte? Bei einem Aufprall kann ich mich doch rasch mit den Händen am Lenkrad abstützen!'", erinnert Weißner zeitgenössische Naivitäten. Also entschloss man sich zu einer drastischen Demonstration.

Weißner und zwei weitere Mitarbeiter Fialas aus der Forschung und Entwicklung von VW setzten sich höchstpersönlich jeweils in einen Golf, gurteten sich an, starteten den Motor und fuhren los – und ungebremst im rechten Winkel in die Fahrerseite eines stehenden weiteren Golf. Krach! Das Ganze fand statt und wurde gefilmt auf dem internen VW-Testgelände. Zugunsten einer besseren Beobachtung der menschlichen Reaktion beim Aufprall hatte man beim fahrenden Golf die Türen ausgebaut.

Selbstversuch: der damalige Bundesminister Hans-Jochen Vogel mit 50 km/h beim Crash mit Gurt im Golf

„War schon ein komisches Gefühl, etwas zu tun, was man sonst nicht so machte", fasst es Testfahrer Weißner rückblickend zusammen. Zudem erinnert sich der spätere Leiter Zentralplanung Produktion des VW-Konzerns und Leiter des VW-Werks Kassel, mit seinem Stuntfahrer-Ausflug bei Lloyds in London versichert gewesen zu sein. Keine andere Gesellschaft habe dieses Risiko tragen wollen. „Aber wir wollten unbedingt zeigen, dass Gurte wirksam sind!" Viele Golf-Fahrer hatten es dann auch geschnallt. Die drei ehemaligen Testfahrer sind bis heute wohlauf.

Volkswagen-Werbung im „Spiegel" aus dem Jahr 1978

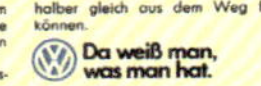

# Schloss Gripsholm und tatsächliche Märchen

**Echt jetzt, Diesel im Pkw? Heute selbstverständlich, na: noch. 1976 hingegen überhaupt nicht. Da kam VW mit einem Selbstzünder im Golf. Auch als Diesel revolutionierte dieser die Kompakt-Klasse.**

Diesel galt bis 1976 als Synonym für lahme, laute Fahrzeuge wie Busse und Lkw. Der Golf Diesel machte es anders! Wenn auch durch Zufall, weil Volkswagen versuchsweise Benzinmotoren umgerüstet, aber keine rechte Freude mit den sogenannten „Schichtlade"-Ottomotoren hatte. Bei denen wird in einer Vorkammer ein fettes Benzingemisch von einer Zündkerze gezündet. Die Flammenfront geht aus dieser Vorkammer heraus und entzündet das magere Gemisch im Brennraum. Ein solcher Vorkammer-Zylinderkopf wurde zum Ursprung des ersten Golf-Dieselmotors mit 1500 ccm Hubraum und 50 PS.

Bei dessen Präsentation in Stockholm waren die Journalisten positiv überrascht. „Entscheidend und psychologisch wichtig war, dass wir dem Golf Diesel mit 50 PS die gleiche Leistung wie dem Standard-Benziner gegeben hatten. Und ähnliche Leistungen und Höchstgeschwindigkeiten", plaudert der ehemalige VW-Forschungsvorstand Ernst Fiala aus dem Nähkästchen. Ziemlich trickreich veranstaltete VW unter den Diesel-Journalisten einen Wettbewerb, wer den niedrigsten Verbrauch herausfuhr. Bestwert waren 5,1 Liter auf 100 Kilometer.

Erst als Diesel (und als GTI) startete der Golf ab 1976 am Markt richtig durch. Über diese Verzögerung war VW insgeheim recht froh. Denn weil VW-Entwicklungschef Dr. Friedrich Goes keine Korrosionsversuche mit dem Golf unternommen hatte („Brauchen wir nicht, VW hat die beste Lackierung der Welt."), gammelte der Golf bekanntlich so schnell, wie ein Wassereis im Wüstenwind schmilzt. Goes kostete das letztlich den Job. Der Golf war eine völlig andere Konstruktion als der Käfer, teils mit mehreren übereinander gepressten Blechlagen. Nur ohne Konservierung in den Falzen, Lack kam dort nicht hin. Dafür aber Feuchtigkeit. Die Legende von sowjetischen Billig-Blechen? Ein Märchen, sagen VW-Zeitzeugen. Besser wurde der Rostschutz am Golf erst um 1978, gut war er immer noch nicht (ein Los, das sich der Golf mit Zeitgenossen anderer Marken teilte).

Die Journalisten auf Schloss Gripsholm erkoren den Golf Diesel zum kompakten, flinken Sparmobil. Als Souvenir von der Präsentation schleppte man Holz-Wikinger mit nach Hause und der finnische Modellauto-Hersteller Stahlberg lancierte rasch einen heute sehr seltenen Plastik-Golf-I im Maßstab 1:25. Währenddessen stieg der Diesel-Anteil beim echten VW Golf auf 67 Prozent Marktanteil und 1978 fuhr Rennfahrer Jochi Kleint mit einem „Zebra" getauften Golf Diesel den Porsches auf der Rallye Monte Carlo um die Ohren. Echt jetzt.

Schloss Gripsholm in Schweden, Ort der Selbstzünder-Revolution

Rallye-Golf Jochi Kleint von 1978

# Rostblock

**Der Käfer lief und lief und lief, der Golf rostete und rostete und rostete. Es war zum Haareraufen: Da baut VW ein komplett neues Volumenmodell und dann versemmeln hässliche braune Flecken und Rostkrümel die quietschgelben und -orangen Lackierungen. VW schaffte heimlich Abhilfe …**

Es war mit bloßem Auge zu erkennen. Und – im Wortsinne – nicht mit anzusehen: Der ursprünglich dem Alfasud zugedachte Schmähruf „Der rostet schon im Prospekt!“ sprang ab 1974 auf den damals neuen Golf I über. Der „blühte“ nämlich auch bereits nach wenigen Monaten rundum: an den Radläufen, um den Antennenfuß herum, an den Kotflügeln, an den Falzen von Heckklappen und Motorhauben. Selbst Anekdoten von verzückten Enkeln („Opa, ich kann die Straße sehen, obwohl ich nicht aus dem Fenster gucke!“) sind überliefert. VW fand die Ursache – ungeschützte Blechfalze, in denen eindringende Feuchtigkeit ihr Werk verrichten konnte –, doch eine schnelle Umkehr war inmitten des Produktionsprozesses nicht so schnell umsetzbar. Was tun? VW griff zur Guerilla-Taktik!

VW-Chef Rudolf Leiding, gelernter Techniker, erkannte den konstruktiven Fehler am Golf-Auspuff umgehend.

In kleiner hoher Runde wurden ungewöhnliche Maßnahmen beschlossen. Tenor: umgehend unbürokratisch einzugreifen, wann und wo immer es nötig war! So kam es, dass immer dann, wenn er einen stark korrodierten Golf I im Verkehr erblickte, VW-Pressechef Anton Konrad seinem Wagen entstieg und den jeweiligen Rost-Golf-Fahrern seine Karte überreichte. Verbunden mit der Aufforderung, eine VW-Werkstatt zu konsultieren. Dort erhielten die Kunden entweder neue Heckklappen, Motorhauben oder Kotflügel oder gleich ein komplettes neues Auto. Dies tatsächlich, man halte sich fest: kostenlos! Kommentar Konrad: „So aber bekamen wir die Rostlauben und das schlechte Golf-I-Image schnell von der Straße. Ich war nicht der einzige VW-Mann, der das praktizierte." Die „eingesammelten" Teile und Fahrzeuge wurden umgehend VW-intern verschrottet, heimlich, still und leise.

Apropos „unbürokratisches Engagement von VW-Führungskräften": In seiner Startphase litt der Golf I an rätselhaften Auspuffrohr-Brüchen. Als Verlegenheitslösung legten VW-Werkstätten ihren Kunden vor langen Reisen tatsächlich Ersatz-Auspuffe ohne Berechnung in die Kofferräume. VW-Chef Rudolf Leiding höchstpersönlich fand schließlich die Lösung, indem er sich kurzerhand unter einen auf der Hebebühne platzierten Golf begab. „Führen wir das Hosenrohr anders und ersetzen wir den scharfen Blechknick hier durch ein flexibles Wellrohr!", rief er nach einem fachmännischen Blick. Ab da war's vorbei mit Auspuffbrüchen aufgrund von Vibrationen.

Golf I: Auspuff, Rohr ab!

# Kolanski

**Während der 1970er Jahre riss sich alles, was in der Wirtschaft Rang und Namen hatte, um Designer Luigi Colani. Der residierte von 1972 bis 1981 auf Schloss Harkotten mit seinem Atelier Colani, bildete Nachwuchs aus und fand sich selbst ziemlich gut. Dann klopfte VW ans Schlosstor.**

Allerdings, muss man sagen, besaß der Kerl auch einfach Charme und hochgradigen Unterhaltungswert. Dies nicht abwertend gemeint. Wer ihn erleben durfte, weiß, wovon die Rede ist. Zu Colanis Habitus gehörte die Titulierung mancher seiner Auftraggeber als „Idioten". Zudem verzichtete Colani auch sonst auf einen vermittelnden Umgangston, um es einmal so auszudrücken. Dennoch hatte ihn Ende der 1970er Jahre natürlich auch VW um Entwürfe gebeten. Zur Präsentation schwebte der Maestro in gewohnter Weise ein. Im Gepäck hatte Colani Modelle und Zeichnungen dabei sowie die einzig wahre Meinung: seine eigene.

Der flamboyante Designer präsentierte also seine Ideen für Scirocco, Golf II und Polo II. Die Entwürfe blubberten, schwelgten, schwollen rundlich über alle Räder. Stöhnen und Kopfschütteln aufseiten der VW-Mannen, die schließlich alles ablehnten, ablehnen mussten. Begründung: unbaubarer Mumpitz! Colani schäumte! Schließlich ließ er sich in seinem berühmt-berüchtigten Stil über diese unmögliche Art der Behandlung, über diese unglaubliche Ignoranz und Borniertheit angesichts seiner phänomenalen Ideen gegenüber VW-Pressechef Anton Konrad aus.

Konrad, ein Kommunikationsprofi und Menschenleser par excellence, hörte sich mit seinem berühmten Pokerface den schnauzbärtigen Maestro eine Weile an. Dann schnitt er ihm mit kalkuliertem Temperament das Wort ab und blaffte mit erhobenem Zeigefinger: „Ludwig Kolanski! Wenn Sie jetzt nicht sofort Ruhe geben, mache ich das Aller-Aller-Schlimmste, was Sie sich überhaupt nur vorstellen können!“ „Ach, soo?“, fragte da der gebürtige Berliner Colani spöttisch-neugierig, „und watt soll dit sein?“ Konrad: „Dann zeige ich Ihre gesamten VW-Entwürfe in aller Öffentlichkeit!“ Kolanski: „Ooooh! Möönsch, Männeken! Watt biste denn so jemein zu mir ...?“

**Nahm er mal ein Blatt vor den Mund, verwelkte es sofort: Ludwig Kolanski alias Lutz Colani alias Luigi Colani war eine facettenreiche Persönlichkeit.**

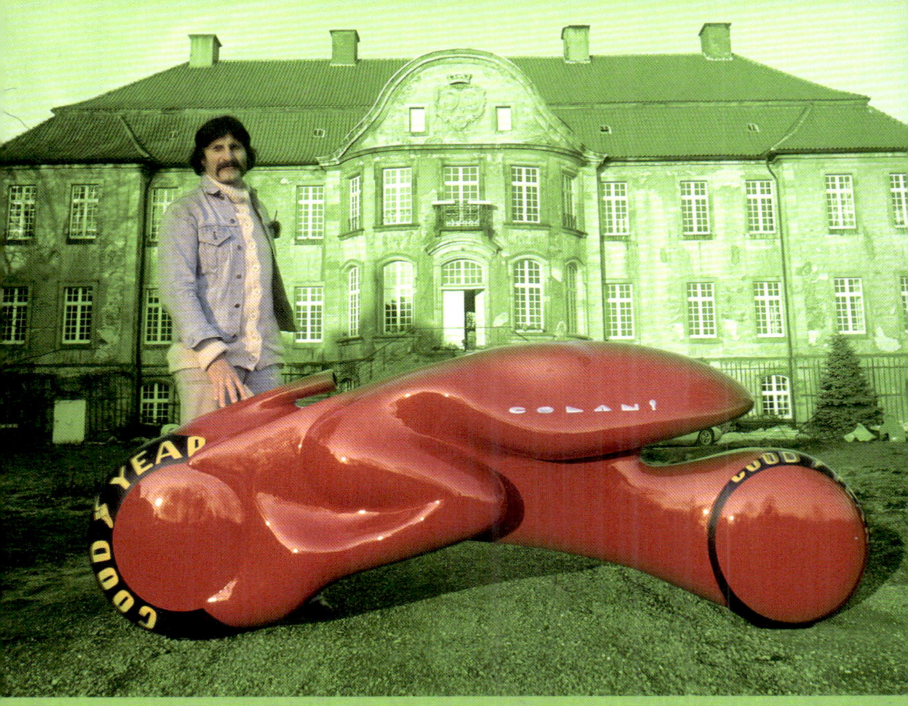

Heinrich Nordhoff

Es trifft nur bedingt zu, dass VW-Chef **Heinrich Nordhoff** angeblich bis zuletzt am Käfer-Konzept festhielt. Zwei Jahre vor seinem Tod im Jahre 1968 diktierte er: „Auftrag an die Firma Porsche, einen Nachfolger für den Käfer zu entwickeln. **Konzeption freigestellt**, große Stückzahlen, Hubraumbegrenzung auf 1,0 Liter." Lieber spät als nie. Beinahe wäre es dennoch zu spät gewesen ...

Rund ein Drittel des damaligen **VW-Vorstands** hegte 1973/74 Misstrauen gegen das neue Konzept namens Golf. Nicht wenige davon wünschten sich – mehr oder weniger heimlich – gar ein **Scheitern** des wassergekühlten Frontantrieb-Wagens.

Weil VW dem Golf die alleinige Nachfolge des Käfers nicht zutraute, sollte ein von Ferdinand Piëch konstruierter Mittelmotor-Wagen namens EA 266 **parallel gebaut** werden.

Nach dem „Aus“ für den glücklosen EA 266 plante VW für den Fall, dass der Golf floppte, diesem rasch den **Polo** zur Seite zu stellen. Ersteres blieb aus. Der Polo kam trotzdem – ebenfalls mit Erfolg.

Am **25. Juni 2002** überholte der Golf den **Rekord** des Käfers und wurde mit **21 Millionen 517 Tausend 415 Einheiten** zum meistgebauten Auto der Welt. Allerdings brauchte der Golf für das, was der Käfer beinahe unverändert schaffte, vier deutlich verschiedene Generationen.

Bis zum Entwicklungsauftrag (EA) 337 (Golf) arbeiteten bei Volkswagen insgesamt nur **28 Stilisten** und Designer.

# Wie Herbert von Karajan doch nicht im Golf I umkam

**Weil der Golf I nicht nur für das Unternehmen VW, sondern auch generell neu war, ließ man ihn besonders promoten. V.I.P.s gehörten dazu. Und manchmal überschlugen sich dabei nicht nur die Ereignisse ...**

Für Dirigent Herbert von Karajan bestand Entspannung aus nächtlichen Vollgasfahrten im Porsche 911 auf der A 8 zwischen Salzburg und München. Zu VW pflegte er eine besondere Beziehung, da er auf Initiative von VW-Generaldirektor Heinrich Nordhoff mit den Berliner Philharmonikern jährlich in Halle 15 des Wolfsburger Werks musizierte. Eine Woche lang wurde dann nicht geforscht, sondern ausgeräumt, gestrichen, Teppich verlegt, Gestühl installiert. Im Gegenzug erhielt Ausnahme-Dirigent Karajan stets Ausnahme-Autos von VW. Daher wurde dem Maestro auch der neue Golf vorgestellt, inklusive scharfen Wedelns durch die Pylonengasse im VW-Prüfgelände Ehra-Lessien. Karajan gab sich beeindruckt, bedankte sich und brauste im 911 davon.

In der Woche drauf durchlief eine österreichische Delegation inklusive kräftig gebauter Staatssekretärin das gleiche Programm: Demonstration von Sicherheit und Fahrdynamik des neuen Golf. Frau Staatsrätin gurtete sich auf dem Beifahrersitz an, hinters Steuer schlüpfte, wie schon bei Karajan, VW-Pressesprecher Anton Konrad. Der gab ordentlich Stoff, lenkte den Golf in die Pylonengasse – und erschrak: Der Golf lag viel zu schwammig! Konrad ging vom Gas, worauf der Rand der belasteten rechten Vorderradfelge sich im Betonboden verkeilte, den Golf steil aufstellte und sich zweimal überschlagen ließ. „Während wir uns drehten, dachte ich: ‚Mist. Jetzt überschlägst du dich und kommst zu spät zu deinem nächsten Termin.'", erinnert sich Konrad. Grund für das Malheur: Der vermeintliche Test-Golf war gar keiner, son-

Wenn in der Pylonengasse die Reifen schleifen: Golf I in Ehra-Lessien

dern lediglich ein nach Fotoarbeiten abgestelltes Presseauto mit zu niedrigem Luftdruck im rechten Vorderrad.

Nach dem Crash lag der nicht angeschnallt gewesene Konrad im Golf wie ein Käfer auf der Staatssekretärin, die sich indes völlig unbeeindruckt gab. Während das aus dem Kofferraum herausgeschleuderte Reserverad munter außer Sicht kullerte (seitdem wurde es verschraubt) und der Golf aufgerichtet wurde, applaudierte die Delegation ob der unversehrten Staatssekretärin. Anton Konrad trocken: „Die dachten, das gehöre zum Programm. Ich habe diesen Eindruck nicht korrigiert." Bis zu seinem Ausscheiden bei VW ließ er der Staatssekretärin am jeweiligen Jahrestag des Ereignisses einen Blumenstrauß schicken – anlässlich ihres „zweiten Geburtstags". Konrad: „Man stelle sich vor, das wäre mir eine Woche vorher mit Karajan passiert. Wir wären beide in die Zeitung gekommen. Eventuell sogar mit schwarzem Rand drumherum."

Nie wieder Schraube locker: Sicherung des Reserverads

# Geisterfahrer

**Unfallforschung begann in den 1930er Jahren in den USA. Doch erst 1973 wurden die beiden ersten wirklich menschenähnlichen Dummys „Hybrid I“ und „Hybrid II“ eingesetzt. Mit Beschleunigungsaufnehmern in Kopf, Brust und Becken und Messgerät, um die Kräfte im Oberschenkel zu bestimmen. Doch das war nicht „lebensnah“ genug ...**

Auch VW untersuchte im Zusammenhang mit der Konstruktion des Golf die Möglichkeiten, Menschen vor Unfallfolgen zu bewahren oder Schaden für Leib und Leben zu minimieren. Allerdings fehlte aufgrund der Technikstandards die Gewissheit, dass die an Dummys gemessenen Belastungswerte tatsächlichen Belastungen des menschlichen Körpers entsprachen.

**Seitenaufprall-Versuch im ESVW I (Golf I) mit Dummys**

**Volkswagen-Werbung 1979 im „Spiegel“: Dummys übernahmen auch bei VW nach und nach menschliche Aufgaben komplett …**

In Kooperation mit dem Institut für Rechtsmedizin der Universität Heidelberg griff VW daher für einen begrenzten Zeitraum auf Versuche mit menschlichen Leichen zurück. Klingt makaber? Yep. Die Unfallforscher betrachteten ihre Arbeit jedoch unter dem Motto: Tote helfen, Leben zu retten. Es ging um Biomechanik und Kybernetik an der Grenze von Medizin und Technik. Um das Begreifen des Menschen als physikalische Einheit. Voraussetzungen für die Leichenversuche waren damals, dass die Leichen unabhängig von der Unfallforschung zur Obduktion bestimmt waren und Einwilligungen der Angehörigen vorlagen. So wurden wertvolle Erkenntnisse hinsichtlich Knochenbrüchen, Verletzungen innerer Organe, Kopfbeschleunigung und Brustbelastung gewonnen. Nur Hirnverletzungen konnte man damals (noch) nicht untersuchen: Tote haben keinen Blutdruck.

# Der weiße Scheinriese

**Opel war gerade so richtig zufrieden mit dem fertig entwickelten Kadett E, als ein futuristischer VW namens „Auto 2000“ durch die Medien geisterte. „Oha! Der neue Golf?“, fragte man sich in Rüsselsheim panisch – und ließ sich famos in die Irre leiten ...**

Der Schock kam auf der Internationalen Automobil-Ausstellung (IAA) 1981. Sämtlichen Opel-Ingenieuren blieben die Lachshäppchen im Halse stecken: WAS war dieses weiße Raumschiff da auf dem VW-Stand ...?

Ein futuristischer Dreitürer mit riesiger Heckklappe, zwergenhaftem Verbrauch von 4,2 Litern Diesel auf 100 Kilometern und einer sichtbar strömungsgünstigen Kunststoff-Karosserie von Designer Lamberto Angelini mit einem cW-Wert von sensationellen 0,25! Dazu ein Interieur, das Comic-Held „Captain Future“ zur Ehre gereicht hätte: Digital-Cockpit mit LCD-Bildschirm, Wegeleitsystem – also Navi! –, speziellen Sitzen aus voll recyclebarem Kunststoff, Scheiben aus Polycarbonat und unter der Haube ohne Kühlergrill entweder Dreizylinder-Turbodiesel mit 53 PS oder mit Kompressor-

Der Keil: Studie „Auto 2000“ – am Ende doch kein neuer Golf. Design von Lamberto Angelini

Aufladung und 60 PS. Damit erreichte das nur 780 Kilo leichte „Auto 2000" satte 186 km/h! Schließlich verbaute VW in einem weiteren Prototypen einen Vierzylinder-Benziner mit 75 PS und nur einem Liter Hubraum, dafür aber ebenfalls mit Kompressor-Aufladung – Kenner horchen auf: Hieraus sollte der G-Lader entstehen. Und unten drunter? Eine Hinterachse aus Kunststoff!

Ablenkungsmanöver: VW-Chef Carl H. Hahn narrte die Opel-Ingenieure.

„Volkswagen ist auf ungebremstem Weg in die Zukunft mit bahnbrechenden Konzepten für die baldige Serienfertigung", diktierte sinngemäß VW-Chef Prof. Dr. Carl H. Hahn den Journalisten in ihre Notizblöcke. Woraufhin Zeitzeugen zufolge bei Opel der Angstschweiß ausbrach. Denn: Zur gleichen Zeit befand sich bei Opel der neue Kadett auf der Entwicklungszielgeraden, mit dem man sich in Rüsselsheim angesichts des „Auto 2000" meilenweit hinter dem Mond fühlte. „Wenn das der von VW für 1983 angekündigte neue Golf wird, dann gute Nacht!", soll es geheißen haben.

Opel schärfte seinen fast fertigen E-Kadett im Science-Fiction-Stil so umfassend nach, bis der die konservativen Käufer so richtig schön verstörte. Und was kam dann? Der Golf II! Mit artigen Rundscheinwerfern im schwarzen Kühlergrill, identisch gebliebener Formsprache und doch recht brav. „Bei Volkswagen ist Evolution stets wichtiger als Revolution", diktierte Carl H. Hahn erneut. Dies wohl so trocken, wie die Kehlen der düpierten Opel-Manager gewesen sein dürften. „Zur Zeit des ‚Auto 2000' haben wir VW-intern viel diskutiert, uns dann aber dazu entschieden, dass der Golf ein Golf bleibt. Das ging ja bis 2019 gut", stichelt Ernst Fiala, Ex-VW-Forschungsvorstand.

Lustige Randnotiz: Gert Volker Hildebrandt, Designer des besagten Kadett E, wirkte von 1986 bis 1989 bei VW maßgeblich mit am Golf III …

Opel traf angesichts des Auto 2000 der Blitz.

# Slow Motion

**Weil nicht sein kann, was nicht sein darf, verfeinerte VW im Jahre 1983 einen von zwei wichtigen Pressewagen. Es war die Zeit des Modellwechsels zwischen Golf I und Golf II, sämtliche Fachzeitschriften testeten den „Neuen“ gegen den „Alten“.**

***„auto motor und sport“*** bestellte damals in Wolfsburg zwei Kandidaten für einen mit Spannung erwarteten Vergleich: Golf I GTI, Sondermodell „Pirelli“, und Golf II GTI – also Alt gegen Neu, das Duell der Ikonen! Und nun raten wir einmal alle gemeinsam, wer am Ende alt aussah ...

Weil VW – zumindest bei Pressetestwagen und dies zumindest früher – wirklich nichts dem Zufall überließ, durchliefen beide Testkandidaten im ersten Anlauf Wolfsburg-interne Messprogramme und Qualitäts-Checks. Wie immer notierten die verschiedenen Fahrer aus der Fachabteilung jedes noch so kleine Knistern hinter den Türverkleidungen, stopften Schaumstoff unter die Fensterkurbeln, klebten zusätzliche Antidröhnmatten an die Karosserie-Innenflächen. Komisches Geräusch aus dem Getriebe? Wechseln, das Aggregat! Dann ab auf die Schnellbahn, Durchbeschleunigen, Stopp der Werte von null auf 100. Mit folgenden höchst unerwünschten Ergebnissen: Der mit 183 km/h Spitze angegebene Pirelli-GTI rannte echte 187 km/h! Boah, ey, geil! Und der Thronfolger? Tja ... Der offiziell vom Werk mit 191 km/h angegebene Golf II GTI schaffte 188 km/h. Boah, ey, wie ungeil! Was tun?

Anderntags sollten beide GTI an die Redaktion übergeben werden! Fieberhaft wurde überlegt ...

Inmitten dieser Situation löste sich ein beteiligter Mitarbeiter der Forschung und Entwicklung aus der Gruppe und öffnete kurzentschlossen die Haube des Einser-GTI. Kurzes Überlegen, dann prüfende Handgriffe hier und da. Schließlich klimperte Werkzeug unter der Haube. Das Ende der Operation ergab eine unauffällig veränderte Position der Feder am Drosselklappensteller des Motors. So, dass man kein Vollgas mehr geben konnte, dies aber nicht bemerkte. Und siehe da: Schon sprintete der Neuling im offiziellen ***„auto motor und sport“***-Test dem Vorgänger knapp davon! Die GTI-Welt nebst natürlicher Rangfolge war wieder in Ordnung. Weil eben nicht sein kann, was nicht sein darf . .

Too fast and too furious:
Golf I GTI „Pirelli“

Bist du zu stark, ist er
zu schwach: Golf II GTI

# Burger, Sushi, Sarajevo

**Jeder hat ja bekanntlich sein Laster, Volkswagen hatte den Golf I Caddy. Heute längst Kult und Sammlerstück wurde der Golf-Pick-up gemäß Bestimmung zeitlebens nicht geschont, sondern bestimmungsgemäß ge- und rasch auch verbraucht.**

„Nicht geschont" in besonders bedrückendem Ausmaß wurden vor allem die 3.000 Mitarbeiter des VW-Joint-Ventures TAS Sarajevo während des Kosovo-Krieges ab 1992. Der ausschließliche Produktionsort des Caddy I wurde zwar zunächst von den Kriegsgegnern Serbien und Bosnien nicht angetastet, weil jede Partei danach trachtete, das lukrative Werk und dessen Wirtschaftskraft nach einem Sieg jeweils für sich zu nutzen. Nach dem Friedensabkommen von Dayton jedoch verminten und verwüsteten serbische Kräfte ganz gezielt den Standort der Caddy-Produktion. Zudem wurden zentrale technische Einrichtungen systematisch entfernt.

Peschkes Inspiration aus Südamerika: It's a Pick-up!

Der kriegsbedingte Komplettausfall der Caddy I-Produktion sowie der nur mühsam gelingende Wiederaufbau in Sarajevo rissen also eine empfindliche Lücke ins VW-Modellprogramm, die nun ausnahmslos der größere, parallel zum Caddy gebaute VW Taro aus deutscher Produktion ausfüllen musste. Dieser Taro wiederum war im Prinzip nichts anderes als ein fast lupenreiner Lizenzbau des japanischen Toyota Hilux. Nach dem mehrere Jahre dauernden Wiederaufbau des Werks in Sarajevo startete man die Caddy-Produktion nicht erneut. Das Modell galt als veraltet. Nicht in Serie ging der übrigens fertige Caddy auf Basis des Golf III – durch die Skoda-Übernahme bot sich VW eine günstigere Pick-up-Plattform.

Gestartet war der Caddy I ursprünglich in den USA – als Pick-up-Variante des US-Golf „Rabbit". Und nach diesem hieß er dann auch. Hätte sonst auch nur Verwirrung gegeben! Denn wer damals in den USA umgangssprachlich einen „Caddy" orderte, meinte und bekam auf gar keinen Fall einen blechernen Golf-I-Pick-up. Sondern einen plüschigen Cadillac in XXXXL! Vom Start weg sehr erfolgreich verkauft wurde der Pick-up-Golf jedoch vor allem in Südamerika. In Ecuador waren für einen Pick-up nur 15 Prozent Importsteuer statt 190 Prozent für Limousinen zu entrichten, wie VW-Ingenieure auf der „Alaska-Feuerland-Tour" (s. Seite 14/15) aufmerksam notierten. Im Hintergrund spielten auch militärische Interessen eine Rolle: Im Konfliktfall hätten die Truppen auf eine Vielzahl robuster Nutzfahrzeuge zurückgreifen können. Guatemala wies zur Zeit der VW-Golf-Erprobung auf der Panamericana einen Pick-up-Anteil von 40 Prozent auf.

Ein Caddy ist ein Caddy ist – nein, nicht immer ein VW Caddy ...

# Grill-Glut

**Die hier haben Glut hinterm Grill. Die heißesten Gölfe aller Generationen. Nie waren sie schneller, stärker, brachialer, irrer als die hier gezeigten Exemplare. Einige in Serie, einige limitiert, einige gar nur ein einziges Mal gebaut. Für was? Für den Spaß. Für die Show. Und für die Ewigkeit. Weil, die hier vergisst du nie. Egal, wie oft oder selten es sie gibt. Denn im Kopf drehen sie Doughnuts. Bitte einsteigen und anschnallen!**

## Golf I GTI

„Den Zauber besitzt nur der erste GTI", urteilt der ehemalige „auto motor und sport"-Tester Klaus Westrup noch 45 Jahre nach dem Debüt des Sport-Golf. 110 PS, 1600 ccm, 0 100 9,2 s, 182 km/h Spitze. Leichtgewicht, dezente Optik, brachiale Dynamik und Power. 1976 mit dem richtigen Fahrer am Steuer definitiv eine Gefahr für jeden Porsche 911.

**Golf GTI 16V**

Schwer hatte es der Golf II gegen seinen Vorfahren, dies in doppeltem Sinne. Er war größer, komfortabler, behäbiger geworden. Erst der Sechzehnventiler ab 1987 brachte ihn wieder ordentlich in Schwung. Heute dennoch gemacht, gesucht, gepflegt und geliebt. Mit was? Mit Recht!

**Golf GTI G60**

Ungefähr jeder zweite bis dritte Testwagen namens Golf GTI G60 verreckte während der Pressepräsentation. Dabei galt der mechanische Lader G-Form wegen des fehlenden „Turbo-Lochs" als die kultivierte Alternative zum damals äußerst angesagten Turbo. Brachte jedoch weder in Serie noch im Motorsport Erfolge. Heute gesucht. 1800 ccm, 118 PS, 0 100 8,2 s, Spitze 219 km/h.

**Golf Limited**

Im auf nur 71 Stück angelegten Golf Limited vereinte sich feinste VW-Technik der Zeit: 1,8-Liter-Vierzylinder. Sechzehnventiler. Mechanische Aufladung durch G60-Lader. Dazu syncro-Allradtechnik mit über eine Viscokupplung schlupfabhängig angetriebenen Hinterrädern. 1800 ccm, 210 PS, 0 100 7,4 s, Spitze 229 km/h. Unbezahlbar.

**Rallye Golf G60**

Etwas proletarisch-präsent wirkt er, der pausbäckig aufgeblasene Rallye Golf. VWs Wunschvorstellung, ein optisch starkes Golf-Modell zu kreieren. Es wurde auch mit gleichgroßen Doppel-Rundscheinwerfern experimentiert, aber am Ende kamen die Glasbausteine. **Kimme – Korn – Kraft: Klare Kurvenlinie, beeindruckende Beschleunigung, das Fahrwerk ist bretthart.** 1800 ccm, 210 PS, 0 100 7,4 s, Spitze 229 km/h. **Wir haben verstanden.**

**Golf II Pikes Peak „Kurt Bergmann"**

Zwei Golf-GTI-16V-Triebwerke, dank Turbo und Digifant-Einspritzung auf jeweils 337 PS gebracht. Zwei Hewland-FT-200-Renngetriebe der früheren Formel 2. Leichtbau im Bereich des Rohrrahmens und durch GFK-Karosse. Irrer Bi-Motor-Golf, erdacht und gebaut von Rennlegende Kurt Bergmann. 1987 damit am Start am Pikes Peak in den USA. Zweitplatzierter hinter Walter Röhrl – wegen eines Defekts 200 Meter vor dem Ziel! Es bleiben für immer die Bilder, wie sie – am Berg! – mit 188 Sachen mitten in die weltweite Aufmerksamkeit hineinfuhren.

**Golf III A 59**

Kompromisslose Renn-Konstruktion mit entsprechender Optik. Alu-Vierzylinder-Benziner mit Turbo und Ladeluftkühler. Standard: 2000 ccm, 275 PS, im Renneinsatz 400 PS geplant. Allrad, hydraulisch gesteuerte Lamellensperre im Mitteldifferenzial und 6-Gang-Getriebe. Piëch killte das Projekt (s. Seite 82/83).

WOB GA 59

**Golf IV R32**

Nicht so leicht wie ein Einser-GTI, doch wie dieser mit Motor aus einem Audi. Brüllt ähnlich wie ein G60. Sein DSG krepiert schlimmstenfalls auch wie der Spirallader. Macht auf Muckis wie Rallye Golf und A 59, nur optisch wie technisch ausgewogener. Leistung? Klar. 251 Sachen Spitze. Sound? Und wie. Da haben sie gezaubert wie beim Einser. Geht **nach Gusto giftig wie Galle oder samtig wie Seide**. 3200 ccm, 241 PS, 0 100 6,4 s, Spitze 251 km/h.

**Golf GTI W12 650**

Anlässlich des GTI-Treffens in Reifnitz am Wörthersee 2007 entwickelte Studie. Die Karosserie wurde um zwölf Zentimeter verbreitert und um acht Zentimeter abgesenkt. 6,0-Liter-Biturbo-W12-Motor vor Hinterachse eingebaut. 650 PS, 750 Newtonmeter Drehmoment, 3,7 Sekunden von null auf 100 Sachen. Die Höchstgeschwindigkeit? 325 km/h. Läuft.

**Golf VI R**

Downsizing mit Spaß: 2,0-l-FSI-Reihenvierzylinder mit Turbolader, 270 PS, 350 Newtonmeter Drehmoment. 4MOTION-Allrad, 6-Gang-Handschalter oder 6-Gang-DSG. Sogar als Cabrio lieferbar. Front mit Bi-Xenon und LED-Tagfahrlicht, Heck mit Doppelrohrauspuff und LED-Rückleuchten, Interieur mit R-Logo und zweifarbigen Sportsitzen, Sportfahrwerk mit 25 mm Tieferlegung, ESP mit Sportmodus. Trotzdem vom Image her a bissl blutleer.

**Golf VII GTI Clubsport S**

2,0-Liter-Turbo, 310 PS, 380 Newtonmeter Drehmoment, ausschließlich mit 6-Gang-Schaltgetriebe erhältlich. 265 Sachen Spitze. Limitiert auf nur 400 Exemplare. Nummer 001 besitzt Benjamin Leuchter, der 2016, mitten in den Jubiläumsveranstaltungen zum 40. Geburtstag des Golf GTI, einen neuen Nordschleifen-Rekord für frontgetriebene Serienautos im Golf VII GTI Clubsport S auf dem Nürburgring herausfuhr.

**Golf VIII R**

Sechs umständliche Bedienschritte braucht es, um den schärfsten Golf VIII zu entsichern, und auch sonst gibt's noch immer Ärger mit aussteigender Digitaltechnik. Sei's drum: Wer die Kohle hat, legt bei seinem Golf VIII R noch ein paar Verfeinerungs-Schippen drauf. Dann gibt's Radau und Performance(-Paket). 270 km/h Spitze. 2,0-Liter-Turbodirekteinspritzer holt 420 Newtonmeter Drehmoment raus. Anders gesagt: Der R hier schiebt. Dich. An.

# Random

**30.514 Kilometer** betrug die Fahrstrecke, die zwei speziell präparierte Golf I von Oktober 1973 bis Januar 1974 auf ihrem Härtetest von Alaska nach Feuerland zurücklegten.

Erstmals ABS und Airbags im Golf gab es in der Generation III – zu Beginn gegen Aufpreis, später serienmäßig.

Auch sie gehört zu VW wie der Golf: Die 1973 von einem Fleischer speziell für VW entwickelte Currywurst feierte im Jahr 2015 ihren bisherigen Absatzrekord mit **7,2 Millionen** Stück. Die „Fleischpeitsche" hat sogar eine eigene VW-Ersatzteilnummer: **199398500**.

Volkswagen Currywurst

Der Golf III ist der einzige Golf, der jemals die Auszeichnung „Auto des Jahres" erhielt.

Niemand bei VW mochte oder verstand den hochbeinigen Golf II Country. Abschätzig hieß es, dies sei „Fialas letztes Spielzeug". Der genannte Forschungschef Ernst Fiala ging 1988 in den Ruhestand.

Golf II. Country

6.500.000 Quadratmeter beträgt die Fläche des Golf-Stammwerks von VW in Wolfsburg. Das entspricht 910 Fußballfeldern.

Die höchste Stückzahl von innerhalb eines Jahres gebauten Golf erreichte der Golf III im Jahre 1992. Grund hierfür war die vorangegangene deutsch-deutsche Grenzöffnung mitsamt Währungsunion und entsprechenden Käufen von „West-Autos".

Jedem Golf-V-Sondermodell „Goal" legte VW ein Tipp-Kick-Spiel bei.

Die Exemplare der Golf-VI-Sonderserie „Edition 35" besaßen angeblich jeweils 235 PS – von denen soll laut damaligen internen Leistungsmessungen aber keiner unter 260 PS rausgegangen sein. Die Motoren stammten aus dem Scirocco R.

Als sie das Golf Cabriolet Etienne Aigner entwarf, überreichte der damalige Aigner-Chef ein Geschenk an VW-Designerin Gunhild Liljequist. Zurück in Wolfsburg packte sie es aus. Kommentar: „Es war Shampoo – und ich hasse Shampoo! Na, habe ich eben zwei Jahre lang den Hund mit gewaschen ..."

# tetra

Es ist Winter in Wolfsburg und wir schreiben das Jahr 1985. Die Tore des internen VW-Sicherheitsbereichs der Forschung und Entwicklung waren gut bewacht, während drinnen ganz spezielle Fahrzeuge auf ihren Serieneinsatz warteten. An ihren Hecks trugen sie die silberne Modellbezeichnung „tetra". Als besonderer Gag bildeten auch die Fäden der Heckscheibenheizungen das Wort „tetra". So sollten die neuen Allradfahrzeuge von VW heißen!

Die Testwagenflotte schwärmte aus, von Wolfsburg aus in die weite Welt, bis Colorado, USA. Dann plötzlich erhielten alle Testwagenfahrer Post aus Wolfsburg. Inhalt: ein Schreiben, nach dem eine Namensänderung der Allrad-VW unumgänglich sei und kurzfristig zu erfolgen habe! Weshalb jedem Schreiben tatsächlich jeweils ein Schraubenzieher (!) beilag, nebst der expliziten Aufforderung, sämtliche „tetra"-Schriftzüge mithilfe des gelieferten Werkzeuges zu entfernen! Hm, was war passiert?

So ist's richtig!

Grund für die Umbenennung war das drohende Veto des Verpackungsherstellers „Tetra Pack". Und vielleicht hatte ja auch ein reflektierter Marketing-Experte mögliche negative Assoziation zu besagter Einwegverpackung erkannt. Also wurden weltweit die Heckscheiben ausgebaut und zerstört, sämtliche „tetra"-Schriftzüge manuell entfernt und vernichtet. Im Bild einer der wenigen Überlebenden.

Innerhalb kürzester Zeit wurde tetra bei VW syncronisiert.

# Hauben-Taucher

Ende der 1970er Jahre mehrten sich Kundenbeschwerden über neue VW Golf mit nach außen gewölbten kleinen Beulen an den vorderen Rändern der Motorhauben. „Unverschämt!“, schnaubten die Kunden. „Was ist das bloß?“, fragten sich schwitzend die Verantwortlichen in der Produktion. Intern lagen die Nerven blank, weil das sporadisch auftretende Phänomen unlösbar erschien, obwohl der Ursache akribisch nachgegangen wurde. Eine extra Kommission wurde gegründet, deren Mitglieder in unregelmäßigen Abständen die Neuwagen inspizierten. Und – Teufel! – tatsächlich hatten die Gölfe mal diese kleinen, fiesen Höcker in der Haube, mal nicht! Schließlich wollte VW es ganz genau wissen und begleitete zu Fuß die gesamte Produktion von der Rohkarosse bis zum fertigen Auto – ohne Ergebnis.

Nur durch puren Zufall wurde das Geheimnis schließlich gelüftet: Ein Mitarbeiter aus der Produktion, der für die Ausführung seiner Montagetätigkeit im Motorraum des Golf dessen vordere Haube öffnen musste, hatte den Grad seiner Arbeitseffizienz durch das lässige Hochwerfen der Haube mit der linken Hand und dem gleichzeitigen Aufwerfen der Motorhaubenstange mit der rechten Hand perfektioniert. Dabei hatte er eine derartige Versiertheit und Routine, dass die Haltestange zwar exakt an der dafür vorgesehenen Stelle auftraf, aber halt die zurückfallende Motorhaube mit ihrem ganzen Gewicht darauf landete. Das Ende der Stange bohrte sich daher in die Blechfläche und sorgte so für „Pickel-Hauben“. Die Kommission hatte bis dato keine Chance gehabt, weil sie ausgerechnet während der Schichten, in denen der verantwortliche Mann am Fließband stand, nicht kontrollierte. Es ist eben überall wie beim Motor-Zahnriemen: Auf das Timing kommt es an ...

# Volkswagenfeste

Weltweiter Bekanntheit erfreut sich das internationale Golf-GTI-Treffen im österreichischen Reifnitz am Wörthersee. Es findet seit 1982 jeweils für vier Tage, beginnend mit dem Mittwoch vor Christi Himmelfahrt bis zum darauffolgenden Samstag, statt. Jahr für Jahr überschütten mittlerweile bis zu 200.000 GTI-Fans den beschaulichen Landstrich mit ihren Autos, ihrem Lärm und

Ganz schöner Brocken: Der Golf GTI aus Granit schwebt ein in Reifnitz.

ihrem Geld. Nun darf jeder raten, was davon den Einwohnern am liebsten ist.

Zwischen 1993 und 1995 wurde es aufgrund zu hoher Krawalle abgesagt. Inoffizielle Treffen waren die Folge, mittlerweile spaltet sich das Fan-Lager teilweise in Anhänger der „offiziellen" und der „inoffiziellen" Treffen, die jeweils kurz hintereinander stattfinden. Am unterhaltsamsten waren die Tumulte wohl 1987, als Sponsor Volkswagen einen in Golf-II-GTI-Form behauenen Granitbrocken per Spezialtransport nach Reifnitz karrte und dort dauerhaft ablud. Der GTI aus schwedischem Granit war behauen von Auszubildenden und Meistern der Steinmetzschule im niedersächsischen Königslutter, einem pittoresken Kaff bei Wolfsburg.

Zur offiziellen Einweihung des Golf-Brockens schaute der damalige VW-Chef Carl H. Hahn persönlich in Reifnitz vorbei. Hierfür jedoch musste der Manager in Nadelstreifen zunächst über massivst alkoholisierte, kreuz und quer am Boden liegende dänische GTI-Fans steigen, die in lustig-unbeschwerten Panzerkombis angereist waren. Derweil interpretierten die Teilnehmer mitsamt ihren GTI die Strecke zwischen Ortsein- und -ausgang als Beschleunigungsstrecke. Davor und dahinter protestierten die damals noch jungen Grünen gegen derartige Raserei und der damalige Reifnitzer Bürgermeister skandierte: „Hängt die Grünen auf, solange es noch Bäume gibt!" Doch wer jetzt meint, das alles oder irgendetwas anderes wäre jemals Grund, diese Volkswagenfeste für immer zu beenden, beißt auf Granit.

# Heide graut

Lange Zeit musste VW bezüglich der Formen seiner Autos den Spott des Volksmundes über sich ergehen lassen. Der Begriff „Heide-Design" schallte böse durch die provinzielle Landschaft, in der das Wolfsburger Stammwerk gewachsen war. Dabei waren VW-Modelle stets von italienischen Namen ersten Ranges eingekleidet worden. Von Ghia (Karmann-Ghia), Pininfarina (VW 411), Bertone (VW 1500), Giugiaro (Golf I). Dazu gesellten sich nicht weniger als 70 (!) Prototypen potenzieller Käfer-Nachfolger von 1946 bis 1968, an denen neben Porsche auch die genannten italienischen Karossiers beteiligt waren. Dass diese Autos, die zusammen elf Milliarden Mark verschlangen, allesamt nicht in Serie gingen, ist ein Buch für sich. Einige der erhalten gebliebenen Entwürfe sind heute als Museumsstücke in Wolfsburg zu bestaunen.

**Wieso dann also „Heide-Design"?**

Ganz einfach: An fast allen italienischen Entwürfen dokterten im Nachhinein Wolfsburger Stilisten herum. So finden sich bereits 1967 verzweifelte Appelle von Vater und Sohn Pininfarina an VW-Boss Heinrich Nordhoff persönlich („Man darf an ein so schmales Auto keine Doppelscheinwerfer bauen! Und das Dach – viel zu hoch und rund! Man muss doch nicht überall mit Hut einsteigen können!") als auch eigenmächtige Eingriffe am Golf I. Ab den 1970er Jahren erstarkte das hauseigene VW-Design unter der Leitung von Herbert Schäfer personell. Zwar entstanden auch dann nicht wenige atemberaubende Renderings, zum Beispiel

Heide, hier blüht dir gleich was!

keilförmige Entwürfe für den Scirocco II eines gewissen Luca Rezzonico, der auch den Passat 32b von 1981 gezeichnet hatte, dies bereits 1973. Fließheck und harte Kanten waren en vogue! Aber dann wurde stets verlangweilt.

Oft existierten zwei grundlegend verschiedene Sichtweisen: Während der Passat 35i, Wegbegleiter des ebenfalls „braven" und formal eher unschlüssigen Golf III, ob seiner geschlossenen Front VW-intern mit dem größten Stolz betrachtet wurde, bezeichneten ihn externe Kritiker gallig als „Kartoffeldesign". Oder gar als „Kotzknolle". „Am Ende kam stets der VW-Vertrieb mit seiner Angst vor Revolutionen", resümiert der erwähnte Rezzonico, „und eben Herbert Schäfer mit gedanklichem Hut auf dem Kopf."

**Der Schäfer wohnt übrigens bis heute in der Heide.**

Zumindest heute ein Klassiker: Golf II

# Der Ernst-Fall

**Michail Gorbatschow sagt, wer zu spät komme, den bestrafe das Leben. Ernst Fiala hat das Leben, also VW, auch bestraft. Jedenfalls zum Ende seiner Laufbahn als VW-Forschungschef. Da verspottete man den Golf Country als „Stelzen-Golf“ oder bezeichnete ihn als „Kinder-Country“. Wie war‘s denn nun?**

Wegbegleiter sagen noch heute über Fiala: Der war mit seiner Forschung der Entwicklung immer mindestens drei Schritte voraus. Und während heute zum Alltag gehört, dass kriegsbemalte Gölfe mit der Modellbezeichnung „Cross“ durch schweres Parkplatzgelände vor dem Supermarkt kreuzen, schüttelten sie 1990 den Kopf: Golf Country ...? Was war geschehen? Nicht weniger, als dass VW den Allrad verschlafen hatte. Schon im Transporter hatte Wolfsburg ihn erst nicht haben wollen! Dann fuhr Ferdinand Piëch mit dem Konzept quattro voraus, VW musste nachziehen mit syncro. Das war chic, doch dem Fiala auf Dauer zu flach.

Ende im Gelände nach nur zwei Jahren: Golf Country

Er hatte den Aufstieg des knochigen Land Rover zum gediegenen Range Rover aufmerksam verfolgt, zudem das Auftauchen neuer Autotypen wie des AMC Eagle. So bekam der Golf Country die Aufgabe eines Versuchsballons, wie VW die Mixtur zwischen Pkw und Geländewagen auf dem Markt etablieren könnte. Oberstes Diktat: Entwicklungskosten ungefähr gleich null. Im Frühjahr 1988 rührte Fiala sein rustikales Rezept an: Serien-Golf CL syncro, im Wolfsburger Versuchsbau einen Rohrrahmen konstruiert, fertig! Ästhetische Unbill hielt Einzug: „Für uns war das eine Katastrophe", erinnert sich VW-Designer Luca Rezzonico, der damals dabei sein musste. „Der Country sah aus, als hätte man die Karosserie mit einem Kran nach oben gehievt und das Fahrwerk wäre unten liegen geblieben." Satte 18 Zentimeter höher wurde der Golf Country dadurch, der nur von April 1990 bis Dezember 1991 durchs VW-Modellprogramm stelzte. Formal und dynamisch 'ne ganz schön träge Masse. Auf mechanische Differenzialsperren sei laut Fiala verzichtet worden, weil in der nächsten Golf-Generation gleich per Anti-Schlupf-System hätte geregelt werden sollen. Prädikat des Country daher: bedingt geländegängig.

Für 42.000 Mark und mit seinem grotesken Äußeren erreichte VW nur rund die Hälfte der avisierten Verkaufszahlen von 15.000 Stück. Der Country wurde zweifellos auch deshalb kein Erfolg, weil er intern ein ungeliebtes Kind war. Wäre es anders gekommen, wäre im September 1988 nicht auch Ernst Fiala aus dem VW-Modellprogramm geflogen ...? Der pensionierte Vorstand und Forscher jedenfalls konnte „seinen" Golf Country ab da nicht mehr protegieren. Und in gewisser Weise verpasste VW zum damaligen Zeitpunkt Modell- und Marktlücke. Träge Massen gibt es eben nicht nur in der Physik, sondern auch in jedem großen Unternehmen.

# Der Weg zum Golf. Mit den wichtigsten Meilensteinen

**1966** Im Herbst erteilt VW-Chef Heinrich Nordhoff Porsche den Auftrag zur Konstruktion eines Käfer-Nachfolgers. Die Revolution umfasst zwei Worte: „Konzeption freigestellt." Alles, auch jenseits von Heckmotor und Luftkühlung, ist möglich. Im Juni tritt der Club dem Verband Süddeutscher Fußballvereine bei. Am 7. Oktober absolviert die Mannschaft ihr erstes Pflichtspiel, schlägt in der Klasse B in der Hinrunde sämtliche Gegner und stolpert erst in der Fastnacht.

**1968** Heinrich Nordhoff stirbt am 12. April. Nachfolger Kurt Lotz („Lotz of Trouble") lässt den Porsche-Auftrag EA 266 mit Unterflur-Mittelmotor weiterentwickeln. Gleichzeitig Arbeiten in Wolfsburg am Konzept EA 276. Idee: Es soll zwei parallel gebaute Nachfolgemodelle des Käfers geben.

**1969** Hans-Georg Wenderoth, ehemaliger NSU-Entwickler, forciert das Frontantriebs-Konzept inklusive vorderer Einzelradaufhängung.

**1970** VW-Chef Kurt Lotz gibt grünes Licht für das spätere Golf-Konzept EA 337. Auf dem Turiner Salon bewerten VW-Vorstände heimlich verschiedene Design-Entwürfe. Daraus folgend erhält der Autodesigner Giorgetto Giugiaro im Januar 1970 eine Einladung nach Wolfsburg. Und den Auftrag, den kompakten Käfer-Nachfolger zu entwerfen. Präsentation des Entwurfs erfolgt nur wenige

Monate später. Abänderungen durch VW umfassen die Länge des Vorderwagens sowie die Neigung der Frontscheibe aus Sicherheitsgründen, Rundscheinwerfer anstatt Rechteckscheinwerfern aus Kostengründen.

Im Oktober muss der glücklose Kurt Lotz gehen. 1971 ...........
Ex-Audi- und VW-do-Brasil-Chef Rudolf Leiding folgt. Killt sofort das desaströse EA-266-Projekt. Forciert Golf und zur Sicherheit den Polo. Der soll den Golf im Ernstfall stützend ergänzen.

Hobbyrennfahrer und VW-Pressechef Anton Konrad 1972 ...........
spricht mit Ingenieur Alfons Löwenberg über die Möglichkeit und Attraktivität eines „Sport-Golf“.

18. März: Alfons Löwenberg schreibt über alle in- 1973 ...........
ternen Hierarchiegrenzen hinweg ein Memo, ob auf Basis des künftigen Golf nicht ein sportliches Modell entwickelt werden sollte. Und verbrennt sich damit erst einmal gehörig die Finger. Rudolf Leiding sagt Giugiaro den von Kurt Lotz in Aussicht gestellten Zehnjahresvertrag über Entwurf, Konstruktion und Prototypenbau für VW aus Kostengründen ab. Giugiaro weist VW auf die Unmöglichkeit der geplanten Modellbezeichnung „VW Pony“ hin. So heißt bereits ein Hyundai, an dem Giugiaro parallel zum VW-Auftrag arbeitet. VW ändert ab in „Golf“.

Oktober 1974 bis Januar 1975: Auto-Schriftsteller 1974 ...........
Fritz B. Busch und ein VW-Team absolvieren mit zwei modifizierten Vorserien-Golf-I die abenteuerliche Panamericana als Marketingaktion.

August: **Debüt des Golf I.** Frontantrieb, Heckklappe, Quermotorisierung, variabler Innenraum brechen mit der VW-DNA des Käfers.
Demission Rudolf Leidings, Nachfolger wird der von Leiding eingefädelte Anton „Toni" Schmücker, sein persönlicher Freund.
Pressechef Anton Konrad bildet seine „Geheimtruppe GTI" mit Verschworenen aus den VW-Bereichen Marketing, Karosserie, Fahrwerk. Höchst konspirativ wird ein Lastenheft zum „Sport-Golf" erarbeitet und im Verborgenen ein Auto aufgebaut.

1975 Im Mai lüftet die Geheimtruppe GTI gegenüber VW-Chef Schmücker den Schleier – der tags zuvor von Konrad ins Vertrauen gezogene Schmücker nickt den GTI artig ab. Der kritische Vertrieb schäumt, muss sich aber geschlagen geben.
September: Vorstellung des Golf GTI auf der IAA in Frankfurt

1976 Markteinführung des Golf GTI
Markteinführung des Golf Diesel, des flinken Selbstzünders
1 Million Golf

1977 Voll fahrbereiter Golf I mit Elektroantrieb, Reichweite 65 Kilometer. Es bleibt bei einem Exemplar zu Forschungszwecken.

1978 2 Millionen Golf
Facelift mit geänderten Stoßfängern aus Kunststoff

Einsatz Golf I Diesel in der neuen Diesel-Klasse, Rallye Monte Carlo. Pilotiert von Jochi Kleint. Aufgrund seiner Beklebung erhält der Golf den Titel „Zebra".

1979

Präsentation des Golf Cabriolet unter lautem Protest der Käfer-Cabrio-Fahrer. Aufgrund des aus konstruktiver Sicht unnötigen Überrollbügels bekommt der Wagen den Spitznamen „Erdbeerkörbchen".
3 Millionen Golf
Golf 928. Extremprojekt von Ausnahme-Tuner Günther Artz. Porsche-928-Basis und -Technik, verkleidet mit Spezialkarosserie in Golf-I-Optik. 30 Zentimeter breiter, 21 Zentimeter länger als ein Golf I. Mit 240 bzw. 300 PS (zwei Stück gebaut).

1980

4 Millionen Golf
Facelift: größere Heckleuchten, überarbeitetes Armaturenbrett

1981

Das auf der IAA gezeigte Konzeptfahrzeug „Auto 2000" wird von Konkurrent Opel für den kommenden Golf II gehalten, woraufhin Opel den fast fertigen eigenen neuen Kadett komplett überarbeitet. Grundlos.
Bau der ersten beiden Golf I CitySTROMer mit Elektroantrieb, Reichweite 50 60 Kilometer
Carl H. Hahn löst den erkrankten Toni Schmücker als VW-Konzernchef ab.

1982 Erster Golf GTD (Turbodiesel)
5 Millionen Golf
Bau von weiteren zwölf Golf I CitySTROMern

1983 6,99 Millionen Golf I
**Golf II – Debüt**
Servolenkung und Garantie gegen Durchrostung als Neuerungen. Äußeres konservativ, Opel ist düpiert.

1984 Zweiter Golf GTI. Weil der Golf I GTI schneller ist als sein Nachfolger, wird ein entsprechender GTI-I-Testwagen künstlich verlangsamt.
Zweiter Golf GTD
Einführung Geregelter Katalysator
Bau und Versuchseinsatz von 50 Golf II CitySTROMern mit Elektroantrieb, Reichweite 50 60 Kilometer

1985 7 Millionen Golf

1986 Facelift: Entfall der vorderen Dreiecksfenster, geändert werden Schriftzüge und Kühlergrill.
Erster Golf syncro (Allradantrieb), der eigentlich hätte „tetra“ heißen sollen
Erster Golf GTI 16V – endlich ist ein Golf GTI wieder angemessen schnell.
ABS für Golf syncro

1987 ABS für alle Golf GT und GTI verfügbar
Golf Pikes Peak. Bi-Motor-Wettbewerbsfahrzeug mit 652 PS, konstruiert und gebaut von Rennlegende Kurt Bergmann. Konnte wahlweise mit Front-, Heck- oder Allradantrieb gefahren werden. Spektakulärer Einsatz am Pikes Peak, USA. Golf-Pilot Jochi Kleint unterliegt durch Defekt nur 200 Meter vor dem Ziel Walter Röhrl.

Es wird heiß unter den Hauben! Pausbacke Rallye Golf G60 und der ultimative GTI namens Golf Limited G60 bereichern (kurz) das Modellprogramm. Vom Limited entstehen nur 71 Exemplare zum Stückpreis von 68.500 Mark. 1988
10 Millionen Golf – dazu gibt's das passende Sondermodell.

Erste Golf-Hybrid-Studie 1989
Öko-Golf: Start-Stopp-Automatik plus Freilauf auch bei rollendem Fahrzeug. Erprobung im Straßenverkehr, keine Serienfertigung.
11 Millionen Golf
Golf GTI G60
Rallye Golf, Auflage 5.000 Exemplare. Der mit den dicken Backen tanzt.

Es erscheint der Allrad-Golf Country. Verspottet als „Stelzen-Golf". Absatzziel wird bis Ende 1991 nur zur Hälfte erreicht. Nicht wirklich geländetauglich, SUV verkaufst du nie – jedenfalls nicht damals. Heute Kult, gesucht sind die GTI-Versionen mit 107 PS (50 Stück gebaut). 1990
Erster Golf GTI mit G60-Motor. Wird zum Kult aufgrund seiner mechanischen Aufladung und seiner Legende. Aber kein Markterfolg, als der Turbo kultivierter wird und der G-Lader erst spät weniger anfällig.
Katalysator für alle Golf-Modelle Serie
1 Million Golf GTI
12 Millionen Golf

1991

6,3 Millionen Golf II
**Golf III – Debüt**
Wegfahrsperre und Geschwindigkeitsregelanlage

Golf VR6 („We are Six"), erster Golf mit Sechszylinder-Benziner
Golf Diesel mit Oxidationskatalysator
Dritter Golf GTI

1992 Ferdinand Piëch übernimmt den VW-Vorstandsvorsitz von Carl H. Hahn.
Fahrer- und Beifahrerairbag erstmals erhältlich im Golf
13 Millionen Golf
Golf VR6 als Top-Modell mit 174 PS, wahlweise als Allrad. Understatement in 7,4 s auf 100 km/h und 225 Sachen Spitze

1993 Erster Golf TDI (Turbodiesel-Direkteinspritzer)
Erster Golf Variant („Der Golf mit Happy End")
Zweites Golf Cabriolet
Zweiter Golf syncro

1994 15 Millionen Golf
Golf Ecomatic mit Schwungnutzautomatik. 2.320 Mark Aufpreis für rund 20 Prozent weniger Verbrauch und gewöhnungsbedürftiges Fahren verbuchen diesen Spritsparer unter der Rubrik „seiner Zeit voraus".

1995 Erster Golf SDI (Saugdiesel-Direkteinspritzer). Ruhiges Temperament, extrem langlebig und sparsam.
Markteinführung des Golf III CitySTROMer. 16 Blei-Gel-Akkus bringen 490 Kilo mit, weshalb der 24-PS-Elektromotor seine liebe Mühe mit diesem Golf hat. Spitze 100 km/h, 0 70 km/h in 27 Sekunden. Trotzdem werden 155 Exemplare verkauft. Zusätzlich zehn Versuchsfahrzeuge für die Insel Rügen.
Elektro-Forschungsfahrzeug „Golf Two Speed" mit 85 Kilometern Reichweite

Erster Golf GTI mit Turbomotor 1996
Golf GTI Sondermodell „20 Jahre GTI“ auch als TDI erhältlich – au weia!
ABS für alle Golf Serie
Seitenairbags
17 Millionen Golf

4,83 Millionen Golf III 1997
**Golf IV – Debüt**
Erster Golf V5 (Fünfzylindermotor)
Karosserie voll verzinkt

Golf 4MOTION (mit Haldexkupplung) 1998
Golf III Cabriolet (Facelift, Basis Golf III, Golf-IV-Optik)
Golf IV GTI – mit verwässertem Rezept, fast alle Motorisierungen sind möglich. Keine reine Sport-DNA mehr.
ESP und Xenonscheinwerfer erhältlich
Bau von zwei Golf IV Electric mit Reichweite von 150 bzw. 110 Kilometern

Golf TDI mit Pumpe-Düse-Technik 1999
Golf 4MOTION mit 6-Gang-Getriebe
19 Millionen Golf
Golf IV Variant
Bremsassistent
ESP in Deutschland Serie

Millennium. Die Erde geht doch nicht unter. 2000
Stattdessen Jubiläum:
20 Millionen Golf

„Jubi-GTI“ der Generation Golf IV anlässlich 25 Jahre Golf GTI. Ist mit 180 PS mal wieder ein 2001

„richtiger“ GTI, 225 Sachen Spitze und in 7,3 s auf Tempo 100.

2002 Bernd Pischetsrieder tritt die Nachfolge von Ferdinand Piëch als VW-Konzernchef an.
Golf FSI (Benzin-Direkteinspritzer)
Erster Golf R32. Legitimer, aber zornigerer VR6-Erbe mit 247 km/h Spitze. Und dann die Werbung! („Drehzahlmesser ...??!“) Mehr als die 5.000 geplanten Exemplare werden gebaut.
Golf mit Erdgasantrieb (BiFuel im Variant)
Nach Front- und Seitenairbags werden auch Kopfairbags Serie.
**Weltrekord: Mit 21.517.415 produzierten Exemplaren überholt der Golf den Käfer.**

2003 Erster Golf mit 6-Gang-Doppelkupplungsgetriebe (DSG) im R32
4,97 Millionen Golf IV
**Golf V – Debüt**. Laserschweißen der Karosserie bringt dem Wagen höhere Steifigkeit, die abgesunkene Detailqualität den Spitznamen „Klapperbude“. Verkaufszahlen sinken, Design und Gesamtkonzept scheinen nicht wie gewohnt zu überzeugen. Allerdings erstarkt der GTI erneut, auch vom Marketing her. Erhältlich sind automatisch abblendender Innenspiegel, Bi-Xenonscheinwerfer, Park Distance Control, Regensensor. Serie ist die Vierlenker-Hinterachse (die laut Werbung auch geradeaus fährt, und dies sogar mitsamt Auto).

2004 Golf V GTI (mit TSI / Turbobenzin-Direkteinspritzer)
23 Millionen Golf

2005 Golf V TSI als Twincharger

(Kompressor- und Turbo-Aufladung)
Golf V R32

Martin Winterkorn wird neuer VW-Konzernchef und Nachfolger von Bernd Pischetsrieder. 2006
Golf Plus, ob seiner Erscheinung vom Volksmund „Elefantenrollschuh“ getauft
Golf GTI „30 Jahre GTI“ mit strammen 230 PS (30 mehr als in der Serie), schwarzen 18-Zöllern, speziellem Interieur. Ein echter GTI.

Golf BlueMotion. Lange Getriebeübersetzung, schmale Reifen sowie aerodynamische Optimierungen senken den Verbrauch auf offiziell 4,5 Liter Diesel auf 100 Kilometern. 2007
CrossGolf (kann nix anderes außer Aussehen)
Golf V Variant
Showcar Golf GTI W12-650. Der brachiale Wahnsinn auf Rädern. Zwölfzylinder aus dem Bentley Continental GT. Angeordnet als Mittelmotor. Sechs Liter Hubraum, in 3,7 s von null auf 100, Spitze 325 km/h. Heckantrieb.
25 Millionen Golf

Golf V mit 7-Gang-Doppelkupplungsgetriebe 2008
Golf-Hybrid-Studie. Mit 1,2-Liter-Dreizylinder-TDI (75 PS) und E-Motor (27 PS). Verbrauch von offiziell 3,5 l/100 km, $CO_2$-Ausstoß von 89 g/km.
3,4 Millionen Golf V
**Golf VI – Debüt**. Streng genommen „nur“ ein Facelift des Golf V – also quasi ein Golf V-II. Erreicht dank lasergeschweißter Karosse fünf Punkte im EuroNCAP-Crashtest. Die Umstellung auf Direkteinspritzer senkt Verbräuche, mit den TSI-Motoren jedoch kommen Probleme mit der

Steuerkette. VW muss eine entsprechende Kulanzregelung auf Fahrzeuge erweitern, die älter als sechs Jahre sind.
Außerdem: Umstieg auf Common-Rail-TDI von Pumpe-Düse
Erhältlich sind zudem automatische Distanzregelung ACC, Berganfahrassistent, dynamisches Kurvenlicht, elektronische Dämpferregelung DCC, Keyless Access (Schließ- und Startsystem ohne Tür- und Zündschloss), Knie-Airbag (Serie),
LED-Rückfahrleuchten, Navigationssystem mit Touchscreen, Park Assist, Rekuperationsmodus, Rückfahrkamera, Start-Stopp-Automatik. Eindruck: Autofahren scheint immer komplizierter zu werden ...

....... 2009 Golf VI Plus
Golf VI Variant
Golf VI GTI
Golf VI GTD (Comeback, gab's nicht im IV und V!)

....... 2010 Golf VI R

....... 2011 Golf Cabriolet

....... 2012 2,85 Millionen Golf VI
**Golf VII – Debüt**. Sein Design vereint das Beste aus dem Golf – laut seinen Designern dem Einser und dem Vierer. Erscheint plausibel. Auto überzeugt wieder. Erhältlich sind Adaptive Cruise Control, Ambientebeleuchtung, City-Notbremsfunktion, Dynamic Light Assist, elektrische Parkbremse, Ergonomiesitz, Verkehrszeichenerkennung (der Mensch hat's vorgemacht ...), Fahrprofilauswahl, Lane Assist, Müdigkeitserkennung, Park Pilot, Runflat-Reifen, Multikollisionsbremse und Zylinderabschaltung (Auto fährt trotzdem weiter).

Golf VII Variant 2013
Golf VII TDI BlueMotion
Golf VII TGI BlueMotion
Golf VII GTI
Golf VII GTD
Golf VII 4MOTION
Golf VII R
Golf VII Sportsvan
(der „Elefantenrollschuh“, auch jetzt noch immer kein sportiver Laufschuh)

Mit dem e-Golf schwimmt der Golf jetzt nicht nur 2014
im Strom, sondern auch durch ihn. Nachfrage bleibt überschaubar.
Erster Golf mit Plug-In Hybrid debütiert.

Der Super-GAU tritt ein: Nach Bekanntwerden 2015
von Manipulationen an Dieselmotoren rollen im VW-Konzern Köpfe. Martin Winterkorn muss abtreten, Michael Müller, bis dato Chef bei Porsche, übernimmt das Ruder in Wolfsburg.

Jubiläum der besonderen Art: 40 Jahre GTI! Zu 2016
diesem Anlass reist „GTI-Mastermind“ Anton Konrad zum GTI-Treffen an den Wörthersee und referiert an fünf Tagen vor der Jugend und anderen Fans, was diese drei Buchstaben so angerichtet haben.

Modellpflege (Facelift) für den Golf VIII 2017
Die Gerüchteküche brodelt:
Wird VW im Zuge der sich ausweitenden Dieselaffäre den Golf fallen lassen und ausschließlich den vollelektrischen ID.3 bringen?

.......... 2018 Erst mal bringt VW den Herbert Diess.
Als VW-Konzernchef und damit als Nachfolger von Michael Müller.

.......... 2019 Entwarnung: **Debüt des Golf VIII**
Er kommt also doch! Allerdings nicht mehr als batterieelektrische Variante wie sein Vorgänger. Als Erster seiner Art wird der Golf VIII nicht als Dreitürer angeboten.
Muss sich mit Qualitätsmängeln rumschlagen. Mangelhafte Lackierungen, Passungenauigkeiten bei Exterieur und Interieur, Ausfall relevanter Digitaltechnik konterkarieren die hippe Sorglos-Golf-Werbung. Auto heißt intern ob seiner Frontoptik „Tapir“. Und nicht verstummen wollen die Gerüchte, dass dies die letzte Golf-Generation gewesen sei.

.......... 2020 Golf VIII Variant erscheint

# Von hoch droben komm ich her …

Im Winter 1973 erreichte Anton Konrad, damals Pressechef von VW, ein aufgeregter Anruf: „Herr Konrad! Hier spricht der Werksschutz von der Teststrecke in Ehra-Lessien. Bei uns sitzt der berüchtigte Erlkönig-Fotograf Hans-Günter Lehmann oben im Baum und fotografiert über den Zaun hinweg die geheimen Prototypen des Golf! Was sollen wir tun?“ Konrad überlegte nicht lange, schlüpfte in Parka und Dienstwagen und begab sich zum Ort des Geschehens.

Dort angekommen stapfte der gewiefte Kommunikator durch dicken Schnee zum Baum, in dessen schwindelerregender Höhe tatsächlich der gefürchtete Prototypen-Jäger mitsamt Teleobjektiv klickend seinem Tagewerk nachging. Konrad pflanzte sich neben dem Baumstamm auf, legte den Kopf in den Nacken und rief: „Aber Herr Lehmann! Es ist viel zu kalt! Kommen Sie doch herunter, wir zeigen Ihnen den Wagen. In allen Details und ganz bequem bei uns in der geheizten Werkstatt! Es gäbe auch Kaffee und einen Imbiss.“ Daraufhin schwankte das Geäst nur noch mehr. Der entsetzte Lehmann ließ für einen Augenblick das Tele sinken und schrie empört herunter: „Sind Sie verrückt? Sie ruinieren mir ja mein Geschäftsmodell!“

# Bumerang

**Ach, Golf III. Da hast du nun viele Jahre bei Wind, Wetter, Sonne und Schnee brav funktioniert – und dann kommt das unweigerliche Stoppschild: Endstation Schrottplatz. Doch dann hatte jemand die Idee, dass Recycling sich auszahlen könnte.**

„Moment!", dachte sich VW Mitte der 1980er Jahre, „die Menschen wollen, dass wir das ändern. Außerdem lässt sich auch noch mit Schrott-Gölfen Gewinn machen – mindestens ein Image-Gewinn in diesen umweltbewegten Zeiten." Gedacht, getan: Im ostfriesischen Leer nahm 1990 die Pilot-Anlage zum sortenreinen Zerlegen und Wiederverwerten von ausgedienten VW die Arbeit auf. Allerdings wurden dort gerade einmal drei Fahrzeuge pro Woche trockengelegt und in ihre einzelnen Baugruppen zerlegt. Dann erhob sich eines Tages im Jahr 1991 Ferdinand Piëch von seinem VW-Chefsessel und verkündete der Öffentlichkeit: Ab sofort verpflichte sich VW zur kostenlosen Rücknahme von Golf III und Vento ab Modelljahr 1992! Später wurde dies auf VW-Modelle bis zu einem Alter von zwölf Jahren ausgeweitet. Ein Raunen ging durch die Automobilbau-Unternehmen! So etwas hatte es noch nicht gegeben! So wurde der Golf III zum weltweit ersten Auto mit Rücknahmegarantie durch den Hersteller Und damit quasi zum Bumerang: kommt immer zurück!

Bereits bei seiner Konstruktion wurde beim Golf III auf Demontagefreundlichkeit und Kennzeichnung der Werkstoffe (PP, PE etc.) geachtet. Zeitgleich propagierte VW den Anteil von Recycling-Material in eigenen Neufahrzeugen. So entstanden Stoßfänger und Heckleuchten mit Zusatz von Recycling-Granulat. Allerdings erreichte man nie die angekündigten Größenordnungen und blieb laut Zeitzeugen weit unter 20 Prozent Recycling-Anteil. Skeptischen Nachfragern, die den von VW besonders herausgestellten hohen Anteil von Recycling-Granulat in Blaulichtern anzweifelten („die gehen doch nie kaputt!"), begegnete man un-

Viele viele bunte Gölfe – und andere VW-Modelle aus 100 Prozent Recyclingmaterial ...

geniert auf Münchhausen-Art. „Doch, weil die Polizei ja oft in Tiefgaragen und Parkhäuser fährt und nicht auf die Durchfahrtshöhen achtet." Bei Kraftstofftanks verbot sich sogar das Beimischen von Recycling-Material – entsprechende Versuche ergaben Sprödigkeit und Rissbildung. Auch das gemeinsam mit der damaligen Preussag Recycling GmbH geplante bundesweit flächendeckende Netz von Demontagezentren wurde nicht realisiert.

Immerhin entstanden lustige Stifthalter in Form bunter VW-Plastikmodelle im Maßstab 1:43 mit der Aufschrift „Volkswagen Recycling". Und zur Abrundung der Salve an Schnellschüssen hatte man vergessen, die entsprechend notwendigen Rückstellungen pro „kostenlos" zurückgenommenem Golf III einzuplanen. Mit rund 400 Mark pro Auto rechnete man schließlich, die man in zehn bis zwölf Jahren hätte parat haben müssen. Klappte dann aber. Knapp.

# Kill Brüll

**„A" wie „Auftragsnummer", dazu die 59 – so nüchtern kann man Emotionen beziffern. Doch der A 59, Über-Golf der Generation III, ist kaum bekannt. Noch weniger sind es die Interna. Hier kommen sie.**

Er ist der Golf, der 1994 mit 400 PS die Rallye Monte Carlo hätte abräumen sollen. Der Über-Golf A 59, begonnen 1992, stattdessen jedoch im Januar 1993 von Ferdinand Piëch vom Tisch gefegt. Begonnen nach dem G-Lader-Desaster in der Deutschen Rallye-Weltmeisterschaft 1990 (drei Einsätze, ein dritter Platz). Mit den Worten „Jetzt machen wir das mal richtig!" von VW-Entwicklungsvorstand Herbert „Berti" Schuster.

Umgehend begannen externe Spezialisten mit Konzeption und Aufbau des A 59, indem sie einen Golf III dort zersägten, wo sie es für notwendig hielten. Statt EA-827-Motor nebst G-Ladern entstand ein komplett neuer Alu-Vierzylinder-Benziner mit Turbolader und Ladeluftkühler. Der schaffte 275 PS und 367 Newtonmeter Drehmoment. Als Sauger ohne Turbo war der A 59 vorgesehen für den Einsatz in der Zwei-Liter-Prototypenklasse in Le Mans und für die Formel 3. Die erwähnten 400 PS dienten als Spitze im weiteren Renneinsatz. Dazu Allrad mit hydraulisch gesteuerter Lamellensperre im Mitteldifferenzial und 6-Gang-Schaltgetriebe.

Mit viel Geld hätte das VW-Motorenwerk Salzgitter das A-59-Herzstück bauen können – doch den Wagen selbst? VW hätte die Fertigung des A 59 weder als Kleinserie im Versuchsbau noch innerhalb der Serienfertigung unterbekommen – viel zu teuer, viel zu aufwendig einzusteuern. Lediglich 2.500 A 59 zu Homologationszwecken waren angedacht. Das wären heute hübsch teure Blechleckerbissen! Weil man damals allen Widerständen zum Trotz nicht aufgeben wollte, suchte man – so ist das bei VW – dem A 59 eben eine eigene Produktionsstätte. Die geeignetste

Option hierfür fand sich in Ostdeutschland. Im Rahmen konspirativer Termine stapfte man daher tatsächlich – durch die Hallen des ehemaligen Barkas-Werks!

Doch Pustekuchen: Im Januar 1993 wurde dem Projekt mit Turbo das Licht ausgeblasen. Offizielle Begründung: „Finanzielle Schwierigkeiten“. Der neue VW-Chef Ferdinand Piëch, bekannt dafür, die eigenen Ideen gut zu finden, die anderer Talente manchmal nicht so, hatte alle verzichtbaren Projekte auf den Tisch beordert. Und „A“ wie A 59 stand am Anfang der Liste. VW überwies also das gesamte Projektbudget vertragsgemäß an die externen Partner und bekam am Ende dafür ein zu 80 Prozent fertiggestelltes Museumsstück. Den Audi Sport quattro unter den Gölfen. Ein Geschoss der Präzision. Dieses Turbo-Tier hätte das Zeug dazu gehabt, das Image des Golf III brüllend nach oben zu reißen. Stattdessen läuft es heute hinter den Gitterstäben von Volkswagen Classic unruhig auf und ab.

Das Turbo-Tier: Golf A 59

POPULÄRER IRRTUM

# Die im Dunkeln

Der Erfolg hat bekanntlich viele Väter. Das gilt auch für den Golf. Am Ende wollen es immer alle gewesen sein. Und, wissen Sie was: Das stimmt sogar! Denn wiewohl die einzelnen Golf-Generationen stets einem bestimmten Designchef zugerechnet werden, haben andere die Arbeit getan. Das räumt mit Legenden auf. Zum Beispiel mit der von VW-Designchef Herbert Schäfer. Der habe zwar stets sich selbst gefeiert, aber keines der ihm zugeschriebenen Fahrzeuge selbst entworfen. Und die Designteams gar alle paar Monate ausgewechselt, „um die Vaterschaft zu vertuschen", wie es heißt. Dafür sei der damalige Forschungsvorstand Ernst Fiala (ob seiner formalen Vorlieben „Sicken-Ernst" getauft) regelmäßig mit eigenen, teils haarsträubenden Designs in den VW-Ateliers aufgetaucht, mit der Bitte um Umsetzung. Das habe größtenteils verhindert werden können. „Der Schäfer hat schon ein Formgefühl, was Autos angeht, war aber nie der Initiator", sagt wiederum Fiala trocken über seinen Ex-Designchef. Oje.
Nun, Grund genug, einmal die vielen wahren Väter der Gölfe ans Tageslicht zu ziehen. Hier sind sie – erstmals alle vereint.

| | | |
|---|---|---|
| **GOLF I** | **VW Designchef:** | Herbert Schäfer |
| | **Interieur:** | Mike Miller |
| | **Exterieur:** | Giorgetto Giugiaro |
| **Golf II** | **VW Designchef:** | Herbert Schäfer |
| | **Interieur:** | Martin Kirchner |
| | **Exterieur:** | Luca Rezzonico |
| **GOLF III** | **VW Designchef:** | Herbert Schäfer |
| | **Interieur:** | Wolf Rieger |
| | **Exterieur:** | German Hornstein,<br>Gert Volker Hildebrandt |
| **GOLF IV** | **VW Designchef:** | Hartmut Warkuß |
| | **Interieur:** | Ulrich Lammel |
| | **Exterieur:** | Karl John Ellmit,<br>Gregory Guillaume |
| **GOLF V** | **VW Designchef:** | Hartmut Warkuß |
| | **Interieur:** | Ulrich Lammel |
| | **Exterieur:** | Marc Lichte |
| **GOLF VI** | **VW Designchef:** | Walter de Silva |
| | **Interieur:** | Ulrich Lammel |
| | **Exterieur:** | Andreas Mindt,<br>Frank Brühse (Front) |
| **GOLF VII** | **VW Designchef:** | Klaus Bischoff |
| | **Interieur:** | Tomasz Bachorski |
| | **Exterieur:** | Andreas Mindt |
| **GOLF VIII** | **VW Designchef:** | Klaus Zyciora (Ex-Bischoff) |
| | **Interieur:** | Tomasz Bachorski |
| | **Exterieur:** | Felipe Montoya,<br>Marco Pavone |

# Zahlenspiele

Mit über **35 Millionen Exemplaren** ist der Golf das meistgebaute Modell aller Zeiten.

Der Golf ist mit rund **19 Millionen Exemplaren** das meistgebaute Modell im Stammwerk Wolfsburg.

Bereits am 17. Oktober 1976 lief in Wolfsburg der **einmillionste Golf** vom Band.

Zwischen Mai 1974 und August 1983 entstanden rund sechs Millionen **GOLF I**.

6,3 Millionen **GOLF II** wurden von 1983 bis 1992 gebaut.

Vom **GOLF III** produzierte VW zwischen 1991 und 1997 rund 4,8 Millionen Fahrzeuge.

4,1 Millionen **GOLF IV** wurden von VW zwischen 1997 und 2003 produziert.

Per 31. Dezember 2008 wies der bereits 2003 eingestellte **GOLF IV** mit **1.558.955** rund doppelt so viele in Deutschland zugelassene Exemplare auf wie sein 2008 vorzeitig abgelöster Nachfolger **GOLF V** mit **786.554** Exemplaren.

Vom **GOLF VI** baute VW zwischen Oktober 2008 und November 2012 **2,85 Millionen**.

Gleich **drei Weltrekorde** über **12** und **24 Stunden** sowie über **5.000 Kilometer** fuhr Rennfahrer Jochi Kleint am 23. Mai 1987 mit dem Prototyp des **Golf syncro G60** mit **236 PS** ein.

Mit ihren Fahrgestell-Endnummern **653** und **714** sind die beiden Golf aus dem Härtetest Alaska-Feuerland die heute ältesten bekannten Vertreter ihrer Art.

Exakt **30** sehr beweglichen Österreichern aus Langenlois gelang es laut Guinness-Buch der Rekorde, sich **1983** in einen Golf zu quetschen.

# Unter Druck

Einiges hat sich ja nicht geändert: Politik und Gesellschaft verändern sich und damit einher gehen diverse Anforderungen – auch und gerade an die Autoindustrie. So war bei VW für den Golf II ab 1985 beim 40-kW-Motor ein ungeregelter Katalysator für 720 Mark und beim 66-kW-Motor ein G-Kat mit Lambdasonde für 1.880 Mark Aufpreis erhältlich. Pikant dabei: Die beiden Erzrivalen Opel und VW waren technisch gleichauf, doch besaß VW einen entscheidenden Vorsprung: Die Wolfsburger hatten lange im Vorfeld in sämtlichen relevanten Gazetten doppelseitige Anzeigen gebucht. Das Motiv – lediglich aus dem VW-Logo und dem Satz „Wir sind bereit." bestehend – war im Prinzip fertig, lag von BILD bis F.A.Z. vor und wurde nur noch VW-intern durch die Hierarchien hinweg abgestimmt. Das ging klag- und kommentarlos bis zum damaligen Vertriebsvorstand W. P. Schmidt. Der las, stutzte, öffnete den Mund, brachte aber vor Schreck keinen Ton heraus. Dann kam das Donnerwetter aber doch. Schmidt tobte! „Warum ist das niemandem aufgefallen! Sofort stoppen! Sofort stoppen!" Wieherndes Lachen aus dem Hintergrund. Prustend und sich vor Lachen biegend kam die Mannschaft der VW-Werbeagentur hinter Schmidts Bürotür hervor. Alles war in Ordnung. Nirgendwo wurde die Anzeigenvorlage gedruckt, die auf W. P. Schmidts Tisch gelandet war. Nirgendwo stand in dicken fetten VW-Lettern: „Wir sind breit."

Moderne Zeiten. Kat sei Dank!

AHA!

# Wie Beethoven das Licht erfand

Über Jahrzehnte diktierte Glas die Gestaltung von Autoscheinwerfern. So auch beim Golf. Im Jahre 1997 jedoch gab es eine kleine Revolution: Erstmals guckte mit der Generation IV ein Golf aus sogenannten „Kunststoff-Freiformreflektoren" in die Welt. Das neue Material der Klarglas-Scheinwerfer ermöglichte auch völlig neue Dimensionen der Gestaltung. Schauen wir dem Golf IV in die Augen, wirken diese fast wie der Blick in das Innere einer Mechanik. Und: Volltreffer! Genau das war das Designthema beim Golf IV – ein symbolischer Transmissionsriemen mit unterschiedlich großen „Zahnrädern". Die entsprechende Idee dazu hatte ein damaliger Jungdesigner namens Michael Werner. Hierfür gebührt ihm zeitloser Applaus. Bis heute übrigens wird Werner aufgrund der Art und Form seiner Haarpracht von seinen Kollegen im VW-Design scherzhaft „Beethoven" genannt. Weshalb das hier die kurze Geschichte war, wie Beethoven das Licht erfand.

Klare Sache: Golf IV-Blick

# In the Klemme tonight

**Es war eine laue Frühlingsnacht, als das Fax (ja, so etwas gab es seinerzeit noch!) in Wolfsburg einging. Weil gerade niemand da war in der VW-Zentrale, sank es leise zu Boden. Von dort hob es am nächsten Morgen jemand auf, dessen vor sich hin gesummte Version des Hits „I Can't Dance" abrupt verstummte ...**

Langsam verfärbte sich das Gesicht des Teammitglieds der VW Sound Foundation. Dies sehr wahrscheinlich sogar in dem Farbton „Violet Touch Perleffect" des damals aktuellen Sondermodells Golf Cabriolet „Genesis". Benannt nach der legendären britischen Band rund um Starsänger Phil Collins, deren Welttournee Volkswagen sponserte.

Pretty in Pink: Col Phil... – äh, Phil Collins

Besagter Collins – respektive seine Anwälte – zeichnete auch als Absender des Schreibens. Und es wurden der Faxe und der Anwälte immer mehr, sodass man bald den hübschen Teppichboden im Verwaltungshochhaus der VW-Zentrale gar nicht mehr erkennen konnte. Was war geschehen? Nun, Collins machte auf die weltweit geplante Anzeige für das Sondermodell Golf Cabriolet „Genesis" aufmerksam, welche die assoziationsreiche Überschrift „In The Air Tonight" zieren sollte. Und das ginge nun mal überhaupt nicht, weil der gleichnamige Welthit zwar auch von ihm gesungen werde, aber nun mal nicht als „Genesis"-Frontmann, sondern als Solokünstler Phil Collins himself. Das sei ja etwas ganz anderes! Bei VW werden sie weltweit gestöhnt haben, stornierten jedoch hektisch in letzter Sekunde sämtliche geplanten Veröffentlichungen mit besagtem Motiv. Das kam vermutlich günstiger als irgendwelche Strafzahlungen. Blöd scheint es in diesem Zusammenhang aber vor allem, wenn die eigene Kunst so austausch- und verwechselbar ist.

Schon mal drüber nachgedacht, Mister Col Phillins?

Pretty in Violett:
Golf Cabrio Genesis,
wir erinnern uns ...

# Designerlei

**Entgegen den Erwartungen kam der Golf V während seiner gesamten Laufbahn (2003–2008) beim Publikum vergleichsweise verhalten an. Ende 2008 fuhren auf Deutschlands Straßen tatsächlich doppelt so viele Golf IV wie Golf V! Irre.**

Dies führte dazu, dass der „Fünfer" zur Golf-Generation mit der geringsten Gesamtproduktion wurde. Und vorzeitig von einem Nachfolger abgelöst wurde, der genau genommen keiner war, sondern lediglich eine Überarbeitung. Eine Tatsache, die in Fachkreisen zu vehementen Diskussionen führte, denn so etwas heißt nun einmal „Facelift". Oder im internen VW-Jargon ganz offiziell „GP" („Große Produktaufwertung"). Beim Facelift oder bei der GP oder beim Was-auch-Immer des Golf V beharrt VW bis heute darauf, damit einen neuen Golf gebaut zu haben. Hat das Unternehmen nicht, denn Plattform und Technik blieben weitgehend gleich. Wichtiger, wenn nicht gar entscheidend war die deutlich gesteigerte Qualität des Golf-VI-Designs.

Der „Sechser" wirkt in Gänze wesentlich harmonischer als sein Vorgänger – und schlägt gestalterisch eine Brücke zu seinem Nachfahren Golf VII. Das mag auch daher rühren, dass Golf VI und Golf VII ein und denselben Designer namens Andreas Mindt haben, wobei das „Gesicht" des Golf VI von Mindts Kollegen Frank Brühse stammt. Mindt allerdings schuf auch das Golf-V-Heckleuchten-Design, das mit zur umstrittenen Gestalt des Golf V von Marc Lichte beitrug. Der damalige VW-Chef Ferdinand Piëch wollte es so. Kaum bekannt war bis jetzt außerdem, dass der Golf VI ursprünglich die Front des Scirocco III erhalten sollte. Dies wurde – wohl auch durch den von Piëch vorzeitig und unsanft vollzogenen Abgang des seinerzeitigen VW-Designchefs Murat Günak – verhindert.

Was für eine Maskerade!

Homogenes Design, aber vom Absatz her ein verhaltener Erfolg: Golf V

# Fisland

**Ordentlich zusammengeschissen hatte er seine Leute, der Martin Winterkorn. In bewährter cholerischer Manier war der VW-Vorstandsvorsitzende durch die Hallen der Forschung und Entwicklung marschiert, als es darum ging, den Golf VI besser zu machen als dessen Vorgänger. Naja …**

Tatsächlich schien der Job dann doch zur vollen Zufriedenheit zu verlaufen: Zwar entfielen wertige Details wie die stoffbespannten C-Säulen, dafür wurden Quietschen und Klappern abgestellt. Nun konnte es also darangehen, den Golf VI offiziell zu präsentieren.

Auf der Suche nach einem geeigneten Präsentationsort meinte eine VW-Delegation, im malerischen Island fündig geworden zu sein. Eine „Location“ mitten in den Bergen wurde festgelegt. Einziges Problem: Dort gab es außer einer phänomenalen Aussicht – nichts. Die Isländer teerten also erst einmal sieben Kilometer Zufahrtsstraße und legten Wasser- und Stromanschlüsse dorthin, wo VW ein fantastisches Präsentationszelt vorschwebte. Das sollte im Anschluss der isländische Golf-Club

Er kam, brüllte und zeltete:
Martin Winterkorn

übernehmen. Prima, so entfielen der teure Abbau und Rücktransport!

Das Zelt mit Panorama-Glasfronten und marmornen Waschbecken wurde errichtet, fiel in sich zusammen und wurde erneut aufgebaut. Winterkorn kam und schrie rum, was für eine Sch… man sich bei der Wahl des Präsentationsortes gedacht habe. Zudem die schlechten Straßen, die uneben und voller umherspritzender Steine waren … Nun, die Präsentation lief gut an. Bis nach exakt einer Woche das Wetter umschlug. Tiefsttemperaturen, Sturm, Dauerregen. Die herangekarrten Journalisten nahmen kaum noch das Auto wahr – „Ah, ein Golf, wird schon okay sein! Wo, bitte, geht es jetzt in die geheizte Teestube …?“ Scheinwerfer und Heckleuchten der insgesamt 75 Golf VI, die dann wohl doch noch nicht ganz dem Serienstandard entsprachen, liefen voll Wasser. Die VW-Mechaniker hatten alle Hände voll zu tun, jede einzelne Leuchteinheit per Fön trockenzulegen. Weil es sich um Heißluftföne handelte, wurde der eine oder andere Mechaniker unfreiwillig zum „Glasbläser“, indem der Kunststoff der Scheinwerfer schmolz.

Aufgrund besagter Beschaffenheit der Teststrecke (Steinschläge!) musste das VW-Team Abend für Abend Stoßfänger nachlackieren. Heftige Windstöße führten zu Beulen in den Türflächen. Ergo gab es Testwagenausfälle, in deren Folge das Werkstatt-Team dazu überging, Präsentationswagen auszuschlachten, um andere einsatzbereit zu halten. Am Ende reiste rund die Hälfte der Golf-VI-Präsentationswagen als Schrott zurück nach Wolfsburg – und die tolle Hülle auch: Aufgrund der drohenden Staatspleite im Rahmen der weltweiten Bankenkrise 2008 hatten die Isländer plötzlich irgendwie andere Schwerpunkte als eine Weltkonzern-Zeltplane mit Marmor und Panoramablick …

# Glaubensfragen. Kuriositäten-Sammlung zum Golf

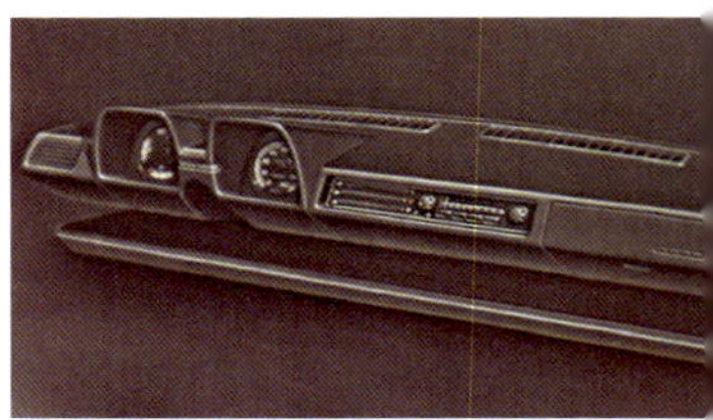

Aus Kostengründen ersetzte VW Giugiaros Armaturenbrett-Entwurf durch ein hauseigenes Cockpit – und plötzlich war der Golf in der arg spartanischen Grundausstattung dem Käfer wieder sehr nah.

Der oft als „Henkel" geschmähte Überrollbügel des Golf I Cabriolets (daher auch dessen Bezeichnung „Erdbeerkörbchen") war aus technischer Sicht nicht notwendig. Versuche mit einem „henkellosen" Prototypen ergaben eine ausgezeichnete Verwindungssteifigkeit. VW bestand jedoch mit Blick auf die sensiblen US-Käufer auf dem Bügel. Die gefrusteten Entwickler trösteten sich: Was bot der Bügel doch für eine perfekte Dachauflage und verbesserte Gurtführung ...

1986 fand erstmals der „Grand Prix Formel E" statt – Rennen mit Elektroautos! „Macher" des Events waren verschiedene Batteriehersteller und Stromkonzern RWE. Sage und schreibe 53 Akkus waren im Elektro-Renn-Golf II von Fahrer Hagen Arlt verbaut. Das Ganze wurde zunächst gekühlt mit Trockeneis. Später dann von einem extra angefertigten Kühlkreislauf mit destilliertem Wasser, das von vier Pumpen mit hoher Geschwindigkeit durch dicke Gewebeschläuche befördert wurde. Die Anfangsleistung: 36 kW!

2003 verzeichnete die Stadt Wolfsburg auffallend viele Diebstähle ihrer Ortsschilder. Grund für das Phänomen: Als Gag zur Einführung des Golf V hatte die Stadt beschlossen, sich einen Monat lang offiziell in „Golfsburg“ umzubenennen – mit allen sichtbaren Konsequenzen. Nicht wenige VW-„Schildbürger“ dürften ihre entsprechenden Beutestücke noch heute in Garagen und Partykellern hängen haben …

Bei seiner Markteinführung war der Basispreis des Golf III niedriger als der des Golf II. Erdacht als Absatz-Turbo des damaligen VW-Chefs Ferdinand Piëch.

Erstmals im Golf III VR6 gab es einen Sechszylinder bei VW. Versuche mit dem kompakten VR6 hatte es ab 1978 bereits in Golf-I- und Jetta-I-Versuchswagen gegeben. VW-Chef Carl H. Hahn hatte den Serieneinsatz bereits im Golf II vorgesehen. Nur ein einziger Versuchsträger, ein weißer Jetta I in Vollausstattung, hat überlebt. Er steht im Wolfsburger AutoMuseum, ist jedoch nicht fahrbereit.

Ferdinand Piëch war ein Freund geteilter Heckleuchten, die Fachleute ablehnen. Ihre Haltung resultiert weniger aus ästhetischen als aus pragmatischen Überlegungen: Erschütterungen beim Öffnen und Schließen von Heckklappen führten ihrer Ansicht nach zu erhöhtem Glühbirnenverschleiß! Dass der Golf IV die von Piëch favorisierten Heckleuchten nicht erhielt, ist dem standhaft gebliebenen Ästheten und damaligen VW-Chefdesigner Hartmut Warkuß zu verdanken.

# Verhinderte Serien-Stars

**Diese Golf blieben allein zu Haus. Oder waren nie zu kaufen.**

## IRVW I

Dieser Golf ging mit Sicherheit nicht in Serie. Aber als Integrates Research Volkswagen Number One (IRVW I) hatte man dem Technikträger allerhand mitgegeben: Neben den massiven Stoßstangen des US-Modells Rabbit wurde die Front mit dickem Gummi abgepolstert – optisch wie bei Aldo Sessanos Seat Bocanegra und Renault 15/17. Dazu kamen ein Gurt-Rückhaltesystem (ähnlich dem späteren „procon-ten“ von Audi), ein damals noch nicht angebotener Vierzylinder-Turbo-Diesel unter der Haube sowie Sicherheitsgurte und Kopfstützen vorn und hinten.

## GOLF ROADSTER

Warum denn ein Golf Roadster? Es ist Juli 1988 und das Golf I Cabriolet fährt Traumergebnisse ein. Da kommt die Wilhelm Karmann GmbH aus Osnabrück mit diesem Vorschlag: Ein Targa-Golf, bei dem das Verdeck entweder komplett, nur über den Vordersitzen oder nur über den Fondpassagieren geöffnet werden konnte. Dazu lackierte dicke US-Stoßfänger in Wagenfarbe, Breitreifen auf Alus, „böser-Blick“-Blende über den Scheinwerfern. Der Golf Roadster ist definitiv cool, wird jedoch nie in Serie gebaut. Denn: Es ist Juli 1988 und das Golf I Cabriolet fährt Traumergebnisse ein …

## GOLF/JETTA VR6

Leckerbissen für Kenner: Dieser Jetta I ist der einzige Überlebende aus der Reihe der Versuchsfahrzeuge, die bereits 1978 den VR6-Motor in sich trugen. Der entsprechende Golf existiert nicht mehr. Angeschoben unter VW-Chef Toni Schmücker, weiterbetrieben von Nachfolger im Amt Carl H. Hahn. Letzterer forcierte den Serieneinsatz des Sechszylinders bereits im Golf II – ein zu ehrgeiziges Ziel. Der VR6 debütierte „erst" im Golf III. Ursprünglich sollte der Motor „RV6" (Reihe-V-Form-6) heißen. Wurde geändert in VR6, weil so die englische Lautmalerei „We are Six" daraus entstand. Wichtiger PR-Gag, extra für den US-Markt.

## GOLF CABRIOLET OHNE ÜBERROLLBÜGEL

Zum Glück sah kein Serien-Golf-I-Cabriolet je so aus! Herrliche Begriffe wie „Henkelmann" oder „Erdbeerkörbchen" wären uns verloren gegangen! Denn im Prinzip hätte es des Überrollbügels des Golf I Cabrios nie bedurft – jedenfalls nicht aus Gründen der Fahrzeugstabilität und Sicherheit. Hierfür hätten der verstärkte Frontscheibenrahmen und die eingeschweißten Bodengruppen-Versteifungen gereicht. Doch Zeitzeugen berichten, Ulrich Seiffert, damals Leiter des Bereichs Forschung bei VW, habe im Hinblick auf den US-Markt auf dem „Henkel" bestanden.

## GOLF II CABRIOLET

Irgendwie sei es mal an der Zeit für ein neues Golf Cabriolet, und zwar auf der Basis der Generation II. Fand Karosseriebauer Karmann in Osnabrück 1985. Also ging man die Aufgabe an, indem man den Golf II aufschnitt, ihm eine durchaus gefällige Seitenlinie verpasste und außerdem ein Entenbürzel-Heck mit Jetta-II-Heckleuchten. Das sah alles wohlproportioniert aus, dennoch blieb es bei einem „Mock-Up" genannten internen Demonstrationsmodell ohne Interieur und Mechanik, das später verschrottet wurde. Weil das „Einser"-Cabrio sich verkaufte wie warme Semmeln, konnte VW sich das Überspringen einer Golf-Cabrio-Generation leisten. Schade eigentlich.

## GOLF I CITYSTROMER

Strom-Parade: 1981 warten die ersten von insgesamt 50 Golf I CitySTROMern auf ihren Einsatz im Rahmen einer Dauererprobung bei RWE. Erstmals hatte VW eine Kleinstserie elektrisch betriebener Pkw aufgelegt, die jedoch nicht für den Verkauf bestimmt war.

## GOLF IV „PLUS 40MM" / BORA „PLUS 80MM"

Dieser Golf IV war echter Durchschnitt – aber wie! Als gedankliche Alternative zu einem komplett neuen Modell existierte bei VW die Überlegung, dem Hauptmanko des Golf IV beizukommen: dem oft kritisierten knappen Beinraum im Fond. Also ging der Golf IV in die Verlängerung, indem der Versuchsbau einen Golf und einen Bora jeweils an der Mitte der B-Säule durchtrennte und in Handarbeit um zehn Zentimeter streckte. Das Ganze wurde ordentlich verschweißt, verspachtelt, geschliffen und lackiert und VW-Chef Ferdinand Piëch präsentiert. Und verschrottet. Weil: dann doch lieber Golf V. Seufz.

Golf + 40mm

Bora + 80mm

## BOSAT

Gehört auch „irgendwie" mit zum Golf, jedenfalls zur Hälfte. Gut, zu einem Viertel: Denn beim „Bosat" verband der VW-Versuchsbau den Vorderwagen des Golf-Derivates Bora mit dem hinteren Teil einer Passat-B5-Limousine (ab deren B-Säule). Warum? „Weil die Chefs was für ihre Hinterhand brauchten, mit dem sie glänzen konnten", sagen Zeitzeugen. Und weil das Budget unbegrenzt war für Spielereien jeglicher Art.

Bosat R6 TDI

Bora V8

## BORA/GOLF IV VR8

Um das Jahr 2000 überlegte man bei VW, ein echtes Muscle Car auf die Räder zu stellen: Golf/Bora VR8! Hierfür wurde ein nagelneuer Bora geopfert und zwei VR6-Motoren wurden entsprechend zertrennt und von einer Spezialfirma in Belgien wieder zusammengesetzt. Das Auto wurde vorne moderat verbreitert, Gelenkwellen und Querlenker wurden verlängert, die Vorderachse breiter, der gesamte Vorderwagen per neuer 50.000-DM-Richtbank eingestellt, die Elektrik komplett von Hand erarbeitet und eingebaut. Alle Vorstände sind mitgefahren, von Ferdinand Piëch bis Martin Winterkorn. Fazit: Ein feines Auto! Kostete rund 500.000 DM, dann wurde das Projekt verworfen. Das Auto selbst sollte verschrottet werden, hat aber werksintern in Wolfsburg überlebt. Und einen Bora V8 bauten sie dann auch noch. Weil sie es konnten.

## GOLF VII GTI ROADSTER CONCEPT

Sowas gibt's auch: dass ein PlayStation-Star Realität wird! So geschehen 2014 mit dem GTI Roadster aus dem Spiel „Gran Turismo 6". Der rollt als „leibhaftige" Skulptur dem Publikum des GTI-Treffens am Wörthersee vor die Füße, voll fahrbereit dank Drei-Liter-V6-Biturbo. 503 PS, Allrad und mehr stehen für alles, was man sonst nicht machen darf im VW-Design. Performance trifft auf Rennsport-Feeling, die virtuelle Welt wird mit der realen verschmolzen. Leider nur einmalig.

## GOLF III CADDY/PICK-UP

Dass er formal etwas seltsam wirkt, wäre allein kein Grund für eine Serienfertigung gewesen. Doch den Golf III ereilte das Schicksal, dass VW sich eine hübsche Tochter namens Skoda zulegte, als intern am Nachfolger des Golf I Caddy geforscht wurde. So gibt es zwar den Golf III Caddy, aber nur als Prototyp. Der offizielle Nachfolger des Golf I Caddy kam dann auf Basis des Skoda Felicia. Das Auto war bei Übernahme durch VW bereits fix und fertig. Nur das VW-Emblem musste noch dran …

# Griechischer Stein

**Wir Normalsterblichen drehen uns auf der Straße ja kaum um, wenn ein Golf an uns vorbeifährt. Warum auch? Das ist schade und ein wenig ignorant, weil hinter jedem Golf eine Design-Idee steht. Beim Golf VII waren die Entwerfer gar mit keinem geringeren Anspruch und Ideal angetreten, als „das Beste des Golf zu vereinen".**

„Glatt, sauber, cool. Neo-Modernismus statt Retro haben wir damals gesagt", verrät Golf-VII-Designer Andreas Mindt erstmals. „Daher unsere Verbeugung vor der sogenannten ‚Schulterfallung', das glatte Übergleiten der C-Säule in die Seitenflanke des Golf I am Golf VII und die parallel zur Heckklappe verlaufende Fuge des hinteren Türausschnitts wie beim Golf IV – die sogenannte ‚Banane'."

Hätte dieser Tempel noch sein Dach, könnte man gut erkennen, was wir erklären möchten!

Bei der Entwicklung der Design-Philosophie des Golf VII spielten auch dystopische Zukunftsszenarien eine Rolle – respektive eine Abkehr von ihnen und eine erneute Hinwendung zum Positiven. Kein Scherz. Denn Designer sind nicht selten auch Philosophen. „Der Film ‚Blade Runner' hat damals Gewissheiten umgeworfen und damit Zukunftsglauben negiert", erzählt Andreas Mindt. Der Golf VII mit seinen Zitaten der besten Golf-Kreationen sollte ein Beitrag zur positiven Deutung der Zukunft sein. Und natürlich gleichzeitig die Marke VW wieder schärfen.

Und weil Designer manchmal auch Architekten sind, immer jedoch Baumeister, kommt jetzt noch die Aufklärung, was, zum Teufel, der Golf mit einem griechischen Tempel zu tun hat. „Ist doch ganz klar", sagt Andreas Mindt, „schon die Griechen haben erkannt, dass wirklich gerade Tempeldächer bei der Betrachtung wirkten, als hingen sie durch. Daher bauten sie Dachflächen, die in Wirklichkeit gebogen waren, die zu ihrem Rand hin quasi ‚beschleunigt' wurden. Den Kniff hat später Mies van der Rohe bei der Neuen Nationalgalerie in Berlin angewandt. Und wir beim Golf-VII-Dach."

Die Götter müssen verrückt sein.

Ohne Durchhänger: das in Wirklichkeit gebogene Dach der Neuen Nationalgalerie in Berlin

# Showdown

**Es war irgendwo in Spanien. Im äußerst spannenden Finale waren zwei VW-Designteams dazu auserkoren, ihren jeweiligen Entwurf zum Golf VII den obersten Entscheidern zu präsentieren. Das ganze Ding wird zum echten Nervenkrieg. Dann knallt's – gefährlich leise ...**

Italo-Western-Star wider Willen: Walter de Silva

Während ein VW-Vorstands- und -Aufsichtsratsflieger nach dem anderen landete, wuchsen die Spannungen zwischen den Teams, die schon längst auf dem Boden der Tatsachen angekommen schienen: Das gibt ein echtes Match! Team Nr. 1 operierte unter Mitwirkung des damaligen Konzern-Chefdesigners Walter de Silva. Der asketisch-elegante Italiener agierte jedoch in diesem wenig souverän bis indigniert, weil ihm der Entwurf des konkurrierenden Teams aus den Jungdesignern Philip Römers, Marc Lichte und Andreas Mindt deutlich missfiel. „Ein Elendsprozess", sagt ein Zeitzeuge, „wir hatten gefühlt alle Magengeschwüre."

Dann Auftritt von Ferdinand Piëch, dem damaligen Aufsichtsratsvorsitzenden. De Silvas Team präsentierte wortreich, der VW-Patriarch blieb wortlos. Näherte sich daraufhin gemessenen Schrittes dem Golf-VII-Entwurf der Jungs. Und sagte den Tonnen wiegenden Satz: „Euer Auto is' schwer wie Blei." Da umtanzte der frohlockende de Silva beinahe den Piëch, „Yes! Look! Our car! It's better!", brach es aus ihm unkollegial heraus, denn als souveräner Designchef hätte er seine eigenen Leute, den eige-

„Euer Auto ist schweer wie Bleei ..."

nen Nachwuchs respektvoll behandeln müssen. Das Ganze geht für de Silva in die mutmaßlich maßgeschneiderte Hose, denn „Godfather" Piëch beschied ihm, sehr, sehr leise und ungerührt: „Mr. de Silva. Your car is much to conservative." Stille. Niemand rührte sich. Dann trat beherzt einer der Jungs vor, veränderte mit einer scheinbar hervorgezauberten Rolle dünnen Tapes konzentriert die Seitenline des eigenen Golf-VII-Entwurfs. Parallel dazu kommentierte und begründete er sein Tun. Fertig. Piëch schaute, legte den Kopf schief und sprach die Erlösung: „Ja, so schaut's heil aus!" Abgang Ferdinand Piëch. Frust und Frost bei de Silva & Co.

Ab diesem Zeitpunkt war Walter de Silva – im Prinzip aus eigenem Entschluss – zum Feind der eigenen Jungdesigner geworden. Welch Paradoxon! Nun, er ist Geschichte. Marc Lichte hingegen Chefdesigner von Audi, Andreas Mindt in gleicher Funktion bei Bentley.

## Schnelles Wissen

Alles, was ein GTI-Fan braucht ...

Am **18. März 1974** schrieb VW-Ingenieur Alfons Löwenberg eine interne **Hausmitteilung**, ob man nicht einen **sportlichen** Volkswagen für junge, begeisterte Kunden entwickeln wolle. Er stieß auf **Schweigen** oder auf **kühle Ablehnung**. Der Grund hierfür war gar nicht mal das sportliche Auto gewesen. Sondern die Tatsache, dass Löwenberg seine Mitteilung an alle **Hierarchie-Ebenen** geschickt hatte. So etwas macht man nicht bei VW!

VW-Chef **Toni Schmücker**, dessen Urteil zum „Sport-Golf" die geheimen GTI-Entwickler nervös erwarteten, war bereits am Tag vor der offiziellen Enthüllung des Projekts von Koordinator Anton Konrad **eingeweiht** worden. Schmücker spielte in der Sitzung überzeugend den **Ahnungslosen**, um letztlich dem GTI vollumfänglich zuzustimmen. Dadurch hatte Schlaufuchs Konrad sämtlichen VW-internen Gegnern den Wind aus den Segeln genommen.
Der GTI konnte gebaut werden.

Toni Schmücker

Die legendären **Schottenkaro-Bezüge** des **Golf GTI** wurden entworfen von **Gunhild Liljequist**. Die gebürtige Berlinerin kam 1964 als erste Frau ins VW-Design. Das rot-schwarze GTI-Muster entstammt Liljequists Vorliebe für **Schottenröcke**, die sie persönlich in den „Swinging Sixties" auf der Londoner **Carnaby Street** einkaufte.

Nachdem der **Golf GTI** offiziell am **18. Mai 1975** beschlossen war, wurden mehrere GTI in Handarbeit für die Präsentation auf der **IAA** im September 1975 aufgebaut. Die GTI-**Motorräume** allerdings blieben **leer**, die Hauben **zu**: Man hatte noch **kein Aggregat**. Das kam, umgebaut von Längs- auf Quereinbau und mit zusätzlichem Ölkühler versehen, kurz darauf vom Spender **Audi 80 GTE**.

Designerin Gunhild Liljequist am Arbeitsplatz

Der amtliche **Mehrpreis** des **GTI** gegenüber den anderen Golf-I-Modellen – es waren über 4.000 Mark – wurde 1975 höchst **willkürlich** festgelegt. Die internen GTI-Drahtzieher wollten damit vor allem **Gegenargumente** des kritischen Vertriebs **entkräften**. Hierdurch würden potenzielle **Rowdys** vom Kauf eines derart schnellen Autos abgeschreckt, die dadurch das solide VW-Image beschädigten, hieß es gewieft.

# Prominente Golfer

Kompaktwagen des Herzens: Die britische **Prinzessin Diana** fuhr 1979 einen Golf I in Miami-Blau.

Ausnahmeschauspieler und „Hannibal"-Darsteller **Sir Anthony Hopkins** orderte beim britischen Traditionshändler Scotts of Sloane Square seinen Golf II GT in Oak Green Metallic.

Ein einziges Mal in seiner Musikerkarriere coverte Superstar **Cliff Richard** einen Welterfolg: Er bestellte ebenfalls wie Hopkins einen Golf II GTI. Ebenso im Lack-Ton Oak Green. Und bei Scotts of Sloane Square.

Für ihre Fahrten zwischen Windsor Castle und den königlichen Pferdeställen benutzte **Queen Elizabeth II.** lange Jahre einen weißen Golf II in spartanischer Basisausstattung. Da der Golf nur innerhalb des königlichen Anwesens genutzt wurde, war er nicht offiziell zugelassen.

Das erste Auto der heutigen **Princess Catherine** war ein 2001 von ihr für 10.000 britische Pfund gekaufter Golf IV. Ein Typ namens **William**, ihr heutiger Ex-Freund und Ehemann, pilotierte den Golf oft.

Die schafft das: Eine gewisse **Angela Merkel**, seinerzeit wohnhaft Schönhauser Allee 104 in Berlin, ließ 1990 einen weißen Golf II CL auf ihren Namen zu. 1995 ging „Angies" erstes West-Auto für ein Jahr in den Besitz ihres Mannes Joachim Sauer über, danach wurde der Zweitürer verkauft. Im Jahr 2012 versteigerte der neue Besitzer den Ex-Bundeskanzlerinnen-Golf für 10.165,02 Euro. Kein schlechter Werterhalt.

Harry, fahr mal schnell den Wagen vor: **Horst Tapperts „Derrick“** fuhr in einigen frühen Folgen privat einen Golf I GTI in Silbermetallic. Böse Buben hatten so noch schlechtere Karten.

Das letzte Auto von Tierfilmer **Heinz Sielmann** war ein weißer viertüriger Golf II CL. Das Auto befindet sich heute in einer privaten Sammlung.

Auch der legendäre **Prof. Dr. Bernhard Grzimek**, Tierfilmer und Zoologe („Serengeti darf nicht sterben“), nannte einen Golf seinen letzten Privatwagen. Es handelt sich um einen bis heute in Sammlerhand bewahrten Golf I GTD – eines der seltensten Golf-I-Modelle.

Schauspieler **Harald Krassnitzer**, Darsteller des Wiener „Tatort“-Kommissars Moritz Eisner, fuhr in diversen Folgen den damals brandneuen Golf V GTI. Klarer Fall von klassischem Product-Placement. Heute aufgrund von Compliance-Regeln untersagt.

Tarnfahrzeug: Neue-Deutsche-Welle-Star **Joachim Witt** („Goldener Reiter“) fuhr bis vor Kurzem einen Golf II Diesel aus ehemaligen Bundeswehrbeständen – natürlich in originaler Flecktarnfarbgebung.

Back to the roots: Rallye-Ass **Hans-Joachim Stuck** schaffte sich 2015 einen roten Golf I GTI von 1982 an. Seitdem pilotiert er ihn in freien Stunden mit Begeisterung über die Passstraßen der Alpen.

# Die Zukunft des Tapirs

**Permanent online und vernetzt. Sagen die einen: Hilfe! Dem Golf VIII entkommt man nicht, denn er übermittelt ständig Daten seiner jeweiligen Nutzer. Sagen die anderen: Tolle Connectivity! Ähnlich dual ist das übrige Wesen des Golf VIII: zwischen Hightech und Qualitätseinbußen. Und wird er den ID.3 überleben?**

Der Golf erkennt, wenn wir müde oder sonst was sind. Ein mobiler Big Brother. Kritikern kann Beruhigung zuteilwerden: Erhebungen zufolge nutzen über 70 Prozent aller Autofahrer die Assistenzsysteme ihrer Fahrzeuge nicht. Zudem funktionieren sie (auch) im Golf VIII nicht immer. Laut VW-Insidern weise rund jeder dritte gefertigte Golf VIII Macken auf und lande in der Nachbehandlung. Häufigste Probleme: Infotainment inklusive Navi fallen aus, die Memory-Funktion für individuelle Einstellungen sowie für die Personalisierung der Digitaldisplays entwickele Gedächtnisstörungen. Zudem arbeite die Touch-Bedienung verzögert. Nervt und lenkt ab.

Dazu kommt der VW-interne Begriff von „transparenter Technik“: Die Lackschichten des Golf VIII seien dünn und wirkten wie Orangenhaut. Wenig Lack in den Schwellerausläufern und auf Türflächen. Aus durchscheinender Grundierung resultierten Nachlackierungen. Interieur- und Exterieur-Teile passten nur ungenau. Schiefe Modellschriftzüge aufgrund fehlerhafter Schablonen. Was ist mit der gerühmten VW-Qualitätssicherung, die noch mal draufguckt, bevor ein Golf zum Kunden rollt? Dazu mal wieder „Entfeinerungen“ gegenüber dem Vorgänger: Haltestange statt Gasdruckfedern für die Motorhaube, einfachere Materialien, Entfall von Dekor und Verkleidungen. Dafür optionales Head-up-Display. Kein Wunder, dass der Golf VIII so traurig und echt seltsam guckt, weshalb sie ihn intern „Tapir“ tauften. Und: „Der Golf VIII gleicht einem deutschen Schäferhund: angeblich perfekt, doch dabei etwas kalt. Das ist kein VW mehr“, findet der ehemalige VW-Designchef Hartmut Warkuß.

Ertappt: der Tapir, das Golftier

Man hört, der Golf VIII sei in der Entwicklung vernachlässigt worden aufgrund der Priorität des Elektro-Popstars ID.3. Zumindest ist verbürgt, dass sie in Wolfsburg wussten, dass der Golf VIII unausgereift war, als die Produktionsbänder anliefen – anlaufen mussten. Ende der ersten Hälfte 2021 soll laut Insidern die Anzahl bestellter Golf VIII nur fünfstellig gewesen sein. Den Golf gibt es aktuell nicht als Elektrovariante, dies in Zeiten, in denen Autohersteller bekunden, demnächst keine Verbrenner mehr produzieren zu wollen. Ob der Golf IX daher ungewiss sei, beantworten VW-Repräsentanten mit so klaren wie höchst inoffiziellen Worten: „Solange der ID.3 so schlecht bleibt, besitzt der Golf einen Vorsprung."

Dennoch irgendwie undenkbar, dass der ID.3 die wahre Zukunft der Marke VW, damit zum Nachfolger des aktuellen VW-Bestsellers würde – so, wie es einst dem Käfer mit dem Golf erging. Oder etwa doch?

Betrachten wir es einmal nüchtern und lassen aktuelle Zahlen sprechen, nach denen rund 38 Prozent der Neuwagenzulassungen auf Fahrzeuge mit alternativen Antrieben entfallen. Derzeitiger Spitzenreiter unter diesen ist der Elektroantrieb. Dass Hersteller oft und gern massenhaft Dienstwagen und Tageszulassungen in die Statistiken drücken, sei auch hier am Rande bedacht. Zudem werden VW-Mitarbeitern zunehmend elektrifizierte Dienstwagen „angeboten". Davon ab jedoch darf man bei den ehrgeizigen Klimaschutzzielen und -vorgaben von heute mit einem erhöhten Anteil von Elektrofahrzeugen auch morgen rechnen. Für VW bedeutete dies, parallel zum ID.3 auch den zukünftigen Golf IX vollelektrisch zu konstruieren, zu bauen und zu verkaufen, wollte man am Traditionsmodell festhalten. Doch warum sollte VW dies tun? ID.3 und Golf (Limousine) wildern im selben Segment. Wird also aus der Golf-Klasse die Generation ID.3?

Auf die Gefahr hin, einem Irrtum zu erliegen, hier eine persönliche Prognose: Wenn alle Golf VIII gebaut, alle Elektro-, Digital- und andere Qualitätsdefizite bei ID.3 und Golf VIII ausgemerzt sind, werden sie bei VW feststellen, dass die Menschen unterm Strich doch lieber Golf fahren. In diesem Falle könnte Wolfsburg den ID.3 leise sterben lassen – so wie Eos, The Beetle, Sharan, Sportsvan – und den Namen Golf neu aufladen. Dieses Mal elektrisch.

Fest steht: Der E-Antrieb und die digitale Infrastruktur sind zurzeit die Achillesferse von VW. Nach der Zerreißprobe 1965 bis 1975 stehen Marke und Konzern jetzt vor ähnlichen Herausforderungen – 2015 bis 2025.

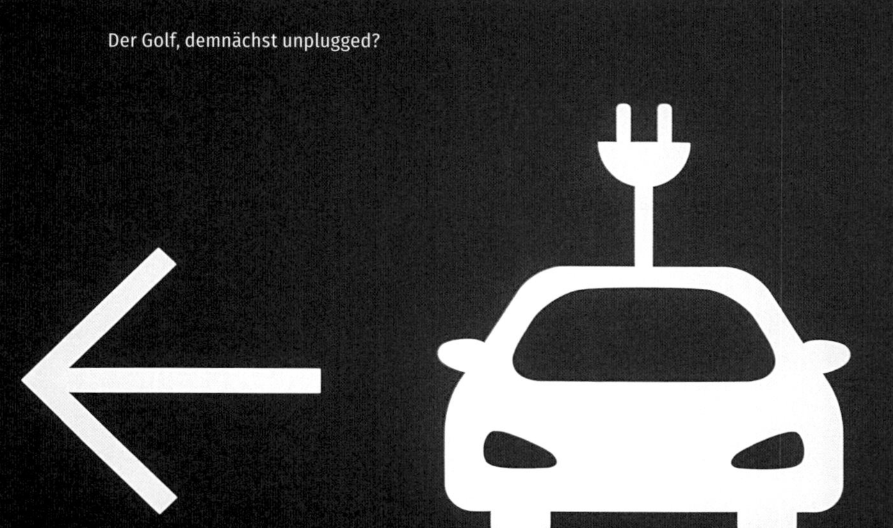
Der Golf, demnächst unplugged?

# Das Quiz für VW-Golf-Experten

**1. Wie sollte der allradangetriebene Golf ursprünglich heißen?**

a) Country
b) tetra
c) syncro

**2. Woran scheiterte das geplante Modell EA 266?**

a) An überhitzenden Motoren
b) An verfehlten US-Crashtests
c) An den hohen Kosten

**3. Welches Auto war direkte Vorlage für einen ursprünglichen Käfer-Nachfolger, der später bei VW do Brasil in Serie ging?**

a) Glas 1300 GT
b) Renault 16
c) Simca 1000

**4. Welches Auto fand Golf-Designer Giorgetto Giugiaro bei seinem ersten Besuch in Wolfsburg als Maßstab für das neue Kompaktmodell vor?**

a) Käfer
b) Opel Kadett
c) Fiat 128

**5. Welcher Modellname des Käfer-Nachfolgers wurde kurzfristig verworfen, existierte aber schon auf Schriftzügen und Prototypen?**

a) Pony
b) Rabbit
c) Dingo

**6. Wer stieß die Entwicklung des Golf GTI an?**

a) Der VW-Vorstandsvorsitzende Toni Schmücker
b) Der rallyebegeisterte Bundesminister Franz-Josef Strauß
c) VW-Pressemann Anton Konrad

**7. Warum wollte VW keinen sportlichen Golf?**

a) Weil man sich auf den Start des Grundmodells konzentrieren wollte
b) Weil man in Wolfsburg „Indschäktschn" nicht aussprechen konnte
c) Weil man keinen sportlichen Motor hatte

**8. Was bekamen Golf-I-Besitzer vor einer Urlaubsfahrt von VW-Werkstätten in den Kofferraum gelegt?**

a) Einen Kasten Bier
b) Luftmatratzen
c) Hosenrohre

**9. Warum gab es einen voll schwimmfähigen Golf?**

a) Weil VW-Ingenieure sehen wollten, wie ihre Vorgesetzten baden gehen
b) Zu Show-Zwecken
c) Ein Sturm hatte den Anleger für die Kutter der VW-Werkskantine zerstört.

**10. Wann schubste der Golf den Käfer vom Thron in der deutschen Zulassungsstatistik?**

a) 2003
b) 1976
c) 1983

**11. Welcher Konkurrent hielt das „Auto 2000" für den Golf II und überarbeitete komplett das eigene Modell?**

a) Talbot mit dem Horizon
b) Opel mit dem Kadett E
c) Ford mit dem Escort Mk III

**12. Die geschraubten Lagerböcke der Golf-II-Hinterachse waren teuer. Warum wurden sie trotz hoher Kosten beibehalten?**

a) Weil die Ingenieur Gummifetischisten waren
b) Weil dadurch das Reißen der hinteren Radkästen wie beim Opel Kadett E vermieden wurde
c) Um den entsprechenden Entfall als Innovation im Golf III feiern zu können

**13. Warum wurden in jedem Golf II Dutzende Kilo Wachs und Bitumen verarbeitet?**

a) Wachs und Bitumen waren leichter und elastischer als Blech.
b) Aus Gründen des Korrosionsschutzes
c) Weil beim Bau der A 39 nach Wolfsburg zig Tonnen Teer übrig geblieben waren

**14. Offiziell wurde beim Golf III die Konservierung aufgrund verbesserter Produktionsprozesse reduziert. Was war der eigentliche Grund?**

a) Die optimal konservierten Golf II brachten zu wenig Umsatz bei Instandsetzung und Ersatzteilverkauf.

b) Wachs und Bitumen wurden knapp auf dem Weltmarkt.
c) Die offizielle Begründung stimmt.

**15. Was bedeutet der Golf-IV-Slogan „Blau macht glücklich"?**

a) Appell an echte Kerle, auf Alkohol hinterm Steuer nicht zu verzichten
b) Werbung für die neue blaue Instrumentenbeleuchtung
c) Bezog sich auf den damaligen neuen US-Designchef Matt Blau

**16. Wie bezeichnet man den charakteristischen Schwung der C-Säule beim Golf ab der Generation IV?**

a) Gurke
b) Ranunkel
c) Banane

**17. Was haben der Golf III CitySTROMer und James Bonds Aston Martin DB 5 gemeinsam?**

a) Das klappbare vordere Nummernschild
b) Bond-Darsteller Timothy Dalton fuhr (privat) E-Golf.
c) Identische Stückzahlen

**18. Was war die Basis für den E-Motor des Golf III CitySTROMer?**

a) Neun in Reihe geschaltete und verstärkte Corrado-Wischermotoren
b) Ein nachglühender Kernbrennstab
c) Ein SIEMENS-Werkzeugmaschinen-Antrieb

**19. Wie heißt VW-intern das digitale Cockpit des Golf VIII?**

a) Firlefanz
b) Mäusekino
c) Pac-Man für Arme

**20. Welches Thema liegt dem Scheinwerferdesign des Golf IV zugrunde?**

a) Das „Terminator"-Auge von Arnold Schwarzenegger
b) Ein Transmissionsriemen
c) Die Kunststoffmulden der „Toffifee"-Verpackung

**21. Welcher Golf-Werbeslogan wurde zur unfreiwilligen Lachnummer?**

a) Wertigkeit neu erleben.
b) Der Golf. Wir sind stolz auf ihn.
c) Der neue Golf. Fährt jetzt auch geradeaus.

**22. Welche Modelle sollten final den Käfer ablösen?**

a) Der Golf
b) Der Polo
c) Golf und EA 266

**23. Welchen Spitznamen hatte VW-Entwickler und Golf-Förderer Hans-Georg Wenderoth ob seines expliziten Sprachgebrauchs?**

a) Grummel-Georg
b) Brüllfrosch
c) Fäkalien-Schorsch

**24. Welche Alternative zum Golf V erprobte VW als Zwischenlösung?**

a) Von Hand zertrennte und um zehn Zentimeter verlängerte Golf IV
b) Golf IV Coupé und Roadster
c) Eine neue Hinterachse, mit der der Golf IV auch durch Kurven fährt

**25. Wie nannte man den Golf Country scherzhaft?**

a) Kinder-Country
b) Stelzen-Golf
c) Fialas letztes Spielzeug

**26. Wie hieß der allererste offizielle Elektro-Golf?**

a) Eco Golf
b) CitySTROMer
c) Power Ranger

**27. Welchen internen Spitznamen trägt der Golf VIII?**

a) Skunk
b) Tapir
c) Marsupilami

**28. Welche Golf-Generationen zitiert das Design des Golf VII?**

a) I und IV
b) II und VI
c) III und V

**29. Was ersetzt beim Golf VIII die Hydraulikdämpfer der Motorhaube?**

a) Eine Metallstange wie beim Golf I
b) Die VW-Fachwerkstatt
c) Ein „Jetzt helf' ich mir selbst"-Büchlein

**30. Was wurde bei Golf-I-Crashtests eingesetzt?**

a) Eigene Ingenieure
b) Leichen
c) Dummys

# Quiz-Lösungen

1. b – tetra
2. a, b, c
3. c – Simca 1000
4. c – Fiat 128
5. a – Pony
6. c – VW-Pressemann Anton Konrad
7. a – Weil man sich auf den Start des Grundmodells konzentrieren wollte
8. c – Hosenrohre
9. b – Zu Show-Zwecken
10. b – 1976
11. b – Opel mit dem Kadett E
12. b – Weil dadurch das Reißen der hinteren Radkästen wie beim Opel Kadett E vermieden wurde
13. b – Aus Gründen des Korrosionsschutzes
14. a – Die optimal konservierten Golf II brachten zu wenig Umsatz bei Instandsetzung und Ersatzteilverkauf.
15. b – Werbung für die neue blaue Instrumentenbeleuchtung
16. c – Banane
17. a – Das klappbare vordere Nummernschild
18. c – Ein SIEMENS-Werkzeugmaschinen-Antrieb
19. b – Mäusekino
20. b – Ein Transmissionsriemen
21. c – Der neue Golf. Fährt jetzt auch geradeaus.
22. c – Golf und EA 266
23. c – Fäkalien-Schorsch
24. a – Von Hand zertrennte und um zehn Zentimeter verlängerte Golf IV
25. a, b, c
26. b – CitySTROMer
27. b – Tapir
28. a – I und IV
29. a – Eine Metallstange wie beim Golf I
30. a, b, c

# Zitate

*„Die Journalisten waren vom Golf I sofort begeistert, die Autokäufer blieben vorsichtig. Der Erfolg kam erst mit Golf Diesel und GTI."*

Ernst Fiala, Ex-VW-Forschungschef

*„Da musst du Knochen im Oberlippenbart haben!"*

Peter Dieckmann, Rallye-Weltmeister auf Golf II (Gruppe A, 1987)

*G.O.L.F. = Gerät ohne lustvolle Funktion*

Volks(wagen)mund

*„Es ist trotz Herbert Schäfer immer ein relativ gutes Design entstanden."*

Ein Ex-VW-Designer

*„Audi hat statt ‚GTI' die Modellbezeichnung ‚GTE' gewählt, weil die Bayern ‚Indschäktschn' nicht aussprechen können."*

Anton Konrad, Ex-VW-Pressechef und Initiator des Golf GTI

*„Die erste Zeit war der Golf alles andere als ein Selbstläufer, er startete erst im zweiten Jahr spürbar durch."*

Anton Konrad, Ex-VW-Pressechef

*„Erst mit dem Golf I lernte VW, Autos zu entwickeln und zu konstruieren."*

Horst-Dieter Schwittlinsky, ehemals VW-Marketing

*„Ich musste als Erstes an die Scheinwerfer ran – der Golf III schielte irgendwie."*

Hartmut Warkuß, Nachfolger von Herbert Schäfer als VW-Designchef